Sewer Balls

STEVEN SCHINDLER

To Bob —

The names have been
changed to Protect
The guilty

Steve Schindler

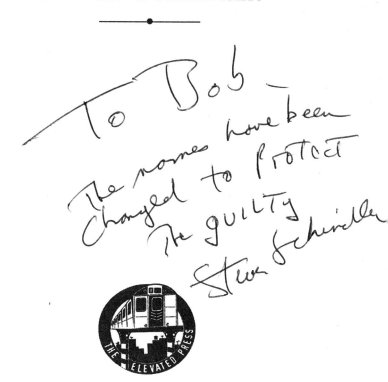

The Elevated Press
PO Box 65218
Los Angeles, CA 90065
USA

www.elevated.com

SECOND PRINTING

Library of Congress Catalog Number: 98-72814

ISBN 0-9662408-6-3

Cover design by *Suddenly Chadwick!* Design Services
Sherman Oaks, CA

*To my mother and father, my brother
and sister, all of my aunts, uncles, cousins,
and my friends from the neighborhood who
made childhood such a wonderful and magical
time.*

*And especially to my wife, soul mate, coach, and
love of my life, Sue, who has made adulthood
even better.*

Sewer Balls

My head is down about two inches from the single piece of loose leaf on my desk. I can smell the page, the desk, the blue Parker ink from my fountain pen. Ball-point pens aren't allowed in any grade in Presentation School. Not even in the 8th. The ink comes in cylinders that fit snugly right into the pen. Sometimes I throw out a cartridge that still has ink in it because I like the way putting in a new one feels. Like loading a gun.

My concentration is broken by Sister Fidelis' shrill voice, "Shelley, keep your eyes to yourself before I smack you silly."

We all snicker at that one.

"Quiet, 8th grade! Or you'll all stay after school!"

That shut us up. Just thinking about staying after school was the worst thing that could possibly happen. Especially during a science test. You were depressed enough. Even though it was freezing outside and not a very nice November afternoon at all, you could still play touch football in the park. Or go to a fort and look at "Playboys" and smoke cigarettes. Or hang out in the laundromat, listen to WMCA, and talk to the girls. We always listened to the "Good Guys" on WMCA. No contest. There were other cool rock 'n roll stations, WABC, WINS, but we listened to WMCA. Everybody on our block did. Well, not the old people. They listened to WNEW, and William B. Williams and Perry Como and Frank Sinatra and Doris Day and other totally old-fashioned junk that we couldn't bear to listen to for more than the time it took to whiz past while looking for a good song somewhere on the dial.

"Shelley! That's it. I'm gonna give you a good crack!"

Shelley could take a crack. Shelley is not a girl. Furthest thing from it. Shelley is Robert Shelley. But nobody except Sister Fidelis calls him that. We call him Whitey. He's the tallest kid in the class, maybe the dumbest, and definitely the one who can get a nun up out of her seat, rush down the aisle in a blur of black cloth with who knows how many layers of underwear rubbing underneath, rosaries and crucifixes swinging, and creating a mad rush of wind and rhythm as she winds to smack Shelley across the head. SMACK. "Hey, ouch,

1

Sister," Whitey says in an annoyed tone of voice.

This isn't one of those vicious attacks. Just the kind to show everyone in the class that Sister Fidelis wasn't going to take ANY crap from anybody in class, especially the biggest boy. She was going to give him a few love taps and even let him block most of the blows.

We knew better than to laugh at Sister Fidelis now. She's in such a state that if we were to make fun of her we'd absolutely have to stay after class. Nothing worse than that.

Suddenly a voice from the unknown.

"Attention all classes."

Wow, what the hell is this? The loudspeaker! Sister Thomas the Principal. It's the middle of the afternoon. She never comes on in the middle of the day, unless it's for a fire drill or an air raid drill. Even Sister Fidelis stops her smacks on Shelley's head.

"All Classes are to stop what they are doing. We have just found out that President Kennedy has been shot."

Sister Fidelis grabs her mouth with both hands and whispers, "Jesus, Mary and Joseph."

"Teachers are to bring all students to the Church right now, sitting class by class, for a reading of the rosary."

Some girls just burst out crying, and everybody looks real scared.

ALMOST everybody.

Whitey tugs the fag tag on the back of my white shirt. "Holy shit! Maybe it's the Russians and we're gonna have a nuclear war. Wouldn't that be neat! This test won't count."

Being afraid of getting caught talking, I just ignore Whitey.

"Shelley! If you make me go over there, you'll regret it for the rest of your life."

"Yes, Sister."

Sister Fidelis suddenly took her intensity to a new level. "Single file, and NOT A WORD."

We listened. The last time we were this obedient was when some Bishop came to talk to the school about vocations. That's when they try to convince us that being a priest or a nun

2

is a great career. We knew better. In the 2nd grade, probably 90 percent of us thought we'd be priests and nuns when the Bishop asked. Now in the 8th grade, when most of the guys had probably tongued a girl, and maybe even copped a feel off Tina Robustelli while standing in line for cookies or something, most of the girls realized how they could make boys do pretty much whatever they wanted to if they smiled a certain smile or even hinted that they thought a boy was cute; so the only ones who still considered being priests and nuns were the really weird ones. Like Joanne Martorana. Her average was 98. All she did was homework. I can't remember ever seeing her out playing, and I'm out playing all the time. Louis Zummo was probably the only boy who still wanted to be a priest. He was a sissy. Didn't play any sports. Hung around with Patricia Anne Dugan all the time. And he watched helplessly as his little brother Eugene drowned down at the river at 225th Street when we were in the 4th grade. He was never the same after that. Jerome Mullooly might still want to be a priest. Both his parents have heavy Irish brogues, and they never, ever let him watch "The Three Stooges." They even pray the rosary every night. On their knees. Their house smells funny. Like old socks.

We shuffle single file out into the cold afternoon, not even stopping to put our jackets on. The girls always go first in alphabetical order. The boys follow. Some guys get to sit behind the girls if their name begins with an A, B, C, or maybe even a D, because the girls sit first seat, first row, and go down the row from there. But being an S, I'm always a few rows in back of them. In eighth grade it's easy to get excited about girls. Just sitting behind them is enough to get aroused. Unless you're right behind Deborah Laturza. She's fat, ugly, and smells so bad that one day in 6th Grade, Miss Gannon actually drenched her with a can of Lysol. I felt sorry for her. She still smelled everyday after that. Miss Gannon left the next year. We heard she was working as a guard in a women's prison.

We're waiting to hear more about the President. All of the nuns are crying and praying on their knees. It's the strangest sight. Nuns never cry. Nuns made kids cry all the

3

time. Even Whitey Shelley. But now they're all crying. Kennedy's like a saint to us. He's Irish, Catholic, and he even lived in the Bronx for a while. OK, it was the Riverdale section where only super rich people live, but still, it was the Bronx. When Kennedy was running for President, it was like somebody from the neighborhood was running. We had to go to rallies, carry signs and cheer. We even had to take the subway all the way downtown one time, and stand on 5th Avenue just so we could be there when he drove by.

Everyone has pretty much realized that the nuns aren't really paying attention to us, so kids are starting to whisper and goof around a little. I can see Bobby Bailey listening to Brian Pratt right next to him, whispering in his ear. Bobby turns around and whispers to me, Whitey Shelley, and the other kids with last names that start after the letter "M."

"He's dead. The Reds killed the President."

Who killed him? The Russians? Are we at war? I gotta know.

"Sssshhhhh!!!" A nun took time out from the rosary to shut us up without missing a word of the "Hail Mary."

We were taught to fear the Russians. Ever since first grade, we would have air raid drills where we'd have to sit in the hall in the dark on the floor, with our heads between our legs and our hands over our heads, as the nuns cruised by reciting the rosary. Those lousy dirty stinking godless Russians who kill the poor Czechoslovakian Catholics!

In the second grade, Sister Thadeus posed the following question: "If a Russian soldier burst into this very classroom, right this instant with a rifle, and asked if you loved Communism or Christ what would you say?" Every one of us knew the answer. I love Christ, not Communism. We'd all rather die. We had no idea what the hell Communism was. But we sure as hell knew it was something awful.

The rosary was over. And Sister Thomas announced we should all go back to our classes in silence, get our jackets, go home, and continue to pray with our parents. My parents were both at work and wouldn't be home till after 5, so we made plans to meet at the flagpoles for some touch football

4

instead.

It's sure a strange walk home today. Like always, we walk in groups, and make fun of the kids in the lower grades. I can't wait to get out of this stupid uniform (white shirt, blue tie with the little "PS" for Presentation School in white, blue pants, and laced black shoes) and put on my play clothes (dungarees, sneakers, striped tee-shirt, zippered jacket). But the grown-ups on the street are silent. Some have tears in their eyes, and some are sobbing.

"I'll call for you as soon as I'm changed, Whitey."

"Alright. Who's bringing a ball? Mine's dead."

"I'll bring mine."

"See ya, Vinny," Whitey says as he bounds up the four steps from the sidewalk and onto the courtyard edged with a green and white wooden picket fence.

Here I am all alone at the flagpoles, usually the scene of many important after school activities, like touch football or fist fights. But it's about as empty right now as Christmas morning, until Whitey finally shows up.

"Wanna play catch?" Whitey asks me.

"Sure."

Nobody else's parents let them out that afternoon. Where the heck is everybody?

There was nothing on TV the entire weekend. Every channel, all day was about the President. People all over the world are crying. Even the old anchor guys on the news were crying. My mother cried all through dinner that night. She even talked nutty.

"What's this world coming to? Why, God, why? That beautiful man! And those children. Why, God, why? I hope they find that bastard and tear him limb from limb."

Every once in a while my parents would say "bastard" or "son-of-a bitch" or "shit." They said "ass," "damn," and "hell" quite a bit. But they never ever uttered the "F" word, or said "dick" or "pussy" or "blowjob" or anything like that. If they said "bastard," you knew they meant business.

5

By Sunday, things were starting to calm down a bit. Sundays were big days. We all went to one o'clock Mass together. Except my older brother, who dropped out of high school last year to work at the new ski slope in Van Cortlandt Park. He didn't go to church anymore. But me, my sister who's a senior in high school, and my parents went every Sunday.

Sunday was usually the day we had company or went over a relative's house. This day we were going downtown to my Aunt Grace and Uncle Cornelius' house. I say house, but it was just an apartment in Peter Cooper Village. That's an apartment complex on 20th Street in Manhattan that looks like a housing project, except there aren't any coloreds or Puerto Ricans. They even have playgrounds, huge trees, benches, and squirrels. My father hates going there because he hates driving all the way down there on the FDR Drive. I'm not sure if dad is too crazy about Uncle Cornelius. Uncle Cornie (we only call him that behind his back) doesn't drink beer, watch sports, or curse at all. Sometimes when my dad's had a few drinks, he says that Uncle Cornelius is a "fairy" nice man. I'm not exactly sure what that means but it gets my mother really mad whenever he says it.

I love going to visit Aunt Grace and Uncle Cornelius. Aunt Grace reminds me of Martha Raye from the Abbott and Costello movies, and they have three kids, Jimmy, Elizabeth, and Walter. They call Jimmy and Elizabeth Irish twins because the were born in the same year, 10 months apart. Walter's my brother's age, but they don't seem to like each other. My brother might be a tough guy, but he sure can be funny. Walter somehow thinks his own jokes are the funniest, even though he's the only one who ever laughs. But he can sure be mean. He once tripped Jimmy for a laugh, and that's why Jimmy has a chipped front tooth. But the real reason I love going there is Jimmy and Elizabeth. They're four years older than me, and they are the two funniest people I know. Elizabeth is really cute and Jimmy's good in sports. He lets me play with him and his friends at the basketball courts. Sometimes.

My mother's taking longer than usual to get ready be-

6

cause we're leaving for Aunt Grace's right after church. I'm sitting in the bedroom watching the extra TV my uncle just gave us instead of throwing out. I say "the" bedroom because we only have one. Three kids, two parents, ONE bedroom. The Eagans, on the 6th floor, they have four kids and one bedroom. The Pisanis, they have five kids and one bedroom. So we don't have it too bad.

They're getting ready to bring the bastard who killed the President somewhere, and they're going to show it live on TV. It's really confusing and exciting, too. They're in a garage or something, and everybody's pushing each other and stuff and....

BANG! BANG! BANG!

"They shot him! Right on TV! They shot him! They shot him!"

My mother rushed out of the bathroom, half her head still in curlers.

"What? Who got shot?"

"They shot Oswald."

"Good, the bastard."

After she said bastard, she spit. Not a real spit. But a sound like a spit. Italians do that when they're really mad.

"Come on and hurry, we'll be late for church."

My father was waiting outside with the '48 Ford station wagon that we have. We pile in, drive the two blocks to Presentation Church, and sit about halfway back like we always do. Church is a good place to think about things. Most of the time you just daydream, and maybe think about stupid stuff, but every once in a while, especially during the sermon, the priest will say something that gets you to thinking about something important. Father O'Shaugnessy is the priest and while I was off thinking about how Aunt Grace always under cooks the roast beef, Father O really got my attention. He sobbed, right on the pulpit, talking about the President, and how he was Catholic, and how if we really believe, we know he's in a better place. I could tell everybody was listening for a change. But after the sermon, I went back to kneeling, sitting, standing, getting Communion, singing, exiting, and pil-

7

ing back into the car for the trip to Aunt Grace's.

"I hate this drive," my dad says.

"Oh, you hate everything," my mother chimes in as she turns on the radio and searches for the only station played in the car besides baseball games...WNEW. But wait! Where's Perry? Where's Frank? Where's William B.? It's all news. The President's STILL dead. Oswald's dead. Over and over and over and over.

The trees along the highway all look dead. Even the telephone poles look like crucifixes. I sure hope Jimmy and Elizabeth are funny today.

"We usually go to the Gristedes over on 2nd Avenue," Uncle Cornelius says, after a long chew on some under cooked string beans. "If you use cue-pons, it's really quite reasonable."

"Yes, those cue-pons are a life saver!" my cousin Jimmy adds. I can tell Jimmy is getting ready to break into a maniacal funny routine.

My mother knows it too. And since Aunt Grace has been noticeably absent for the past five minutes, she decides to try and cut Jimmy off while she still has a chance.

"Shut up, Jimmy, you little brat. When you have to pay for something around here you'll be using cue-pons too."

"Aunt Angie, why you pickin' on me? I LOVE cuuuueeeee-pons." Jimmy's getting very close to taking off. Elizabeth, who never is the one to start trouble, is just waiting for Jimmy to go nuts, so she can follow closely behind. That's one way to avoid being the one who gets smacked; just be second.

Jimmy knows that without hardly trying he can have me rolling on the floor. But getting the rest of the kids to join in isn't so easy. I can tell by the way he doesn't even look in my direction that he knows I'll go berserk any minute. I'm already laughing with my mouth full. I know better than to look over at my father, but my mother is giving me that stare, where she looks like she's trying to see if she can crush her teeth by clenching her jaw.

"Alright, James," Uncle Cornelius says, knowing that

Jimmy is on the verge of going off, "that's enough."

We all try not to explode with laughter as Jimmy opens his mouth, revealing a tunnel full of mashed potatoes and points at himself like, "Who ME???!!!" Uncle Cornelius obviously doesn't think it's funny at all.

Uncle Cornelius doesn't look or sound anything like my dad. He's tall and thin. Everything on him is thin. Thin eyes, lips, hair, arms, nose, legs, hair, and neck. He has a big office job for some big downtown company. My father says he's loaded. Nobody's scared of Uncle Cornelius. Especially his kids.

"Excuse me, I'll go see what's holding up Grace." Uncle Cornelius dabs his mouth with a cloth napkin and walks down the hall to the big bedroom. They have three. Three kids, three bedrooms. Wow.

Aunt Grace comes out of the bedroom with Uncle Cornelius. You could tell she was crying. Everyone looks around at everybody else at the table. Things aren't funny anymore.

"Come on, Grace, your food's getting cold," my mom says. She always has a knack for knowing how to change the subject and keep things going. Everybody knows why she was crying. Kennedy. She even volunteered at the parish for him during the campaign.

"I'm just not hungry. I've got to do some stuff in the kitchen," Aunt Grace says just as she starts to blow her noise real loudly. The honk is followed by a long silence.

"We usually go to the A and P." I look up from my under cooked roast beef in disbelief. My father talked at the table.

He even had something else to say. "The Grand Union near us is filthy. I saw the bum there sneeze into his hand while he was slicing my ham and keep going like nothing happened. After he wrapped it up, weighed and marked it, I said, 'You expect me to buy that with your snot all over it?' And he goes, 'What are you talkin' about?' I haven't been back there since."

"Frank, that was 20 years ago," my mother reminds

9

him, like she does every time he tells this story.

"So what! I'm still not going back there."

"That old German deli guy is dead and buried."

"Yeah, probably from eating that snotty meat." My dad made a funny! And a good one at that.

This is it. I can tell by the look of anticipation on Jimmy's face that he knows the time for action is now! He picks up the most under cooked piece of blood-red roast beef off the large blue-and-white china plate which has about a half-inch of beef blood, sticks his finger in it, and pushes it right up about two inches into his nostril.

"Snotty meat! I love snotty meat, too!!!"

All of us kids lose it. Me, my sister, Elizabeth, even Walter, who's usually a total sour puss, are roaring uncontrollably. In the midst of the pandemonium, I can see that the adults at the table are stunned. I can tell my mother doesn't know whether to laugh or cry. Uncle Cornelius and my dad are seething. But like an express train roaring through the local station, Aunt Grace storms out of the kitchen heading straight for Jimmy, "You little bastard." She pulls the meat out of his hand, throws it down into the china plate which splashes everyone at the table with splotches of cow blood and makes everyone scream and the girls squeal even louder. She winds up like Whitey Ford and lands a good loud smack on the back of the head. "Don't play with food. Now finish and get out of here."

"Vinny, shut your little trap," my mom warns me. But I can't stop laughing. Jimmy's got this exaggerated look in his face like he's in unbelievable pain from the smack on the head and the back of his skull's gonna fall off. His writhings are ignored by the grown-ups at the table, but sending us kids into uncontrollable fits of laughter.

Then after a particularly flamboyant head roll he says, "God, now I know how the President felt." That was it. The final straw. You could see Uncle Cornelius, my mother, my father, and Aunt Grace stop chewing. Not a sound even from the kids. Then, like in slow motion, Aunt Grace jumps up from her chair, already swinging with her face all contorted and weird and she goes totally nuts, throwing smacks, punches, elbows, anything she can at Jimmy's face, back, head, and body; anywhere she can.

"You little wretched son-of-a bitch. God have mercy." Everyone is screaming now. "Stop it!" "Don't!" "Grace, no!" and just squeals of panic mixed with excitement from me, my sister and Elizabeth. Jimmy finally manages to slip out of her clutches and runs like hell down the hall and into the bathroom, slamming the door behind him.

Nobody's laughing anymore. Just total silence. The white table cloth is splattered with pieces of blood-red roast beef and red meat juice looking like a war just took place on it.

Aunt Grace looks around at everyone like she just woke up from a dream and sits down in her chair as if nothing happened. "Angie," she says, "would you like some more meat?" "No, Grace, I think we've had enough." my mom says. "Let's start cleaning up before dessert." With that, they start cleaning up the mess on the table in total silence.

We kids just look at each other, figuring that this is our cue to go away from the dining room table in the corner of the living room and go plop in front of the TV set.

Cleaning the table off didn't take too long. My mother, Aunt Grace and Uncle Cornelius had cleared everything away and were starting to bring out the next batch of plates and silverware for the Italian pastries, cakes, cookies and coffee. My father is sitting with us in front of the TV. I'm flipping the channel changer trying to find something good and keep going back and forth, till my father lets out with his usual, "You won't be satisfied till you break the damn thing."

The grown-ups have their coffee and we were just getting ready for ice cream and Italian pastries when Jimmy appears. Uncle Cornelius gives him a thin stare. "You just sit down and behave yourself," Uncle Cornelius says in a dead serious tone of voice. Jimmy didn't utter a word. He looked inconvenienced.

"Jimmy, you think anybody'd be at the courts?" I asked. Before Jimmy could respond, Aunt Grace sternly said, "Nobody's going anywhere. This is a school night."

11

"We have to leave soon anyway," my mother adds.

"Can we play with your car race set."

"Nah, we gave that away," Jimmy sheepishly admits.

"Wanna listen to records?" Elizabeth chimes in enthusiastically.

I was up for anything. "Yeah! Let's do that." Even my sister, who only talks a little more than my father, says, "Yeah, let's go." Even Jimmy has a look of joy on his face. "By George, Liz, you've done it again! Records it is!" he says, imitating an Englishman.

Walter the sourpuss quickly interjects, "Don't touch any of my records."

"You mean we can't listen to the Singing Nun! Oh darn!" Jimmy continues in his mock English accent.

Me, my sister, Elizabeth and Jimmy go down the hall into Elizabeth's room. Yup, she has her own room. And on a table, a brand new Magnavox portable hi-fi. Stereo! The lid lifts off and has a speaker in it. It's got a long wire, and you can put it on the other side of the room for stereo sound!

Jimmy pulls off the shelf a 45 box. He opens it, and pulls out a card with every record listed, in the best penmanship possible. Each record in its original sleeve, and separated by a file card from the other records. It even has a special number, glued right onto the label, so you knew where the record was supposed to go in the box.

At our house, none of the records were filed at all. In fact, most of them didn't even have sleeves or anything, and were just thrown in a 45 box, all rubbing against each other like sandpaper. My mother even left a whole box of them on the radiator once, and they all got warped. Our record player was lousy too. Hi-fi, not stereo.

Jimmy inspects his list. "Wait'll you hear this."

He pulls out a record that had a plain black label with a plain white sleeve.

"Hey, Vinny, have you heard of The Beatles?"

"Sure," I say. I had heard OF them, but I couldn't remember what they sounded like. "They're those English guys."

Elizabeth turns to Anne Marie, "You've heard of them

haven't you, Anne Marie?"

"Oh yeah. The girls at school talk about them all the time."

"Do you have any of their records?" Jimmy asks.

"No, not yet."

Jimmy slides his prized possession out of its sleeve and looks across the grooves, looking for the slightest amount of dust. He thinks he sees a speck and blows across it. He holds it by its edges, like the way the priest holds the really big wafer in church called the Host. He gingerly puts it on the spindle, turns on the hi-fi, waits for it to warm up, and places the needle on the edge of the record.

It was like an explosion. A rat-a-tat crack of drums and

SHE LOVES YOU YEAH YEAH YEAH
SHE LOVES YOU YEAH YEAH YEAH
SHE LOVES YOU YEAH YEAH YEAH

It was loud. I never heard anything like it before. It sounded nothing like Elvis, or the Four Seasons, or Gene Pitney, or Neil Sedaka.

All I could hear was YEAH YEAH YEAH YEAH YEAH YEAH. And they sing some words really weird like "yesterday-yay" and "say-yay" and "mie-yind" and then all off a sudden they went "Woooooooooh."

Jimmy and Elizabeth mouth every word and beat their laps in rhythm.

And at the very end of the song, The Beatles sounded like they were going to stop and cry or something, and then they paused and then screamed again, YEAH YEAH YEAH.

I wasn't sure what that was all about. I never saw my cousin Jimmy sing along with a record that sounded like a girl's record. You know, like The Shirelles or something like that.

"What'd you think, Anne Marie?" Jimmy had to know.

"It's good. They have nice voices. Are they cute?"

"Yeeessss!" Elizabeth says in a very deep, throaty, raspy, funny-sounding voice.

She pulls out a box with a bunch of magazines from under the bed. "Look at them. Aren't they adorable!"

"They write almost all of their own songs," Jimmy adds matter-of-factly.

"And did you hear that guitar work? They play all their own instruments too. I just got this yesterday. I've got some others here. Wanna hear 'em, Vinny?"

I had to think for a second. What else could there be? I already heard them once. I didn't really get all the words. I usually like stuff like "Itsy Beeny Teeny Weeny Yellow Polka Dot Bikini" or "Alley Oop" or even "All Shook Up." Well, what the heck, I thought.

"Yeah, let's hear something else."

"Great. This was their first release." He searches through his box for another.

" 'Love Me Do' it's called."

Just then, my mom pokes her head in the door. "Come, on kids. It's time to go."

"Awww, we don't want to go now." My sister and I plead.

"Now. Let's go."

"Aunt Angie, have you heard of The Beatles?" Jimmy had to know.

"Yeah, I step on 'em whenever I see one. Come on, let's go! Now! Bye sweeties."

My mother crosses the room and gives big Italian smooches to Jimmy and Elizabeth.

Back on the FDR going uptown to the Bronx. At least there's something besides news on the radio. Frank Sinatra sure sounds old-fashioned. My mother knows every word.

The Kennedy dirge went on for weeks. This winter is terrible. Wet and really cold. Not light fluffy piles of white snow that closes school and means a few extra days of sleigh-riding in the park. Or even so much snow that you can actually take a sled from the very top of 238th Street at the stumps and go right down the middle of the street, all the way through the traffic light at the intersection to the bottom at Bailey Avenue. No cars, no buses, no grown-ups yelling. It's a cold, damp, freezing winter. Sleet and globs of gray, heavy, frozen, filthy wetness mixed with road oil, dog poop, banana peels, candy wrappers, crushed beer cans and anything else swept down the gutter by the always-flowing, not-quite-frozen run off.

Instead of snow men, we'd build huge dams in the middle of the hill, made up of whatever snow and garbage we could make stick together. Make it as high and wide as fast as we could. That would create a deep pool of water, curb deep and several feet across that some unsuspecting rushing sucker might not see and step right into. And it meant that a freezing concoction of slush and street swill would go right over their galoshes and into their boot. We never actually saw anybody fall for it, but I'll bet they did. Maybe.

Christmas came and went. 8th grade meant no more toys. Just clothes. New Year's Eve was for grown-ups and older kids. My parents went to a Knights of Columbus party every year with my mother's friends from Fuhrman's Department Store where she works. I had no idea what they did at those things until the next week, when the Brownie snapshots came back with my mother sitting on my father's lap, wearing a flapper feathered head band, and my dad wearing a green plastic derby left over from St. Patrick's Day, with an expression on his face he never had around the house....you know, goofy looking.

My sister is upstairs on the 2nd floor of our building at Mary Ellen Lynch's house, with a bunch of other girls from ours and other nearby buildings gossiping and giggling about boys while Mrs. Lynch sits in the kitchen with Mrs. Ryan gossiping and not giggling at all.

My brother is around the corner in "Grecco's Bar" probably drinking whiskey and maybe starting fights. I could almost see Grecco's from out the bedroom window. It's below us, but we can't see the front of it. Just the cars parked and double parked out front, and whoever wasn't old enough to be inside hanging out on the cars. The tires squealed almost all night, dropping kids off and picking kids up. New Year's was a lot like every other night except the cars came and went longer, the fights seemed louder, there were more kids hanging out on cars, and the bar stayed open until the old ladies walked by

15

with looks of scorn on their face as they headed for 7 o'clock mass.

For me, New Year's meant sitting at home and watching TV with Whitey Shelley. My sister would pop in every hour or so to make sure we aren't setting the house on fire or drinking my father's Dewars or Rupert Knickerbocker beer. That, of course, didn't stop us from using the telephone. Dial any random number... "Hello, this is the phone company. We're repairing the phones in your area so please be patient while we try and locate the problem. Thank you." Wait about three minutes and call the same number. "Hello this is the phone company again. For the next five minutes, our repair man is working on your line. Please do not pick up the phone for any reason. If you do, our repairman could be injured from an electrical shock. Thank you." Four minutes later, call back, and when the person picks up, you yell, "AAAAHHHHH, I TOLD YOU NOT TO PICK UP, AAAHHHHHHHHHHHH!!!!!"

So much for New Year's. It's not really like the end of the year anyway. Everybody knows the year ends when we get out for summer vacation and begins when we go back to school.

Winter break was over. Back to school. Back to the drudgery of winter, and mid-terms, and day after day of old nun bad breath, spitting through yellow teeth, smacking the boys, calling the girls tramps, and trying to teach us sex education by telling us that going to the bathroom and sex were disgusting animal acts. "Don't ever touch yourself... there! Shelley, get your hands our of your pocket. I know what you're doing."

Johnson is now President. He told the country that he would carry on the legacy of Kennedy. Johnson was like a foreigner to us. He talked with a heavy Southern accent and had those huge ears and when he talked, his whole face would shake like the gristle on a fatty corned beef right out of the pot. He was old and looked mean. He wasn't anything like Kennedy. My mother said she thought that Johnson had Kennedy killed

16

so he could be President. Other suspects were Castro, Khrushchev, the Jews, the coloreds, the Chinese, the Vietnamese, Protestants, and Rockefeller.

One thing I noticed about Johnson was he talked about Viet Nam (rhymes with ham) a lot. And I started noticing they showed actual war footage on the TV news. Sometimes even bleeding guys. My friend Jimmy Joe Clancy's brother is in Viet Nam. He got a huge block party before he left. The biggest one I've ever seen. Free soda, beer, and even baskets of clams on the half-shell. My brother got so sick my mother thought about bringing him to the hospital. But after he threw up out the window a bunch of times, they figured he was OK.

Everybody in the neighborhood knows me because they know I'm Schmidt's kid brother. My brother is big. Tall and wide. His hair is jet black and with the Vitalis he drenches it with, it looks almost blue. He looks really Italian too. My mother is Italian, and my father's German and Irish with green-gray eyes. Joey's skin is even darker than my mother's. They call him Spade. If you can imagine such a thing, he almost looks like a chubby Elvis. He dresses real Italian too. Tight peg-legged pants. Pointy shoes. He calls them Puerto Rican "cockroach-in-the-corner crushers." Funny but it seems all the guys he hangs out with dress the same way. I say funny because all his friends are Irish. Murphy, Eagan, Stanton, Walsh, Roach, O'Connor, Mulvaney, Carroll, all look like extras in a Sal Mineo movie. It seems everybody who's cool in the neighborhood has that look. Like Frankie Valli and the Four Seasons, or Dion and the Belmonts, or Frankie Avalon, or Fabian, or Joey Dee and the Starlighters, and Elvis.

Hair greasy, combed back, with a thin, greasy strand hanging over one eye. Everybody smokes. And they aren't angels.

It was really late one night. Probably three in the morning. The house was dark and quiet. There was a loud banging on the door that woke everybody up, and probably everybody else on the floor the way the tiles in the halls made even the slightest sound reverberate from one end of the building to the other. My sister and I snuck over to the doorway where we could see the front door. My mother in her flannel pajamas and my dad in his underwear went to the door.

"Who is it?" my mom started.

"It's the police. We've got your kid here."

"Oh, my God," my mother said under her breath as she opened the door, "What happened, Officer?" My father didn't say a word.

"Step inside."

Two cops came into the narrow hall of our apartment with my brother, looking really scared. I had never seen my brother look scared before.

"We caught your kid in a stolen car," the younger cop said.

"What! You no good son-of-a-bitch" my mother screamed as she started to really smack the hell out of my brother.

"Hold on, lady," the older cop said, pulling them apart. "He wasn't alone in the car, the others got away, and the man whose car it is says he won't press charges as long as the damages are paid for."

"Damages! You crashed it, you little bastard," she yelled, starting to smack him again..

"Lady, stop. The guy's out here in the hall. Sir, get some clothes on, come out here and we'll settle this, OK? Otherwise your kid's going to jail."

My father went for his pants and wallet, "I'll be right there, Officer."

The two cops turned to leave, one paused and added, "And lady, tell your kid if he's out looking for trouble, don't wear gold pants."

The smacking continued, followed by plenty of "It'll never happen again."

Then my mother ran to the front door, "Frank, come over here please." She whispered something to him.

The door opened and a black man in his 50's came into our house. That was a first. My mother grabbed my brother and took him over to the man. "Go ahead, talk to the man whose car you stole and almost wrecked."

My brother lifted his head up. "I'm sorry we stole your car. Really. We were drinking..." My mother started in again. "Drinking! You lousy bastard! I told you not..."

"Angie! Stop!" my dad got her back under control, as my brother continued...

"We were really jerks and I'm sorry."

"Well, I'm sorry too," replied the man, "I hope you've learned a lesson young man. You've got fine parents here, and you should listen to them. You got off easy. If I was a mean man, or if those were mean cops, or if you had mean parents, you'd be a lot worse off than you are now. Good night, and stay out of trouble. Thank you folks."

"We're so sorry, I don't know how we can ever thank you!" my mom sounded for real.

"Just keep that kid in line or you'll have big problems soon. I know, I have four boys myself."

"Thank you sir." She closed the door and turned to my brother. "Now you! Who was with you?"

"No, no, I ain't squealing!"

"Oh yes you are, or I'm calling the cops this time!"

"I ain't, leave me alone, goddammit!"

My father had enough. "Goddammit" is one of those words that my parents could get away with once in while, but not a kid.

"You little son-of-a-bitch" my dad screamed and started throwing punches at him. Joey blocked most of them, but a few were hitting him. My sister and I were terrified. So this is what happens late at night, when everyone else is asleep, and kids are out drinking.

The fight stopped. My brother went into the bathroom. My mother was crying. My father was rubbing his arm like he hurt it. Joey didn't squeal. We all went to sleep. My brother too.

Whitey Shelley and I are best friends. We weren't always. Most of the kids in the 8th grade have been together since the 1st grade. Whitey Shelley is a relative newcomer, since he moved into the neighborhood in the 5th grade. He has

19

two older brothers. Even though they live right across the street in another apartment building, I've never even see them. One was real old. Maybe almost 30. He was a cop. The other one went away to college somewhere. Both his parents worked, just like mine, so we were pretty free to go and do what we wanted at our houses until they came home.

Whitey has a huge apartment. It has four bedrooms. It even has a dining room. His building seems a little seedier than mine. We both have elevators, but my building has an incinerator. That's a little hatch that you could dump your garbage into, right on your own building floor. Actually ours isn't a real incinerator anymore. They used to just burn all the garbage in the incinerator. But last year they took away the incinerator part, and made it a garbage compactor thing. You still put the garbage down the same chute, only now, we have about a million times as many roaches. There's no stopping them. My mother cleans and scrubs, and plugs up holes with wooden putty, plaster, Brillo, silly putty, everything... but now that the roaches aren't getting burned to death once a week, they are everywhere. At night, when you have to go into the kitchen for something, and turn the light on, you can't even kill them fast enough. They scurry away like little elves carrying microscopic pieces of Italian bread, Twinkies and meatballs back into their secret hiding places. At night we can't even breathe because my mother sprays so much Raid in the air. Mostly the roaches are in the kitchen, because the kitchen was actually right next to the garbage chute. But every once in a while, you'll find a roach in the living room, or the bathroom or even in bed. And whoever is the unlucky one to wind up with a roach on their leg or head or whatever, would rant and rave about what a dump we live in and how filthy and disgusting it is to live there and why did we have to live in such a horrible place. Then they'd kill the roach, and things would go back to normal.

Whitey has roaches too. Big deal. Everybody does. So what. We had other things to worry about. Like girls. How the heck were we going to get to feel one up?

We had been kissing a few of the girls on the block for

several years already. Spin-the-Bottle, Kiss-O-Leerio, and Post Office were handy introductions to the opposite sex, but we wanted more. Guys a little older than us talked about getting laid and blowjobs, and before you knew it, Whitey and I found out what those two things actually were. Imagine that!

In Whitey's building there's a family of Irish kids named the Fitzgeralds. Four boys, all about two years apart. The youngest, funniest, and meanest of the lot is Fitzy. He's a year older than us, and of course that much the wiser. Fitzy is the kind of guy who makes you laugh by throwing eggs, water balloons, bags of dog doo, or whatever else was readily available at whoever was conveniently right under his 6th story window. Of course, Fitzy only had loyalty to family members and people he knew would beat the living tar out of him. Anyone else could fall victim to his nasty deeds. Whitey and I were occasionally victims, but no more than other kids on the block. That meant he liked us. Especially since if I asked my brother to kick his ass he would, gladly. But I never have. I'm not a squealer. Fitzy likes that.

Fitzy is also creative in his mis-deeds. The best acts of vandalism are the ones that require the most planning. One time he and Mike Clooney spent hours collecting two garbage cans full of bottles, only to throw them at the motel down the block from the top of the hill overlooking the place. No reason. They just felt like it.

Fitzy heard there is a girl in our class who has a reputation. If someone has a "reputation," you don't have to ask if it's good or bad. Her name is Tina Robustelli. She's not cute, smells for some reason like sour milk, has two really strange sissy brothers named Francis and Ambrose, but has really huge boobs. So naturally, she was popular. It was also said that Tina "did it." I didn't know anybody who would admit to it, but the word was out. Tina wanted boys to feel her up, and then she would let them "do it."

Fitzy had a plan. He had been sweet talking Tina, and he thought today was the day he would get her. He knew how to open a door to one of the storage rooms in the back of my building's basement and that's where it was going to happen.

21

Here was the master plan or plans of Fitzy Fitzgerald that would allow us to see and, yes, perhaps cop a feel off a naked girl. Whitey and I would hide behind the piles of old coin-operated radios that were stored in the room, along with the cases of air raid fallout biscuits and tubs of emergency nuclear attack water, and wait for our cue from Fitzy; a loud sneeze. At that point, Tina would be totally nude, and we'd rush out from our hiding spots, get a glimpse of those big boobs, maybe get a grab, and have the laugh of a lifetime. Fitzy had vision.

Down to the basement we went. Through the dank stone and cement halls that smelled and looked exactly like a dungeon. Nothing was painted. Open drains were just black holes to nowhere. Doors were locked with several padlocks. Some were just nailed shut. An old man, Mr. Patter, sat in one of those rooms for hours, under a bare, dim light bulb. My parents said he made his own soap down there. Soap? It was one of those things that old timers seemed to do for no apparent reason. Just a few doors down from there was the boiler room. A huge furnace roared 24-hours a day, unless of course it was the coldest day of the year, then it was stone cold. No steam heat. No hot water. Nothing. I had lived in this building my whole life, and there were still cubby holes and doorways that even I was too frightened to explore. And at the very end of the long cellar hall that turned to the right and dead ended, there were two doors. One was the old dumbwaiter door, where people used to lower garbage and stuff from a small door in the kitchen for the porter to dispose of in the basement. The other door was the door behind which Whitey and I would for the first time see a girl naked, live, and actually have a chance to feel a real naked boobie.

"This is it, Whitey. I hope the super doesn't come back here."

"Does he ever?"

"Nah, not really. Fitzy said the key was up there, can you get it?" Whitey was taller than I was and easily got a key off the door frame on top. He opened the padlock, and we gave each other looks as if we were about to enter Aladdin's cave of treasures.

"Come on."

The room was filled with stacks of old-time radios with coin slots on them. At one time, they'd have these in bars, and people would drop nickels in to be able to hear it for a while. But all of the romantic songs and great radio dramas that once came through those speakers didn't compare to the rush of sexual excitement that Whitey and I felt. I wasn't going to tell Whitey, but I already had a boner.

"Hey, Vinny, I'm getting a boner."

"Shut up, you jerk. Back here."

We climbed over the radios and found a spot where we could sit down, and peek through a narrow space. And we waited. And waited. And waited.

"Shit. What's taking him. We've been in here an hour."

"Shut up, Whitey, it's only been about 20 minutes. He's got to get her in the mood, you know."

"In the mood? Oh, like Alfalfa and Darla?"

Whitey had a thing for Darla of "The Little Rascals" and started his imitation of Alfalfa singing... "I'm in the mood for looooovvvee, simply because you're near meeeeee. Darling oh when you're near me, I'm in the mood for loooooovvvveeee."

We all had a thing for Darla. She had the same effect on most of us that Betty Boop, and Annette on the Mousketeers had. Of course feeling like that about Darla was when we were real little kids. And it always amazed me that Alfalfa could just stand there in front of a whole club house filled with kids and sing right to Darla that he was in the mood for love. And Darla would get that look in her eye, and start showing off those dimples. But now that I'm older it's starting to make sense.

"Shut up, listen...."

Footsteps. In the hall. Voices. Listen. A moan. More moans.

"Oh Tina, oh Tina."

More moans and groans.

Whitey and I looked at each other. I probably looked just as stupid to him as he did to me. Eyes bugged out. Mouth

23

open grin. Head shaking. A combination of terror and bliss.

The creaking sound of the door opening.

"Come inside, Tina. There's nothing to be afraid of."

Then in barely a whisper, "Oh Fitzy."

"Here, sit down here."

We looked through the crack but couldn't see them.

I whispered to Whitey, "Shit, he's on the other side of the room."

"Oh Tina, you're so beautiful..."

There was a rustling of clothes. More moans and groans.

"Oh Tina, take off your coat."

"OK."

Groaning, moaning again.

"Take off that sweater, Tina."

"OK."

"Oh Tina, you have such great... such a great body."

"Oh, Fitzy."

We could hear definite smooching going on now. The sound of big wet kisses.

Whitey could hardly control himself, "This is unbelievable!" He panted.

"Oh Tina, please strip."

"No, Fitzy, no."

"Please Tina."

"No Fitzy."

"I love you, Tina."

"OK."

We heard a zipper, the rustle of clothing.

I mouthed to Whitey. "She's doing it!!!"

"Oh, Tina. You are unbelievably beautiful naked."

"Oh, Fitzy."

More moans and groans and smooching.

Then silence. Total silence. More silence.

A little bit of rustling. Nothing.

"AAAAAACHHHHOOOOOOO."

Whitey and I jumped up, knocking over several radios, ran around the corner of the room where we heard the sounds we had been waiting a lifetime to hear in person, and now was

24

a moment of naked glory......

SPLAAAASSHHHHH.

A flash of light. Another flash of light.

Owww. That hurt. I'm soaked.

I rub my eyes. Jumping up and down right in front of us is Fitzy Fitzgerald and Mike Clooney, roaring in laughter. They had just bombed me and Whitey with several water balloons, then took several pictures with a Brownie flash camera.

"You assholes!" Fitzy gloated having pulled off his best stunt ever.

"You fuckin' idiots! Oh, Fitzy. No, Fitzy. No, Fitzy."

It was Mike Clooney imitating Tina the whole time. He began kissing his hand passionately making the smooching sounds that made us hard. There were several pieces of clothing on the floor, and some water balloons that they'd probably save for some other suckers later in the day.

"You two are the two biggest assholes in the world."

Whitey and I were speechless. We knew Fitzy was right.

I hardly ever see my brother since he turned 20. This Winter he got a job at a ski slope. In the Bronx. That's right. Some city government planner apparently thought that what the people of the Bronx needed was a ski slope. Because once you got your exercise pounding on the radiators with a hairbrush or plunger or a hammer, trying to convince the super that a little steam on a freezing cold day seemed like a good idea... and after you killed a few thousand cockroaches in the kitchen, and finished cleaning the vomit off the hall floor in front of your apartment door, because if you waited for the porter to do it, it would be there until the fourth of July. After all that what better thing for a Bronxite to do than GO SKIING.

I don't know one person who has skied there. Although the times I went up there to look in disbelief at the people holding on to tow ropes, to go up the 18th hole on the golf course, it was jam packed. The only people I knew up there were my brother and his cronies who worked the place. Actually, they ran the place. The rental equipment, the snack bar, the tow rope, the locker room, everything.

And from what I could figure out, since my brother sure wasn't going to tell me, they had a pretty good racket going. They probably stole a little from the cash register, locker rooms, and ski equipment, drank all day, went skiing, fooled around with the tow ropes, made fun of rich boys from Riverdale and Westchester, and picked up rich girls from Riverdale and Westchester.

As Whitey and I watch the operation from up a tree on a hill across the snowy fairway, we just dreamt that one day, we should be so lucky to have such a racket.

Joey, my brother, would come home late at night. I was always already asleep on the top bunk against the opposite wall, and he hardly ever woke me up when he came in. Once in a while, I'd hear him throwing up out the window. Occasionally, he'd forget to close the window, and we'd freeze to death, since at night they usually turned off the steam to save a few bucks, and it was already impossible to stay warm. And it was real hard to warm the room back up after closing the window.

My sister sleeps in the bottom bunk, with a big blanket stretched across so you couldn't see in there. She has a little reading lamp clipped on the headboard, and even has a small bulletin board on the wall. It's her only private space. It's a lot like submarine movies. You know, people putting up curtains, and treating their bunks like it was their only place for solitude. In fact, the whole apartment is like a sub. My dad's a plumber at New York University, but he's also an expert electrician and carpenter. So anyplace there was wall space, my mother instructed him to BUILD BUILD BUILD. We have cabinets and closets everywhere. From wall to wall. From floor to ceiling. Sure we were only renters, but who cared. My parents hadn't had the landlord in the apartment since the day they moved in 1944. My father painted, did the plumbing, repaired broken windows, plastering, everything. It wasn't just an apartment. It was our HOUSE. And we did as we pleased.

As cramped as we were... as cold as it got... no matter how many roaches were living in small appliances, it was our HOME. It was clean, painted, wallpapered, carpeted, and it was ours.

But I could tell that with three teenagers, it was smaller than ever. My brother came home later and went our earlier. My sister stayed at school later, and did her homework at the library or at a friend's house. And any chance I could come up with a good excuse, I was out of there too. And by the time mom and dad got home from work, all they wanted to do was fix a meal, clean up, plop in front of the TV for a while, then open the Castro convertible for a good night's sleep.

I was fast asleep. "Vinny. Vinny." Someone was whispering. It was Joey. In the dark. He smelled like Sen-Sen. The stuff teenagers use to hide booze. "Wake up."

"What's the matter?" I was scared.

"I'm going away."

"Waddyuh mean?"

"I need to go away. I'm enlisting in the Army. I wanna go fight in the war."

I was shocked. I never had anybody go away. Oh, in 2nd grade, the two girls from the 2nd floor moved. In 3rd grade, Raymie Hands moved away somewhere. My grandmother died when I was five or so, but nobody ever went away. My parents were always there. My sister. My cousins, uncles, aunts. Almost everybody in my class has been with me since the 1st grade.

"I've got to do it," he said.

"Why?"

"When you're older, you'll understand."

"When are you going?"

"I'm going to stay at Jimmy O'Connor's place upstate until the Army accepts me. Then I'll be going in."

"Don't go." I think I was going to cry. I didn't want to cry. Maybe I was crying a little.

"Kid, if it wasn't for you, I would have been out of here

a long time ago. I'm leaving a note for mom and dad. Bye."
He turned and left.

The next morning, I got up. My mother was in the kitchen. She didn't see me. She was crying. I went back to bed.

February is always the worst month. It's the coldest part of Winter. No more days off from school. Spring seemed a million years away. Mid terms. And now my brother might be going to Viet Nam.

When Jimmy Joe Clancy's brother went, I thought it was great. Imagine, I knew a guy in Viet Nam, sort of. But now the thought of my brother going really scared me. I watched the news. I saw the boys on the stretchers, with bloody bandages, and the helicopters looking down on the fallen soldiers below, and the big cargo planes unloading the flag-draped coffins. I knew about that stuff now.

I hadn't seen my brother in almost three days. I guessed that pretty soon he'd knock at the door with a crew cut and a uniform on, give us a salute, and that would be the end of that. I can't think about him dying. No, not him. He's too smart. Too tough.

Almost all of my uncles were in World War II, and none of them got killed or even injured. My mother says that's because Grandma Pappalardo (her mom) died just before they left for war, and in a dream she told her not to worry, that she had to die so she could take care of her brothers during the war. And she was right. But who would take care of Joey? This is the longest three days ever.

The next day I came home from school in a blazing rush as always. Out of the blue-and-white uniform and into play clothes. I opened the door to the house, ran in, and sitting at the kitchen table is Joe. No crew cut. No uniform. No salute. Just his old duffel bag and a can of Rheingold.

"Joey! What are you doing here?"

"Well, kid. Looks like I ain't going to Nam. Your big brother's 4F. 4F for fat, fucking high blood pressure, fucking

28

bad feet, and for generally being fucked up!"

"Really? You're not going?"

"Not to Viet Nam, but I'm going nowhere fast. What're you doing'?"

"Meeting the guys for touch."

"Come on, I'll go with you."

"Really? Are you sure?"

"Let's go before I smack the shit out of you."

The guys at the flagpole were shocked. My brother wasn't the kind of guy who was known for playing sports. You'd see him playing poker on the stoop, or driving by in somebody's hot rod or fighting outside the bar, but not playing sports.

Some of my friends were really good at sports. Charlie Trotta was scouted by tons of high schools for three sports. Jimmy Joe Clancy was small, but was as good as Joey. Gerard Adams was almost 6 feet tall. Me and Whitey and the rest of the guys were OK.

My brother had a paper bag with cans of Rheingold. He immediately took over the show.

"Go deep." He threw a bullet to Charlie, 40 yards down field. Charlie caught it in his bread basket. He didn't flinch, but I'll bet it hurt. I went out next, tried to do the same thing, but I dropped mine.

"You're a bunch of little faggots. Come on, let's play tackle."

After a bunch of other kids dropped passes, or didn't do something right and got yelled at, it stopped being fun for me and everybody real quick.

Behind the fence in the distance you could hear, "Hey, Spade! Spade!"

There they were. Several of the neighborhood older kids. My brother's friends. The tough guys. Somebody had a car, and they wanted him to go along.

"I'm coming." He shouted in their direction. He then kicked the football as high as anyone of us had ever seen a ball go. A perfect spiral that hung for hours. By the time it hit the frozen ground he was in the '52 Plymouth, peeling out. Going nowhere fast.

We chose up sides and played until dark. On the way out of the park, we noticed a small group of guys. We couldn't really tell who they were, but if they were in our park, we thought for sure we'd know them. We got closer and closer and just as we were passing them, we smelled something really strange; like rope burning. We didn't seem to recognize them either. They were older, but didn't look like any of the older guys from the neighborhood. In fact, they didn't have slicked back hair, or Puerto Rican cockroach killers on. Their hair was weird, kind of like Moe in the Three Stooges. And they were laughing hysterically as we walked by, smoking... something.

We walked by in total silence. Once we were far enough away, Whitey said, "Know what that was?"

"What?" we all wanted to know.

"Those guys were smoking pot."

"What's that?" I asked.

"It mary-wanna. It's illegal."

"How do you know?"

"My brother Alfie goes away to college. He told me all about it. He even showed me some once." Whitey proudly admitted.

Charlie wanted to know more, "Isn't that a narcotic or something to do with hallucinations?"

"Yeah, I think so." Whitey didn't seem too sure. "Maybe we'll get high from smelling it?"

"Shit, you think so?" Jimmy Joe Clancy seemed very concerned.

"Forget about it, those guys are just beatniks," I pronounced self assuredly. "My father works at N.Y.U. and he's always complaining about the sloppy beatniks and radicals on campus. They're usually communists too. Against the war."

"Which one?" Whitey wanted to know.

"The war in Viet Nam, doofus."

"Don't call me doofus, you little shit, Schmidt," Whitey said as he chased me to put some noogies on my short haired skull.

With that, we were out of the park, back on the side-walks, and headed home. Great! Only one more day till the weekend. That's what we live for. No school.

It's a cold Saturday. I don't feel like playing football. I call for Whitey, and we decide to go down to the laundromat because he heard two girls from his building who are in our class are going to be hanging out there. Carrie Vitelli is one of the few Italians on the block. Most people don't think of me as being Italian, because of my last name, plus I don't look it. Everybody knows my brother is Italian, despite his name. Donna Murphy is one of 10 kids. She and Carrie are both really cute. And we know for a fact that they make out with guys. Yes, they know how to kiss. Not with Whitey or my-self, but other guys like Jimmy Joe Clancy and Gerard Adams, who are more worldly, and better at sports than we are.

The laundromat is an oasis. Sure, you have to put up with a few old ladies doing their wash, and you can't smoke or read "Playboys" or curse out loud. But believe me, in my neighborhood, no matter how old the person is, they wouldn't think twice about giving you hell on any of the above. And, if you had some really bad luck, you could even piss off a real nut job of an old coot. Like Mr. McCugh.

Mr. McCugh lives on the 6th and uppermost story of my building. And from the top of the highest TV antenna to the bowels of the basement, Mr. McCugh is the unofficial en-forcer of 118 West 238th Street. He's short and old. Real old. But you don't want to mess with him. He's what my mother calls "shanty Irish." Mostly that means he's probably a first-generation Irishman who grew up in Hell's Kitchen, White Harlem, or some other tough ghetto for Irish Catholic poor people. He wears black T-shirts with chinos and sneakers, kind of like the way some teenagers dress, actually. He even has tattoos that are so blurry with age you can't even tell what they are, and sometimes keeps a rolled-up pack of Luckies under his shirt sleeve. Nobody, but nobody messes with Mr. McCugh. Not me, not my brother, not even the Walsh kids who live in an apartment in the basement of my building, a couple of whom

31

served time in jail for armed robbery.

In the summer, we call the roof "tar beach" because you could sit up there in a beach chair and relax as if you were at the beach. But the tar beach on our roof has the meanest lifeguard you could imagine. Mr. McCugh. If he knows you and your parents, and you sit in your chair and keep your radio low, then you were alright. But if you had any thought of loud horseplay of any kind, Mr. McCugh would show you his sawed-off black baseball bat, and you got the message but quick. He knew what kids were up to, and he wasn't about to let it go on in his building. He's also a drinker. A heavy drinker. In fact, Mr. Walsh once told me, he has ropes nailed up all over the apartment; to walls, cabinets, woodwork, doors, even the ceiling. That's for when he falls down drunk, and needs a little help getting up.

The laundromat is always steaming hot. With the dryers spinning, hot water heaters boiling, and radiators blasting, it's always nice and toasty even on the coldest days. And if you're relatively quiet, just a few of you, no more than four, you could sit there for hours. You could even listen to the radio if it wasn't too loud.

Whitey and I make our move. We walk by the window and we could just barely see Carrie and Donna sitting right between the gumball machines and laundry soap machine through the foggy plate glass window. There's a wide ledge right by the front window with steam heat radiators underneath. Perfect for a cold winter's day hangout. As we slowly approach the window, trying to be cool, Carrie spots us and starts whispering frantically to Donna. That could mean anything. It could mean that Carrie or Donna hated or liked Whitey or me or just about any other combination. Well, Whitey likes Donna, and I like Carrie, and here we come...

"Anybody out today?" I nonchalantly inquire.

"What's the matter, we're not good enough for ya," Donna blurts out.

Strike one.

"No, I was just wondering if any of the guys were around."

Carrie isn't even looking at me. She's mouthing some song on the radio.

"Well, Jimmy Joe, BB and Ralphie were here, but they made too much noise and Mrs. Fitzgerald chased them out. I think they went to the fort by the bridge."

"Oh. Want some gum, Whitey."

"Yeah, get me a jaw breaker."

Above the jaw breaker machine is a sign with a "Snidely Whiplash" kind of character in a coffin holding a lily on his chest. The sign reads "NO DYE-ING HERE PLEASE"

Jaw breakers are huge and hard as rocks. A dentist's dream. How anybody could enjoy them I'll never know. But there are lots of things about Whitey that nobody could understand, the least of which are jaw breakers.

The girls aren't saying a word. Whitey began crunching the jaw breaker, and every bite sounds as if his molars are exploding. The washing machines are chugging away, water sloshing everywhere, and dryers humming. And just above the din, there he is, not going "Aaaaaa-Vay! Hoh!" but Murray The K is going bonkers on the six transistor Japanese radio that Carrie Vitelli is holding with two hands, pointing back at her and Donna. He sounds like his pants are on fire. "They are HERE, BABY! And Murray the K is with them!!! Here's John!"

"Hello W.I.N.S" A monotone English accented man says.

"Here's George!"

"Hey, baby, Wins is cool!" (That must be George himself.)

"Paul!"

"Ten ten wins is it!"

Yup, it's the Beatles playing along with Murray the K!

"And Ringo!" Murray screams through Carrie's speaker.

"W.I.N.S. is the greatest, baby, and we know GREAT when we hear it don't we lads?"

"Yeaaahhhh."

Wow. They're cool!

33

"And this is Murray the K...and I tell you I'm gonna be the fifth Beatle, baby...let's spin some sounds, here we go... with "Love You Do!!!....

(an unidentifiable Beatle in the background could be heard... "Love ME do!!!)

"Love ME Do!" Murray adds.

"Hey, that's really The Beatles, right?" Whitey says.

"No kidding. Where have you been? They're gonna be on Ed Sullivan tomorrow night." It sounds like Carrie was pissed off or something. "I wish I could get in the audience" she says, obviously quite hurt.

Whitey took time from trying to demolish whatever teeth he had left. "My brother at Cornell says that the Beatles are just a fad. He says folk music like Bob Dylan and Pete Seeger is the real new sound."

I figured it was my turn to add my two cents. "My brother says they're faggots."

At that moment, I knew that unless I was Sherman and Whitey was Mr. Peabody, and we could set the "way back machine" about five minutes, I had made an awful mistake.

"They're not faggots. And anybody who says that is just jealous, 'cause they're ugly slobs and have no idea what being cute, and singing, and music is all about. And just because they have long hair doesn't mean anything. They aren't followers like every idiot guy around here who hangs out on the street corner playin' cards and drinkin' beer and has a filthy mouth and drops out of school to work in a freakin' gas station or something. Come on, Donna, let's get out of here. It's stifling."

Whitey and I just stand there, stunned, and watch the two girls we thought we'd try to impress put on their sweaters, coats, gloves, hats and scarves, and head out into sub freezing temperatures rather than be in a nice warm place... with us.

"Boy, I'm glad I didn't talk about what my other brother said about them, 'cause he said exactly what your brother did."

Whitey buys two more jaw breakers and hands me one.

"Here, kid, this'll cheer ya up."

I thought I'd give it one more try..."Owwwwwwww."

I almost broke a tooth and spit it into the garbage can. "Let's get out of here," I say in total defeat.

Just a few doors over from the laundromat is "Snookey's." It's a candy store, like all the other candy stores of all the neighborhoods of New York. Whether on my block, or up the hill where mostly Jewish people live, or downtown just a couple of blocks over from 5th Avenue where the rich people live next to where the St. Patrick's Day parade is every year, or out in Brooklyn where we have relatives or even in Hackensack where more relatives are, there's a candy store on just about every block. Snookey's also has a grill where you can get hamburgers, french fries, or grilled cheese, so as far as most candy stores go, this was a pretty fancy one.

Sylvia is a big Italian lady with bugged-out eyes, a scratchy voice, and a short temper. She runs Snookey's with Tony, her husband. You can tell Sylvia runs the place, keeping the kids under control, the orders going smooth, and the place clean. Tony's always got a cigarette hanging off the end of his lip; and whenever possible, leans on one elbow at the end of the counter and talks to Vito the shoemaker from across the street, Mr. Walsh, or any of the other old timers from the neighborhood who always seem to be talking about Jews, coloreds, beatniks, Communists, hoodlums, the track or baseball. Tony works the grill, cleans up, and whatever Sylvia yells at him. There is no Snookey.

The rumor is that when they opened the business about 10 years ago, their nephew had just come home from the war in Korea. Supposedly, his nickname as a kid was Snookey. Probably the real story is the one where the neon sign guy got stuck with a custom neon sign that said "Snookey's Place" and they got a deal on it.

Sylvia knows every kid in the neighborhood, their older brothers and sisters, and maybe even their parents. And she can tell the good kids from the bad ones. That was easy in a candy store. Good kids sat quietly on the red vinyl stool, drinking an egg cream, eating a pretzel rod, reading a "Sad Sack" that they just bought, until the egg cream was done, pretzel eaten, comic finished, bill paid, and out the door, maybe even with some "Good 'n Plentys" for the road. Bad kids were a different story. They stormed into place, jumping down the three steps from street level, practically busting the door open. They'd be continuing whatever crazy talk was going on just before they entered; "Give me the thirty five cents you owe me, you jerk." "I don't owe you nothin'." "You better give it to me or I'll knock your teeth out." "Go ahead and try it, asshole."

"Alright! That's it, you little creeps. Get your asses out of here before I jump this counter and smack everyone of ya's." Sylvia was quick to nip it in the bud.

I never saw anybody defy Sylvia other than a few mumbled come-back lines. But my brother told me that one time, Studs O'Gorman from Review Place once stood up to Sylvia in a big way, and that's when Tony came from the back of the store with a baseball bat in one hand and a kitchen knife in the other. I think everybody in the neighborhood knew about that story.

Whitey and I aren't bad kids, but we aren't totally good either. It kind of depended on who we were hanging around with. And that could mean a lot of different things. There were so many kids in the neighborhood, or on your block, or even in your own building, that there was almost anything you wanted to try. And almost everyone of the groups that was doing whatever it was they were doing was usually happy to have somebody new hanging out with them. Not that you were really "new," because you knew these guys and their families your whole life. If you were really totally "new" in the neighborhood, you can bet that the only way people would let you hang out with them, was if you let them humiliate you on a daily basis. If they know you, and even though you've been hanging out with some other guys, well, maybe you came around to our way of having fun.

In my building, there were the Walsh boys. There were a couple of girls in there too, but it was the boys who were legendary in our neighborhood and all the surrounding neighborhoods. From the oldest, named Brother, who rode the number one train "el" from 242nd Street all the way to the tunnel at Dyckman, and had the top of his skull scraped off when he hung on for his life; to Harold, who once fell off the roof of our building, six stories up, while showing off and only survived because on the way down he managed to slow himself down by grabbing onto the many clotheslines strung across the back courtyards; to Terry, who everyone called a "fairy" all the way down to Albie, who was a few years older than me, but younger than my brother. Albie was probably the most famous of all the Walsh boys. He had the good street looks that Hollywood is always trying to capture. The kind of kid that wears a "ginney" tee (a tank top undershirt) and a pair of dungarees, and the girls go bonkers over him. Even though we've all heard the stories from rape to robbery to drugs, Albie was the guy the girls wanted and the cool guys wanted to be like.

My building also has the Lutz's, the Eagans, the Pacciones, the Caputos, and the Doyles... and Whitey's building across the street has the Stantons, the Vitellis, the Murphys, the Fitzgeralds, the O'Connors, and the Howes. And those are just two of the buildings in our neighborhood. Plenty of families, brothers, and groups to hang out with. And don't think that just because guys were brothers that they were in the same group.

Whitey and I are playing the part of good kids in Snookey's, sitting on the red vinyl stools. Whitey starts to spin around and Sylvia stops him fast, "Quit your scootchin'." We didn't know what "scootchin'" really meant but figured it must've meant something like "breaking balls."

"Hey, Vinny, there's Jimmy Joe and the guys, let's go!" Whitey says, after noticing them walk by the front window of the store.

Having already paid up front for our egg creams and pretzel rods, we were free to run out and catch up with Jimmy Joe. To me, Jimmy Joe was another newcomer to the neighborhood. He didn't show up until the 4th grade. And he didn't really live on our block. He was from almost 10 blocks away, but hung around on my street because that's where most of the kids in class lived. Jimmy Joe was like the leader of the kids who weren't in our class from 1st grade.

"Hey, where are you guys goin'?'" Whitey shouts to the guys walking up the hill.

"Pin darts in 118," Jimmy Joe calls back.

Oh shit. First of all, why the hell do they have to play in MY building? I know why. Because there are so many connecting hallways and elevators and stairways and hiding places. But people there know ME and I'll be the one to get in trouble.

"I ain't goin', Whitey."

"Oh come on, you chicken."

Chicken. Yeah right. Actually, I am chicken. Chicken to play in my building. But that's not what Whitey means. He thinks I'm chicken to play "pin darts." Pin darts is the most dangerous of all indoor city sports. Here's how you play. You take the large kitchen size match sticks, then cut off the red tip with a razor blade. You take the razor and cut two slits in one end. Then you take two pieces of paper and stick them in the end, like flights on a dart. Then you take a sewing needle, a big one, and insert the "eye" end into the other end of the match stick so the pointy end is sticking out. Now you have a pin dart. You choose up sides, and the object of the game is to stick as many darts as possible into the opposition's body. No aiming above the neck. Sure.

"I'm not chicken. Why don't we play in your building?"

"My building is no good. Mrs. Fitzgerald'll call the cops."

"Oh yeah, like that's worse than Mr. McCugh chasing you with a baseball bat."

"You haven't heard of 'McCugh Rules Apply' no above the 5th floor."

Once inside my building we meet at the rear staircase for the ground rules. No above the neck. McCugh rule #1: no above the 5th floor. McCugh rule #2: no in the basement. McCugh hung out down there sometimes with Mr. Walsh. And 3: maximum three darts each. First team to make three hits wins. No jackets or sweaters. Then it was time to choose for sides.

It was understood that Jimmy Joe was the best shot and the fastest among us so would choose two others for his team. His cousin BB wasn't really the next best, but Jimmy Joe thought he was because he is his first cousin, so those two would be captains and choose for sides.

"Odds or evens for first pick," Jimmy Joe challenged BB.

Without any hesitation, BB let out, "Evens, once twice three, shoot."

BB put out one finger, Jimmy Joe put out two, making him the winner. "I'll take Ralphie," Jimmy Joe had his first team mate.

"I'll take Bobby." BB had his first.

"I'll take Ralphie," Jimmy Joe had two.

"I'll take Vinny." I'm with BB.

"I'll take Whitey." All the teams are complete.

I hated it when Whitey and I were on opposite teams for pin darts. It wasn't like choosing up for ring-o-leaveo or Wiffle ball or curb ball or stick ball. Pin darts could make enemies forever. Amazingly, no one has ever had an eye knocked out with the deadly pin dart, but I've seen pins stuck in guys' necks or heads or ears and then the fisticuffs take over. Phillip Kitt still hates Jimmy Joe from a pin darts game two years ago, and hasn't been back on our block since.

Jimmy Joe was ready to command his troops. "Choose you for first go-out."

BB responds, "Evens, once twice three shoot."

Jimmy Joe wins again, and with that they're off while we count 10 Mississippis. Any more than that would be too big an advantage.

My building is so big that there are four stairways from the lobby. One on each end of the building, and two in between, and they could all be accessed.

We separate with three pin darts in hand searching for the other team lying in wait for us. Most of the guys creep along slowly, crawling or hugging the walls. I jump around, quickly, hoping that if somebody saw me, they'd have a hard time trying to hit me.

As I was jumping up to the fourth floor, Whitey charges to the railing and lets loose with three quick shots. I didn't have a chance to fire back. I threw my arms up to cover my head and "OOOWWWWWW" a direct hit on my wrist.

"You asshole."

Whitey comes running down the stairs, "Where'd I get you?"

"You asshole."

I look down at my arm where the pain is coming from, and blood is pouring out of the tiny hole where the pin dart was still stuck.

"I'm sorry, Vinny, I didn't mean it."

I pull out the dart, just as the other guys come running over. BB, my team captain, had a blood red spot on his skin-tight white dungarees on his right thigh about three inches in diameter. Ralphie, on the other team, was nursing his arm like he just had a vaccination. And my other teammate Bobby Bailey had a red blotch right over his heart. Looks to me like we lost this battle.

Jimmy Joe wants to know what exactly happened, "Where was your wrist when it hit?"

"Over my head."

"Whitey, you asshole, no above the head."

"Shut up, Jimmy Joe."

"Fuck you, Whitey."

Uh oh. The "F" word. I could see Whitey is really shaken up. He's big, but Jimmy Joe had a reputation for being a good fighter, even though we never really saw him fight.

Whitey went over to Jimmy Joe and stood in front of him. I could see he was thinking real hard. Jimmy Joe looks up at Whitey, ready for action. Suddenly, Whitey pushes Jimmy Joe in the chest with both hands. For some reason, it seems all fighters who don't really want to fight start out this way. Jimmy Joe was shoved back a couple of feet, and then put up his two hands, like in a John L. Sullivan stance, and yells, "I'm calling you out, Whitey. I'm calling you out," which reverberates through the tile-lined halls. He isn't exactly going after Whitey

40

or anything, he just keeps putting his arms up like he was going to punch him, but actually is backing up a few inches at a time. Whitey stares at Jimmy Joe and looks back down at me, "Come on, let's go get a Band-Aid."

"You big pussy," Jimmy Joe calls after Whitey as he walks with me down the hall to my apartment. Luckily no one was home.

It really wasn't that bad a cut. I put some cold water on it in the kitchen, pressed on it with a wet paper towel, and it soon stopped bleeding.

"Jimmy Joe can be a real little shit sometimes," Whitey said as he looked through the refrigerator.

"He sure acts like a big shot. Have you ever seen him in a fight?"

"To tell you the truth, the only time I saw him almost hit somebody was when he called out Sister Anita last year in class."

"Yeah, remember after he did it and he realized what he was doing, he started to bawl out loud crying and everything, right in front of everybody, and saying he was sorry and he never would have really hit her."

"And then Sister Anita said, 'You would have PULVERIZED me! You would have PULVERIZED me!' "

Whitey holds up something he found at the back of the refrigerator, "Can I have this?"

"What is it?" I ask, not wanting to give away something that somebody was saving.

"It looks like roast beef." Knowing that was probably left over from an Aunt Grace doggie bag, I figured it was OK. "Go ahead, but you owe me half of the next package of "Sno-Balls." (Those are those round cupcakes covered totally in pink marshmallowey stuff and coconut.)

"Deal," Whitey says, as he starts coating the old meat with salt and pepper.

"When does your family get home?" he asks between chews.

"My sister usually gets home around six because she stops at the library. My dad gets home at five, but then he goes to pick up my mother at work, and they get home around 6:15. My brother's hardly ever here."

"Yeah, that's like my house, except my one brother's away at school and my other brother Brian, the cop, is either hanging out in our old neighborhood in a bar or working weird hours."

I knew that wasn't the whole story. I knew that Whitey's father is a cripple, and a real drunk too. He walks with a bad limp and always has a different job. His mother works steady at Ehring's Bar and Restaurant on 231st Street. I think Whitey's father was pretty mean sometimes. He was in the hospital a lot too. His older brother Alfie was real smart. He went to Bronx High School of Science which is a public school for really smart kids, and then got a scholarship to Cornell. His oldest brother, Brian, was a cop. My brother told me he sees him in uniform sometimes at Grecco's Bar.

Whitey and I have been best friends since 7th grade. I had two other best friends before then, but those guys, Michael and Jerry, somehow started hanging around "Review Place" down the street with some other kids. I think they like the girls down there better. Me and Whitey just kind of bounce around from group to group. Plus, there's more big kids that hang around by us when it's not so cold, and mostly everybody hangs out on the stoop or on the stump or on the roof or in the alley. The bigger kids kind of let us hang out because they know our older brothers are pretty tough. Well, my brother Joey is, and Whitey's brother Brian is. Nobody talks too much about Alfie.

Just as Whitey finishes the last piece of meat, he says, "I think I better go home now. Can you go out tonight? It's Friday."

"I'll have to ask. What do you want to do?"

"Want to go skating?"

"Yeah, I'll call you."

"See ya."

Whitey was gone. I pull the wet towel off my wound, and a tiny drop of blood comes out. "That's the last time I'll ever play that game," I thought to myself. I hoped I was telling myself the truth.

42

Skating is the one place we can go on a cold winter Friday night. Our parents knew that if we actually went there, there wasn't much trouble for us to get into. The rink is called Kelton's and believe it or not, it's part of a family-owned recreation center right in our neighborhood. In the winter, there's an outdoor skating rink and in the summer there are tennis courts and even a huge swimming pool. I've never been to the pool because you have to be a member for the whole summer to go there. The funny thing is, that the complex is right next to the "el." So there you are at a private club paying a whole summer's worth of dues and you're under the freakin' "el" just like every other slob in the neighborhood. Next door there used to be an actual amusement park. It closed a couple of years ago and now it's just an empty lot, but when I was a little kid we used to go there all the time. It was called "Joyland" and had all kinds of kiddy rides. I still have a picture of me kissing the real Bozo the Clown on the nose there. And across the street there's another empty lot. Going back as far as I can remember it has been pony rides, then trampolines, then miniature golf, and now it's an empty lot. I guess people must've thought we lived in a resort area or something.

It looks like skating isn't going to be very eventful this night. As usual, when they announced it was "couples only" Whitey and I pretended we would ask a girl to go around with us, but we never get the nerve up to actually ask someone. That's too bad, because there are some real cute girls who go skating. Some of them are great skaters and have really nice skates. They must come down from Riverdale. That's where the Keltons live.

These girls seem to know the guys that we don't know. The guys seem like real wise guys and all have really cool speed skates. Whitey and I have hand-me-down hockey skates. I think I've seen some of those guys on Van Cortlandt Lake playing hockey. They've got all the equipment. Whitey's not too good in hockey, but I am. If I get a job, I think the first thing I buy will be real hockey equipment, instead of taping

43

pillows to my shins.

Skating ends pretty late, around ten. I like walking home at that time. Even when it's freezing cold, like it is tonight, you get to see what goes on in the neighborhood at night. There's always a crowd of old men waiting by the corner cigar store for the "Night Owl" edition of the Daily News. That's the next day's paper that you get the night before. I asked my father why he never gets that one, and he says because he'd have nothing to read on the way to work. You hardly ever see those old guys talking to each other. They just hang around outside the store, usually smoking cigars. And once the paper arrives, the old man in the store can hardly cut the string on the bunch quick enough before they each grab one and rush back home with the paper. I wonder what they read the next day.

There are three or four bars on the way home. The first three are what my brother calls "donkey" bars. That's where the old Irish men from the neighborhood go. They sit at the bar with their caps on, and don't listen to the juke box unless it's a special occasion like New Year's Eve or Saint Patrick's Day. One bar is called McNichol's and even though it's a donkey bar for old men, I hear it's the toughest bar around. One time, two colored guys walked in and held the place up. One crook grabbed a guy sitting on a stool and put a gun to his neck and said he'd kill the guy if anybody tried anything funny. Then the other guy jumped over the bar to the cash register. What they didn't know was that the guy who had the gun to his neck was Andy Fucci. First of all, everybody in the place hated Andy Fucci. He was Italian, he never shut up with his crazy stories, and he thought it was real funny to secretly wipe his snots on you. So all the Irish guys in the bar jumped the crooks even though they threatened to kill Andy and had a gun at his head. And yes, they pulled the trigger and shot Andy. But they jumped them anyway, and put the colored guys on the floor, and blew their brains out with their own guns. And every guy in that bar swore on a stack of bibles that those two guys came in for a beer, got in an argument and shot each other. Oh, Andy did get shot in the neck, but much to the disappointment of the rest of the regulars, it was only a flesh wound, and he was out of the hospital in a few days.

The last bar on the block is Grecco's. That's where the wild teenagers and younger people hang out, including my brother. On a cold night like this, they'd all be inside, not spilling out onto the street like usual. Whitey and I peek in the window and see the wild party going on. The jukebox is blasting "The Lion Sleeps Tonight" by the Tokens with all the guys singing in that really high falsetto...

"eeen the jungle, deee mighty jungle, dee lion sleeps tonight, HUT HUT, een the jungle, dee mighty jungle, dee lion sleeps tonight, HUT HUT, a weem a wa, a weem a wa, a weem a wa," etc., and it's a riot to see these tough guys singing along to this song. It's like "Alley Oop" and "Teeny Weenie Yellow Polka Dot Bikini" and "Yakety Yak" and "Surfin' Bird." Cool songs that are fun. Nobody knows what they mean in those songs, they're just fun to sing.

The next song to come on was "She Loves You" by the Beatles. And almost as soon as it starts, even before the the "yeah yeahs" end, Jackie Morrissey kicks the jukebox in exactly the right way so that the needle skips across the record and goes on to the next song. "No English fags allowed," Jackie shouts, and all of a sudden all the girls start chanting, "We want the Beatles, we want the Beatles." But the chanting stops once the Four Seasons started singing the opening to "Sherry." Whitey looks at me and says with the most serious look he could muster, "Don't start." I knew what he meant, because to taunt Whitey with "Shelley" sung like "Sherry" meant you'd have a real fight on your hand, and even though he was my best friend, I knew he would kick my ass. I assured him, "Whitey, I don't hear a thing."

I wasn't sure why, but I was beginning to realize that music sure pissed some people off.

Aunt Gina and Uncle Carmine live in Brooklyn, but they come over to our place for dinner at the drop of a hat. I think Uncle Carmine likes my mother's cooking better than Aunt Gina's, who's my mom's sister. But then again, some

45

people think the best-tasting food is free food. It's Sunday, and Aunt Gina and Uncle Carmine are here for dinner. They didn't have any kids, but Uncle Carmine acted as if he was one. His favorite TV show was "Sing Along with Mitch," he was in two barber shop quartets, and he brought his guitar wherever there was a free meal, or a captive audience to be had.

My Uncle Nicky lives right in our own building. Some of my relatives don't like him anymore, even though they don't talk about it, because he got divorced last year. He doesn't have kids either. But my mom really likes Uncle Nicky. He's the youngest of the nine kids and the only one younger than my mom. She won't let anybody bad mouth Uncle Nicky when she's around. Uncle Nicky and my mom love to sing when Uncle Carmine brings his guitar. They actually can sing pretty good together.

After the usual way-too-much food, first a plate of antipasto with several cheeses, black olives, green olives, Progresso artichokes, celery, hot radishes, and pepperoni, then the lasagna and the bread and some sausage, then the plates are cleared, then comes the roast beef, the mashed potatoes, the sweet potatoes, the boiled green beans, peas, spinach, the broccoli, the gravy, more bread, the butter, and seconds, then the salad, with everything that was in the antipasto and some iceberg lettuce, then the table's cleared again, then the coffee and cakes, and pastries.

Then my father gladly takes over in the kitchen. He can't stand Uncle Carmine's guitar playing and singing. On this Sunday, he'd rather do the dishes than sit in the living room and listen to Uncle Carmine, my mother, and Uncle Nicky go through, "Apple Blossom Time," "By the Old Mill Stream," "In the Streets of Old New York" for the umpteenth time in almost three-part harmony. My father hates doing the dishes.

Uncle Carmine goes into his routine, "Angie, do you have a small chair with no arms?" I don't know why he asks. It's only the four millionth time. My mom brings out the same chair, and Uncle Carmine takes his guitar out of its case. All I know about this guitar is that it's really beautiful dark wood.

Not a scratch on it. He also takes out of his case an old empty fishing line spool and a yellow cloth. He starts to wipe the guitar with the cloth, and puts the spool just in front of his right foot, which he immediately uses and starts to tap with his right wing tip.

I just hope my mother doesn't try to get me to sing with them. In the 3rd grade, I was picked out of the class and forced to sing lead in a class play. Ever since then, she thinks I'm another Frank Sinatra. Singing in front of others makes me real nervous.

"OK, one, two, three, four," there's no stopping Uncle Carmine now, "Down by the oooooollllllllldddddd millllllllllllll streeeeeeeaaaaammmmm" My mother and Uncle Nicky look at Uncle Carmine like that dog in the RCA ad looking at the Victrola. When one of them needs help, Uncle Carmine makes all kinds of funny faces with his eyebrows going wild, trying to tell them to go up or down a few notes for harmony, and sometimes sings the parts they should be singing.

My sister sits next to me on the couch, laughing at the scene. Now I hear the front door opening. It must be my brother. He never has Sunday dinner with us anymore. He walks past everyone, and with a big phony smile, says, "Hi everybody, just passing through." Everyone waves to Joe, not wanting to interrupt the "you were sixteen, not seventeen" part. Joe goes into the bathroom for a few minutes, and then goes into the bedroom. All of a sudden all I hear coming over the TV in the bedroom, blasting away, is screams. One constant roar of high-pitched screams coming through the three-inch speakers on our old Motorola TV, piercing the slowed down finale "ooooooollldddd millllllllllllllll streeeeaaaammmmmmmmmmmm."

My sister and I jump up and run into the bedroom. My brother's sitting on the edge of his bed changing his socks. "What's going on?" I yelled. And without missing a beat my brother says, "Someone just got shot on the Ed Sullivan Show!"

"Oh my God! Really?" I ask. After all, I saw Oswald killed on TV.

"I swear to God." He reassures me.

"You liar," my sister butts in, "The Beatles are on The Ed Sullivan Show."

"Oh yeah." I remember. The Beatles.

My brother always does stuff like that. One time I asked him if there really was an Easter Bunny and he told me with a straight face that there used to be but he was crucified. I cried after that one, but I was really small. He was a good liar, with a good sense of humor.

On our lousy second TV, with bad reception, it was hard to make out what was going on. Just lots of screaming girls and shots of the audience. They never show the audience on The Ed Sullivan Show, unless some Prince or something is sitting in the audience and he stands up and takes a bow, but on this show they're showing the crowd go wild almost as much as The Beatles. It's really strange, because all the girls aren't just screaming, some of them are sobbing, crying uncontrollably. It's hard to make out what The Beatles look like because of our lousy reception, in fact, except for the drummer with the big nose, all three of the guys singing look alike.

My brother seems more interested in shining his pointy black shoes than paying attention to the show. "Joey, do you like them?" I ask.

"The only reason these fairies are on Ed Sullivan is because somebody got paid off, " my brother says matter-of-factly, all knowing.

"I like them," my sister says meekly.

I didn't know what to think. But wow, all those girls in the audience going wild, screaming, crying, smacking each other and pulling their hair out... something must be going on, and I hope I can find out what it is.

The Beatles were just finishing their first song, when Uncle Carmine decides to give up on "Down By The Old Mill Stream" take 967 and check out all the hubbub in the bedroom.

"What's the big racket in here?" Uncle Carmine asks as if he had heard a train wreck.

My brother quickly snapped, "Ed Sullivan just got shot on TV!" My mother knows what a wise ass my brother is...

48

"Vinny, what's going on?" she asks.

"It's The Beatles on Ed Sullivan, you should see the girls in the audience, pulling their hair out and screaming."

"I was in the audience when Frank Sinatra was at the Paramount, and you should've heard the screaming there! Oh my God, and it was so hot, I almost fainted," mom says.

"Stop it, Angie," Uncle Carmine is incredulous, "at least that was music, with an orchestra and real tunes, this is just noise, 'yeah yeah yeah yeah yeah yeah,' that's not lyrics, that's a racket. And those electric guitars, sheesh, they have all that screaming because they don't want you to hear how terribly they play those instruments."

Uncle Nicky, who was listening to Uncle Carmine with a serious look on his face was ready to put in his two cents, "Oh, Carmine, you sound like my father when we used to listen to Benny Goodman do 'Swing Swing Swing.' He said it was trash because he liked the opera."

"That's different. Have you heard this stuff, Nicky?" Uncle Carmine asked.

"Not really, but..."

Uncle Carmine interrupts, "Well, wait until you do! It's God-awful! Believe me, I know music!"

There's something strange about this whole thing. Uncle Carmine seems really upset over this. I never heard him ever once say anything about the music kids listened to. And now he was red in the face, jowls jiggling and big ears flapping about it.

Aunt Gina, his wife, comes into the room, "Carmine, we really must be going now."

"OK, sweetie pie." Uncle Carmine then turns, and looks right at me. "Vinny, do you like The Beatles?" Now I really had to think. My brother and his friends hate them, my sister and almost all girls like them. They do look like fairies with that long hair, but... "Yeah, I think they're cool." I couldn't side with Uncle Carmine on this one.

"Oh boy! Angie, keep an eye on that kid, next thing you know he'll be playing with dolls. So long, everybody."

Aunt Gina and Uncle Carmine leave with Uncle Nicky,

and my brother was gone soon after, "just out"... And mom and dad exhausted from the big Sunday dinner event.

My sister went into the kitchen to do some homework, and I was in the bedroom. I had to cram in my homework for Monday morning. Usually I put the TV on while I do it, but there was nothing on Sundays after Ed Sullivan... I didn't like "Gunsmoke." So instead I pulled a transistor radio out of the top drawer with all the junk (string, cards, rubber bands, pens, used batteries) and decided to listen to the radio. I wanted to check out what the cool stations were playing... I wanted to hear more Beatles. But Sunday nights, all you could hear on the radio was religious shows and news talk shows... so I turned to page 54 of my math book and did questions 1 through 10, showing all work... no music. It sure was quiet and boring. And I couldn't wait to get to class tomorrow and talk to the guys... and yes, the girls, about The Beatles on Ed Sullivan.

It was freezing all last night. My mother's poking me real hard like she always does when I have to get up in the morning. My sister is already dressed, and ready to leave for school since she has to take two buses to get there, and I guess my brother didn't come home again last night. His friend "Smoker" has his own apartment. I hate to get out of bed on these mornings when the radiator's stone cold. My mother has all the gas jets on the stove burning and the oven on for heat. It's not too bad if you wrap yourself in a blanket and bring your clothes and underwear into the kitchen to dress. And it's really great if you put your clothes on the kitchen table and stand on a chair to dress. I swear, it's about a hundred degrees up where your head is. Maybe in another kitchen somewhere in the city, standing on the kitchen chair in your underwear and squirming into long johns might be frowned upon, but here it's just survival. Breakfast today is the same as almost every other day... scrambled eggs on Wonder Bread. My mom is the best at Italian foods, but when it comes to eggs, you're better off just getting scrambled.

My mom leaves for work just after I leave for school, and she's already got a wash in the washer. Most of the other kids think we live in luxury because we have a washing machine right in the kitchen. With it sitting there, we hardly have enough room for a table up against the wall, but my mother swears she'll never go to the laundry room in the cellar again. Something about her catching a drunk doing something disgusting into one of the washers.

Usually, we hang the laundry up on two outdoor clothes lines. One of them goes out the kitchen window and goes clear across a courtyard and attaches to Mr. Slattery's kitchen window. I always thought that was really cool of Mr. Slattery to let us do that. He's been our neighbor for as long as I can remember. The only time I ever was in his house was when my father took me with him to attach a pulley to the window sill outside his kitchen when I was about 4 years old. We have another clothes line out the bedroom window. That one is even more ingenious. My dad took a length of pipe about 10 feet long and attached it to the fire escape somehow, so it was sticking straight out. And with a pulley on the end of the pipe, and another pulley at the window sill, we had a good 12 feet of clothes line in the bedroom and about 10 feet in the kitchen. We never put the laundry all the way over to Slattery's window because my mother said it would be rude. But on freezing-cold, damp winter days, even more ingenuity was in order. I've been in lots of friends' and relatives' apartments all over the city, and never have I seen the likes of the contraption hanging from the ceiling in our tiny kitchen. Since it's usually empty, you probably wouldn't even notice it, and, since when it's not in use it's right up next to the ceiling over the washing machine, by the kitchen window. It's a rectangular grid made of steel tubing, with about six thick wires going from end to end, like a mini-clothes lines with clothes pins already in place. And through a series of pulleys and hoists and rope like you'd see on a pirate mast, this grid is lowered down, right over the washing machine. It's then loaded with a whole load of heavy, wet laundry right out of the washer. Each piece of laundry is wrung as dry as possible, and then hung into place on one of those thick wires, and snapped into place with a wooden clothes pin. After the whole load is hung, man is that thing heavy. In fact,

51

it becomes a two-man operation. My mom always mans the hoisting rope, and then I take an old mop handle that has two steel prongs on the end still on it in a V shape and put it up to the end of the grid furthest from the wall. On the count of three, I push the end of the grid up as far as I possible can, while my mother yanks on the rope with all of her might, giving usually three big tugs and grunts until she can wrap the slack around a thing my father attached to the wall that looks like a thing you see on a dock, called a cleat. And magically, just about when dinner's done that evening, the whole line will be dry. Then it'll be time to do another load of family laundry and continue the ritual until we can retire it until the next cold, damp winter.

I hate long johns, but my mother is a big believer in them, probably because she doesn't have to sit in a small desk in a warm classroom all day. But giving into little things like long johns sometimes means you can trade for other stuff. So I go for my first try of the week, "Mom, could you get me a record at work today?"

My mother works at Fuhrman's department store, which is this store on 231st Street that has been there for like a hundred years or something. It even has gas lamps. "A record? Which one?"

"I want the new Beatles album."

"Oh, are you kidding me?"

"No, I really want it, and Anne Marie does too."

"Well, I'll see if I have time at lunch."

I knew that was a done deal. In my house a "maybe" was almost always a "yes" and a "no" was always a "no."

As usual, I was just a little bit late for school. Even though it was freezing cold, the nuns still make us wait in the school yard until it was time to go into class. The principal, Sister Thomas, comes out in her extra heavy winter nun costume and rings a huge bell. That meant stop in place and wait for the next bell, which meant walk over to where your class lined up and get into size places, double file, boys behind girls, and wait for the next bell, which was walk into school, into class, to your desk, and into the world of Sister Fidelis, our 8th

52

grade teacher.

Sister Fidelis was in an unusually jolly mood this day. She even got a big laugh right after doing morning prayers by striking a prayer pose and asking the class who she was imitating. With her hands lazily intertwined, and thumbs pointing apart, and held down below her rosary belt, head cocked to one side, looking up to the ceiling, mouth crooked and all weight on one leg, the other leg bent and one shoulder slouched, we all knew... "Bobbbyyyyy Dicostanzo."

Dicostanzo, with eyes bugged-out, turned as beet red as an olive-skinned Italian possibly could, and was to never strike the pose again for the rest of the school year, and probably the rest of his life. The power of a nun was never to be underestimated.

Morning was like most of the mornings at Presentation School. Burning through as many subjects as quickly as possible while students were captive and distracted enough not to be counting the minutes until the end of the school day. Before I knew it, we had gone over the math problems on the board from homework, and didn't have to hand it in, much to the relief of most of the class, but really pissing me off since I did it. We got through some general science learning like we did every year since 4th grade that the sun was 93 million miles from earth, and light travels at 186,000 miles per second, and some kids still don't get it. The most fun is watching Sister Fidelis dissecting sentences on the board with all those lines and spaces for nouns, verbs, adjectives, pronouns, adverbs, and all those other things that wind up almost to the bottom of the blackboard, because she always screws it up somehow, and it just so happens that Joanne Martorana always corrects her mistakes, much to the chagrin of Sister Fidelis. And it was already time for lunch. Luckily I lived close enough to school where I could walk home for lunch and eat whatever I wanted since my parents both worked, rather than go to the school cafeteria and be forced to eat everything from baloney to spiced ham on gooey white bread with butter on both sides and nothing but white milk to drink.

I could go home to my own refrigerator and have a leftover meatball sandwich on Italian bread washed down with a sixteen-ounce Coke in a bottle. But best of all, I could hang out with Whitey, who also went home for lunch. And since his parents weren't home either, it was no problem for him to come over to my place for real Italian meatballs. He stopped off at his apartment to pick something up, while I got a head start on getting lunch together. I was just about done when there was a banging on the door. (Our doorbell hasn't worked since as long as I could remember.)

"Who is it?" I shouted through the heavily locked steel door.

"Whitey."

I opened the three locks and Whitey bounded in.

"I've got it! Right here!"

"Got what?"

"Meet The Beatles!" Wow! He beat me to it. The rat. I was hoping to be the first in the class to get it.

"Great, let's put it on!" I said.

But Whitey, always more hungry than I was, didn't agree.

"No, we'll eat first, then listen."

"OK, grab a sandwich and we'll go in the bedroom to put it on."

We grabbed our plates of cold meat balls and sauce on crispy Italian bread and went to the bedroom. Whitey may have been impressed with the food, but he wasn't impressed with our hi-fi. "This thing is a mess. When was the last time you had a new needle on this thing?"

"I don't know. Does it matter?"

"Are you kidding? I ain't gonna ruin a brand-new record. Look at all those dirty old 45s on that thing. Don't you know you're not supposed to use those stackers? The records scratch against each other."

I couldn't believe it! My brother listened to "Yakety Yak" and "Peter Gunn" and "Get a Job" and tons of other records a million times, and I never noticed them getting wrecked and of course we used the stacker. How else could you listen to a bunch of 45s in a row without getting up every three minutes to change a record? In fact, just about all we listen to are 45s. We have boxes of them, and just a few thirty three and a third LPs. Plus, I never once thought that a needle could screw up a record. "Just put it on, I want to hear it." But Whitey refused, with cold sauce dripping down his face and onto his white shirt, "Nope. I just got it and I ain't gonna ruin it with no crummy needle. We'll go to my place after school and listen there."

"Alright. Let's go back into the kitchen."

We finished lunch, I cleaned up. I never knew Whitey could be fussy about something like that. I didn't think Whitey could be fussy about anything.

Back in class again with everybody still excited from lunch-break freedoms. "Alright class, calm down. We're going to music class with Miss Schmelzer." The class let out a common groan. Oh no. Not Miss Schmelzer. She's even older than Sister Fidelis, and believe it or not, not even as much fun. We all get up and as soon as the classroom door opens we can hear that rickety old piano playing some kind of march just like the kind they play on "Romper Room." I mean, she's been playing that same song since 1st grade and we thought it was corny then. Back in 1st grade, I thought I was going to like music class because Miss Schmelzer let me and Teddy McKenna sing the "Good 'n Plenty" song in front of the class. But lately, the song we've been singing in the schoolyard the most, sung to the same tune, goes: *Once upon a time there was a Cuban-eer, Fidel Castro was his name we hear. He had a country and he sure had fun. He used machine gun bullets to make the people run. Castro says, love Nikita Khrushchev. Castro says, really think he's swell. Castro says, hate the USA. I'm gonna kill the President so he can go to hell."* I don't think we've sung this since the President died. I don't think the nuns or Miss Schmelzer would think this version was too cute. Especially sung by a couple of smart-ass 8th graders.

So here we are sitting in the music class. First thing we do to warm up is sing through the scales. Miss Schmelzer pounds a chord on the piano and we respond, ah ah ah ah ah ah ah. CHORD. ah ah ah ah ah ah ah. CHORD. ah ah ah ah ah ah

55

ah. CHORD. Through the entire scale all the way up the piano. Miss Schmelzer leads us in the singing by opening her mouth as wide as a human being possibly can, and probably wider than lots of different kinds of animals. It's so wide open that you can see straight down her throat and count her fillings. Then she starts with those stupid flash cards and rhymes... "two sharps "b" and "c" brings us to the key of "d." Whatever the hell that means. Then after this drill, it's time to sing. "Open your books to page 9, let's start with 'Ave Maria'." Another favorite of hers since grade one. During the last chorus, the boys in the class have a little fun, and both Sister Fidelis and Miss Schmelzer are well aware of it. It finishes up with a bunch of "Ave Marias" and it just so happens that "ah'vay" is a very popular sound right now. Murray the K, the crazy DJ from WINS has this thing where he does this tribal chant thing. It goes something like this,

MURRAY the K: "aaaaaaaaaaaaaahhhhhhhhhh. VAY!"
CROWD: "HO!"
MURRAY THE K: "aaaaaaaaaaahhhhhhhhhhh. VAY!"
CROWD: "HO!"

Murray then answers with a long chant of gibberish, and the crowd follows him with a deafening war cry of chants, gibberish, and profanities at the top of their lungs.

So the "ave's" in the final chorus are followed by a soft "ho" which gets louder with each "ave" until the last one, which is shouted loud and followed by a loud semi-yell of gibberish. Instantly followed by a simultaneous crash of a piano chord and even louder yell from Sister Fidelis in the back of the class, "Stop, you idiots! Can't you behave even for a sacred hymn? You asinine morons!"

Most of the girls are terrified by these outbursts, but a few of them, and most of us boys, get a huge kick out of them and laugh under our breaths whenever she makes a fool of herself like she just did. Whitey, however, was not good at laughing to himself.

"Shelley, you're the biggest moron of them all," she yells as she gains momentum down the aisle, getting more steamed with every exhausting step. Without missing a beat, she picks up Whitey's hard-covered hymn book and bangs him over the head with it. "Now shut up." Whitey was half smiling, but it was gradually turning into a stunned look of realization that he just received a pretty good whack on the head.

"Now, 8th grade, " Miss Schmelzer regained control of the class, "last evening I tuned in The Ed Sullivan program on the television set, and saw and heard what many of you saw and heard."

I couldn't believe my ears. I can't imagine Miss Schmelzer watching TV at all, never mind tuning in to catch The Beatles.

"How many of you saw The Ed Sullivan program last evening?"

The entire class' hands shot up faster than volunteers to go bang blackboard erasers outside the school. Well, almost the whole class.

"How many did not see The Ed Sullivan program last evening?"

Jerome Mullooly, Mark Fay, Mary Fanning, and Joanne Martorana. That was it. The four quietest, most studious, most pious, most lame kids in the whole class.

"Well, I'm glad to see there are some parents who still have control over their children! Now for the benefit of the rest of the class, I'm going to teach you a little lesson on what it was that you heard last night, because it certainly wasn't music."

Miss Schmelzer began to draw her five-line music staff on the blackboard, "Now slowly, sing that yeah yeah song." Dead silence. Miss Schmelzer turns to face the class with a look of total disgust on her face like she's going to make us all drink castor oil for our own good.

"Go ahead, sing the yeah yeah song."

Whitey and I are in shock. Miss Schmelzer asking us to sing a rock-n-roll song! And not just any song, but the coolest, most popular song on the radio. The closest we ever came to singing rock-n-roll was when she let us sing "How Much is that Doggie in the Window."

And from the back of the room, Sister Fidelis commands us, "Sing the yeah yeah song!"

Whitey and I start to lead the class in a verrrrrryyyyy slow, and embarrassed tone, *"She loves you, yeah, yeah, yeah."* And with each syllable, Miss Schmelzer frantically writes the notes we are singing on her chalk music chart. *"She loves you yeah yeah yeah. She loves you yeah yeah yeah yeah yeah."*

"Stop right there!" Miss Schmelzer orders us. "Do it again." This time with every word we sing, she writes the word out on the board underneath the note. And when we were done, there it was, the entire opening chorus of "She Loves You" written out on the board with notes and all on Miss Schmelzer's blackboard.

"Take a look at what we have here, class." Miss Schmelzer is really worked up. "Jerome Mullooly, stand up and read these lyrics out loud to the class."

"She loves you yeah yeah yeah. She loves you yeah yeah yeah. She loves you yeah yeah yeah yeah yeah." Jerome Mullooly reads in a monotone voice, like he was reading off the planets in the solar system.

"Jerome?"

"Yes, Miss Schmelzer?"

"Are these good song lyrics?"

"No, Miss Schmelzer."

"And why is that?"

Jerome Mullooly looked to the left, to the right, to the ceiling, to the floor, back up to the ceiling, picked his nose once and said, "Because they say 'yeah' so many times. We're not allowed to say 'yeah' in my house."

The whole class laughs out loud.

"Quiet!" Sister Fidelis rumbles.

Miss Schmelzer is getting almost animated. "Joanne Martorana, stand up, please, and count how many different notes are used in this so-called song."

Joanne Martorana stands and points at the board from her seat. "One, two, three, four. Four."

"Very good. Four notes for 20 words. Four different notes for 20 words. Class, that isn't music. This isn't music. This is rubbish. And if you listen to this music, your brain will stagnate as much as the poor misguided souls who write and sing this material with no musical training. It's merely an animalistic urge for instant gratification and primitive lusts and desires. I think Sister Fidelis will agree that if music could ever be sinful, this is certainly is."

Sister Fidelis rises from her chair, "You could be right, Miss Schmelzer."

I couldn't believe it. Miss Schmelzer never ever even let on that she knew rock 'n roll existed, and here she is trying with all her might to convince us that the absolute coolest song that has everbody in the whole city going nuts is junk. How come she never did this with something like "Itsy Bitsy Teeny Weenie Yellow Polka Dot Bikini" or some other really silly song? If she and Sister Fidelis are making that big a deal out of it, The Beatles must be even cooler than I thought.

Without another word, Miss Schmelzer steps over to the piano and starts pounding out that silly march music. "Let's go, class, step lively." Sister Fidelis took control of the troops once again.

"Hey, Whitey, wanna sin after class?" I whisper.

"Bless me father for I have sinned, I sang 'yeah' a hundred times, and jerked off once." Whitey shoots back at me.

It looks like the rest of the school year might be more fun than I thought.

Going to Whitey's apartment was like going into another world. I mean our furniture wasn't new, but Whitey's looked like the inside of a bungalow in Rockaway Beach; really old and worn-out Oriental rugs, ancient dressers and cabinets, oversized but tattered stuffed chairs and a huge crushed velvet couch with tassels on the bottom. They even had a couple of large cases with glass doors that had foreign looking knick-knacks in them caked with dust. I mean our stuff was old, but at least my mother sewed the holes up, and the stuffing wasn't hanging out or anything.

Whitey takes me into his room. It's huge. His bed wasn't pushed up against the wall. It's practically in the middle of the room, and there's still lots of room around it. The stuff might be ancient but at least he has his own desk, his own closet, his own dresser, and even his own cork bulletin board on the wall. He has the same two autographed pictures of Yogi Berra and Sam Huff that I have from the time the Safeway Supermarket opened down on Broadway and 232nd Street a couple of years ago. He cut out a picture of The Beatles from The Daily News and put it on the board so that it was partially covering a photo of Mickey Mantle and Roger Maris together. On the desk he has the same kind of 45 box that my cousin Jimmy has. He also has a larger box that's the size of 33 1/3rd LP albums.

"Here's where I keep my new record collection," Whitey says, as he gingerly opens the 45 case, revealing maybe three or four records.

"Are those your records?" I ask.

"Yup. I've got four. I can buy one single a week with my allowance."

"You get an allowance?"

"Yeah. don't you?"

"Nah. I just ask for money or something, and either I get it or I don't."

"Let's play the album," Whitey says as he opens his brand-new album box and takes out one of the two albums in there. It's called "Introducing The Beatles."

We head into the living room and against the far wall is something I had never noticed before, a huge console hi-fi. "Wow! When did you get that!"

"Well my big brother Brian the cop bought if for the family for Christmas. It's stereo."

Whitey took the album carefully out of its sleeve and put it on the turntable with a carefulness I had never seen before. He twisted a couple of knobs and things started to move automatically. Next thing you know, something that sounded like somebody shouting "fah" followed by fast strums on electric guitars. I read the back of the album jacket and saw this one was called "I Saw Her Standing There." It was a totally new sound to me, and with the great new stereo system, it was like nothing I've ever heard before. The next song, though,

60

didn't thrill me quite as much. It was a slow song called "Misery." And then there was even a song on that side called "Boys." I had heard it before I think, but not sung by guys. "Hey, Whitey, isn't that a girl's song?"

"Why?"

"They're singing about kissing boys aren't they?"

"No. It's just a song."

Well, even after "Boys," I still liked the fast songs a lot better than the slow ones. We went through Whitey's four 45s and his two albums, the other being "Meet The Beatles," over and over and when I looked at the clock, I had five minutes to get home before dinner. Sweater on, jacket on.... "See ya, Whitey, I got to go," and out the door, fly down the 6 stories, across the street, into my building, and open the three locks. Jacket and sweater off. To the kitchen, but no dinner. Past the kitchen and into the living room with a sight I've never seen before. My brother, Joey, sitting on the couch with a strange girl. What the heck is going on here. My father's sitting in the stuffed chair, and my mother's sitting in another chair, looking like she's been crying.

My brother has never brought a girl over. In fact, I don't think he ever talked about having a girlfriend.

My mother looked up at me and gave me a weird smile, like she was drunk or something, even though my mother never drank. "Come here, sweetie." I went over and sat next to her, and she gave me one of those too-tight hugs with a big kiss on the cheek like I just got back from fighting in a war. She looked at me strange and said, "Your brother is getting married." I looked at my brother, and he didn't look happy.

In fact, he looked about as depressed as when he told me he didn't get into the Army. "Yeah, kid. This is my fiancee, Peggy."

Peggy? I never saw her before. She was kind of cute, except she had thick glasses.

"Hi, Vinny," she said barely above a whisper.

"Hi. When's the wedding?" I ask. My mother looks at my father, my father looks at my brother, my brother looks at Peggy, and Peggy whispers to my brother, and my brother says,

"April 1st."

I thought that was pretty soon... "April Fools!" I yell.

"Shut up!" my mom says yanking on my arm, and I could see Peggy's eyes widen like I said something awful about her glasses or something.

"Well, I better be going," Peggy said, rising.

"Yeah, me too," my brother says joining her.

"Come on, Vinny," my mom said as all four of us follow to the front door, without saying a word until they had their coats on and walking out into the hall. "Bye," my mother manages to say. That was it. They were gone.

I looked at my father and asked, "Why are they getting married so soon?"

"Ask your mother," he grunts as he goes into the kitchen. There we were, in the narrow hallway of our tiny apartment next to the coat hooks, under the painted-over doorbell, just next to the string with a glow in the dark traffic signal connected to a light fixture. I look to my mother and she says, "Because somebody's going to have a baby, now go get washed for supper."

Boy! Imagine that! My wild brother, going to get married and have a baby! I'm going to be an uncle! Gee, I hope I get his bed! "What's for supper?!"

"Franks and beans," my mother snarls.

This IS my lucky day.

Finally. The big thaw. It seemed like years since it was a jacket and no-sweater day. Sixty degrees isn't bad for March 17th. And 60 degrees for Saint Patrick's Day is unbelievable. I would think that in most neighborhoods in America the big holidays would be Christmas or the 4th of July or Thanksgiving, but not in my neighborhood. Yeah, Christmas is big, but there's so much of a buildup for it that by the time it comes, there's always some kind of letdown. The 4th of July is big, but the cops are really starting to crack down on blowing stuff up, and not everybody even cares about it. Thanksgiving looks to me like an excuse for everybody to be a bigger pig than usual. But St. Patrick's Day is the most special. It just kind of sneaks up on you. There's no big fanfare, or count-down... only 23 more shopping days... It's not a big govern-ment holiday when the President goes to some cemetery to talk about dead people. And even though it's the only real holiday for a saint, it's not even a religious holiday.

My mother sometimes makes fun of the Irish. She calls them those dirty shanty Irish if it's somebody she thinks is dirty. Like the time she got stuck in the elevator with Mr. and Mrs. Fanning. You can tell both of them have terminal B.O. just by walking past them on the street, so getting stuck in an elevator for a half hour is torture. Plus, even though my par-ents and the Fannings have lived in the same building for about twenty years, they don't even say hello to each other. Natu-rally, I don't say hello to them either, even though I don't know why. In fact, there are several families in the building we don't say hello to.

But even my mother, Italian on both sides, puts on her greenest clothes and talks the entire day in her best brogue, unless she gets really mad about something. And my dad, who's half Irish, will even blurt out a line or two from "McNamara's Band" or "When Irish Eyes are Smiling" or "Danny Boy." Now that's rare.

There are lots of rituals and traditions that go with St. Paddy's Day. Every year, sometime in the wee hours of the morning, somebody paints a green line right down the middle of 238th Street. And it goes down to Bailey Avenue, where right in the middle of the intersection is painted a perfectly huge green shamrock. Not an outline of a shamrock, but a totally filled-in green shamrock. I don't know who does it, but the story goes that it's the leprechauns. And for the little kids of the neighborhood, the green line leprechaun is just as real as Santa Claus, the Easter Bunny, and Bozo the Clown.

Another tradition of the day is to get drunk. You see old people, parents, the guys at the meat counter in the market, high school boys and girls, priests, even cops looking like they're stewed. Smiles everywhere... cop hats on backwards... girls with big boobs and Irish sweaters who normally don't even hang out, wearing "Kiss Me I'm Irish" buttons, and if you ask, they'll actually let you... sometimes.

But the real thing to do on Saint Patrick's Day is go downtown. The Saint Patrick's Day Parade that goes UP 5th Avenue is the place to be. As any New Yorker can tell you, 5th Avenue is a one way street that goes DOWNtown. But on this day, it goes UPtown. Downtown is what most people think of when they think of New York City. But what they don't know is that it's the people who don't live downtown that really make up the city. Whether you're in the Bronx or Queens or Brooklyn, if you're getting on the subway to travel south, or west to go into the heart of Manhattan, the sign says "downtown." That's where the rich people live.

5th Avenue is a place to "sight-see." To gawk at the windows of the stores where you never would think of going into. The hotels with uniformed people blowing whistles and directing human and auto traffic past their red carpets on the sidewalk. And the apartment buildings that have awnings and names and doormen and balconies. But on St. Patrick's Day, the people who work in those stores and hotels and apartment buildings as doormen and janitors and elevator mechanics and window washers and cleaning ladies, who take the subway downtown every morning and uptown every evening, take over 5th Avenue and make it go uptown instead of downtown.

I've been to a bunch of St. Patrick's Day parades with my parents. We'd take the subway down, and stand for an hour or less, and head back home. But this would be the first time I was going to the parade without my parents. And of course, I'm going without telling them.

I knew what went on at the parade. In the 8th grade, kids start to get the word on the street about certain things that older people know, like what a blow job really is, some parents still have sex, faggots are really homosexuals and don't just act like sissies but actually have sex with each other, and the action at the Saint Patrick's Day Parade is at the turn on 86th Street. For some reason 86th street is where kids can get drunk, go wild, grab girls, and nobody cares. The parade does go uptown on 5th Avenue from about 42nd Street, but at 86th

Street it takes a right turn and goes a few more blocks. Well, right there, where it makes that turn, on the Central Park side of the street, is where the Catholic kids of New York City, no matter which "uptown" direction they came from, gather on the sidewalk and in the park to do what they usually do hidden away in the parks and empty lots and cellars and on rooftops and in forts and under bridges and down by the river and over by the railroad tracks and in the stands, under the stands, under the boardwalk, behind the billboard or wherever...they're here today, on Saint Paddy's day, to do it "downtown," on 5th Avenue, where the rich people live. They drink everything from Schaeffer to Chivas Regal stolen from secret hiding places under the sink, to scream, yell, dance, goof, ape, imitate, climb trees, piss, puke, grope, laugh, cry, fall, get up, march, sing, strip, flirt, make out, fall asleep, break bones, fight, argue, insult Jews, coloreds, fat people, old people, and do whatever the hell they think life is going to be when they grow up, right there in the heart of downtown, 5th Avenue, the bull's-eye of New York City.

And today, Whitey and I are going downtown, on the subway, by ourselves, with 10 bucks and a pretty good idea of where to go and what to do to really make Saint Patrick's Day the best holiday of the year.

My parents think that I've taken the subway downtown without them only twice. Once earlier in the year when several of the boys in the class took the train down to take the entrance exam for Saint Regis High School (a Catholic school for boys that's free, but only accepts the smartest 100 or so kids from the city each year. Nobody passed, but we had a hell of a time and almost got caught ditching a lunch tab in our school uniforms), and once when Whitey and I went to the car show on a Saturday afternoon. But I've been on the subway without my parents two other times. One time I took the train down to Inwood because Whitey knew where we could buy fireworks, and another time we took the train down to 42nd Street, went across the platform, got right back on the return train, and back to 238th Street just to do it. We chickened out

65

from buying the fireworks because we had to go up to a total stranger selling them out of his trunk right on Dyckman Street. And we were scared to death on the ride to 42nd Street. We thought we'd go up to the street and check out Times Square, where all the dirty bookstores and theaters are, but after all the scary people we saw in the subway going through Harlem and the rest of Manhattan, we didn't have the nerve to go up to the street.

Today was our day. We knew where we were going and what we were doing. We got on the train at the elevated platform on our street, 238th. You buy your token from a guy in an old wooden token booth with an iron gate in front of him, like a teller's window in a cowboy movie. After you give him the money, he slides your change and the token across a wooden counter worn so smooth it hardly takes any effort to do it. The token and coins land in a wooden well, about the size of cigar ash tray. The well was probably painted army green maybe 50 years ago, but the natural wood color shines brightly. The turn-stiles are huge wooden things that you really have to push to get through. And next to the door that leads out to the plat-form, there's actually a pot belly stove that I've never seen used. But my dad tells me that it used to be fired up all night long in the olden days, before I was born.

The platform is filled with people. Unlike the other times on the train, this group of people aren't gloomy workers in their dark pea coats and blue wool caps. This is a happy group of red or wavy black hair, freckles, green berets, green scarves, green buttons, Irish sweaters, green ribbon bowsand green ties. Young and old, men, women and children, all tell-ing stories and laughing, shaking hands and slapping backs, pinching little cheeks, and sneaking a sip from silver flasks. Most are familiar faces we've seen in church or at Connelly's Market or waiting for the "Night Owl," or walking a dog, or playing hand ball.

We look north to 242nd Street and can see the light of the on-coming train headed for us. And no sooner did it screech to a halt steel on steel, we all pile in. And out of nowhere comes a wild call of teenage boys screaming, "Hold the doors!

Wait! Don't go!" and a herd of about a dozen guys and girls all older than us, probably high school juniors and seniors, storm into our car in a frenzy of pushes, shoves and yelps. I just know that on any other day, the parents in our car would've feared for their lives, with a rowdy group of teenagers invading their car, but this is Paddy's Day. Parents and kids alike are smiling and laughing along with, and at, the loud teenagers... one big happy Irish Catholic family.

Whitey and I sort of recognize some of them, but don't really know any of them that well. We just sat there, watching, listening, knowing that one day, we'd be part of a gang just like this.

The car rolled on to 231st, 225th, 215th, Dyckman, and at each stop, another battalion of Irish Catholics would get on the train, looking and dressing just like the group before them. After Dyckman Street, we went underground and the sunshine was gone. But the roar of good cheer continued.

"Hey, this reminds me of the time we took the bus down to the Natural History Museum in 8th grade," one of the boys who got on at our station yells. "Hey, we're on a class trip!"

And the others joined in, "Yeah, class trip, class trip, class trip!" And without any introduction a voice starts singing, "Ohhhhhhhhhhhhhhhhhhhhh."

He looks around at everyone in his group, and they join him, "Ohhhhhhhhhhhhh!" He jumps on the seat, holds onto a strap and looks down to the other end of the car waving his free hand, "Ohhhhhhhhhhhhhhhhh", and lo and behold, the other end of the car joins in too, "Ohhhhhhhhhhhhhhhhh" waiting for their cue, and then the leader begins: *My name is MacNamara I'm the leader of the band, although we're few in number we're the finest in the land. We play at wakes and weddings and all the fancy balls, and when we play at funerals, we play the best of all. Dah dah dah dah dah dum dee dah.....* " A whole subway car of strangers is singing "MacNamara's Band" like they're all relatives at a friend's house. The train roared through the tunnel, and the group continues, second verse same as the first, and after that, a rousing round of applause for the group.

"Hey, Mr. McGowan!" the leader of the gang yells, as he spots a middle-aged man halfway down the car, with the look known by all as "black Irish" (alabaster white skin, rosy pink cheeks, thick wavy black hair, and bushy black eyebrows). "Hey guys, it's the singer from church, Mr. McGowan, let's hear one from Mr. McGowan," leading the whole car in a rhythmic clap for Mr. McGowan. And through the clickety clack roar of the tracks and claps and yelps rose a pure note, higher than a schoolboy's, cutting through everything, and making everyone stop in their tracks and listen... *"Oh Danny boy..."*. We couldn't hear the noise of the train anymore, all we could hear was a real Irish tenor, going through "Danny Boy" better than Dennis O'Day on The Jack Benny Show. Old ladies were crying, little kids stopped crying, young girls had the look of love, and old men took a pensive sip from their flasks, wiping a tear away. Even the people who weren't going to the parade and who weren't part of this clan watched and listened in wonder, while Mr. McGowan reminded the crowd what love and sentiment and sorrow and hope and beauty and poetry and family and love was all about. With one song. One Irish song sung on the subway on the way to the St. Patrick's Day Parade.

When he finished, the crowd applauded, but at 168th Street, about half the car got out to catch the express, and a whole group of non-revelers got on. It wasn't the same. The singing stopped, and the men pulled out their newspapers to read while the ladies quietly chatted. It was like a subway car once again. Not like a class trip anymore. There were even a few scary looking people in our car now.

"Where are we getting off?" I ask Whitey.

"86th Street. Man, if the subway ride is this good, imagine what the parade's gonna be like."

Just then a smelly bum comes through the door next to us from another car, stops right in front of us, hocks up a big wet loogie, spits right onto the floor, and lets out a big disgusting fart. He pushes his way through the car, yelling, "Happy Saint Patrick's Day!"

The train was jam packed by 86th Street, our stop. We push our way through the strap hangers onto the platform.

"How do we get out of here?" Whitey asks me.

"Just follow the crowd that's going up."

The stairs put us out on 86th Street and Broadway with not too much St. Paddy's Day green around, but whatever green there was, it was headed that-a-way, so we followed the smiling faces with green accessories toward the parade.

We crossed the Avenues going east, and eventually came upon Central Park. "5th Avenue's right on the other side of the park," I said. I knew this from the trips downtown at Christmas time, and trips to visit Aunt Grace and Uncle Cornelius. Sometimes when we went to Aunt Grace's, my dad didn't take the highway. Instead we went up Broadway on the West side, and when we got uptown, past the 90s and into the 100s, he'd start to say things like, "That used to be a ball field over there," or "I worked in that Gristedes Market when I was a kid," or "that used to be the Jimmy Ryan Democratic Club that sponsored our baseball team," or "it looks like a jungle around here."

Halfway through the park, we could hear the sounds of drums beating, trumpets and trombones blaring, glockenspiels glocking, and bagpipers piping. We're almost there. And just about when we started hearing the sounds of the official parade-goers, we started noticing the unofficial ones. A girl not much older than us came out of the bushes still zipping up her pants, wearing a plastic green derby, a crooked shamrock painted on her cheek, and an Irish sweater with an oversized "Kiss me I'm Irish" button on it. She was just about right next to us as we walked past, and Whitey gave me a nudge and said, "Hey I'm Irish, do I get a kiss?" The girl looked dazed, her eyes searching for the source of the offer. She settled on Whitey and slurred, "Come back when you get some hair on your balls, junior."

I roared in laughter at that one, and so did the few other people within earshot. "Hey, Whitey, I didn't realize you already knew her!"

Whitey gave me a punch in the arm, "Shut up, you little queer," as he joined in the goofy laugh we were having at his expense.

69

The closer we got to the end of the park, the louder the music became, and the more wild-eyed high school kids we saw coming out of bushes, up in trees, pissing in plain sight, groups of 6 or 12 arm in arm in circles singing, bottles and cans in the air, bottles and cans littered everywhere, just follow the piles of puke. We must be about 50 yards from the wall that separates the east end of the park from 5th Avenue and there are hundreds if not thousands of wild partying, screaming, groping, drinking, singing, people. Some teenagers, others in their 20s and even 30s, but all of them in a huge crazy party, right next to the wall at 86th Street just shy of 5th Avenue.

Whitey looks at me with a big smile on his face, "Jesus, this is freakin' unbelievable."

We're walking a little slower now, blending in with the crowd, totally unnoticed, each step revealing another up-close look at the things we only heard about. A guy with a girl up against a tree, one hand up her sweater, the other down her pants, both locked at the lip. A group of kids about our age chanting "chug chug chug chug" as the smallest one downs a can of "Rheingold." A group of about 15 high school girls with their sweaters tied around their waists in the warm St. Paddy's sun, dancing to the drummers on the avenue.

"Vinny, do you want to stay here, or you want to go up to the street?"

"Let's go up to the street and see what that's like."

Kids weren't bothering with the stairs just down a half block, they were jumping up the wall to the avenue, or jumping down into the park.

"Whitey, I'll give you a boost up, and then you help me from up there."

I positioned myself in the familiar "give-a-boost" stance. Up against the wall, hands locked together, knees slightly bent. Whitey puts one foot in, and up the wall. Then he leans down with a hand and pulls me up. There we are. From on top of the wall we can see down 5th Avenue, an incredible endless sea of marching bands and bannered groups, and probably a million people on both sides of 5th Avenue watching and just hanging

70

out. there were even people out on the balconies of the luxury apartment buildings, which you never see. And looking straight across 86th Street where they make the right turn, the huge snake of a parade goes on for blocks and blocks. All of a sudden "wham" we're both pushed off the wall from the side and go crashing onto the sidewalk about four feet below, with a sound of laughter coming from a group of kids just next to us. Luckily, we don't get hurt.

"Hey, you little pussies!"

I look at Whitey next to me on the sidewalk. "That's our cue to skidoo."

We got up, brushed ourselves off, and quickly start walking away. An empty beer can is thrown by our feet, followed by more laughs.

"Freakin' assholes," Whitey says under his breath, "if there weren't so many of 'em I'd kick their ass."

"Yeah Whitey, let's just go down here a little ways."

We didn't see any families or grown-ups. Just groups of drunken kids, going wild.

I was starting to get a little worried. "Maybe we should walk downtown a ways. We usually watch from the 60s when me and my family come down."

"What are you scared?"

"No shit, Sherlock."

"Yeah, me too. Let's go."

We started our walk downtown, hoping no one would notice two 8th graders from the Bronx, scared shitless, trying to avoid fights, insults, piss, puke, and poured alcoholic beverages over our heads.

"Hey wait! Holy shit, there's my cousin!" And there sitting on the wall was my cousin Jimmy, with a group of about eight friends.

"Jimmy!"

"Hey, Vinny! What the hell are you doing here?"

"Me and my friend Whitey took the train down."

I hadn't seen Jimmy in over a month, and he looked really different. His hair had gotten really long, like almost to his collar in the back, and about an inch over his ears, and was

71

combed just like a Beatle, with bangs in the front. And his guy friends that were there had the same kind of haircut. And his group of girls and guys weren't rowdy like the others, they were kind of quiet, sitting there, almost like it was just any other day to be hanging out. And not one of them had anything that was green.

"Hey, everybody, this is my cousin Vinny who's in the 8th grade, and his friend Whitey. Vinny, this is my girlfriend, Mary."

Wow. I couldn't believe it. Mary was about the cutest girl I had ever seen. She had that black Irish look, with pure white skin, dark eyes, and jet black hair that looked like she had ironed it. Instead of a "Kiss me, I'm Irish" button, she was wearing an oversized button that read "I Love The Beatles." She stuck her hand out to shake with me, "Hi, Vinny. Gee, you're cute just like your cousin Jimmy."

I suddenly got all hot, and I'm sure I was turning deep red.

"Vinny, don't tell your mother or anybody that you saw me here, I'd be dead.'"

"Hey, same for me, are you kidding!" I felt like a big shot now.

Jimmy reaches into his back pocket and pulls out a pint-sized bottle. "Either of you guys want a little blackberry brandy."

I look at Whitey, waiting to see his reaction. Whitey looks at me, and back to Jimmy and puts his hand out, "Yeah, I do."

"Not me," I say.

Whitey takes the bottle, looks around, and takes a big gulp. "Thanks."

"You sure you don't want any, Vinny?" Jimmy asks again.

"No, I'm sure."

After seeing the reception my brother usually got when he came home with liquor on his breath, I knew that was something I didn't want to even attempt. I know what happens when you surprise my parents with something bad. I'll never forget

72

the beating I got in the 1st grade, after I found some cigarettes hidden behind a wall with some matches and decided that it would be great to try them. A neighbor caught me doing it and brought me to my parents who both happened to be home on this Saturday afternoon, and gave me the licking of my life.

"I don't drink."

The whole group laughed out loud. I'm not sure why.

Whitey and I just stand there, hanging out with this group of high school juniors and seniors. Big kids. And boy were they cool. They were making fun of the parade of drunks that passed us, but only to each other. And when they weren't doing that they talked about music, or boyfriend/girlfriend stuff, like who's going out with who, and where they were going to hang out that night. Not much St. Paddy's Day banter at all.

"Vinny and Whitey, come with us," Jimmy says as he takes Mary by the hand.

We jump over the wall, and head over to a clump of bushes and small trees which we sort of got inside of, so no one could see us.

Jimmy pulls out a pack of Marlboro's. He opens the lid, and instead of pulling out a cigarette, he pulls out a really thin crooked-looking cigarette and licks one end of it. He then looks me straight in the eye and says real serious, "Don't ever tell anybody about this. Swear to God?"

"Swear to God," I say, real quick.

Jimmy looks at Whitey, "You too?"

"Swear to God," Whitey shoots back.

Jimmy then lights the small cigarette. This is pot. Holy jumpin' shit. He sucks on it real hard and slow, and hands it to Mary. She does the same. Jimmy takes it from Mary and holds it out for me. "You want some?"

I thought for a second, and flashed on the shellacking I got the first time I got caught smoking a cigarette. "Nah, not today."

"How 'bout you, Whitey," my cousin asked.

"Nah, not today."

Jimmy and Mary take turns on the cigarette till it was about half gone, then he puts it out and sticks what's left back

73

in with his Marlboros. Jimmy looks at me very seriously, straight into my brain, "Now we both have a little secret."

"Yeah, I guess so," I say.

We go back to the wall, but this time, boosting each other up becomes a bumbling ordeal. Jimmy tries to boost Mary, but she keeps falling or he drops her, and they wind up laughing hysterically on the ground, rolling in the dirt. Finally, Mary makes it, and then it's Jimmy's turn. The same thing. Falling, laughing, falling, laughing, and Mary sitting on the wall watching us ready to split a gut. We get Jimmy up, and Whitey and I make it up without a problem.

As soon as we got back to the group, Jimmy takes out his Marlboro box and flips it to one of the guys. Then that guy along with another guy and two girls hop over the wall, down to the same clump of bushes where we just were. And a few minutes later, we could hear them screaming hysterically as they attempt to get up the wall.

The guy flips the pack of Marlboros back to Jimmy, "Hey, thanks for the trip to Marlboro country."

Now the conversation isn't as subdued as it was earlier. A drunken old man staggering by isn't just viewed by the group and snickered at. Now it's cause for really loud hysterical laughter. Teary-eyed, roll-on-the-floor, uncontrollable laughing fits. Whitey and I didn't get it. The parade was a lot funnier to them now than it was before the trip to the bushes. We felt like real outsiders all of a sudden.

I whisper to Whitey, "Hey, let's walk downtown," and he nods in approval, just as a group of green-bereted drunken teens came stumbling over.

"Hey, McGuire," the smallest one yells at my cousin, "When did you get the fuckin' fag haircut. You look like a fuckin' fag Moe from the The Stooges."

"Yeah well you look like a fuckin' fag Shemp, you little asshole Sweeney."

Without another word, the little green-bereted drunken one lunges at Jimmy. My cousin was taken totally by surprise, and did his best to hold on as Sweeney tried to push him off the wall. Girls start screaming, guys yelling, as Sweeney has Jimmy

74

half over the wall, trying to push him over head first.

Sweeney's yelling as he holds onto Jimmy's throat, "You fuckin' faggot McGuire, I ought to kill you." I don't know what to do.

Two cops come running over, right off 5th Avenue over to the action, as we all try to push and shove and get Jimmy off the wall and out of danger. "Alright, what's going on here?" one cop says. That was enough for Sweeney to let go of Jimmy.

"Are you alright?" the other cop says.

"Yeah," Jimmy says as he gets himself together.

"Now you, you little asshole," the cop says while pointing his billy club right in Sweeney's face, "get the hell out of here, and if I see you again, I'll put your ass in jail."

Sweeney and his friends, without saying a word, were gone into the crowd, and so were the cops.

"Are you OK?" I ask Jimmy.

"Yeah."

"Where are those guys from?"

"They're from Peter Cooper Village. A couple of playgrounds over from where we hang out. Fuckin' hitters."

Hitters. I knew what that meant. Some kids were called "hitters" and that was what they were. They'd go to dances, other neighborhoods, parties, the beach, bingo, christenings, it didn't matter, and they'd go for one reason...to pick fights. And not just with people they thought they could easily beat up, like my cousin Jimmy. They'd go after big Italians, Blacks, Puerto Ricans, Jews, anybody they came across that they didn't like. Even guys from the same neighborhood.

"Well, me and Whitey have to get going."

"See ya," Jimmy mutters in a not very friendly manner in our general direction.

"Yeah, see ya."

So Whitey and I head down 5th Avenue once again.

Walking against the parade is the only way to go. If you walk with it, you wind up with the same group the whole time. If you go against it, you see all the different groups as you walk past.

I'm always amazed as I look into the faces of the people on the sidelines. Somehow, they all look like people I should know. They dress like people I know, they talk like them, but I've never seen any of them before. Even the people who are on the balconies on the other side of 5th Avenue sipping drinks from fancy glasses, with scarves blowing in the breeze, in the super-rich apartment buildings look like they could be from my neighborhood. But I'm sure they aren't. I'm sure the only time they go to the Bronx is either to the zoo or to Yankee Stadium.

"Want to head back?" I ask Whitey.

"Yeah."

The ride home was crowded, but it sure didn't feel like a class trip anymore, and as usual, for dinner it was corned beef and cabbage, and I luckily didn't have to lie about going to the parade because I just said that Whitey and I hung around all day. It's not really a lie. I don't think.

March holds the first signs of Spring, but opening day at Yankee Stadium is Spring. Yeah, it could be cold or rain or even snow on opening day, but who cares. That's the real start of Spring.

The Yanks ended last year lousy. Swept four games to none by the LA Dodgers in the World Series. Everybody hates the Dodgers more than anything. They left Brooklyn about eight years ago. I was small but I remember the headlines and all the mad, crying people on TV. A couple of years ago, the Mets started. They really stink, but they're fun to watch because their manager is Casey Stengel. Casey's really old, and you can hardly understand what he's saying, but he says the funniest things. This year Yogi Berra is the manager of the Yankees. He's one of my favorite players, next to Mickey Mantle and Roger Maris. Yogi's the second funniest guy in baseball.

We can never go to opening day because it's almost always a school day, so we're going to the first Saturday game. Last summer, after not too much arguing, my parents finally let me go to Yankee Stadium alone since it's only one bus that you get and it takes you right to the Grand Concourse and 161st Street, just a couple of blocks from the ball park.

This first Saturday of the season is one of the biggest games of the year for us... bat day. That's the day when every kid at the game is handed a real baseball bat for free.

Whitey invited a younger kid from his building, Mike Vitelli, the younger brother of Carrie Vitelli of our class. He's two grades behind us, but sometimes we let him hang around because he's funny, and because his sister is Carrie.

The bus goes right down the Grand Concourse from up by us, at Mosholu Parkway, and goes down Concourse, right through the heart of the Bronx. Once you get down by the Stadium, there are a lot of coloreds and Puerto Ricans around. That's why my parents yell at me to be careful, even though nothing has ever happened to us.

Today, we got here early so we can watch batting practice and stand way out by the foul poles to try and catch a ball. We came close, but it's harder to catch one with only one hand, since you have to hold onto the bat with the other one.

As usual, our seats are out in right field. There are usually more home runs hit out there. We always scream our heads off during the game, but today I guess we're screaming louder than usual because a lady told an usher on us and he threatened to kick us out. We'd scream for anything. At the top of our lungs. We also stomp on mustard and ketchup packages that shoot out over the railing onto the people below. One time, I even threw a tin foil ball I made from the tin foil on my baloney sandwich and made it all the way to the first base umpire in foul territory. He picked it up and threw it into the Yankees' dugout. I couldn't see in, but I wonder if maybe Mickey Mantle picked it up. Wow, imagine that. I guess that's why we all want baseballs so bad. To think that an actual player touched something and it could be yours to keep. So maybe that tin foil ball was being tossed around by Mickey and Yogi.

When the game ended, we rushed down to the Yankees' dugout. I noticed there was the Yankee line-up card still on the dugout wall, and there was a worker cleaning up.

"Excuse me, sir."

"Yeah, what do you want?"

"Could you give me that line-up card off the wall?"

Whitey and Mike Vitelli look at me in disbelief.

And much to my surprise, the guy tears it off the wall and hands it to me. A real line-up card, signed by Yogi Berra, with the entire Yankee line-up written out!

"Gee, thanks, mister!"

Me, Whitey and Mike are totally amazed. Here it is right in my hand, and it's mine to keep. Just then I hear a kid's voice, "Officer, officer!" I look over and some kid I'd never seen before wearing a tie and a jacket is pointing at us. "Officer, those boys over there went into the dugout and stole that piece of paper." The cop comes over to us and we're petrified.

"Where'd you get that from?"

"A guy in the dugout gave it to me."

"Yeah well, there's nobody in there now, is there?" With that, he takes the card out of my hand, walks around to the front of the dugout and puts it on the bench.

I was brokenhearted . I wanted to bawl out crying, but I held it in. I think. The cop went away. The kid was gone.

Whitey banged his bat on the top of the dugout, "Let's get that little faggot and bust his head open." But I didn't have a sense of rage at all. Just defeat. "Nah, let's go home."

I tried and tried to understand why a kid would do something like that. He was dressed like the kind of kid who probably had box seats and souvenirs and everything. Why? Then I just thought that to some people it didn't matter what they got, what mattered was making sure that other people didn't get it. One time my father told me that some people are born on third base and think they hit a triple. I think I understand what he was talking about.

The bus came pretty quick. Mostly everybody from the game was gone by now, so it was almost empty except for a few old ladies with shopping bags. I looked out the window all the way home and didn't talk about the line-up card once. I don't think I'll ever talk about it again.

Spring really is here. The snow isn't coming back, and

78

the trees in the empty lots are starting to get leaves. And everybody is hanging out now. After school, everybody rushes home to tear off the uniform and into their hang-out clothes. The older kids like Billy Paccione and Richie Lutz aren't hanging out on the stoop next to my building anymore. Last year they were on the stoop everyday. It's the perfect place to hang out. It's at the top of the hill right next to my building, and right under a big tree that has pink blossoms when the spring starts. There are two "stumps" about four feet high that my father says once had fancy light fixtures on them, but now they're just flat platforms about four feet high. Perfect for sitting on, putting the radio on, or playing cards. And there are steps that go down into an alley, also perfect for sitting on. With the tree overhead and my building next door and a house right next to that, there's always shade there.

But no older kids are there now, perfect for us to take over. All I have to do is sit there and I just know kids'll start to show up. Whitey's the first one to arrive.

"Where's Paccione and those guys?" he wants to know right away. The last thing we would want to do is think that we could hang out on the stoop, and then have the older guys come back and kick us out.

"They're over in the park playing basketball and probably drinking. I saw Paccione earlier and he said they hang out in the stands now."

The stands is where guys hang out just before they start hanging out in bars. It's a huge seating area next to the football field in the park. It's across the street from the pool hall, has its own bathrooms during the day, and it's near the basketball courts. And if you sit on the top, at the end, nobody bothers you as long as you don't break any bottles.

I could see Whitey was excited. "I'm gonna go home and get my radio!" He turns around and tears down the street. I just sat there, enjoying our newly inherited hang out, and two little kids came by, Frankie Ryan, and Tony Pisani, from my building.

Frankie has the reddest hair I've ever seen on anybody. He has really white skin, and always seems to have a green

79

booger hanging from his nose. Tony's an Italian kid. But they were inseparable, and would probably grow up to be bigger ball busters than me and Whitey. "Hey, Vinny, wanna know something?" Frankie asks.

"What's that, Frankie?"

"I saw Holly's pee pee, and you know what?"

"What's that Frankie?"

"It's inside out!" I started to crack up, and so did little Tony Pisani and so did Frankie. But I guess Frankie did have a point there. Not that I've ever seen a grown up girl's privates, but when you see it on a little girl it does look inside out. And the only magazines where they show between a woman's legs, it's one of those "nudist colony" magazines where they get rid of the hair and the nipples, and they're playing volley ball or something and you can't tell what the heck it looks like.

"Can I have a dime?" Frankie asks.

"Get the hell out of here," I tell him.

"Oh, come on," Tony chimes in.

"Get lost before I tell your mother on you."

"For what?" Frankie demands.

"I'll think of something, now get out of here."

They went down the stairs into the alley. The alley led to some cool things. There was an empty lot behind my building that was connected to the roofs of some stores. You could play on the roof and look in the skylights of the stores. Or throw rocks at pigeons, or if you were really lucky, at rats. Or maybe you could climb fire escapes if you could get up that high. Some kids drink back there, but I think Frankie and Tony have a few more years to go. Even for them. One time when I was about Frankie's age, I dropped a dirt bomb right into the middle of some teenager's card game from the roof. If I wasn't "Schmidt's little brother," I'm sure I would've been beaten really bad instead of just kicked in the ass and smacked in the face a few times. It was worth it.

Whitey's back with the radio. Breathless. "I ran into Carrie Vitelli and Donna Murphy, and I told them we were hanging out at the stumps and they said they were going to call for Eileen Moran and maybe come by."

"Really?" I was surprised by that. They haven't given me the time of day since that day in the laundromat. "What station should we listen to?" I asked, trying to look like I didn't care that the girls were coming to hang with us.

"I said Carrie and Donna and Eileen are coming HERE," Whitey says as is if The Beatles were going to drop by."

"Big deal." I say, trying to be cool. "Let's listen to MCA."

Although WMCA used to be the number one station when we were hanging out, we're listening to Murray The K on WINS a lot more. They play more Beatles, and Murray the K was still calling himself the "Fifth Beatle" playing back the tapes he got of them when they were here doing The Ed Sullivan show, and he was actually hanging out with them in their hotel suite. But Murray The K was famous for other stuff too. Like watching the submarine races. That's what you tell the cops you're doing when they catch you making out by the river or the ocean, "We're just watching the submarine races, baby!" And the "aah vay... hoh" thing is still big.

It seems like every five minutes they're playing "I Want To Hold Your Hand" and "She Loves You" and "Please Please Me" and "Twist and Shout" and "Can't Buy Me Love" and even the strange new one called "Love Me Do." It's not fast like the others, and it's not slow, just kind of spooky.

Whitey and I are kings of the hill. And we know it. The bigger kids have moved onto the stands, and we're the first ones from our class to take over. And now the girls want to hang out here too. And up the street I can see a group of guys on bicycles; Ralphie Quigley, Jimmy Joe Clancy, and BB Flannery, the guys from the dart fights over the winter.

"Hey, it's the Cannon Place brigade" Whitey says referring to the street most of the guys live on.

Jimmy Joe, Ralphie and BB put there bikes down on the ground. Now I know we've taken over. Three bikes taking up the whole sidewalk, five guys and a radio blaring. I guess we're the big kids now.

It's been quite a while since the bikes have been out,

and we've had more than four guys just sitting outside, not having to play football, or hiding in a hallway or basement somewhere because of the cold. You almost forget what you used to do on these 65 degree blue sky days. But BB does. "Hey, let's play something."

One of the other reasons that the stumps is a good place to hang, is that it's a great location for many games. Right next to the stumps, the wall of my building is a good spot for "King-Queen." King-Queen is a big game. Downtown where my cousins live it's called "Kings." Some other places they call it "King Ball." The wall is good because the windows there are high enough off the ground to bounce the ball off the wall, and the boxes on the sidewalk are the right size. The game consists of everybody lining up in a box, facing the wall. The first box is called the ace, then king, queen, jack, 10, depending on how many kids you have. You have to make the ball bounce only once before it hits the wall, and lands in someone else's box. If they miss, they go to the end of the line (the far right) and get a point. The ace always delivers, and doesn't get a point even if you miss. You just go to the end of the line. I'm killer at this game because in addition to being good at it, I'm the only lefty.

"Anybody got a spaldeen?" BB asks.

We look at each other... nope. "Anybody wanna go buy one?" BB asks another dumb question.

Suddenly, I realize it's time for another first rite of spring.

"Sewer balls!" I yell.

I knew this would be an instant crowd pleaser. It's like being the first one on Halloween night to say "chalk fight" or "snowball fight" during the first snow storm, or "cannon ball" at the first swimming pool outing.

A sewer ball is just that. A ball from the sewer. Sewer balls are mined from the sewers of the city by city kids like country kids go looking for... I don't know... whatever the hell country kids go looking for when they want to play something. During the summer, it's a fact of life that balls will go into sewers. Wiffle balls, spaldeens, tennis balls, jax balls, handballs. And it's not easy getting them out. First of all, little kids don't know anything about the art of getting sewer balls out of the sewer. And the balls they lose are just as good as a big kid's balls. Girls never go after their balls after it's in the sewer. And some guys won't even do it. But me and Whitey happen to be sewer ball experts. We're the perfect combination. Whitey is tall and strong. I'm small and light, but not weak. But the important thing is trust.

The best sewer on our block for sewer balls is across the street from the stumps. All kinds of balls from all around wind up in there. Even balls from up the city steps, in a totally different neighborhood we call J.T., for Jew Town, sometimes can end up in that sewer. Another reason this sewer is one of the best, is that it has a man hole cover on the sidewalk that's right over the sewer.

The only accessory you need is a wire coat hanger. I kind of know the guy in the dry cleaners, Johnny Bazzicalupo, so he lets me have one for free because he likes me and my brother, because my mother is always reminding him that even though our last name is Schmidt, that her maiden name is Pappalardo and she's full-blooded Italian, which is good for rounding a tab off to the dollar.

You take the coat hanger and straighten it out. Then you take the round part and bend it so it's perpendicular to the long part, sticking straight out. You bend the round part so that it's even rounder and just the right size to pick up a spaldeen. It's the same principle as the wire thing you use to lift the colored Easter egg out of the purple stuff. The reason for this thing is obvious. Everybody knows you don't want to be sticking your hand in sewer water. Not for anything. Not even for a brand new spaldeen.

You also need somebody with strong fingers. When the sewer workers lift up a man hole cover, they use a big crow bar. Whitey uses his fingers. I can't do it. Not many people can. But Whitey's got some strong fingers. Once the manhole cover is off, I'm the one to make the inspection. Spotting a ball in sewer water is pretty easy, even an amateur could do it. But spotting a game-worthy spaldeen is a job for an expert.

Plus I don't wear glasses. You have to lean way down to look, and one time Whitey did it, and his glasses fell off. Luckily I got them out for him, but he says he can still smell the sewer stench from them whenever it gets really hot. So I lean in for the first look. "I see one, two, three, holy shit, it's a bonanza down here, four, five, six... six balls, and let's see, one... two.....three spaldeens, two are questionable, one looks like it's pretty good, maybe new."

I say "questionable" because after a ball has been sitting in sewer water for too long, the ball becomes really hard and won't bounce enough. It might even crack in half if you hit it with a stick ball bat. And if you don't have bouncy balls, you might as well not play a game. Spaldeens are usually the best. They're actually "Spalding" balls, but for some reason everybody calls them "spawl-deens." Even my cousins downtown and in Hackensack call them that. But there's also a new brand that's getting some use these days, "Pensy Pinkies." I don't like "Pinkies" myself. The surface is too smooth. Not enough friction. Ritchie Lutz, one of the older guys in my building goes nuts if he sees a "Pensy Pinky." If he sees you using one, he'll yell and scream and "roof it" (throw it up to the roof of the building... a real pain in the ass since you got to go all the way up to the roof to find it, and you could run into old man McCugh up there). Actually, some guys won't play certain games with sewer balls. Even I don't like to play "curb ball" or "off the point" or "stoop ball" with them. But for "call ball," or if the game is just for fooling around, it's OK. But if it's a real game with real stakes, forget it. Got to be a regulation "spaldeen."

Buying a spaldeen is a rare and special moment. An expert will always take one ball in each hand and drop them from the same height to see which one bounces highest. He'll then measure that winner with every ball in the box until the candy store owner yells at him to quit wearing the balls out and buy the damn thing. And since they're so expensive, that's why sewer balls are the way to go.

Now comes the trust part. I get down on my knees and lean into the manhole over the sewer and slowly inch forward, while Whitey holds my waist first, then lowers me into the hole, until eventually he's holding onto my legs, with my feet hooked under his armpits. Now that's trust. I don't even trust my own brother to do this. That's because my brother has already: put my head in the toilet and flushed it, dropped me in my mother's steaming hot bath water fully clothed before she got in it of course, sat on my face and farted many times, and painted my face with blue polka dots with a magic marker and threw me out into the lobby with my long johns on.

"A little lower... lower... whoah! Right there." Now comes the hard part. It stinks in here. I take the wire scooper and delicately put it into the water, fishing for sewer balls. If you drop them, they can get lost, and you could get splashed with sewer sludge. I get one, and stick it in my pants pocket. It's not too bad. I get another and it's a lousy one. The sewer water stain has eaten through the rubber. But the third one is good. Hardly stained, with the familiar sewer ball, half-dark half-light look.

"Pull me out of this stink-hole!"

Out of the smelly sewer, I emerge to the blinding light of day with three free balls. One lousy, one OK, and one real good. I give Whitey one, and Jimmy Joe one, and I take one, and we each bounce the ball as much as possible to test the ball, and get the sewer off of it.

Now we've got everything. "Call ball!" I scream. We all know what that means. We race past the stumps, down the steps, through the alley, into the courtyard, the most perfect "call ball" place in the world. Wow. What a day.

I'm good at a lot of games. But call ball might be my best. I've got a good arm, I can catch good, I run fast, and I know everybody else's weaknesses. To play call ball, you throw a spaldeen up as high as you can and call out someone's name. That person has to catch the ball. If he drops it, everybody else runs until the guy picks up the ball and yells "halt" and stops in his place. Everybody else has to stop running at that point too. The guy with the ball gets to take three steps from his place, and on the third step he has to hit someone with the ball. If he misses, he gets a point. If he hits the guy, the guy gets the point, and whoever gets the point runs back to the courtyard to throw the ball up and call out another name.

There are many subtleties to this game. If you run too far when somebody drops a called ball, you'll be too far away to get back in time when everybody rushes back for the next throw after a point. Hitting a guy with the ball isn't so easy even if you're just a few feet away, because the guy you're aiming at is allowed to pivot on one foot to avoid getting hit.

And you have to throw the ball up at least three stories high, so that somebody has a chance to get back in time to catch it when the ball is thrown. You should also try to throw the ball as close to the wall as possible, because it's harder to catch. We call those "skimmers." And to make it even tougher, there's about a two-inch ledge at the bottom of the second story, and if the ball hits that ledge and bounces across the courtyard, it's impossible to catch... tough luck, my friend. So even the guys who never drop a ball get an unlucky break.

The courtyard where we play is the best "call ball" location ever. The building for some reason has this U- shaped courtyard with three walls making a playing area about 20 feet by 20 feet, and about seven stories straight up. And for some reason, there aren't any windows in this one courtyard. No old ladies to throw stuff out at you if they get pissed off because you're making too much noise. Old lady Gazedda once threw a pot of boiling water at my brother for playing Chinese school on the front steps of our building. She just missed him. Seems Gazedda's windows were always getting broken after that.

During the mad rush to the courtyard amidst the Curly "whooop whoops" and other favorite sound effects, Jimmy Joe let out with the first war cry of the spring, "Moons up!" I thought to myself, "Uh oh."

Whitey stopped running and looked around to the other guys, "Wait, I don't want to play for moons up." I shook my head, "Sorry, Whitey, it was called, that's it." Everybody including Whitey knew this was the truth. Once it was called, that was it. No going back. It was like calling out some secret magic spell that once spoken, could not be reversed. Thinking quickly I yelled out, "Threesies." I figured I better get that in before Jimmy Joe yelled out fivesies or even tensies. Threesies is the minimum.

"Moons up" is what keeps little kids and girls from playing with us. Moons up turns any game, whether it's Chinese school (a little kid's game played by guessing which hand holds a pebble), curb ball, stick ball, or call ball into a fierce competition. Moons up is serious business. And in a game like "call ball" where there's only one loser, not a whole team, it's not only a pain in the ass, it's total humiliation.

"Moons up" is when the loser of a game, whether it's one person or an entire team, has to go around to the front of my building, get down in a low, crouched position in front of the old coal door, and stick his ass (sometimes called a moon) up in the air. The winners line up across the street and using the curb like it's a rubber on pitcher's mound, throw a spaldeen as hard as possible at the guy's ass. And if the guy getting "moons up" doesn't have his legs together, the ball can go through the legs and get him right in the face. And don't think that getting hit in the ass doesn't hurt. It can sting like hell from a good thrower like me or Jimmy Joe. It can leave a red mark that'll be there for days. Plus there's the element of humiliation. Don't forget this happens in the front of the building, right on 238th Street. And with a sewer ball, it can sting even more. There's no mercy in "moons up," just like there's no mercy in pin darts, dirt bomb fights, sling shot fights, Johnny-on-the-Pony, Black Joe, or Ringo-Leeveo. So if you play for "moons up," you've got to try to win, but more important, you better not lose.

With five guys playing we had to choose to see who threw first. It took a few rounds of odd man wins (you know, everybody either throws out one finger or two, and whoever is the only one to have a one or a two is it). Whitey won.

I can see that he's really psyched. The last time we played with these guys was pin darts, so I know Whitey's still pissed at Jimmy Joe and sure as hell doesn't want his ass sticking up in the air on 238th Street in the middle of the afternoon with busses, cars, little kids, baby sitters, old ladies with shopping carts, delivery guys, big brothers and sisters, and the whole world passing by with four guys laughing their heads off while your ass is the bull's-eye. And don't think that people just walk or drive buy. A good "moon's up" will attract a pretty good-sized audience from the block. Especially when it's a big goofy guy like Whitey getting it from a bunch of smaller guys like us with good arms.

Whitey is squeezing the sewer ball in his hand and I can see his mind working. He knows as well as I do, as does everybody else, how good everybody is. Me and Jimmy Joe are probably tied for best. (Although Jimmy Joe can throw higher, I'm better at skimming.)

After us, it's BB, Whitey, then Ralphie. Ralphie's not too good at any sports except running. He can run faster than anybody in the class, but when it comes to games or sports, he just doesn't have it. Can't hit, can't catch, can't shoot a sling-shot.

Whitey rears back, his hand with the ball almost touching the ground, teeth clenched, face all screwed up like he's constipated and, just as he starts to throw yells, "Ralphie!" Good throw. Too good. It goes onto the roof. That's a point. Everybody's moaning and groaning now about how long it's going to take to get it, we may not find it, you've got a point already, you dick, and other stuff that drives Whitey crazy.

"Alright alright. I'm going to get it. Anybody want to walk me?" Whitey looks at me. "No thanks, I'll wait here."

It'll take Whitey probably five minutes to go around to the front of the building, take the elevator up to the 6th floor, take the stairs to the roof, find the ball, throw it down, then run back. But a lot can happen in five minutes.

Whitey runs off, and we all just sit on the ground and wait, glancing up to the roof.

"What's taking him so long?" Jimmy Joe wants to know, "Anybody want to go to the park and throw rocks at the rats on the tracks?"

"Wait a minute," I say. "He'll be right back." I hate throwing rocks at rats. I used to like it, until I hit one.

Suddenly a swoosh sound, and a "boink" as the ball came flying off the roof and landed just over from where we were sitting. And there's Whitey's big, toothy grinning head sticking over the edge of the roof. "I'll be right down." Whitey says and disappears. Back to the game.

Just then an unexpected yell from the roof, "Schmidt!" I knew this was serious and looked up to see a panic-stricken Whitey peering over the roof edge. "McCugh is coming with the bat!"

"Holy shit!" I was off and running. McCugh doesn't know Whitey at all, and who knows what he'll do if he's really stewed. I know that if I'm there he won't do anything just because he sort of knows who I am if he's not too drunk.

"Let's go," Jimmy Joe yelled as he got up to go with me.

"No, that'll be worse. Let me go alone." No argument there.

I ran into the building and didn't bother with the elevator. Six long stories to the top floor and another story up to the roof. The roof is a scary place. It's a lot bigger than you'd think it would be, and with all the courtyards and stairs and stuff you can really get turned around and not know where you are. And the wall at the edge isn't too high. It would be really easy to jump off or fall off. Too easy. I checked out the roof from the door and there he was. Old man McCugh lurking about, black Tee-shirt and black baseball bat. I didn't want to surprise him. By the time he realized who I was, I'd have a backwards "Louisville Slugger" emblem across my ass for good. And there, about 20 feet in front of McCugh, I could see Whitey hiding behind some kind of vent thing. I was scared to death and totally out of breath, but I had a pretty good chance of stopping McCugh if I played my cards right.

I slowly approached McCugh from behind. I got closer and could hear him mumbling, "Come on out you son of a bitch. You little thief. I know what you're doing up here and I'm gonna bash your skull in." I knew he wasn't too drunk if he was talking so good.

"Excuse me? Mr. McCugh?" I said. He quickly turned and stared me in the eye. I could see his brain trying to figure out whether he knew me. I knew I had to help him. "I'm the

Schmidt kid from the first floor, and me and my friend are up here looking for a ball."

He looked at me suspiciously holding the bat casually on his shoulder. "You're the Schmidt kid?"

"Yeah, you know my brother Joey, and my sister Anne Marie, and my parents, Mr. and Mrs. Schmidt."

"Oh right. You're the ones who scrub the tile in front of your door."

I guess he noticed that there's always a semicircle of perfectly clean white tiles around our front door, and since we live right next to the elevator and he lives on the 6th floor, he would notice. My parents are always scrubbing that semicircle. The rest of the tiles in the hall may be black with filth, but we have a clean, white semicircle in front of our door.

"Yeah, that's us. We're up here looking for a ball."

"Well OK then, but you know this is a dangerous place. You could get killed up here."

"Yes, thank you," I said as I inched past him to where I knew Whitey was hiding. "Hey, Whitey, did you find it?"

He came from behind the vent thing. "No, uh, Vinny, I can't find it."

McCugh came over by us. "Do you live in this building, son?" I could see Whitey was just shy of ruining his BVD's.

"No sir. He does." Whitey said pointing at me but continuing to stare at McCugh in terror.

"Where do you live, chubby?" McHugh grunts at Whitey.

"Across the street in 137." "Well, OK then." McCugh seemed satisfied with that reply.

I figured it was time to go. "Let's forget the ball and go, Whitey." We started to walk past McCugh. "I don't want you kids up here. Hear me?" Now he had the bat in one hand, banging it into his other hard leathery hand. "Now get!"

We ran our asses off, down all 7 flights, up the hill, and into the call ball court yard. The guys were gone. Nobody there. They took the ball too.

We sat on the ground to catch our breath. Whitey just shook his head. "I'll take moons up over that any day. Shit!

My radio!"

In the crazy rush to sewer ball, call balls and from old man McCugh we lost track of Whitey's radio.

"Man, I hope those jerks didn't just leave it sitting here when they left," Whitey said as he hopped around fuming. I tried to calm him.

"Maybe they have it with them. They probably went over to the park."

Whitey agreed, "Let's go." Just as we turned to head around the stumps and down the hill, here they come. Donna Murphy, Carrie Vitelli, and Eileen Moran. Carrie had Whitey's radio and they were all chomping bubble gum to the music. I've got butterflies now. The three of them, obviously coming to bring back Whitey's radio that one of the other guys, who left, had given them to hold onto.

"Let's just sit here like we didn't know they were coming," Whitey said nervously.

So here we are, two jerks, not doing anything, waiting for the three cutest girls on the block to bring back Whitey's radio, now playing "I Want to Hold Your Hand." Not blasting like most guys do. Playing at a normal level. I'll bet anything all three of them are mouthing the words. The song is getting louder and louder as they approach. I wonder if Whitey remembers that I'm the one who likes Carrie better. I hate this butterfly feeling. That's what makes me say stupid things. Like the time in 6th grade when I had a crush on Betty Thigpen at the beginning of the summer, and stayed out until 9:00 at night sitting next to her, hardly saying a word until I finally blurted out, "Will you go steady with me?" I was trembling as I stared straight ahead waiting for her reply. In a totally calm voice, she said, "yes." I haven't said a word to her since.

I know Whitey's as scared as I am. Carrie, Donna and Eileen usually hang out down the hill, in front of Carrie and Donna's apartment building. (The same building that Whitey lives in.) I can't imagine what it is they do down there all day. Us guys are almost always playing some kind of game, and they just seem to sit and talk whenever we see them. But now that the big kids aren't hanging on the stumps and it's just

Whitey and me, and they have Whitey's radio, and they're walking up the hill to give it to Whitey, they probably want to start hanging here. With us. Talk to us. Us. Yipes.

I've always liked girls. Even when I was four years old I remember wanting to hold hands with Mary Jane Hopkins who lived on the second floor. I remember we used to play Popeye and Olive Oyl, and she used to make me eat the leaves from the hedges, pretending that it was spinach. One time, I punched my good friend Raymie Hands in the stomach, because he wanted to hold hands with her. I did hold hands with her one time for about three seconds after eating a mouthful of hedge leaves. I had incredible butterflies then. And that was way before I knew how really different boys and girls are. You know...nude. And now that I realize what they can do... wow. Talk about butterflies.

Carrie's leading the way, with Donna right behind her holding the radio, and Eileen right next to her. I can smell the Bazooka bubble gum already. "Whitey, here's your radio," Carrie says as she takes it from Donna, turns it off, and hands it to Whitey who's sitting down.

"Thanks," Whitey says with a stupid smile across his face.

"You're welcome," Carrie shoots back as she turns around in an about-face with Donna and Eileen doing the same. And in silence they were gone. Not another word. Whitey and I stare at each other. And jump up to watch them disappear as they walk down the hill away from us. They walk slowly, heel first, and wiggle their butts in that skinny girl way. Especially Carrie. When they're about a telephone pole away, all three of them burst out laughing and keep going.

Whitey's shaking his head in disbelief. "I thought for sure they were finally coming to hang out with us."

"They did. Now they want us to go and hang out with them. Which we ain't doing."

"We ain't?" Whitey said, like I was a moron.

"Nope. They'll be back in a little while. Just put the radio on and wait."

We waited. They didn't come back today. But they

will.

It's almost May, and my brother still isn't married. I hardly ever even see him these days. My Uncle Donald, on my father's side, got him a job at the phone company, and he works the night shift. He doesn't even stop by the park to play or hang out or even drink beer, as far as I can tell. It's actually a lot more quiet in the house now that he's hardly here.

But now that the wedding date is set, I am pissed. My mother told me that I have to be an altar boy at the wedding. I haven't been an altar boy in over a year. Everybody except Mark Fay, Louis Zummo, and Jerome Mullooly has dropped out of it, and the only reason those three are still in it is they still want to be priests. Seventh grade is usually the cutoff. To tell you the truth, I do miss the altar boy outings. Last year we went to Lake Hopatcong in Jersey. I don't know why they picked that place. We've got Rye Beach, Palisades, and Rockaway all a lot closer, but there we are going to Jersey. But now I love Lake Hopatcong. Not only is it real cheap there, but way in the back of the place, next to where they rent out the row boats, is an arcade where they keep the really, really old stuff. And I'm proud to say that it was I who discovered what has become THE most popular attraction of the Presentation altar boy outing. Just by accident, I found out that they actually have, way in the back of the room, through a door, around a corner, a place where they have real penny arcade movies. The old-fashioned thing that you stick your face into an eyehole and turn a crank around for a penny and a light bulb pops on as you start to crank, and lo and behold, these old cards with tattered edges start to flip, revealing an actual nude strip show from around the year 1900. Now I've seen a few nudie magazines like Playboy, or the nudist colony ones where they cover up the nipples and the crotch with black bars, or even totally erase them somehow, but I have never seen a totally nude woman doing a striptease! Well, one time I remember that Gypsy Rose Lee was on TV and she did a dance with some giant feathers, but you couldn't see anything at all. And she was ancient. But for one lousy penny, you can turn that crank and see a totally naked lady doing a dance. Most of the nudies are pretty plump. I'd even say fat. But who cares!

Once the word got out about the great show for a penny, of course it became THE place to be. Nobody was allowed to tell Fay, Zummo, or Mullooly because they'd tell Father O'Shaughnessy and that would be the end of it.

And now, after almost two years, I'll be an altar boy at my brother's wedding in Presentation Church. The reception is up in Riverdale at a VFW hall. I found out my parents are paying for the whole thing because her parents said it was her fault for getting pregnant and married and she had to start taking responsibility for herself. My mother says she feels sorry for them, and is planning a heck of a spread.

I can't figure out, though, why my brother doesn't look too happy about the whole thing. I would think that getting out of the house and moving into your own apartment with a girl you're allowed to have sex with would be great.

"Put on something nice, we're going over to meet your brother's fiancee's family," my mother says while putting tin foil over the leftover macs.

"Tonight? I was supposed to do something tonight," I say, hoping she doesn't call my bluff. Anything would be better than that.

"Neveryoumind, put on something nice, we're leaving in a half hour," mom says in a "don't-mess-with-me-I've-got-bigger-worries-than-you" tone of voice.

My father looks about as thrilled as I am. He doesn't usually like to be around relatives he already knows for 20 or 30 years. Meeting new soon-to-be relatives means HE has to put on something nice too. He hates that. He's happiest when Uncle Nicky comes over with a few bottles of Knickerbockers, and my dad pulls out the Dewars and they watch a Yankee game on TV in their undershirts.

My sister is already dressed up, sitting on the sofa, watching "What's My Line?"

"2 down, 3 to go. Miss Kilgallen?" host John Bailey says in his accent that sounds like one of the rich hoi polloi on the Three Stooges. He calls everybody Miss or Mrs. or Mister,

or Master. And they're all dressed up like they're going to the opera. The women even wear gloves. I've never seen anybody in real life who looks or sounds like the host or the panel members... Mr. Cerf... Mr. Levinson... Miss Francis... The only people that seem real are the people who try to stump them....
"Are you the hat check girl at the Stork Club?"
"Oh right you are, Miss Francis! Congratulations!" Mr. Bailey says, flipping over all the cards.
I put on my newest, coolest clothes. No-collar jacket, skinny black tie, white shirt, skintight peg leg pants, and pointy black shoes with white socks.
"You're going like that?" my sister says in disgust.
"Shut up, I like it. What do you know?"
"Show off."
I can see my dad put on the same tie and shirt and pants and jacket and shoes and probably socks from last week and the week before that when we had to go see relatives he didn't want to see.
"Don't wear that shirt!" my mother screams from the kitchen.
"Why?" Dad screams back.
"It's filthy!" my mom yells, topping herself.
My father starts to undo his tie to get off his shirt and, in his usual phony falsetto, starts to imitate my mother, "It's filthy! It's filthy! It's filthy!"
"Fraaaaaaaaaaaaannnnnnnnnnnnnnnnk," mom growls through clenched teeth.
Dad stops.

Here we go. The four of us all dressed up to meet the parents of the girl my brother will marry this coming Saturday. I think the last time our whole family was together for a function like this was Uncle Klaus' funeral. His wife, my mom's sister, Aunt Louise, went totally nuts and jumped into the coffin on top of him screaming. She's been in and out of mental wards ever since. She hits herself in the head with her fist, making her head and her hands bleed, and mumbles over and over, "Oh, my God. Oh, my God. What am I going to do?

95

What am I going to do? Oh, my God." I hope tonight isn't one of those nights. I want to get home early so I can go to a dance in my new, cool clothes.

And next time I go to the barber, I'm hardly getting anything cut. Things are going to be a lot different. I can tell.

Into the station wagon we go. Not a word among us. We sit in our usual places: dad drives, mom in passenger seat, me behind dad, my sister behind mom, my brother absent as usual for the past few years.

"Put on the Good Guys?" I ask, and no sooner finish, when my father chimes in, "Put on the Good Guys, PLEASE."

"Put on the Good Guys PLEASE." I know this drill.

My mother turns on the station and we wait for it to warm up. After about 20 seconds you can hear a crackly voice in the distance getting louder and louder until it reaches its full level. This can't be WMCA, home of the Good Guys. This is Steve Lawrence singing "Go Away Little Girl." This song is one of the weirdest. Last year during one of those TV tele-thons, Steve Lawrence came out to sing this song to a poor little poster girl who was all messed up with huge, thick glasses and sitting in a wheelchair with big braces on both legs. I felt so sorry for her. And for some reason Steve Lawrence starts singing right into her face, telling her to go away. I still don't know what that song is about, or why he was telling that poor little girl to go away. I can't blame her for crying her eyes out uncontrollably. And you can bet that if she wasn't stuck in a wheelchair with huge braces on her legs, she sure as hell would've run away faster than Mickey Mantle chasing a ball around the monuments. Who wouldn't?

"Change the station, this isn't MCA," I plead.

"Be quiet, I like this song," mom says, knowing she's in control of the radio.

I can tell that the radio is on WNEW, the old people's station. Actually, playing this song is pretty unusual for them. It was just out last year. Usually the stuff they play is from years and years ago. To me, it seems most of the stuff they

96

play, and most of what they talk about has something to do with World War Two. That's when my parents got married. 1944.

My mom talks about how sad it was during those years. Her mother had just died, and all four of her brothers were overseas fighting in the war. You couldn't buy as much food and gasoline as you wanted, either. You had to have coupons to buy stuff.

But most of the songs they play on WNEW from those years are really jolly ones. My favorite is The Andrews Sisters singing "The Boogie Woogie Bugle Boy From Company B." It was in an Abbott and Costello movie. Abbott and Costello are on TV every afternoon on "The Abbott and Costello Show." It's all repeats, but it's better than anything that's on TV except for maybe Soupy Sales. Me and the guys are always doing routines from Abbott and Costello like "Niagara Falls." Slowly I turned. Step by step. Inch by inch. And then, beating up on whoever the sucker for the day happens to be. Or "The Susquehana Hat Company" routine. How dare you remind me of someone I hate. Smack!

The trip to Peggy's house is only about five minutes away, right down Bailey Avenue which is the street our building is right next to. But five minutes away in a car means about two miles, and that's a lot of blocks and a couple of neighborhoods away. I wonder how my brother even got to know somebody from all the way over here.

Finally, Steve Lawrence finishes the song I hate. "Now can we hear the Good Guys?" All of a sudden, the absolute worst song of all time comes on, "Dominique" by the Singing Nuns. I knew it would be a while longer before I was able to hear anything that was good. It was bad enough to have to spend my whole life listening to nuns in a classroom, now I have to listen to them singing on the radio. And nobody but nobody knows what the hell this song is about. It's in French or something.

Peggy's building is a lot newer than ours. Probably about five years old. The halls are really nice, and the elevator has automatic doors. (All the elevators in my neighborhood have doors that you have to pull open.) We pile into the elevator and nobody says a word all the way up to the top floor, the 6th, and right to apartment 6A.

This has to be the stupidest meeting of families of all time. I mean, both families are total strangers, and I just know we're going to be talking about things that somehow have something to do with my brother and their daughter getting married. Real important stuff, like that we go to the same Grand Union, aren't there more coloreds around 231st Street (the biggest shopping street around), and both moms agree that taking baths is much better than taking showers. You HAVE to soak. Me, my sister, my brother, and Peggy don't say a word.

During dinner, which was steak, mashed potatoes, and peas, but no salad, nobody said a word outside of "pass the salt."

After dinner, we had chocolate layer cake from the bakery on 231st Street. Discussion of that particular bakery was another 10 minutes of conversation.

"Gee, hasn't it gone downhill?"

"I hate that man, the owner, he's filthy."

"I bought a cake there last Christmas and it was stale."

"Those Entenmann cakes in the Grand Union are very good, and cost a lot less."

"Remember how crowded that bakery used to be on Sunday afternoons?"

After some more awkward good-byes, we head for the door, the car, and home.

Having kept to myself all night, I ask the question I've been on best behavior for...

"Can you please drop me off at the auditorium for the dance?"

"OK, but be home by 11:00."

Wow, 11:00! I would've settled for 10.

Pulling into the church parking lot, I could see Whitey sitting by the steps leading down to the auditorium under the church. Whitey sees our car now. Nobody else has a 1948 red-and-white Ford station wagon. It looks like a delivery truck or something. I can tell that he has a cigarette cupped in his hand. He discreetly drops it and puts it out in the dirt just before we pull up next to him. He knows damn well that my mother would give him holy hell and probably tell on him if she saw him smoking. She'd also give me hell for hanging out with him. Some things are just better kept secret.

"Come straight home after the dance," my mother sternly commands me as the brakes squeak to a halt.

"Yeah. Bye," I reply, closing the car door that sounds like a bank vault door slamming.

As the smoke from the exhaust goes out onto the street, I know they're gone and not coming back. In no time my dad will be in his boxers sitting on the couch, and mom will be in a housecoat with the ironing board set up in the living room, watching the Lawrence Welk Show. My sister will probably go over to Cathy Kelly's house with a few of her other girl-friends. I don't think they do anything except talk.

"What kept ya?" Whitey asks as he pulls another Marlboro out of the box, and lights it up.

"Are you nuts, Whitey? If somebody sees you with a smoke, you'll be in big trouble."

"Nobody's gonna see me. This dance stinks. Let's go in."

Whitey takes a long drag on his cigarette, then care-fully puts it out on the bottom of his imitation Beatle boots and places it back into the box.

Oh great, I thought to myself. I've got on the only cool clothes I've ever had in my life: skinny tie, pointy shoes, col-larless jacket, skin-tight peg leg pants, and the dance stinks. But as soon as we opened to doors to the outer room leading to the auditorium, I knew Whitey was right.

Sitting at a table just next to the door leading the audi-torium was Miss O'Boyle, who was my 2nd grade teacher and still teaches the 2nd grade. My sister had her, my brother had her, just about anybody under the age of forty had Miss O'Boyle in 2nd grade if they went to Presentation. She's as strict as any nun that's ever been at the school. Including Sister Marguer-ite, who I never had, but my mother and all the other mothers of the neighborhood still talk about her, kind of in the same way they remember Hitler. In fact, my mother even blames Sister Marguerite for my brother's bad luck. Ever since 2nd grade with Miss O'Boyle, my brother's gotten into trouble, in and out of school, didn't get into a good Catholic high school, dropped out of the lowly Bishop Malloy High School, dropped out of the huge Roosevelt, even though my Uncle Nicky who is a teacher there tried to keep him in... and well, it didn't work. My mom says that Miss O'Boyle and Sister Marguerite both had it in for my brother. Sister Marguerite wanted my mother to sign something that said she had permission to hit kids if she wanted to. My mother said no way. From then on it was downhill for my brother.

Miss O'Boyle was sitting at the table with a roll of tickets and a cigar box. She had on the same black dress she always has on, and she has big balls of cotton sticking out of her ears. Her hair is a strange sort of blonde color, real short, and kind of pulled up over her ears real tight with black bobby pins. Kind of like those hairstyles you see in those really old movies, with flappers and bunches of girls doing dances in a big circle, and when you see it from overhead it looks like a flower or something. I think it's called a "bob."

"You two birds going in to the dance? Let's go, get a move on. No loitering in the vestibule! Weren't you already in the dance, young man?"

"Yes, Miss O'Boyle," Whitey sheepishly responds. "I went outside to meet my friend."

"OK, well, let's go, tickets are a dollar, and who are you, young man?"

Gosh, I can't believe Miss O'Boyle has to ask me who I am. I had her for a whole year of school, and she always blasted me with the old "don't turn out like your brother...your brother was such a little brat... you're gonna get what your brother got" stuff.

"Vincent Schmidt," I meekly answer.

"Schmidt? Oh yes. And how is that brother of yours, what's his name?"

"Joseph."

"What is he doing these days?"

"Oh, he's getting married."

"Married! Oh my Lord, is he out of college yet?"

"Uh, he didn't go to college. He's just getting married."

"Yes well, good for him. You just make sure you graduate college before you get married, young man. Here's your ticket, and no horseplay! Understand?"

"Yes, Miss O'Boyle."

As we opened the door to the auditorium, I could really see what Whitey meant. The auditorium looked empty. It was a lot darker than usual because it looks like they put some orange crepe paper left over from Halloween on top of the florescent lights. On the left side there are chairs lining the wall with maybe seven girls sitting. On the right side, there are chairs against that wall with maybe seven guys. On stage is Billy Bean, a guy from Whitey's building who's a senior in high school and a real square. He still uses butch wax to push up the front of his flat top.

He's got one of those small portable hi-fi's on a table and he's got stacks of 45s. Right now, the scratchy sounds of "Duke Of Earl" are barely reaching the back of the room.

"Oh my God, Whitey. Nobody's here except the class pets. Where's like Jimmy Joe and Ralphie, and Carrie and Donna and those people? They said they were going to be here."

"They were here for about 15 minutes and said they were going to the pizza place, and left. I had to sit here talking to Louis Zummo about him going to pre-priest school at Cathedral for an hour waiting for you. He said his parents want him to be a priest so that he can pray for his little brother that drowned."

Just then I heard a commotion on the girl's side of the floor. Father O'Shaughnessy, one of the parish priests and head of the altar boys, just walked in. The girls all flocked around him. Father O'Shaughnessy was a different kind of priest from all the others. He actually talked to us and asked us questions. Most of the other priests we had just said Mass, said prayers, and lectured us. Father O'Shaughnessy even kidded around with us sometimes. Just as I looked over to where he was, he looked up and saw me and Whitey, and made a b-line right for us.

"Oh crap, he's coming right at us," Whitey mutters.

Every boy and every girl watches as Father "O" walks across the empty floor, just about in step with the chorus of "Yakety Yak" playing on the hi-fi now, with his long black robe swaying back and forth. With all the class pets on both sides of the room, like Joanne Martorana, who has a 98 average and never uttered a word out of order in class since the 1st grade, and Mark Fay, who has squealed on more kids in class than that rich kid in the Little Rascals, what was he doing coming right over to us?

"Well, look who's here?" Father "O" was saying really loud before he even reached us. "Roberto Shelley and Vincenzo Schmidt-ario! How are you ecclesiastically, Whitey?"

"Fine, Father."

"And Vincent, I see you're coming out of your retirement from the altar boys to serve at your brother's wedding, isn't that exciting!" And with that, he reaches over and grabs my earlobe, and pinches the heck out of it.

"Yes, Father, owwww." He releases his grip.

"Where are you boys going to high school?"

Whitey goes first. "I think I'm going to Regis, Father."

Before Whitey can even start laughing at the absurdity of his reply, because Regis is the hardest school in the city to get into, Father "O" grabs Whitey's earlobe and squeezes it even harder than he did to mine.

"Oh, very good, Mr. Shelley! And what about you, Vincent, you're not going to Regis, are you?"

"No Father. Maybe Cardinal Hayes." That was a safe response. Hayes was the Catholic Boys School most kids went to, being the largest in the whole city, not just the Bronx.

"You boys should understand something. In 8th grade, you decide you don't want to be altar boys anymore. Then you go to high school, and first thing you know, you're no longer sitting in a pew, but you're standing in the back of the church

102

for mass. Then sophomore year, you're standing in back only some of the time. And by senior year, you're out the door completely. And many find that they spend more time in the corner bar than they do in Church and the library combined. Don't let it happen to you."

"No, not us, Father," Whitey and I mumble.

"Vincent, I want you to stop by the rectory some time this week to talk about your brother's wedding and the altar boy outing this spring, can you come over?"

"Yes, Father."

"Tah tah."

Father "O" turns around and heads over to the boys from our class who can't wait to talk to him.

"What was that about?" I ask Whitey.

"I don't know, but let's get out of here."

"Yeah."

The pizza place was right down the block. It was a nice night. People were hanging out in front of it, and also older kids from the bar next door. And it was only 9:15.

"I think I see Jimmy Joe and the other guys," Whitey says.

"Yeah, and there's Carrie and Donna," I reply.

The closer we get, it seems like even more people are coming out of the pizza place and the bar next door and onto the sidewalk. Luigi's Pizza is a long, narrow store, with a big open front, where you can order pizza right from the sidewalk. And with the front door always open, it's like a totally open fronted place, with the music on the jukebox way in the back filling the intersection of Review Place and 238th Street with the sounds of the 45s spinning away under a dull needle. I always wondered how the jukebox always has the latest top records that the radio stations are playing. I know Luigi sure as hell isn't putting them in there. The last row of selections are Italian songs that nobody ever plays unless Luigi is in there by himself, or with one or two kids around. Since there are more Irish brogues on this block than Bronx accents, Luigi knows how not to piss anybody off with that "greaseball eyetalian" music, as the Irish like to call it.

Right now "Walk Like A Man" by the Four Seasons is spilling onto the street. I can tell that Whitey knows it, and I know it, and we are walking like men. Men out to do whatever we want. All dressed up with somewhere to go.

"Jimmy Joe!" Whitey says as we're halfway across the street. Jimmy Joe doesn't say anything, he just gives one big neck thrust up, pushing his chin as high as it will go. A cool way to acknowledge somebody's arrival.

As we approach the group, it's obvious that Whitey and I are the only two people who put on our coolest clothes tonight. We even put a little dab of Brylcreem on our hair to get a little bit of that "Jeff Stone" on the Donna Reed Show kind of look. For some reason, in that Brylcreem commercial on TV, when the girl puts her fingers through the guys hair she says it's "disturbingly healthy." The Beatles hair-on-the- forehead look is way too much for anybody on our block.

"Shelley, I can't believe you stayed at that lame dance for all this time," Jimmy Joe yells at Whitey before we even stop walking. "What, were you making out with Joanne Martorana or something?" Ralphie, and BB, Jimmy Joe's constant shadows gave big "naaaaaaaaahhhhs" to Whitey with fingers pointing right on cue.

"MAKE OUT with her? Are you kidding? She gave me a hand job while Miss O'Boyle counted a hundred Mississippis." Whitey may be kinda dumb in schoolwork, but when it came to being a cut up, he could go toe to toe with the best of them. And Whitey's line didn't just get a bunch of "naaaaaahhhhhhhhs" from a couple of guys. Everybody laughed out loud who was within earshot. Even Luigi who was up front pretending to be reading the Daily News gave a laugh. Luigi doesn't talk much. And none of the locals chat with him too much. Unlike another Italian up by my building: "Vito the Shoemaker."

Vito the Shoemaker has a store right next to "The Modern Market." The Modern, as we call it, is one of the few non-supermarkets around. There are lots of delicatessens around, almost one every few blocks. But there are only a few of the larger markets that have butchers and stuff in them ever since they opened The Safeway, about five blocks away. Vito the Shoemaker's shoe repair store is pretty much the social center for the non-bar going men of the neighborhood. Every day, from 8 in the morning till 6 at night, you can see Vito at his workbench, which of course he placed right in the front of the store looking out the front window onto the street, so he can see the comings and goings of everybody on the block. And all day long, men go in and out, just to stand next to his counter, or sit in one of his shoe shine chairs and chew the fat with Vito. Sometimes you see as many as five or six guys in there. And for some reason, even the old Irish men like Vito.

Vito knows me and I think he likes me, but there was something about him that always confused me. That is until I solved the mystery by accident. Whenever you walk by Vito's store front, Vito always has a big hello and a smile and a wave of his hammer for whoever goes by. But I noticed that most of the time, when he waved and smiled and mouthed a big "hello" through the window, his visitors inside the store would burst out laughing. Not every time. But most of the time. But whenever I was in the store picking up my father's work shoes that were getting new cat's paw half soles, and Vito said hello to somebody outside, there was nothing funny about it, and no laughter from his several cronies.

Then one day the mystery was solved. I was up on the roof of Vito's store goofing around with Whitey, and seeing which store skylights were a little broken so we could drop a pebble or spit on something or somebody below in the store. We snuck over to Vito's skylight very quietly because we knew damn well that if Vito caught us, he'd take the time to chase us and whack the hell out of us. We've seen him do it to other kids. So we crawled on all fours across the tarred roof, trying not to make the crunching sound that comes when you walk across the ancient rooftops. We peered over the chicken-wired skylight glass that you couldn't see through, but there was a tiny two-inch hole on the side of the glass. We could see and hear Vito with his five friends. Vito was holding court. He'd take a couple of whacks with his hammer onto a shoe, with three or four nails in his mouth, and each time he ran out of nails in his mouth, he'd take a swig of whiskey from a small bottle swoosh it around his mouth and swallow. We could see Mrs. O'Leary walk by, and Vito with a big smile says through the window "Hello" real loud as she walks by with a smile. No laughter from anybody. Then we see Mr. Von Fett, the owner of the little deli up the block and the only guy around with a heavy German accent, go by the window, and Vito says real loud "Hello", but real soft we can hear him say "cock-a-de-suck" followed closely with chuckles from his friends. Next to go by is Mr. McDermott from my building, who's a real drunk with a wife and a kid, and I even caught him drinking cough medicine in the basement one time. Mr. McDermott waves hello to Vito, and Vito responds with a big smile and "Hello" followed softly by "you fuck." Bigger laughs from the crowd. Then walking past is Christine Campiglia, the hottest teenager in the neighborhood, who everybody knows is screwing every hot rodder on the block, she waves to Vito and gives him a little wink, and Vito follows with a big friendly "Hello" and quietly mumbles "you little fuckin' whoo-ah, would I love-a to banga you just-a one time mamma mia." Now the old timers are going nuts. Laughing their asses off. Banging their legs with a rolled up "Daily News."

At that moment Whitey and I both knew the secret behind Vito the Shoemaker and the world of adults behind closed doors. Even glass ones.

I ask Whitey, "Hey, you want a slice?"

"Two and a large grape," Whitey says quicker than quick.

"Three slices, a large grape and a small grape," I say in the general direction of Luigi from the sidewalk counter. He doesn't even look at me. He just picks up three slices from the pizza tin next to him, tosses them into the oven and puts the white Dixie cups under the bubbling plastic tank filled with purple grape drink. I put my dollar on the counter, he takes it and gives me back a dime, without saying a word. A minute later our steaming-hot pizza is placed on the counter on three thin sheets of wax paper. We fold our pizza slices in half and start eating, careful not to let any of the grease from the crease get onto our ties or shoes.

"Who's got a quarter for the jukebox?" a female voice says just behind me and Whitey. Uh oh. It's Carrie Vitelli. The girl I like. But nobody really knows it, though most suspect it. She's so close to me that I can smell that smell. The sexiest smell in the world. The smell that only girls can make so sexy. Cigarettes mixed with Bazooka bubble gum.

"I only have a dime left," I say, with a half a slice of pizza in my mouth.

"I'll take it. That's good for one song anyway." Carrie strikes a pose with one hand on her hip and the other with palm up, waiting for me to deposit the coin in it. I can't figure it out. She's never been so... direct with me. Like flirty. She's got her eyebrows raised up and her lips like pouty, as she continues to chew her bubble gum.

I put down my slice and dig back into my pocket for my dime and put it into her pink waiting palm.

"Thanks. I'll pay you back. Someday," she says, and turns on her toes and heads to the back of the pizza place to play a song on the jukebox which is now silent. As I pick up my slice again, I turn to Whitey for his reaction. Whitey contorts his face into a cross-eyed, open-mouthed, tongue-wagging look of total confusion. I agree. We watch her as she studies the songs on the jukebox. She carefully pushes one of the square red buttons, then another. I hear the innards of the jukebox whirring as Carrie turns around and looks right at me with a big smile. Not a goofy smile. An actual... sexy smile. I have this weird feeling that this song is supposed to mean something. The needle meets the vinyl. A big scratchy sound of silence fills the sidewalk in the split second before the needle is in the groove, then WHAM, "I Want To Hold Your Hand" blasts through the night. The jig is up. There it is. Holding hands. I know it doesn't sound like much, but holding hands is the first big step. A real big step. Carrie walks by me in a slow sort of slinky way, and now she doesn't look at me at all. She goes right past and over to Donna and Jimmy Joe and the other kids who are sitting on and leaning against a car parked in the street. She knows I'm looking at her. I can tell she knows I know.

"Hey, Vinny," Whitey says whispering, "I think she loves you."

I couldn't believe he said that. "She loves you." Just like the song. That's what's so cool about "She Loves You." I think it's the first time a song talked about how kids talk to each other. We'd never tell a girl we liked her. A girl would never tell if she liked you either. But friends are always telling secret messages like "she likes you." But she loves you; that's almost too much for a friend to even say.

"Get out of here!"

"OK, she likes you then."

And then, more silence as the juke box needle lifts off the scratchy end of the 45. What's next? Maybe it'll be "Alley Oop" or "Hello Dolly" or.......

> *"She loves you, yeah, yeah, yeah.*
> *She loves you, yeah, yeah, yeah.*
> *She loves you, yeah, yeah, yeah, yeah.*
> *You think you've lost your love*
> *Well, I saw her yesterday.*
> *It's you she's thinking of,*
> *and she told me what to say.*
> *She says she loves you..."*

I can't believe this. Too weird. I have to snap out of it.

"Alright. I'm not sure if I like her."

"Well, you better make up your mind soon, 'cause BB DOES."

"AAAAAH, BB, you jerk," Carrie yells, followed by the sound of a pissed-off girl smacking a guy on the back of his windbreaker.

> *"You know it's up to you,*
> *I think it's only fair..."*

"Yeah, you're right," I say to Whitey.

The loud bang of the door swinging open and smashing against the outside wall startles everybody. We all stop what we're doing to see Sean Symington come staggering out of the door. Symington is only a two years older than we are, a freshman in high school (he was left back) but he looks like he's twenty one, and gets into just about any bar he wants to, since the drinking age is 18. Symington is a hitter. We call him "Simple" as in Simple Symington. But not to his face. If he was Italian, he'd be a greaser, but because he's Irish, he's a hitter. He's over 6 feet tall, with a tiny, flat-topped head, and already has the makings of a prominent Rheingold tumor, or beer belly, as most people say.

"Oh crap, " Whitey says softly, but with a quiver of terror in his voice, "Symington's gonna kick our ass."

"What are you talking about? He never bothered us before," dismissing Whitey's fear.

"Yeah, well, he never saw us dressed like this before." Whitey says.

He's right. Symington is known to kick somebody's ass just for wearing a Mets hat or getting good marks in school or simply because he felt like it. We all know that he gets drunk a lot, and I know that he's one of the guys who hangs out under the Major Deegan overpass bridge next to the railroad tracks and leaves behind tons of empty airplane glue tubes and paper bags. I've even seen him down there by himself.

And here me and Whitey are wearing the latest stuff from Fuhrman's Department Store, worn for the first time, and sticking out like sore thumbs in our pointy high-heeled shoes, collarless jackets, skinny ties and peg legged pants, and frozen in front of Luigi's counter staring at Symington, wondering if he's too messed up to notice us.

"Holy shit!" Symington yells right at us. I guess not.

"Schmidt and Shelley, what the fuck are you wearing, you little queer motherfuckers, I'm gonna kick you're little fuckin' faggot asses."

This could be really bad. Whitey and I are motionless, thinking about our options...run, kick him in the nuts? Symington takes one giant step towards us and slips on some

109

slop that was dropped earlier, falling right on his face, and in his drunken state scrapes up his face pretty good and bloody. Whitey and I knowing an opportunity when we see it, waste no time and run as fast as we can in our pointy shoes and peg legged pants up the block towards home.

"I'm gonna get you little bastids for this!" Symington screams at us from the front of the pizza place as we're already a couple of hundred feet away.

"Goddamn, now we gotta watch out for that asshole," Whitey says as we slow down to a steady trot.

"You think he'll remember?"

"With his face smashed up like that, he ain't gonna forget nothin'."

Whitey's right. We're marked. Even Symington's friends are gonna probably be after us once Symington tells them that we tripped him while he was drunk or some crap like that.

"Screw him. He'll have to catch me first," I said to Whitey defiantly, knowing full well that it was only a matter of time when Sean Symington would catch up with us, somewhere, sometime, and running won't be an option.

I've never been to a wedding before. Some of my older cousins have gotten married, but they never invite kids to the wedding. My mother says that's because we have so many older relatives, that if kids were invited there'd be too many people. But today, I'll be there because it's my own brother. And because Whitey is going to also come out of altar boy retirement for the wedding, he can go to the reception too.

It's going to be real strange to see my relatives in the same room with my brother's friends. My brother has got some friends with weird names. There's "Smoker" who smokes Luckys nonstop and started in the second grade; and "Wig," whose pompadour is so elaborate that some people think it's a wig; and "Murph the Surf," named after a popular Irish gangster; and "Jig Saw" whose eyebrows look like two jig saw blades, and "Muff." I have no idea how he got that one but I

110

think it must be dirty because my brother refuses tell me. And there's "Roach," not named after his similarity to the cockroach, even though I swear there is one, but because that's actually his last name. I've never seen any of those guys dressed up. My mother doesn't like them and blames them for being a bad influence on my brother. Funny, but Muff's brother is a friend of mine, and his mother says the same thing about my brother.

I didn't get to see too much of the wedding in church because being an altar boy, there's actually stuff you have to do. I could see that my mother was crying a little, and that my brother was looking around laughing and winking a lot at his best man, "Wig." Whitey and I both really had to watch the priest, Monsignor Moriarity. He's a real mean one. If you're even a second late on ringing a bell or turning a page or getting the cruets, he'll mouth the insults he's gonna use for real at the top of his voice once you get back into the sacristy afterwards. One time, when I was serving mass with him, he knocked over a whole chalice filled with blessed hosts all over the rug. When he did it, he said under his breath, "Oh, you motherfucker!" Boy was I shocked. I guess he was pissed because the hosts were already blessed and only a priest is allowed to pick them up. I didn't know priests ever even heard of that word.

The reception is at a VFW hall in Riverdale, just a few minutes away by car, but in a really nice part of the Bronx where there are front yards with lawns and apartment buildings with doormen. My brother's friends are all over the place, wearing dark shirts with light-colored ties, dark jackets, and baggy iridescent pants they call sharkskin. And they all have so much grease in their hair that it looks like they just got out of the water. Muff and Smoker are behind a big portable table with bottles of scotch, Coke, and different kinds of buckets with bottles of Rheingold beer. The reason there's only scotch is that about 20 years ago, when my father started working at NYU as an plumber, somebody asked him what kind of liquor he liked and my father said scotch. So for the past 20 years, my father gets bottles of scotch for Christmas from guys who sell faucets, pipes, ladders, work gloves, and snakes. We've had boxes of scotch under beds, in closets, under the sink and everywhere else, with the hope that someday we'd be able to use them for something. And finally we can. I tried drinking scotch one New Year's Eve and threw up immediately.

There's another big table with huge trays of lasagna, sausages, meatballs, chicken cacciatore, and a giant metal bowl filled with salad. And in the front of the room, right between the liquor table and the food table, there's a rock-ola jukebox just sitting there in silence.

People are arriving by the second. You can tell who's who just by the way they greet each other. All my mother's brothers and sisters (she has eight of them) come in and scream each other's names real loud, Angie! Enrico! Nicky! Al! Grace! Marie! Roma! Louise! Dominic! One after another. Whatever kids are here try to keep their distance from the action, because being too close means getting caught up in the hugging, kissing, squeezing, lifting, rubbing, pinching, shaking, hand holding frenzy that embarrasses all kids over 8 or so with any sense of trying to be cool. My father's brothers and sisters (he has three of them) are just as loud, don't touch as much, and have really strong handshakes. Where my mother's family all have jet black hair and darkish skin, my father's family are all kind of red-faced. One thing that everybody seems to share is big noses. My mother's side the classic Roman curve and my father's side the classic German bulbous ones. And it's just beginning to dawn on me that as I continue to grow, there's no way I can escape the curse of the nose.

All of a sudden, from behind, I'm trapped and lifted off my feet by a big bear hug.

"Oh, Vinny, you look so cute!" as my breath is being squeezed out of me.

"Stop it, Whitey, you big ape, you're torturing me!" Thankfully, Whitey releases me.

"Hey, this food is great! Where'd they get it from?" Whitey says as he picks up his paper plate overloaded with sausages, meatballs, and lasagna.

"My mother made it."

"Wow! She's a good cook." Whitey barely mumbles

between swallows, "Hey, let's check out the jukebox."

We snake through the liquor and food lines. I hear no less than four people saying, "Waddyah mean, all there is is scotch?" The jukebox is an old one, probably 10 years old at least, and by looking at the songs, maybe older. Glenn Miller, Frank Sinatra, Benny Goodman, Louie Prima, Artie Shaw, Count Basie, Duke Ellington, Stan Kenton, Harry James, Louis Jordan, who ever heard of half this stuff? In the last column is a couple of Irish songs, a couple of Italian songs, a couple of polkas, and at the very bottom, "Rock Around the Clock" by Bill Hailey and the Comets, and something called "Rock and Roll Music" by Chuck Berry.

"This is gonna stink," I say to Whitey. "There's nothing but old fart music."

"Is that so!" I hear from just behind me, punctuated with two index fingers jabbed right into the part of my sides where even slight pokes send me wriggling, so this one has me almost jumping out of my pointy shoes. I manage to turn around to see who it is... "Uncle Dominic, stop it!" I plead. I've got some funny relatives, and I've seen some funny people around the neighborhood, but Uncle Dominic makes me laugh more than anybody. He looks a lot like that comedian on The Ed Sullivan show, Buddy Hackett.

And even though he's probably not even that old, maybe 40 or 45, he's got false teeth, and is always popping them out for comedic effect.

"Old farts, huh? Well, let's put on some of this old fart music and see if you little shits can keep up with it." Uncle Dominic starts pushing the red buttons real fast like he knows every song on the jukebox. And he's not putting in any money.

"Hey, this thing is free!" Uncle Dominic shouts as he pounds out one red button after another.

"Yeah, great," I say glancing over to Whitey, knowing full well that means Uncle Dominic's songs will be blasting out for the next hour at least.

"You kids think you invented good music," Uncle Dominic screams over the blaring horns of a song called "In The Mood." "Listen to Louis Jordan, Count Basie, Nat King

Cole, and The Mills Brothers some time and we'll talk about music. On the radio in the Army they called them race records, but the white guys in the army called it nigger music, not me, the bigots. But nobody calls it that anymore. Today you call it Rock and Roll, but Elvis Presley didn't invent it, believe you me."

Whitey and I looked at each other, knowing that Uncle Dominic was giving us one of those "in my day" lectures.

"Hey, Vinny, come by later, and I'll show you how to make mozzarella cheese come out of your nose." Uncle Dominic turned around and bounced away to the music, I think looking for a dance partner.

Just as Uncle Dominic was chasing my sister, I saw my cousins Elizabeth and Walter come in. Their parents, my Aunt Grace and Uncle Cornelius, were already here for 10 minutes or so, but I still haven't seen Jimmy. I haven't seen him since that crazy time at the St. Patrick's Day Parade, and I was anxious to talk to him about it. Then I couldn't believe my eyes.

There was Jimmy. I've never seen anything like it in person. His hair was so incredibly long down the front of his face it was practically covering his eyes. It was a little over his ears, and over his collar in the back. Needless to say, he was the only person at this bash with that look. And pretty soon, somebody would let him know it. But good.

"Man, isn't that your Cousin Jimmy?" Whitey says.

"Yup."

I never felt such a strange feeling. Jimmy is my favorite cousin. Even one of my favorite people in the world including my friends from the block. But I felt all funny inside. I didn't want to go over to him. It was like he was naked or something, and I didn't know how I'd react standing next to him. But more than that, I was worried what everybody else would think about me if I was next to him.

And through the crowd I could see him peering, looking around, till he looked right at me. I froze. But he breaks into a big smile and heads right for me, pushing through the middle of the party.

As he did, all I could see was the faces of shocked,

114

disgusted, amused, perplexed relatives, friends, kids looking at this strange creature bopping through the crowd knowing full well that all eyes were on him. Who dared to come to a party, a WEDDING no less, looking like such a...queer. It was one thing to see The Beatles, and the other groups that started to pop up looking just like them... The Dave Clark Five, Gerry and The Pacemakers, and Peter and Gordon... but they were only on TV. And all the way from England. But here was somebody right here. Right now. With that look. No grease, no part, not combed back, but FORWARD! Like bangs. Like a girl.

"Man, your cousin's hair got really, really long," Whitey says to me, never taking his eye off Jimmy. I didn't say anything. That's what everybody in the place was thinking. Those that know him anyway. All the others are probably thinking... "Who the hell is THAT?"

"Vinny! Congratulations!" Jimmy says, with a level of excitement that could only be used for comedic effect.

"Thanks." I didn't know what to say. I wanted to say..."Do you know that everybody in the whole place is staring at you, wondering who the hell you think you are... and don't you know that one of these big greasy micks who thinks that anybody who doesn't look like them is a queer and kicks ass at the drop of a hat... and how could you possibly have the balls to do this, 'cause somebody is gonna say something and you ain't a hitter... you are going to be a hittee."

"Did you see my brother yet?" I managed to ask.

"Yeah, saw him outside. He's polluted already! What a gas! What's there to drink?"

"You saw Joey outside?"

"Yeah."

"And he didn't say anything?"

"Like what?"

"Oh, never mind. There's Cokes and beer and scotch at the table, but you better not let my mother or father catch you with any booze, she told me she'd kill anybody underage caught drinking."

Is he leaving something out? Didn't my brother say

something about the way he looked. If I looked like that, my brother would get a razor, leaving me looking like Curly. He's done worse.

"Follow my lead. Come on." Jimmy motions to Whitey and me and walks over to the liquor table, manned by Muff and Smoker. Now he's had it. I just know it.

Jimmy walks over and speaks right up.

"Hello, gentlemen. Three Rheingolds and three cups, please."

Muff's in the middle of laughing at something with Smoker. They both have lit cigarettes in their mouths bouncing up and down with laughter. Without even looking at Jimmy, they hand over the beers and the cups.

"Let's find a table and relax," Jimmy says triumphantly.

The three of us find an empty table and sit. Jimmy pours each beer into a white wax Dixie cup and places the empty bottles with a bunch of others on the table next to us. He then places each of the cups about two feet away from us.

"This way we can say that they're not ours," Jimmy says as he takes a sip from a cup. "Have a drink."

I know I'll get caught. "No thanks, not me," I say.

Whitey looks around, and says, "Yeah, I will."

"You better not get caught," I tell Whitey, knowing full well I'll be the one to catch hell if he does.

"Don't worry about it," Whitey says as he reaches across the table for the cup like it's the forbidden fruit. He takes a quick sip that leaves a white beer head mustache on his upper lip.

"Wipe off the mustache, doofus," I tell him. He does.

"Don't call me doofus, shithead Schmidthead."

"Vinny, did you get 'Meet The Beatles'?" Jimmy asks me.

"Yeah. It's really cool. I know all the words to a couple of songs."

"There's another group from England that's gonna be on The Dean Martin Show soon called The Rolling Stones. They're The Beatles' favorite group."

"Wow." I never thought of a famous group as having a

favorite group. I thought that was kinda like Kris Kringle recommending Gimbles when he worked at Macy's in "Miracle on 34th Street." "Let me know when they're gonna be on."

Jimmy reaches over for another sip of beer, takes a huge gulp, lets out a big "aaaahhh" and says, "Did I tell you I'm learning how to play the guitar?"

"Really? How are you doing that?"

"I know a guy who plays and he's teaching me. I already know some chords."

"Maybe Uncle Carmine can give you lessons!"

Jimmy bursts out laughing, "What are you nuts?" and continues to laugh hysterically.

I thought it was a good idea. He can play any song pretty good. But I sure felt like a jerk now with Jimmy busting a gut over it.

From out of the crowd at the liquor table, Uncle Dominic reemerges and heads right over to Jimmy.

"Holy mackerel! Elizabeth! How ya doing?"

Since Elizabeth was Jimmy's sister, it was obvious that Uncle Dominic was the first to come out with what everyone else was thinking.

Uncle Dominic grabs Jimmy's ears and plants a big kiss on his cheek.

"Stop, stop, stop," Jimmy pleads.

Uncle Dominic does and pulls something out of his pocket.

"You kids ever roll dice?"

"Hey cool!" Jimmy says, "Let's play!"

"I don't know how," I say.

"I'll teach you," says Uncle Dominic, as he starts blowing on the dice in his hand, and motions for us to crouch down under the table.

"First, everybody puts up two bucks, but not yet, then the first guy rolls the dice. If he gets a 7 or 11 he wins all the money. If he gets a 2, 3, or 12, that's craps, he loses, and the next guy goes. If he gets a different number than 7, 11, 2, 3, or 12, whatever that number is he tries to get that number again, without getting a 7. If he hits the number he keeps all the money. If he gets the 7, everybody else splits the pot, unless..." At this point Uncle Dominic looks up from the dice he's been rolling, picking up, blowing on, over and over, and looks at the three of us who must have the look of total stupidity across our mugs.

"You guys don't get it, do you?" Uncle Dominic says looking really disappointed. He looks at Jimmy and says,
"Jimmy, how old are you?"
"Seventeen," Jimmy replies.
"Seventeen, huh? You ever think about smoking pot?"
Jimmy looks totally stunned, as Whitey and I probably also do.
"Ah, no. Never."
"Well, don't," Uncle Dominic says with a wink, picking up his dice, and heads back over to the liquor table.

The three of us just look at each other in amazement. Jimmy, being the older and wiser of the three of us, gets up and says, "Come with me. Vinny, where's your mom?"

"She's probably in the kitchen."
"Come on, I want to ask her something. Take us there."

I lead the guys through the crowd and into the kitchen and there's my mom, with an apron on mixing up another bowl of salad.

"Oh finally, some relief for me, put on an apron, fellas. Hi, Jimmy sweetie, how are you?" she says as she gives Jimmy a big hug and a kiss.

"Fine, Aunt Angie! How's everything going?"
"Good good, now what do you want?"

Jimmy puts on this big goofy smile and says, "Aunt Angie, can I ask you something... a little bit touchy?"

"Oh, stop the b.s.ing, Jimmy, get to the point; I've got to put in another tray of lasagna."

"Did Uncle Dominic ever smoke pot?"

"How dare you, you little brat!" Mom says, all pissed off and picking up the giant plastic salad mixing fork like she's gonna rap Jimmy in the chops. "Don't you ever say anything like that about Uncle Dominic. I can't believe the gall of you kids."

118

Then she stopped dead in her tracks, and kind of looked up at the ceiling and back down. "Is pot the same as reefer?" she asks in a very deliberate manner.

"Yeah," Jimmy answered.

"Well, then yeah, he did. But that was a long time ago. Now get out of here unless you want to start cleaning some dishes."

Jimmy had the look of someone who had just unsolved a mystery of the ages. "I knew Uncle Dominic was cool. I knew it."

I was in the state of shock. Uncle Dominic? Smoked pot? Maybe he still does. Maybe that's why he's so funny all the time and can do stuff like make mozzarella come out of his nose. And I can't believe my mother knows about it and even knows the word "reefer." I wonder if my father knows? Wait a minute... I just remembered a bizarre story that my mother used to tell about how my dad actually used to know Uncle Dominic way back before he even met my mother. Nah. No way. Not my dad. He was a jock from day one. He played semipro baseball in and around New York City, when that was where the major leagues scouted most of their talent. He even played with Eddie Lopatynski, who was a great pitcher for the Yankees, who goes by the name Eddie Lopat. There's other guys who are managers and coaches now that my dad says he played with. One time, when I had to bring my father something when he was at work at NYU, one of the workers there said my father was a better third baseman than Clete Boyer. Now he hardly ever even plays catch with me, and seeing the Rheingold tumor he's got, I can't imagine him diving head first for a ball going down the line.

"Hey, let's see if we can play some music on the jukebox," Whitey says, snapping me out of my daydream.

"Whitey!" Jimmy yells, grabbing the both of us by our arms, "YOU are a genius! Vinny, I like this guy! He's alright." Even though you could never tell if Jimmy was breaking your chops or if he meant it, I felt real good about Jimmy liking Whitey.

Just as we turn to head for the jukebox, our path is

blocked by a big goon. Not just any big goon, but a particular big goon who tripped and cut his face and blames me and Whitey for it. Yup. Sean Symington. What the hell is he doing here? He doesn't hang out with my brother.

"Hey, Schmidt, bet you didn't know that we're related now?" he says, poking me in the chest. "Your brother's wife's father is my mother's cousin. I thought I'd stop by and do a little celebrating."

Holy shit. Symington. Here me and Whitey are wearing the same clothes we had on the other night, and here's Jimmy, looking like he's the fifth Beatle. A fact that the big dumb asshole immediately picks up on.

"Schmidt. Who's the faggot?"

That's it. The jig is up. The party's over. Should I run for help? Scream for help? Who's gonna help us anyway. Look at Jimmy. He's just asking for trouble with that hair, and those clothes, and now he's gonna get his ass kicked just like he knew he would when he first walked in the place. But Jimmy doesn't look scared. But he sure looks different. He's sticking his jaw out and clenching his teeth, reaching into the inside of his jacket, staring at Symington the flat-topped fool.

"Look," Jimmy says real quietly, "don't mess with me, 'cause I've got a fuckin' switchblade in my hand and I'll stick you, I swear to God."

I couldn't believe it. Is Jimmy for real? No way. No way he's got a switchblade. Symington is gonna kill him.

I can see Whitey's got white knuckles from holding his fists so tight. I don't know if I'm going to cry or run. I can see the wheels spinning in Symington's pea brain. He turns around without saying a word and disappears through the dance floor.

Boy, am I relieved. "Man, Jimmy, you faked him out."

Jimmy opens his jacket slightly, revealing a closed switchblade. I couldn't believe it. A freakin' switchblade. "Holy shit!" I say in a gush of gasps as Jimmy pulls the knife out into full view. He pushes the button and out comes not a 5 inch knife, but a 5 inch comb.

Jimmy gets that big goofy grin back on his face, "Come on, let's get some rock and roll on that jukebox."

And as we make our way to the jukebox, probably to play the only two songs on there that aren't old time music, it seems to me that people aren't staring at Jimmy at all like he's some kind of freak. Everybody seems to be laughing, drinking, eating, dancing, telling stories, hugging, kissing, and just plain talking with whoever the hell they happen to be next to. And the three of us look cooler than anybody else here. What a night.

We managed to play those two songs as many times in a row as the machine would take. And I really like that "Rock and Roll Music" by Chuck Berry. Even the old people danced to it. The later it gets, the drunker most everybody gets, and luckily there haven't been any more hassles that I've seen. And young people aren't the only ones who cause fights. Uncle Dominic gets into trouble all the time when he drinks, grabbing girl's asses and dropping his drawers, but fortunately tonight nobody seems to mind too much except for his sisters, including my mom, who calls him a filthy pig every once in a while.

I didn't even see my brother and his wife leave. Tonight, he's officially out of our house. I think I'll get down off the top bunk and sleep in his bed, over by the window this evening. And if my sister goes away to college this fall like she says she might, I'll actually have my own room. I can't wait.

There are just a few stragglers left in the hall, with a big mess left behind. My parents and my sister are sitting at a table drinking coffee. Me and Whitey are throwing the dice Uncle Dominic gave me, trying to get 7s and 11s on the table next to them. The jukebox is turned off, and there's a small radio tuned to the corny sounds of WNEW.

After rolling 5 sevens in a row, the record for the session, Whitey says, "My father's gonna move to Florida." What a bombshell.

"Whaddyuh mean?"

"He's just moving to Florida, I guess."

"Where in Florida?"

"Fort Lauderdale."

"That's where the Yankees have spring training."

"Yeah. Maybe I'll get to visit sometime and get some autographs."

"That would be great."

"My brother's coming back from college to live at home and go to City College because it's free."

"Wow. I'm losing a brother and you're getting yours back."

Whitey didn't look too happy. "I think I'm going to walk home."

"Are you sure? We can give you a lift."

"Nah, I 'd rather walk."

Whitey dropped the dice and got up.

"Bye, Mr. and Mrs. Schmidt, thank you for inviting me."

"Want to take home some lasagna?"

"OK."

My mom got up and gave Whitey a big bag of food. He took out a piece of Italian bread and started chomping on it as he walked out the door for his long walk home, through the tree-lined streets of Riverdale, down the big hill, underneath the "el" on Broadway, and up the cobble-stoned 238th Street to the big old apartment building he called home.

Spring is definitely here. Now that we've already taken the co-ops (tests that Catholic school 8th graders throughout the city take to see what Catholic high schools they can get into), Sister Fidelis seems a little less concerned with teaching us the math that she has so much trouble figuring out and more concerned with strange lectures that pop up out of nowhere, and are supposed to send us, on our way, out of grammar school and into the real world. She keeps bringing up the horror of birth control and what a sin it is to take the pill. She never once, though, told us what either of those things are. And she really goes nuts when she catches a boy with his hands in his pockets. I mean, what boy doesn't put his hands in his pockets sometime, but Sister Fidelis is sure that anytime a hand is in a pocket, it's doing something dirty. Now that's weird. Just think, every time she sees somebody with their hand in their pocket, she actually thinks he's trying to play with himself. I wonder where she gets her information from?

Playing with yourself, or "jerking off" like it's called, is a hot topic these days. But to tell you the truth, I don't like to talk about it, and I think it's kind of strange that some guys do. In fact, one time Tommy Kowalzyck brought in a pill bottle that had some really disgusting slimy stuff in it. He claimed it was "scum" from you-know-what the night before. I couldn't get far enough away from that idiot. Kowalzyck claimed he was the first kid in the class to have "scum." Maybe he was, but I sure as hell wasn't gonna take him up on a bet. Kowalzyck hangs out with older kids on the block. I know for a fact that he drinks beer every weekend and sometimes sniffs "Carbona." He even says he's screwed girls. I think he's full of crap.

As the days grow warmer in this month of May, it's hard to believe that in a month we'll be set free from this place. From the classroom, it's easy to see the leaves coming out on the trees across the street in the park. And college kids, who get out of school earlier than we do, are practicing baseball and track. We won't have to hide in laundry rooms or hallways anymore, hiding from the cold and nosey neighbors. With a huge park, there are plenty of places to hide and do all kinds of things. And being too old for Little League and the altar boys, and the weather the way it is, it seems like everyone is out every afternoon. There's a whole world of kids out there, and always something to do. I can't wait till 3.

"Shelley! What are you doing, you retard?" Sister Fidelis comes flying down the aisle, swaying back and forth with a look on her fat face like she's really pissed off not that she has to yell at Whitey, she's used to that, but that she has to get up out of her chair and rush all the way down the aisle to see what Shelley is up to. I know what he's up to. I've been watching him all day, since he's right next to me. The latest thing in the class to get through the boredom of the day is to take a couple of ball bearings and make a kind of an obstacle course on your desk with erasers, rulers, pencil sharpeners, pens, pencils, pocket combs, whatever you can think of, and put them in an arrangement where letting the ball bearing go on the top of the desk and rolling downhill, it goes through and around and up, and across, and back and forth and over the ramped edge of an eraser, and maybe plops into a pencil sharpener bottom that's taped to the edge of the desk. Whitey's been working on his set-up for a while. It's really hard to get a good one going because if Sister Fidelis sees something fishy, or decides to take a walk down the aisle, she might see what you're doing. That's why you only use normal school supply items; that way you can just push stuff around and it looks like you're just sloppy with your stuff, and not mapping out some home-made pinball game. But because Whitey's in the back of the classroom, all the way down the aisle, next to the windows, he can sometimes work on his project for hours, perfecting it for the amusement of the 2 or 3 kids sitting around him who can watch while Whitey lets his ball bearing go... across the pencil, hit the eraser, drop to the ruler, across the pen, actually moving the pen slightly, so the ball drops back the other way, straight down, up the ramp edge of the eraser and over, hit another pencil and drop right into the bottom half of the pencil sharpener, the one that looks like a rocket ship. But this time Sister Fidelis saw something was going on, right in the middle of working out a long division problem on the board, which she always has trouble with, and winds up getting frustrated and yelling and asking one of the smart girls like Joanne Martorana to help her solve it without letting the rest of the class know that she's stumped. But here she comes, flying down the aisle heading straight for Whitey.

"Shelley, you big doofus! What in heaven's name are you concocting here?"

"Nothing, Sister."

"Nothing Sister? You have exactly three seconds to let me in on the nature of these shenanigans or it's down to the principal's office."

Whitey was pushing all of his devices to the center of his desk into a giant mess of school supplies. That what his big mistake. Too many items. Yeah, his ball bearing obstacle course was a good one, but he used too many things to make it work. Now there's no way to cover. The real art of a good ball bearing desk obstacle course is keeping it simple enough so that if you are caught, you only have a few things on your desk and might be able to talk your way out of it. Whitey went too far, and now he'll pay for it.

"What's that in your hand?"

Uh oh. Whitey's dead now. What's in his hand, of course, are the dreaded ball bearings. Foreign objects to the class. The one item that will surely get you nailed.

Whitey opens his hand, revealing two gleaming ball bearings.

"And what may I ask do you do with those, Mr. Shelley?"

Whitey was making a big mistake. He was thinking. Hard.

"They're for my slingshot."

Oh no! Whitey made the worst, most stupidest mistake possible; he tried to conceal what he was doing, but came up with a cover that was worse than what he would get in trouble for in the first place!

Whitey's turning deep red now. He knows he screwed up big time and there's no turning back.

"Hand them over!" Sister Fidelis says, like she's asking for the bullets that killed JFK. "Where's the slingshot?"

"It's at home."

"Don't lie to me, Shelley!"

"I'm not, Sister, it's at home."

"You bring it in tomorrow, with a note from your father explaining why you have a slingshot and ball bearings."

"Yes, Sister."

Whitey's screwed. He admitted he had a slingshot, that he uses ball bearings as ammunition, and will have to explain why he can't get a note from his father since he's probably moved out by now.

dingalingadingalingadingalingadingaling

The three o'clock bell is ringing in the hall. Sister Fidelis stares at the class just waiting for someone to jump out of their seat without permission. Nobody does.

She continues staring with those squinty mean eyes, looking back and forth and, through clenched yellow teeth, says, "Class dismissed. Quietly!!!"

I know why Whitey stupidly said that the ball bearings were for his slingshot. Because that's our latest kick now... slingshots. Of course, you'd want to use ball bearings as ammo, but are you kidding? You know how expensive that would be? Plus you probably would kill somebody with a ball bearing. So we use rocks. Nice round rocks. And we haven't killed anybody. Yet.

Today, we're meeting at the construction site up on Orloff Avenue. We're going to choose up sides and have a slingshot fight. One rule. You're not supposed to aim for the eyes.

We make our own slingshots out of branches from trees. You've got to find the perfect size "y" in the limb and cut it with a saw. Then you've got to get special thick rubber bands from a stationery store. Not the usual thin kinds of rubber bands. And the hardest part is finding the right kind of patch for the ammo. Leather is best, but it's hard to find. You never tell other kids how to make a good slingshot. You never tell where you got the great rubber bands, or the saw for the tree, or the great leather patch or how you put the rubber bands together and attach them to the ammo patch. If you did that, then they might have a slingshot as good as yours and you don't want that to happen. Slingshots are serious business. Especially when the idea of a game is shooting at each other from "I" beams in a construction sight. The worse somebody else's slingshot is, the less likely you'll get slammed with a round stone in your face.

My brother taught me about slingshots and I taught Whitey, but that's it. And Whitey's got to be on my side. But first things first. We've got to make a new slingshot for Whitey to bring to Sister Fidelis tomorrow. One that looks so rinky dink that you couldn't hurt a fly with it. Whitey's real slingshot could kill a big rat with the right ammo. Maybe even a person.

126

The neighborhood used to have empty lots all over the place. You didn't even have to hang out in the park, because there were so many lots to either play in if you're a little kid or build a fort in if you're an older kid. When we were little kids, there were all kinds of things to do in the lots. In the lot up the hill, you have to climb up rocks to get into the lot. We call it the "mountains." We used to have great dirt bomb fights there. A dirt bomb is when you take a stick and stick it in a certain kind of dirt about a foot down, and then when you push down on the stick on an angle, it makes chunks of dirt. You're not allowed to throw dirt bombs that have big rocks in them, but anything else is OK. Dirt bombs don't usually stick together too well when you throw them, so the likelihood that you're going to hurt somebody seriously isn't that much of a big deal. Once in a while you'll get a big chunk of dirt in the face, but it's not that bad. Unlike slingshots.

The last couple of years, constructions have started in lots all over the place. They go in, cut down all the trees and bushes, bring in bulldozers, dig a huge hole, and then start building. This is why it has never been more fun to live in this neighborhood.

You wouldn't believe how much wood is left around at construction sites. Sometimes they even leave tools, especially shovels. It's all there for the taking. We don't take the real wood that they build the apartment building with. But they leave around all kinds of wood that they use to make temporary walls and sheds and stuff like that. The shovels are the real thing. Sometimes we even find huge barrels filled with nails. So, with the great wood and tools we find, it's a cinch to make the best forts the neighborhood has ever seen. It seems that every group of kids from all the different blocks have built their own kinds of forts. The little kids in 3rd and 4th grade have little rinky dink shacks; but even kids in high school are building forts, and you should see those things! Sturdy like you wouldn't believe, with locks on the doors, and secret escape hatches. They don't even hide them too much, because everybody knows not to mess with those forts.

127

But the real thrilling thing about construction sites is that once they start to build the foundation and put up a story or two of "I" beams, there's no better place to play. Once a building gets 3 or 4 stories high, they usually put a watchman there around the clock. But, when it's just a story or 2, there's usually just a day watchman, and he leaves at around 4 or 5 in the afternoon. Perfect for after-school fun.

Sometimes we just play Ringo-Leaveo in the construction site. That's when you choose up sides and you have to find the other team and grab them for as long as it takes to count to three "ringo-leaveos" and put them in a dungeon, then the other team has to try to free them without getting caught. But it seems we've outgrown the fun of Ringo-Leaveo. Now it's slingshot fights.

I don't know exactly who it was that thought a slingshot fight would be a fun thing to do, but that's what we're doing today. There's a construction site up on Orloff that's got 2 stories of "I" beams and no day or night watchman, so that's where we're meeting. There are kids that are too chicken to join in. I wish I was one of them.

Tommy Kowalzyck usually hangs out with his older brother and his friends, but when he heard we were having slingshot fights in the construction site, he wanted to be included. Right now it's me, Whitey, Jimmy Joe, Ralphie, BB, and Kowalzyck. Kowalzyck reminds me of that really bad kid in Pinocchio that gets turned into a jackass.

"Let's make up sides," Jimmy Joe announces once we're all inside the chain-link fence.

"Me and Whitey are on the same team," I say, hoping nobody challenges me. Nobody does.

"Alright," Jimmy Joe says, "and you take Ralphie."

I knew he'd say that. Ralphie's got the weakest little slingshot you've ever seen. It's like a twig, with regular rubber bands, and for a patch he uses an old tongue from a pair of canvas sneakers. That's OK. Me and Whitey have fine slingshots. Cut from solid trees. Rubber bands from behind the counter at Robert's Bookstore. You have to know to ask for them. Leather patches cut from old baseball gloves. Then I see what Kowalzyck pulls out of his pocket. Oh my God. It's one of those "sure shot" slingshots that you buy from a hunting store upstate. He sees that everyone has taken notice.

"My old man bought this for me up in the Adirondacks." We were all in awe. We had heard of the deadly "sure shot" but had only seen them in catalogues. Now we would have to face one in battle.

The rules in slingshot fights are simple. Choose up teams. One team takes a position behind the part of the newly laid foundation that looks like the top of a castle's fortress, and the other team roams around the "I" beams. The object is to hit the opposing team at least three times. The real object is not to get permanently maimed or killed, but nobody says it. For ammunition, we use perfectly round rocks that are in great abundance at the site for concrete mixing. Guaranteed a good shot with one of those could knock a tooth out, knock an eye out, and I don't want to know what might happen if you hit somebody right in the temple. I hope it ain't me. Oh yeah, like I said, no aiming for the eyes.

We fill our pockets with rocks. Whitey lost the odds'n'evens choose, so we were out to the "I" beams in a hundred Mississippis.

As we were running through the site still counting, I said to Ralphie, "You keep counting out loud so we know how much time we have. Whitey, you and Ralphie go to the first level on the left side over where the shed is and shoot from there. I'll go up to the second level and lay low until they start to get cocky and come out to try and get you guys."

"99 Mississippi. 100 Mississippi. That's it," Ralphie says, out of breath from all those freaking Mississippis.

"Let's go, Ralphie," Whitey says as he and Ralphie snake around the concrete walls with rebar sticking out of them.

I slowly head up a ladder and onto the second story and over to the right. There's a temporary plywood wall there, and that's where I'm going to hide until I see my chance.

It's eerily silent. Every once in a while I hear a rock explode against an oil drum or into a piece of plywood. But not a word spoken. This is war.

129

I hear a flurry of rocks pelting the side where Whitey and Ralphie are supposed to be. I peek around the wood and see Kowalzyck, a big dumb smile on his face in perfect profile, pulling the patch on his "sure shot" all the way to the limit. This is it!

I stand up, pull my ammo all the way back, just hoping no one sees me. I feel invisible, nobody can stop me. I see Kowalzyck in slow motion, pulling back, back back, smiling, leering. He's got Whitey in his sights, I know he does. All I see is that dumb grin. He thinks he's such a hot shit because he hangs out with his older brother and drinks beer and sniffs Carbona and has scum in a bottle. Well screw him. THWACK. I let loose and in a split second I'm terrified. Oh my God! It's a perfect shot, with a perfect rock, heading right for his fucking temple and if it hits him right there I'm going to kill him and there's nothing I can do about it but watch.

"AAAAAAAAAAAHHHHHHHHHHH," Kowalzyck screams, both hands grasping at his face; he collapses to the ground, almost falling off the wall onto the debris below.

Holy shit. I'm dead.

I climb down the ladder, run across the nails, boards, beer cans, sand, up the hill to Kowalzyck, where the other guys are already around him.

All I see is blood. Blood on his hands, blood on his shirt, the ground, his face. He's crying.

"Where is it?" I scream, "Where did he get hit?"

"Let me, see Tommy!" Whitey screams to Kowalzyck.

Whitey pulls Kowalzyck's hands apart and there, in the middle of his forehead, is a nasty cut. Thank God. Not in his temple, not in his eye, not in his mouth. Probably in the best place possible. The middle of the forehead, just above the ridge of the eyebrow.

"I'm alright. I'm OK. Take me home," Kowalzyck says as he gets to his feet.

Boy, I would've gotten killed if I was just a little bit of a better shot.

Kowalzyck only lives down the block, and seeing that he wasn't going to drop dead, I thought it would be a good idea if I didn't go with the guys who were walking him home because his mother was bound to ask who did this awful thing to her son. She wouldn't understand that it was just us kids having fun. He just happened to be on the other side. That's the rules of the game.

I was wondering where Whitey disappeared to, and he came out of the bushes across the street. "Hey, lookit what I got! My slingshot!" He held up the most pathetic looking twig in the shape of a "Y." "I'll put a couple of rubber bands on it, and hand it in to Sister Fidelis tomorrow."

"What about the note from your father?" I remind him. Whitey's excitement turned into depression.

"Damn. I forgot."

"How about your brother Brian the cop? He's a grown up! Maybe he'll do it."

"I don't know, he's not around too much."

"Come on, let's go see if he's home."

"Well, OK."

Whitey doesn't seem too thrilled with the idea. I know that his brother works a lot and doesn't hang out in the neighborhood because he still hangs out in his old neighborhood down in Inwood. I've heard stories about his brother Brian the cop. He's a real wild man. He gets drunk and takes his gun out in the bar and sometimes shoots it into the air or even into the ceiling of "Vinegar Hill" where he hangs out. I even heard a story of how some colored guy was holding a lady in a car as a hostage, and Brian somehow walked by the car and blew the guy's brains out with one shot. I've never even met him.

Whitey's building is pretty much like mine, except he doesn't have an incinerator, so he has to take the garbage down to the basement because all the buildings in the neighborhood nailed the dumbwaiters shut because too many houses were getting robbed through them. One interesting thing about Whitey's building is that it has these cool stairwells, where there's a big opening from the 6th floor all the way down to the lobby. When you're up there looking down, it sure looks like a long way down. One time we dropped a watermelon from the top and the whole thing just splattered like hell all over the tiled first floor.

Whitey lives on the top floor, the 6th, so we almost always take the elevator up and down, unless it's broken which is pretty often. We never took the elevator if we were doing something bad, like dropping watermelons down the stairwell. You could get caught doing that.

"Let me go in first," Whitey says as he unlocks the three locks on the steel brown door to his apartment and goes in.

After a minute or so he comes and peeks his head out. "Come on in. Nobody's here." Whitey's house is different than mine. First of all it's huge. But it's real dark, and kind of has a dusty kind of smell to it. And the furniture is even older than ours, and we got ours from my Uncle when he bought a house in Queens. There's even stuffing sticking out of the sofa in a couple of places. My mother sewed ours up so you couldn't see it.

The kitchen has a table in it pushed up against the wall. One of those Formica jobs with chrome on the side. The red vinyl chairs have some stuffing sticking out of them too.

"You want something to eat?" Whitey asks as he opens the refrigerator.

"No, I'm gonna eat dinner in a little while."

"I'm going to have my dinner now," Whitey says as he takes a bottle of milk out of the fridge and reaches for a box of Kellogg's Cornflakes out of a cabinet that's been painted so many times the doors won't shut anymore.

"That's your dinner?"

"Yeah, I'll grab some more stuff later."

"Well, I guess I'll just go home now. See ya."

"Yeah, see ya."

BANG BANG BANG.

Three loud bangs on the door startle us.

"Who's that?" I wonder.

"Shit. It's probably my brother, he's always forgetting his keys."

BANG BANG BANG.

From the other side of the steel door, a voice echoes in

132

the tiled hall, "Let me in! Who's home? Let me the fuck in!"
"Uh oh. It's Brian. He's drunk. I better let him in."
Whitey gets up from the table and slowly walks over to the
front door. He opens it.
"Boy, am I glad you're home, you little squirt."
Brian is nothing like what I picture a cop to look like.
He looks like a teenager, even though I know he's 23. He's
pretty fat too. Rheingold tumor no doubt. A big round red
face and a strawberry blond flat top with a little butch wax
push-up in front. He is drunk. Stewed.
"I work all fuckin' night chasin' spics and I see one
right in my own elevator. Shit! I need some sleep. Good night,
Whitey, and be fucking quiet or I'll strangle you and your little
fuckin' faggot friend."
I could see Whitey was scared of Brian, but he was
trying to get out some words... "Uh, ah, Brian, could you write
me a note for school?"
That stopped Brian cold. "A note? Sure. Sure, kid.
Sure. Get me some paper and a pen."
Brian stumbles into the kitchen and sits in the chair
right next to me. He reaches down, under the table down by
his ankle. "Shit, this thing is killing me," he says as he struggles
with something under the pant leg of his baggy chinos. He
brings up a gun in a holster that he had strapped around his
ankle and bangs it on the kitchen table. "That's my equalizer,
kid," he says in my general direction.
Whitey comes back in with a piece of paper and a pen
and places them in front of Brian. "Here you go."
"OK. What do I say?"
Whitey looks over to me with a big "I don't know"
written across his face.
So I start..."Dear Sister Fidelis comma" as Brian begins to write...
"Spell Fidelis."
"F-i-d-e-l-i-s."
"F-i-d-el-i-s."

Please...excuse...William...for...having...a...sling...shot...period.

133

He's...allowed...to...have...one...because...we...spend...our.
..summers...
u p s t a t e . . . i n . . . t h e . . . c o u n t r y . . . p e r i o d
. . . h e . . . w o n ' t . . . u s e . . . i t . . . i n . . . t h e . . . c i t y .
Sincerely...Mister...Shelley"
      "OK, you little prick, now don't get in trouble anymore
and I ought to kick your ass for getting in trouble. Now good
night and don't wake me."
      Brian takes his gun and bounces off the foyer wall into
his bedroom. I look at the note and it's a mess of drunken
scribbles.
      "Oh no! Sister Fidelis will never believe this. It looks
like a drunk wrote it," I say to Whitey.
      "So? Then she'll really think my old man wrote it."
      I don't think Whitey was joking. I didn't see Whitey's
father too often. I don't know what he did for a living. I just
know he worked a lot of different jobs, and he walked with a
pretty bad limp. He's a big guy. Not fat, but big. Barrel chested.
We don't really talk about our parents much. I don't know
why that is, but I'm still not sure why his father is going to
move to Florida.
      Whitey's back to eating his corn flakes.
      "How come your father's moving to Florida?" I blurt
out.
      "I don't know. I guess 'cause my parents fight all the
time."
      I know what that means. They're getting separated. I
don't know of anybody whose parents have been divorced, although I know a few kids whose parents are separated. The
Catholic Church doesn't allow divorce. If you do get a divorce, that's a mortal sin, and a mortal sin means that you're
going to hell, unless you go to confession and do the penance
that the priest tells you to. Confession is really weird. When I
was younger, in the 5th grade or so, confession was simple.
You just said you lied to your parents once or twice and maybe
disobeyed them a few times. We used to talk to each other
before going in to see what the other guys were saying. You
never wanted to come off as too good or too bad. For a few

134

venial sins, the priest would tell you to say ten Hail Marys and a couple of Our Fathers and that would be the end of it.

But now confession is a very touchy matter. First of all, most of us actually have real sins to confess, and the priest darn well knows it. And those sins are sure hard to confess when the priest can actually see you through that screen. So you've got to be real careful to come up with enough sins so that the priest doesn't get suspicious that you're not telling him anything. If you're in 8th grade and you still say you lied to your parents and disobeyed them twice, the priest knows you're holding back and he's going to ask you to be more specific. He's done it to me. Then you've got to come up with quick sins to back up your story, like... "er ah, I didn't take the garbage out when I was told to, and um, I told them I didn't have any homework when I really did." The big sin we came up with to go along with our maturing is the "impure" sins; "Bless me, Father, for I have sinned, it has been two weeks (it's actually been eight weeks, but saying that could arouse suspicion) since my last confession. I was disrespectful to my parents four times (disrespectful is much more in keeping with an 8th grader than simply "lied to." Four times is not too many, but believable), I lied to my teacher twice (again, not too much, not too little), I had impure thoughts three times, and committed one impure act. (The "committed one impure act" is the clincher. It means you jerked off one time in two weeks. A big lie, but enough to keep a priest from asking a question in the box... continuing...). I am sorry for these and all the sins of my past life, especially for committing one impure act. (The obvious choice.) Penance has increased up to twenty Hail Marys and ten Our Fathers, but that's about it. I have no idea what would happen if I told the truth in confession, but I'm not about to find out.

So in our neighborhood, divorce is out of the question unless you want to go to hell or spend a really long time in the confessional telling the truth to a priest. Separation is definitely the way to go.

"What about your other brother, Alfie?"

"He's coming home when the college semester ends at

135

the end of the month."

"That'll be cool."

"Are you kidding, Alfie and Brian hate each other. See that hole there?"

Whitey points to a thin one-inch gash in the wood work of the doorway.

"That's where Alfie threw a harpoon at Brian. Come with me and be real quiet."

Whitey gets up and takes me down the dark foyer hallway. I can feel little pieces of grit crunching under the black-and-white checked linoleum.

"Feel this here."

Whitey takes my hand and rubs it against the living room wallpaper, where I feel a rounded indentation. "That's where Brian smashed Alfie's head into the wall. And look at these." Whitey moves the sofa a little, revealing three tiny holes in the wallpaper in a row.

"That's where Brian just missed Alfie with the BB gun. He fired four times. The other BB is still in Alfie's leg."

"Wow. It'll be exciting around here, won't it?" I say with a big smile, trying to look on the bright side.

"Yeah. So exciting I hope I don't drop dead from it," Whitey says in a way that has me believing him.

"OK. Well, see ya tomorrow, and don't forget that deadly slingshot you've got to hand in."

I decided to walk down the six flights. I looked up from the bottom floor and it looked really far up to the top. And for the first time as I gazed up through that six story high stairwell, made up of cast iron railings and marble stairs, standing on that cold tile floor, it occurred to me that this is a dangerous spot.

Now that my brother's been out of the house for over a month, there's a lot less tension in our house. No more drunken fights in the middle of the night or arguments about what to do about my brother's staying out all night. In fact I heard my mother tell my father that he's "on the wagon." That means he isn't drinking anymore.

My sister has decided that she's going to go away to college next year, so she's already talking about moving out. I'm going to finally have my own room. But September is almost five months away and a lot can happen between now and then. There's my graduation and all the graduation parties that all the kids will be throwing. And Anne Marie's graduation. And maybe I'll get a summer job. And I still have to make the final decision on what high school I want to attend. And will I have a girlfriend? Will it be Carrie Vitelli or someone I haven't even met yet? Will I drink beer? Can the Yankees come from behind and win another pennant? Will I get to feel up a girl?

But until then, I share a room with my sister. We have dinner at 6:30 every night. My dad takes the subway home from NYU, and gets home at 5 every day. He usually has a cup of ice cream and then watches TV until 5:35, when he goes to pick up my mother from work at Fuhrman's on 231st Street. Sometimes I go with him, or both me and my sister go. If we go, my dad finds a parking spot, and my sister and I go by the employees exit door where all the other people of the Bronx go and wait for their moms and dads to come out. Sometimes I can't believe it, as people stream out of the door, that I don't know any of them. They look like people I should know.

We're usually home by 6:20 and dinner is on the table in less than a half hour. Frozen steaks that my dad took out when he got home at 5 are thrown into the electric broiler that sits on a counter next to the stove. Into a pot of boiling water goes a frozen block of spinach, and into a boiling pot of oil goes a basket filled with frozen french fries. My mom is busting up a head of iceberg lettuce, slicing tomatoes, and making her own recipe of salad dressing in an old mayonnaise jar. And before you know it... there's dinner! All hot and ready to be eaten. And it's gobbled up a lot quicker than it took to make. My mom yells at me to eat more and for my dad to eat less. We don't.

And it's the only time of day to bark out a few important family matters. Usually by my mom.

"Let's go to the World's Fair this weekend, Frank."
"It's gonna be too crowded!" my father says between bites of rib eye.
"Oh so what, let's go anyway. It's been open a month already, and I want to go and see the Pieta."
"Well, we've got to leave early," my father warns us. Not likely. Early to us is out of the house by noon. With all the arguing and screaming, and threats over every little stupid thing like, "Where's the toilet paper?", "I don't want ham for lunch.", "You're not going out of the house in THAT outfit!", etc., we're lucky we get out at all.
"We'll go on Sunday right after mass," my mother decides.
I can tell that's that. We're going.
Boy, I can't wait. I've seen the World's Fair on TV and it looks really cool. You can sit in a brand-new car and go through this huge thing that's like driving into the future, and Abe Lincoln comes to life and people are coming from all over the world to see it. I've never been to a World's Fair. I went to Freedomland a few times. That was supposed to be New York's answer to Disneyland, and it was in the Bronx. It was a lot of fun, but only lasted two years. It was huge. Bigger than Disneyland! They had a building that burned every hour, and lots of horse drawn-carriages. There were also lots of piles of horse shit. I remember stepping in a pile that came up over my shoe and my mom said it was good luck. My sister made us go to see Paul Anka at a concert there. It was crazy with all the girls screaming like lunatics. But they tore the whole place down. Now they're building big apartment building projects there, and I'll bet you they don't look anything like Disneyland.

I hate morning prayers in the classroom. It's really hard to remember all the words to some of them. The "Our Father" and the "Hail Mary" are simple, but in the 8th grade, they expect us to know them all by heart. The "Act of Contrition" you have to learn when you get receive confirmation in the 4th grade, but in 6th they start with some tough ones like the

138

"Apostles Creed" and the "Confiteor." When I first started the altar boys, you had to know the entire mass in Latin, and the "Confiteor" was the longest. It went *"Confiteor Deo, omnipotenti, beate Marie, semper Virgini..."* But right around here it got really hard, so you just kind of mumbled till you got a line or two down to "mea culpa, mea culpa, mea MAXIMA culpa." That means *"through my fault, through my fault, through my most GRIEVOUS fault."* That seemed to be the theme of all the prayers, and teachings and lectures from the 1st grade, right up till now. I'm not sure what exactly was my fault, but everyone is sure pissed off about it, and they aren't letting me forget it.

The rest of the prayer was pretty much a repeat of the first part, so you if you could fake your way through this, you could get through the rest of the Mass.

The "Apostles' Creed" is another long one that's supposed to be a guide for all good Catholics. If you don't believe in all the things it says, then you're not really a Catholic. That's according to every priest and nun I've ever had. This morning, Sister Fidelis has decided that today's religion lesson will be all about the "Apostle's Creed." She goes through every word and tells us why we have to believe it to be a true Catholic.

This is usually the ideal time for daydreaming or sneaking in some little things if you're lucky enough to sit towards the back of the classroom. If you're good at keeping your head up, you can even get some sleep. Some people can do homework on their lap, or write notes about who likes who to each other, or read "Mad Magazine" or maybe even a book, or just stare blankly out the window at the park. But for some unknown reason today, I'm actually listening to Sister Fidelis talk about the "Apostle's Creed." She writes on the board in big letters "I BELIEVE" with a very carefully drawn line underneath. And she's making a list just under those words, starting all the way on the left side of the board, like she's expecting to go all the way to the right side of the room with her lesson on the board, which is quite a feat since the blackboard actually takes up the whole front wall of the class. And she goes through the entire prayer, saying the words and then writ-

139

ing them on the board, pressing too hard on the chalk.

She says "I believe" then writes as she says "In God the Father Almighty. Jesus Christ. The Holy Ghost. The Virgin Mary. The Holy Catholic Church."

I don't know why, but she's acting like she really cares about this stuff more than ever before, and as she writes "the Resurrection of the Body and Life Everlasting, Amen," on the word "Amen" she pushes the chalk really hard, creating that awful, awful, sound of scratching on the blackboard that sends chills up your spin, and breaks the chalk in half. I think she may have even hurt her finger, but everyone in the class is startled out of whatever little world they were in, and all eyes are on Sister Fidelis and her lesson on the board.

"If you don't believe in every word on this board, with all your heart and soul, then you don't belong here. You don't belong in this class, this school, this church, this parish, this diocese! You are not a Catholic. And you can't get into Heaven. Do you understand that? You can't get into Heaven."

For the first time in all my Catholic schooling and Mass going and sacrament preparing and reading of the catechism and taking religion exams these words struck me like they never struck me before. "If you aren't a Catholic, you can't get into Heaven." That means that Jews can't go to Heaven, and President Johnson can't go to Heaven, and my Uncle's wife who's a Protestant can't go to Heaven?

I raised my hand.

Sister Fidelis looked at me like I was volunteering to go into a wrestling ring with her.

"Yes, Vincent."

"Sister? Does that mean that Jewish people and Protestants can't go to Heaven?"

"Haven't you been listening? That's exactly what I'm saying!"

Sister Fidelis might as well be in a wrestling ring. She's Bruno Sanmartino right now, and I'm ... Arnold Stang, the guy from the Chunky commercials.

"Jews can't go to Heaven. Protestants. Muslims. Buddhists. Hindus. Pagans. None of them can get into Heaven without the one true only Catholic and Apostolic Church."

Now she's really going nutty. She picks up the broken piece of chalk and starts to underline Holy Catholic Church, time after time after time after time, till it's underlined so many times that it's one huge blob of chalky stuff flaking onto the floor and getting onto her jet-black habit.

The class is in total terrified silence. Like one word will set off a nuclear bomb. One move will make the whole Bronx collapse into a hole to hell. Sister Fidelis is actually out of breath. Breathing heavily. She's eyeing the class, looking for takers.

I raise my hand again.

My heart is pounding. But for the first time in my eight years of school, I feel like I have to ask this question. I don't know why it matters, but I feel like if I don't ask this question, Sister Fidelis will be getting away with something that she shouldn't get away with. It doesn't seem right. She looks into my eyes. She's ready.

"Yes, Vincent."

"Sister. How do we know that the Catholic Church really is the only one true Church?"

It looks like Sister Fidelis has stopped breathing now. Her facial expression becomes totally blank for a split second and drained of all color. Her lips are shrinking even thinner as she starts to bare her yellow teeth. Now as she opens her mouth, color is rushing back into her face, like the red climbing up a thermometer.

"How dare you."

She's inching towards me like a giant, fat, cumbersome, old black panther.

"I sit up here day after day, month after month, year after year, teaching you little spoiled brats about religion. About God. And you have the nerve to ask me how I know the Catholic church is the one true, holy apostolic Church!"

She's almost on top of me. She's spitting through those yellow teeth, and I'm trying to shield myself from the spit and her smell.

Her answer is going to explode all over me, and I will

know HOW she knows, HOW the priests know, HOW the bishops, the cardinals, the Pope knows.

She pounces. "You think I'd be walking around in this stupid, ridiculous outfit for 40 years if it wasn't the ONE TRUE Church?!!! Because I KNOW it is! I SAY it is."

That was it. Because Sister Fidelis told me so.

Her fit stopped. She slowly turned and walked to the blackboard. She picked up the eraser and started erasing her morning lesson.

And with it went all the years of memorizing those Baltimore Catechism questions. *"Who made us? God made us. Who is God? God is the Supreme Being, infinitely perfect, who made all things and keeps them in existence. Why did God make us? God made us to show forth His goodness and to share with us His everlasting happiness in Heaven."* Because as the words were rubbed out by the weary arms of Sister Fidelis, and faded from words to blurs and then to just a cloudy blob of chalk, those words were no longer etched in stone on huge tablets hovering over me like Charlton Heston holding the Ten Commandments on the mountain top with thunder and lightning behind them, shaking, trembling, threatening, commanding me. If that was the best reason Sister Fidelis could come up with, it looks like the whole thing is on pretty shaky ground.

Erasing the board was wearing Sister Fidelis out. Usually, she makes a kid from the class do it. But for some reason she's doing it herself and it's taking forever. One reason that she doesn't take the time to erase the board when it's a big job is that it isn't safe to have your back to the class for too long. Sometimes just a walk down the aisle can mean dangerous exposure to a nun's back. Lately, some of the guys in the class have been spitting big loogies onto Sister's back when she walks down the aisle. I think that's pretty mean. I did, however, pin a "I Love Ringo" button on her back. She wore it for the whole morning until Mark Fay squealed on me just before lunch. I got a lecture about disrespect. I gave Mark Fay a lecture about getting his ass kicked for squealing.

Sister Fidelis is finally done with the board. She walks over to her desk and picks up a box.

"This morning is the Queen of the May program." As she speaks, she walks over to the first seat in each row, and gives out pieces of paper, and envelopes to be passed out. "Everyone must write a personal prayer to the Blessed Mother and seal it in the envelope. There is to be no talking. The prayer is between you and the Blessed Mother, not your neighbor. You are to keep it a secret."

Queen of the May program is the one cool program of the year. There are lots of strange things that they make us do, like on Good Friday, when they take this special super-realistic-looking crucifix with open bloody wounds on Jesus out of storage and put it in the front of the church on a purple pillow and you stand in line and then bend down and kiss the bloody feet of Jesus and an altar boy wipes it off after you're done. Or on St. Blaise Day when you go to the front of the church and the priest makes an "X" with two beeswax candles and sticks it against your adam's apple so you don't get sore throats. But Queen of the May is the most fun.

There's a quiet excitement in the classroom. Everyone trying to think of the perfect thing to write to the Blessed Mother.

An announcement comes on the loudspeaker from the principal, Sister Thomas.

"It is now five minutes before 10. At the sound of the next bell, at 10 o'clock, all classes are to commence the Queen of the May procession. Students are forbidden to get too close to the fire."

The loudspeaker crackles off.

"Let's go, class, write your prayers and seal the envelopes," Sister Fidelis urges us.

I don't know what to write. I could write something stupid, but no one would really know except me, so to be on the safe side, I write, "Dear Blessed Virgin Mary, Please bless my mother and father, and my brother and my sister. Amen."

There goes the bell.

"Alright, class, single file out the door, and not a word," Sister Fidelis commands us.

The hall is dark, even though it's a sunny day outside.

Since we're the oldest class, we will be the last ones in the procession. Hands together, as if in prayer, with our little envelopes between our thumbs and our index fingers. If I could only know what the other kids wrote to the Blessed Mother. Most of them probably played it safe like I did. But I'll bet some kids have dark deep secrets in their soul that no one, not teachers, friends, or parents, know, except maybe one other person. We've heard stories about kids like Tina Robustelli, whose father left her mother. Stories about Tina's mother, Vilma, a weird fat lady, standing nude in the living room and instructing her two son's Ambrose and Francis to touch her private parts to learn the facts of life, and makes Tina have sex with them.

Or stories about how Deborah Laturza's uncle (she doesn't live with her parents) beats her with a belt buckle. Who knows how many dark secrets are sealed in these little white envelopes.

As we exit the building, you can hear Miss Schmelzer at the old pump organ, which usually sits quietly in the back of the music room but was now somehow plopped in the middle of the school yard. This is the only day I ever see it used. And it's comical to see Miss Schmelzer's legs pumping up and down, frantically trying to get enough air through the drafty old organ to keep us marching and singing, *"Oh Mary we crown thee with flowers today, Queen of the angels, Queen of the May..."*

But even the silly sight of Miss Schmelzer, sitting right in the middle of the school yard pumping away, can't take away from what we all know is just around the corner of the school. I can already smell the fire burning.

Next to the rectory is what looks like an old steel drum, with a smoke stack sticking out of it. But it's no ordinary incinerator. It's a blessed furnace. This is where things that are too holy to be dumped in the trash are deposited and burned. Ever wonder what the altar boys do with the incense and charcoal from the thurifer (the thing that he swings that's filled with burning incense)? What happens to old priest's garments? Or what they do with consecrated hosts that have been dropped?

They go into the blessed furnace where they are torched. But today, the old steel drum isn't just a blessed furnace. It's a beautiful, perfect telephone to Heaven.

The teachers of the lower grades take the envelopes from the little kiddies and drop them into the burning bundle of newspapers and incense for them. They then stand in awe as their own little scribbled letters, tucked away in secret envelopes, are dropped into the fragrant flames and instantly turned into black smoke that lifts the letters to Heaven. We're taught that Jesus rose bodily into Heaven. That Mary rose bodily into Heaven. Not their spirit. Not just their souls. Their actual bodies rose into Heaven. They are the only two that did it. And now smoke from our paper is rising to the blue May sky. Little girls asking for new dresses and baby brothers. Boys asking for muscles and Mickey Mantle's autograph. Say hi to Granpa in Heaven, please, Mary! Tell Jesus we're sorry he got crucified. Help daddy find a new job. The smoke lifts every letter, every word, higher and higher, so high you can't see it anymore. It must be in Heaven.

We older kids get to drop our own letters into the fire. Feel the heat. Smell the holiness that has burned before in this container over the years. I wonder what words floated to Heaven on this May morning.

As the smoke rises up, I can't help but think of Indian smoke signals. Secret codes mixing with the clouds, and the Blessed Mother sitting there alone with Jesus in Heaven, deciphering all the messages from all the children from all the Catholic schools in the world. I wonder if she gets upset at the notes that are a waste of time. She should. With all the real stuff that she could be working on. You know, prioritizing requests to present to Jesus, so he could carry out the really difficult ones, leaving the easier ones for her to handle. And she's got to sift through "Bring back Otto, my dead hamster." and "Make my freckles go away." But when she gets to "Make daddy stop hitting mommy." or "Help me to get into Bronx High School of Science because it's free." she's got to figure out how to make it work. Stuff doesn't just happen magically, although the nuns and priests would like us to think otherwise. They want us to believe in all the magic stuff. Like... "indulgence." That's the time you get off for good behavior out of purgatory. Purgatory is temporary hell. And you're assigned time there like a prison sentence for venial sins. If you kill somebody, forget it, you're in hell forever. Nonnegotiable. But something like cursing bad, or say, punching somebody out for no reason, and you are going to purgatory. Really really good people go right to Heaven. You know, like the Pope, cardinals, priests, nuns. But most people who aren't so good all the time have to go to purgatory. But there is a catch. If you do certain things that they tell you to do, you can get time automatically deducted from your time in purgatory. For instance, every time you make the sign of the cross, they take off a hundred days. And if you do it with holy water, you get 300 days off. If you say the "Act of Contrition" you get 3 years off! Go through the rosary and a "Hail Hail Holy Queen" and you can subtract another 5 years off your sentence. I'm not making this up. Just look in the "Official Revised Baltimore Catechism Number Two." It's all in there. Now the tricky part is, the priest will never tell you how much purgatory time you get for specific venial sins. If he did that, you could then figure out that saying the rosary might get you out of purgatory for the exact time you got for stealing a dirty magazine. But I have a feeling that the penance the priest gives you after confession is tied to some kind of formula they don't want us to know about.

Once everybody has dropped their envelope into the burning bin, we line up class by class in the school yard. Here comes the finale.

Everyone is lined up. Quiet. The sun's reflection off the boy's white shirts is blinding.

Miss Schmelzer is watching Sister Thomas like a hawk. Sister Thomas is eyeing all the students, just waiting to make an example of somebody who dares to mock this sacred rite. I look over at Whitey and once he notices that I'm looking at him, he begins to very slowly go cross-eyed, and his tongue starts to ever so slightly come through his lips. But no way am I going to start cracking up here.

Sister Thomas gives Miss Schmelzer a nod, and with

146

that Miss Schmelzer begins to frantically pump the two pedals on the organ. Her skinny body rocking back and forth on the piano stool. She senses she has enough air built up and opens her mouth wide open in that silly, exaggerated facial expression that means we should all be ready to start singing. She looks like some kind of weird amusement park mannequin, spindly legs up and down, rocking her bony butt, mouth as open as a mouth can get; so much so that her entire head is contorted into some Halloween mask look, and then... *"Ave Ave Ave Maria..."*

The whole school launches into "Ave Maria" as the littlest girl from 1st grade walks out from her class with a small bouquet of flowers and places them at the feet of a Mary statue that was especially brought out to the school yard for the occasion. No more worried looks on the nun's faces. Another "Queen of the May" program off without a hitch. You can see that this is the world the nuns want. Secret messages sent to the Blessed Mother in mystical wisps of smoke, and all the little boys and girls not making a sound. Everything in order, neatly obedient.

White shirts and plaid skirts. Anklets and blue ties. All is right within these chain-link fences. For once. For all. So it seems to nuns on a bright Queen of the May morning.

But I see Kowalzyck with a big double-wide Band-Aid right in the middle of his forehead. I see Tina Robustelli's sad, pimpled face. I see Theresa O'Neil, slumping over because she's the tallest person in the school. I see Deborah Laturza pretending she doesn't notice that everybody keeps a couple of extra steps away from her because everybody knows she stinks. I see Whitey trying not to look like he cares that his family might be falling apart. I see Bobby Bailey trying to get somebody, anybody, to look at the way he can make his pants move by wiggling his dick. I can smell Deborah Laturza's B.O.

And cutting through the white shirt and knee socks silence comes the squeal of a carload of day-off teenagers, roaring down the side street next to the school yard. It's hard to see the faces packed into the late '40s dark sedan with the bright sun casting dark shadows inside the car, but there's no mistake

147

that there are four or more teenagers out for laughs in an old jalopy, and they found the biggest laugh of the day as they screech to a halt. Miss Schmelzer pumps more ferociously, trying to drown out the sounds of kids outside the fence. Kids outside the domain of stern nuns and pump organ music and smoke signals to the Blessed Mother.

"Hey look, there's those two faggots Schmidt and Shelley."

No doubt about it. Fitzy Fitzgerald. I just hope he doesn't yell something about Tina and the time he snagged me and Whitey with his plan to get Tina nude, and we jump out from behind the old radios to cop a feel, water balloon in the face trick.

"And look, there's Tina-va-va-va-voom-Robustelli."

The principal, Sister Thomas, isn't going to let this go any further, she's walking as quickly as possible over to the carload of loudmouths.

"Oooooh, here comes Sister Mary Ferris Wheel, let's get out of here, guys." Fitzy's squeaky voice can be heard over the uneven noise of the ancient Plymouth, followed by a very good, rubber burn pull out, and whoops and hollers.

I hate Fitzy Fitzgerald. But at the same time, I sure wish I was in that car with him right now.

Once they're gone, Ave Maria is completed and we end the programs like nothing ever happened. Good thing nothing did happen. I could have really gotten it.

Back in the classroom, Sister Fidelis continues to teach religion. Thank God she didn't ask me or Whitey or Tina who the hoodlums were in that car.

"Everyone take out your Catechism and study questions number 259 to 271. You're responsible for 268 to 271."

Darn. That means they have to be memorized. She hardly ever does that anymore. She must have something important to do. Like grade tests are something, because that's usually the only time she asks us to memorize something in class.

The Catechism is the corniest. It has the strangest illustrations that are drawn in a real old-fashioned, almost stick-

148

figure kind of way. This chapter is about the seventh, eighth, ninth, and tenth commandments. Don't steal, lie, tell secrets, take bribes, cheat, and stuff like that. The cartoon at the top of the page has two boys, one wearing a beany, and he's pointing at a store that has three signs; one reads "meats" another "groceries" and another "vegetables." Inside the store you can see a fat bald man with an apron standing next to a scale, and in front of him is a fat lady with her arms crossed. The caption above the pointing boy reads, "That's a good store! They give honest weight." This one cracks us up so much that it's a running gag that whenever we pass by a store, somebody will stop and point and say, "That's a good store! They give honest weight."

"Mr. Shelley."

Uh oh. Sister Fidelis remembered her order for Whitey to bring a note from his father.

"Yes, Sister."

"Come up here, please. Class, continue to work."

I'd be nervous as hell if I was Whitey, going up there with that chicken-scratch note. But he looks pretty calm, although he is a little bit redder than normal. I can tell a lot by how red he gets.

As Whitey is walking up and I'm flipping through the Catechism like I've done a million times before, looking at the silly cartoons; the one with the ghosts floating up out of graves with tombstones marked "RIP" and the one with all the faces of sin, and the one that says "covetousness" has a guy that looks Jewish, and the one that says "anger" has a guy that looks like Hitler if you put a mustache on him, like every boy in the class has done. But suddenly I notice something new. After all the times I've flipped through these pages, knowing every one by heart, here's something I've never noticed before. And unbelievably it's the first illustration in the whole book, above Part I, "The Creed." It's supposed to be showing how Jesus is above everyone (He's wearing a crown and robes and is nailed to the cross) and below him are workers of the world (a Chinaman plowing, a black man in a lab, a white sailor, a guy sawing wood), but unmistakably, as I look a little closer, there's

149

a father walking with a son. The father is wearing a fedora and suit and in his hand is a book, probably a missal. His other hand is on his son's shoulder. And in the boy's hand, and this is hard to see because it's just an outline drawing, the boy is holding a freaking slingshot. No doubt about it! If that's not an endorsement, I don't know what is. Especially since we learned what Imprimatur means. In the front of any book that has teachings about the Catholic Church of any kind, it has to have the word "Imprimatur" in the front. If it does, that means that every word and illustration in the book is approved by an authority of the Church and is the truth. That's it. The absolute, infallible truth.

I've got to tell Whitey. He can use this. I look up and Sister Fidelis is reading the note. She's trying to speak in hushed tones, but I can hear her.

"Regardless of what your father says, you do not have permission to have such a device while you are a student in this school, do you understand me?"

"Yes Sister."

"Did you bring it in?"

"Yes Sister."

And out of Whitey's pocket comes the flimsy slingshot he put together just for the occasion.

Sister Fidelis looks shocked. Her hushed tone is gone.

"Don't you know you could knock someone's eye out with one of these!"

I look over at Kowalzyck and the big bandage on his head. Yeah, or worse.

"I have a good mind to send you to the principal's office."

A dilemma. Do I open my mouth on this day. The day I had Sister Fidelis worked up into a spitting frenzy, admitting that her stupid black pioneer woman nun outfit even embarrasses her. I could do more harm than good by bringing the picture to her attention. She might explode all over again.

Why not? My hand shoots up.

"Sister!"

She looks at me blankly, and then as she recalls her

tirade of a couple of hours ago, a look comes across her face, like when Moe realizes that Larry just did something really, really stupid and now he has to pull his hair out and poke him in his eye.

"What is it?"

"Can I show you something in the Catechism? It's important."

"Come up here."

Whitey has a look of total confusion on his face; a darker shade of red. Sister Fidelis, still with the enraged-Moe look on her face, is just waiting for me to say one wrong word.

"Sister, here on page 10 of the Catechism, you can see the father figure with a missal in his left hand and his right hand is on his young son's left shoulder, and if you look in the boy's left hand, right here, you can clearly see that the boy is carrying a slingshot. See? So it's OK? Approval by Jesus himself!"

I look up to see how I did. Not good. I think she's redder than Whitey.

She really does look like she wants to pull out my hair and poke me in the eye, but all that comes out of her mouth is, "Take your seats."

That's it?

We sit down. I look at Whitey. He looks at me. Sister Fidelis rises up out of her chair. She's baring her yellow teeth, shaking her head, slowly taking center stage at the front of the class.

"This class has gone too far. Every day I try to instill spiritual values that you take out of here, and into the real world. But you refuse. Well, I'm sick and tired of trying. I've made myself sick trying to get you people to defy the streets and obey the rules of the church, the rules of this class, the rules of your parents. But you continue to be hoodlums, tramps, hooligans, whores, with your street language and short skirts and beatnik ways. Well, no more! I don't care what you do! I no longer intend to make myself sick for you undisciplined, wild Indians! Go ahead, do whatever you want. I don't care what you do! I don't care if you... get up and start dancing on the desks!!!"

She's lost it. In a split second I knew that not only has Sister Fidelis gone madder than I 've ever seen her before, but at the same time, someone was about to make this one of the funniest days in Presentation history. I look over to Whitey and can see that he will be the one to do it.

He pushes out his desk, steps onto his chair and up onto his desk top, immediately doing the craziest mashed potato-twist-pony time- hully gully-watusi-swim-hitch-hiker frenzy imaginable. And before you know it, here goes Bobby Bailey, Jimmy Joe, Kowalzyck, and I can't take it anymore who cares, here I go onto the desk for the dance of a lifetime. I'm not up there for 3 seconds when I feel a tug on my arm, forcing me onto the hard tiled floor, hard, bony fingers smacking my face, and once I open my eyes, the same for the other four jokers who took Sister Fidelis literally and are now paying the price with pulled hair and hard knuckles in the eye.

But not a word from Sister Fidelis. Just the hardest, not-kidding-around slaps in the face ever. We all get the picture. In Techincolor.

Sister Fidelis is breathing real heavy. But just walks back to her chair. Triumphant. She's still the boss. But she already admitted with her speech, she won't be the boss for too much longer.

I knew it. Leave early for the World's Fair my eye. My father went to get the car a half hour ago, and my sister still isn't ready. We've already missed the 9 o'clock mass, which is fine with me, because that's the "children's" mass, and you're supposed to sit with your class, and your teacher sits with you too. It's like being in school on Sunday. So if we can get my sister out of the bathroom now, we'll only be a minute or so late for the 10.

"Anne Marie, get the hell out of there this instant or I'll smack you silly," my mother screams at the door. I'm in the living room watching Chuck McCann on "Let's Have Fun."

152

He used to be my favorite when I was a little kid. One time, when there was a newspaper strike and we weren't getting our Sunday funnies, he would dress up like the comic strip characters and act out what they were saying. He was really big and chubby, but he'd put on this stupid makeup and become Dondi, the semi-retarded orphan. (He's not really supposed to be semi-retarded, but who else would say such dumb stuff?) Then he'd put on a hat and draw these lines on his face and become Dick Tracy. But the funniest of them all was when he'd put on a little dress, a frizzy wig, and place two white milk bottle tops over his eyes and become Little Orphan Annie. He'd dance around in that dress and it was hilarious. But Chuck McCann isn't my favorite anymore. The most popular TV funny man is Soupy Sales. He has a show on in the afternoons, and it's not just for kids. It's real silly, with "White Fang, The World's Meanest Dog" and "Black Tooth, The World's Sweetest Dog" who are both just huge puppet arms that come in from the side of the camera. "White Fang" isn't really mean, and he talks with Soupy by going, "Ooh wah, ooh wah, oooh ooh, wah wah wah wah," in a deep, gruff voice. "Black Tooth" talks in a real high-pitched voice with a bunch of oooos and waaaahhs. "Pookie The Lion" is a hand puppet that appears out the window. Soupy doesn't just do little kid humor. He does stuff like belch and say, "Boy, I've got enough gas to drive to Cleveland." And right now he has a hit song called "The Mouse" that he's been doing on his show for weeks. He's going to be appearing at the Paramount Theater downtown in a Murray the K Rock and Roll Show, and I'm going to go. I hope.

"I'm counting to 3," my mother yells right into the crack of the door, "and if you're not out of there, we're leaving without you."

Finally the door opens, and my sister glides out as if nothing ever happened. I just hope Monsignor Moriarity isn't saying the 10, his sermons go on forever.

Thank God. It it's not Moriarity but Father Balzarini, an Italian priest with a heavy accent who speaks such bad English that his sermons have to be short. But people react exactly the same to the sermons, whether it's Father Balzarini stumbling through some broken English lecture about the fear of hell; or a full-length, unabridged sermon by Monsignor Moriarity going round and round about how Christ died because of our sins; the reaction is the same... none. But the end of the sermon, no matter how long, means the mass is three quarters over, and soon we'll be out of there and into the car for a trip to Flushing, where the future is.

At the Triboro Bridge, which connects the Bronx with Queens, my father hands the toll booth guy the money. He's colored, and I remember when we were real little, we used to sing, "Daddy shook hands with a colored man, daddy shook hands with a colored man." I don't know how it started, but we don't do it anymore.

There's a sign, "N.Y. World's Fair next exit." My sister, my mother and myself all scream, "There's the exit!" which gets my old man really pissed off. He hates it when we all scream together.

All around us are cars from all over the place. New Jersey, Connecticut, even Massachusetts. Slowly making our way up the ramp and into the parking lot.

We gather our stuff and head for the main gate, up a foot bridge, over the railroad tracks and into the World's Fair. They've been talking about the fair for months on the TV. It's at the same place where they had a World's Fair in 1939. My mother went to that one, and she said that was where they saw TV for the very first time and they couldn't believe it. And I hear there are all kinds of things that are being shown at this Fair for the very first time that will be part of our lives in the future. Maybe even something as important as TV.

When you come in, you're up above the Fair and can get a view of the whole place. And from up there, it's an unreal sight. Crowds of people on walkways, in sky trams, in little mini trains, and in every direction strangely shaped buildings in bright colors make up a weird skyline. A giant tire is a ferris wheel. Huge crystal towers, steel giant globes, big domes, with water-shooting fountains into the sky all over the place.

154

It's hard to know where to start, but I know I've got to see GM's Futurama. I saw on TV that it shows what the future will be like. But unfortunately it's way the heck on the other side of the Fair. But since the Vatican Pavilion is near it, we head that way. The Vatican is the one thing my mother wants to see. They have Michaelangelo's Pieta on display there. And they say that later in the year, the Pope is going to say Mass there and it might be open to the public. She's already talking about going to that. What a mob scene that will be. Probably the only thing bigger would be The Beatles.

One of the first things we pass is a building called The Festival of Gas Pavilion, which makes mom really laugh as she points to my dad, "Look, Frank, you should be one of the main attractions in this exhibit!"

"Very funny. Har har HAR dee har har," my father shoots back.

My father's more interested in finding the Chung King exhibit, where you get a full Chinese dinner for 99 cents.

My sister says she wants to see the IBM Pavilion, where people sit in a giant electric typewriter and see all about computers.

But as we're walking, I see something that changes all that. Never mind the future of GM and IBM, never mind that the Pieta is on display in this country for the first time, never mind the 99 cents dinner at Chung King, up on a sign it reads, "Today Live! At the Singer Bowl! Soupy Sales!"

"Mom, mom, Soupy Sales live! I've got to go! I've got to!"

"We didn't spend $2.50 per person to see Soupy Sales! You can see him on TV for nothing," my mother says trying to put an end to that. But I won't hear it. This would be my first rock-and-roll show ever and I wouldn't hear no for an answer.

"No, no, no," my dad says.

"Come on, I'll never get to see Soupy Sales live anywhere else. I have his record. I know all the words. I even know all the words to Pachalafaka," I plead.

"Paka-what-aka?" my mother says as she giggles.

"Paka-what-aka!!!" my sister screams as she laughs

155

uncontrollably, pulling on my mother's arm.

"Pachalafaka!" I say. "It's the flip side of The Mouse."

"Well, if you sing it all the way through, maybe I'll let you go." My mother says shaking her head.

What a deal.

"Here it is!" And I begin the song, *"Pachalafaka, pachalafaka, they whisper it all over Turkey. Pachalafaka, pachalafaka, it sounds so romantic and perky. Oh I know that phrase will make me thrill always, for it reminds me of you my sweet. Just the mention of, that tender word of love, gives my heart a jerkish, Turkish beat. I won't say se bon, or l' amour toujors, for they don't express just what I am feeling, or even mairzy doats, or other foreign quotes, doesn't seem to be quite so appealing. But pachalafaka, pachalafaka, takes me back with you to passionate desert scenes. And it's there we'll stay, till the very day, we find out what pachalafaka means, we find out what pachalafaka means."*

Needless to say throughout the entire song, my mother and sister were laughing hysterically and my father was morti-fied. Passersbys probably from all corners of the country and the globe even, would stop dead in their tracks and look in amazement at the sight of a 13-year-old boy crooning such an old-fashioned song. But I could care less. It was the only way I was going to get to see Soupy Sales.

Through the laughs my mom managed to say, "OK, OK, you can go."

The heck with the future. Soupy Sales is now!

The line for Soupy was ridiculous. It looked even longer than the one for the United States Pavilion which was right next door.

"Oh my God," my mother says as she gazes on the hordes of teeny boppers, "We're not waiting on that line. Let's get out of here."

"Oh, come on! Let me just stay. I'll meet you over there by the United States Pavilion."

Since neither mom nor dad jumped down my throat immediately, I could tell they were actually considering my plan. This might turn out better than I thought. Not only am I at the World's Fair, I'm going to get to see Soupy Sales in-person, and all by myself!

Mom has that look on her face like she's going to give me permission, but I shouldn't think I'm getting away with something. "Well, OK, the show starts in a half hour, it's 12:30 now, so we'll meet you in the front of the U.S. Pavilion at 2:30. Don't be late!"

And there they go. The three of them turn around and waddle down the Avenue of Europe, past the giant Belgian waffle building on the way to the Pieta. And as I look around, I make another discovery. The line is loaded with girls! Me and the guys are always talking about Soupy's jokes and imitating White Fang and Black Tooth, but I guess now that they're actually playing "The Mouse" on the radio, he's got girl fans too. I mean even Murray The K plays "The Mouse." So somehow, Soupy has gotten in on what everybody calls "the British invasion."

I wish I dressed better. If I knew I was going to be with all these girls, I would've put on my coolest clothes instead of my low black PF flyers, dungarees, striped polo shirt, and plain old baseball-type jacket. Funny how when you wear cool clothes, you actually feel cooler. And when you don't, you don't. Especially when there's kids around you who are dressed cool.

Most of the boys do have their cool stuff on; pointy shoes, peg legged pants, some even have on suit jackets with the velvet collar. And the girls have those teased hairdos and tons of make up.

It seems that everybody except for me is in packs of 3 or 4 kids. Kids who look like I should know them, but I sure don't. This could be a good time to meet some new girls. I will be going to high school next year, and will definitely be meeting all kinds of new girls then. And this is the perfect place. Right behind me is a group of three kids, maybe a little older than I am. One Italian looking guy with slicked-back hair and Beatle boots, and two really cute girls. I'll bet I could hang out with them if I wanted to. Just say hi, and then we'd

157

be two couples just joking together about Soupy and talking about rock-and-roll music, and how cool "Shindig" is compared the corny "Hullabaloo." Or what kind of beer we like, and how we ride the subways whenever we want to go wherever we want and how we hang out with our big brothers and sisters and do all kinds of cool stuff that older teenagers do, like ride around in fast cars and hang out till midnight in the park, so what the heck I turn around and open my mouth, "Hi, how you doin'?"

They look at me. My face, my hair, my shirt, shoes, socks, shoelaces, buttons. The girls look at each other and cross their eyes. The boy looks at them and back to me. The girl with the high black hair and too much eye makeup snaps her gum and says, "Get lost."

I was paralyzed. I wanted to yell every curse word I knew and beat the hell out of all three of them. But I just turned around and didn't say a word, and all of a sudden, all these kids who seemed like kids who I could know and be friends with seemed like enemies. Like kids who I'd never want to know in a million years.

As the line inched forward, all I could think about as I stared straight ahead pretending to be invisible, was that these three kids were laughing at me. They knew they humiliated me and made me feel like the snotty nosed, short haired, uncool looking, little nobody that I am. With each shuffle forward, I knew I couldn't enjoy anything. Not even Soupy. Who cares. I wish I was older. I wish I was cool. I wish I had a car, and a girlfriend and a Beatle haircut and a bunch of cool friends who hung out with me all night long riding around the city and meeting new cool kids and having fun. Who cares? I'm leaving.

I walked off the line and headed for the giant Belgian waffle. Screw it. I'll see Soupy some other time. I figured I would meet my family at 2:30 and pretend I had a great time. The future isn't as much fun as I thought it would be.

All Junes are great. School ends. But this June will be

unbelievable. Not only is school ending, but finally, at last, I can't believe it, graduation from grammar school. It's still almost a whole month away, but to know it's THIS month is enough. A month used to be an eternity. I remember at the start of 1st grade, our class was called 1-A. Sister Joan, our teacher told us that if we were good, we would be promoted after Christmas break to the 2nd level of 1st grade, 1-B. Of course it was a lie. 1-A and 1-B were one and the same. There was no promotion to the second half of the year, but once I heard that there was something to look forward to, something in the future, 1-B, time seemed to stop. I thought 1-B was a long, long time away. And each day, Sister Joan would write the day's date on the board, erasing the number, and leaving the month up there for 30 whole days, and it seemed like years before she erased the month and wrote down the next one. When A finally turned into B after the New Year, there was no ceremony, nothing different, it was a big letdown. And that A-B scam went on for several years until about the 4th grade, when we finally figured that there was just 4th grade and no promotion to the second half of the year. But in 8th grade, things move a lot quicker.

I already know where I'll be going to high school next September; Cardinal Hayes. It's a really big school, almost 3,000 students. Compared to our rinky dink little school with fifty kids in each grade, all jammed into the same classroom, with the same teacher all year long. They have priests and brothers and regular lay teachers and a gym and all kinds of great sports teams. I've never had a man teacher before. So far, I'm the only kid in the class who's going there. Whitey still hasn't decided, but he didn't make Hayes yet. He's on the waiting list. But that doesn't matter because even if he goes to a different high school than I do, lots of guys who are best friends go to different schools and stay best friends. I think.

And this month is the month for parties. There's going to be lots of graduation parties at the end of the month at kid's houses, but the real party is going to be the one we throw for ourselves in the stands at Van Cortlandt Park. That's going to be the one to remember.

Whitey's elevator is broken again. I hate walking up these long six flights, but I told him I'd call for him, and then we're going to the lake. It's pretty warm today. Since it stays light so late, we can go fishing or look for frogs or goof around in the swamp, or shoot slingshots at rats or maybe try to hop a freight.

Whitey's doorbell doesn't work for the same reason mine doesn't. It's been painted over so many times that the bell just doesn't make any noise that can be heard. I bang on the door like usual. A second later it opens. But it's not Whitey, it's not his mom, it's not his brother Brian. Who the heck is this?

"Uh, does Whitey live here?" I ask like a moron.

"Yeah, come on in," says the stranger.

Boy! I thought my cousin Jimmy looked outrageous. But I've never seen anybody look like this on our block. He's got blonde hair, not combed Beatle neat, but wild hair that comes forward way down into his eyes, over his ears on the side, and almost touching the crew neck of an old T-shirt in the back. Across the front is written "New York Department of Sanitation." Plus he has a scraggly blonde peach fuzz Maynard G. Krebs goatee, real short dungaree cut-offs that are unraveling at the bottom, and no shoes. He's got a bottle of milk in one hand, and it looks like a peanut butter and jelly sandwich in the other.

"How ya doin? I'm Whitey's brother Alfie. I just got out of school at Cornell, upstate. Who are you?"

"I'm Vinny. Whitey's friend. I live across the street."

"Hi, Vinny. You in Whitey's class?"

"Yeah."

"Don't believe the nuns."

"OK."

Alfie is alternating gulps from the bottle and big bites from his sandwich as he turns pages of the New York Times at the kitchen table. He yells, "Hey,Whitey, your friend's here."

I hear from the back of the apartment, "Hey Vinny, come on back."

Alfie looks busy eating and reading, so I just head back to Whitey's room. Whitey's putting on his Cons. (Chuck Taylor Converse All-Stars, that is.) The coolest sneakers made.

"My brother's home from college. He's looking for a job for the summer," Whitey finishes tying. "Let's go." We walk past Alfie. "See ya," Whitey says, matter-of-factly. Alfie grunts acknowledgment without looking up from his Times.

We go down the long six flights. "Is Alfie pissed about something?" I ask Whitey.

"No. He's just pissed at dad. Wanna hunt rats?"

"OK." And it's off to the swamps.

First we stop off at The Modern for a couple of 16-ounce Cokes. They're cheaper there than in Snookies. The bottles might come in handy later if we see any rats.

Just down the block are the railroad tracks. Up until about 10 years ago there was a passenger train that used this track. Now only freight trains use it twice a day. Once in the day time and once at night. It goes all the way downtown going south and all the way upstate going north.

We jump the fence next to the highway and meander down the garbage-strewn hill, and carefully jump the swampy puddles onto the gravel-bottomed single railroad track. You hardly ever see anybody else down here. Maybe a kid sniffing glue under a bridge or maybe a bum sleeping. But never parents or any regular adults out for a walk. And you don't see many little kids down here because they still obey their parent's warnings about the train and rats and swamps and disease and bums and filth. That's why we like it down here.

Whitey walks over to a new pile of beer cans dumped there over the weekend, "Hey, let's hit some cans."

"Alright, over the wall is a home run," I say as I look around for a good-enough stick to whack cans with and before you know it we're hitting can after can, fungo style. "Hey Whitey, look, I'm Frank Crosetti," I say as I smack a can from a really low angle, like the old third base coach on the Yankees, who everybody agrees is the best fungo hitter in baseball, even though he's 70 or something.

161

"Yeah, well, I'm Mickey Mantle," Whitey says as he smacks a Rheingold can, that still has a gulp of beer left in it, splattering us a little bit.

"Hey fucko!" I yell, "don't get me stinking of beer, I'll get my ass kicked."

"Sorry Charlie, Starkist wants tuna that tastes good."

We pretty much went through the latest pile of Schaeffer and Rheingold cans, and I'm not sure who hit the most home runs. But we held onto our sticks and walked up the tracks, toward the lake.

"Do you want to fish or look for rats?" Whitey asks.

"I don't know. If we don't see any rats, we'll fish."

Whitey and I both keep drop lines in our pockets. That way you can just get a stick and tie the line and hook on the end whenever you feel like fishing. It's not that often you see rats around, but if you do, that's the preferred activity.

We decide to go to the far end of the Van Cortlandt Lake, which is actually a big pond that's fed by a stream and dumps into the sewer at one end. We go through a hole in the fence and walk up the path.

We come upon our favorite fishing spot. There's a big tree that fell over into the lake, and you can sit on it and use your drop line without even bothering with a pole. I had a piece of Wonder Bread in my pocket, which makes the best bait when you roll it up real small. Fishing, like everything else, is a contest. We never keep the fish we catch. Just throw 'em back in. Mostly you get little sun fish, but once in a while you'll land a really tough catfish that'll give you a hell of a fight once you hook him.

Because it's a weekday, there's hardly anybody in the park at all, and it looks like we're the only kids fishing on this side of the lake. And being out on this tree, it's like we're in the middle of nowhere.

"Hey Whitey, do you know Johnny Bazzicalupo in the cleaners on 238th Street?"

"Yeah."

"My brother told me that he said his wife goes to the bathroom on him while he holds Saran Wrap over his face."

162

"Get outta here."

"He says he brags about it."

"Number one or number two?"

"Number two."

"Ahhhhhhh!"

We were always hearing stories from somewhere about Johnny Bazzicalupo. He always hired kids from the neighborhood to deliver for him at the dry cleaners, and he actually talked about having sex with his wife. I've heard guys talking about feeling up girls and getting screwed, but I never heard anybody talk about doing stuff with their wife! That's one of the reasons it's so hard to get a job at Johnny's.

As we were sitting on the tree, things got really quiet as they usually do when you're seriously trying to win a fishing contest. Whitey was winning 4 to 2. I thought I heard something in the bushes off to the side. It could be a rat or a squirrel or maybe even a rabbit or a pheasant. That would be cool. It's not. I look over, and standing next to a bush is a guy. A grown up. He's just standing there, and he's staring at us. He's got black greasy hair, a black tight T-shirt, black shiny shoes, and tight black pants.

I whisper to Whitey, "There's a guy over there, Whitey."

"Yeah, so what."

"Well, nothing, except while he's staring at us, he's rubbing his dick."

Whitey shoots his head over and sees what I saw. This guy is standing there with one hand in his pocket and the other hand on the outside of his crotch, and he's rubbing it real slow.

"Are you sure?" Whitey asks me.

"Yes. He's rubbing his dick."

"Oh shit."

We've been hearing stories about perverts in the park. Guys who take girls to the most remote, hidden places imaginable in this 1,700-acre park seem to find that just when they get a bra unhooked or even more, they hear something and shit, if there isn't some guy whacking off in the bushes. We even heard stories about girls AND boys getting raped by psychos.

This guy was big, though. About six foot or more, and looked pretty strong. I've heard about rapists who rape boys too, although I'm not exactly sure how that would work, but I sure as hell didn't want to find out. My heart was pounding every time I saw him massaging his zipper.

I whisper to Whitey, "Just do what I do."

"OK."

I slowly get up from my position on the tree and walk to the shore, pretending I don't see the guy, with Whitey right behind me. I pick up the big stick we used to whack the cans and scream at the top of my lungs, right at the pervert. "You motherfucker, we're going to kill you if you don't get the fuck out of here." And Whitey follows me, "You cocksucker, I'm gonna fuckin' destroy you!"

We both start to jump up and down, screaming every curse and threat we can think of, waving our sticks at this guy, like we mean business. And we actually get about five feet from him. He's just standing there now. No more rubbing his balls. No more blank stare. He's twitching. "What's the matter with you kids, I'm just standing here minding my own business."

"Bullshit!" I yell like bloody murder, "get the fuck out of here before we kill you, you faggot motherfucker!"

I don't know how scary we look, but I think he took us seriously. He turned and ran his ass off. We won.

"That fucker's the pervert that jerks off all over the park," Whitey says sitting down, catching his breath.

"Yeah, that's the asshole," I say, joining Whitey on the ground. "You feel like fishing anymore?"

"Nah."

"Me neither."

We walked back to the tracks, sticks in hand, thinking we might see him again the whole way back to the block. He wouldn't dare show his face there. You always feel safe on your block.

The days are getting really long now. It stays light out

164

until 8:00. That means it's pretty easy to get permission to go out after dinner. And more and more kids are hanging out. I guess that's partly because it's near the end of the school year, and probably because parents are pretty sick of having kids around all the tiny apartments. Something else that I've noticed is how some kids are taking sports really seriously now. Some are even talking about playing for high school teams next year. And that isn't easy. Catholic high schools in New York City take sports very seriously. They even recruit from local playgrounds for future stars when kids are only in 7th grade. There's a guy from St. Jude's down in Inwood who's seven feet tall name Lew Alcindor. He's from the projects and is a senior at Power Memorial High School. They say that colleges from all over the country are offering him scholarships. The best white guy around is named Billy Champion from Our Lady of Angels.

So some guys from the block spend every minute at the basketball courts, playing really serious games. I like to play and I'm not bad, but there's no way I'd ever make a high school team. Besides, that's all some of those guys do is play basketball and I have other things I'd rather be doing.

Me and Whitey are going to meet some guys at the stumps next to my building. Jimmy Joe, Ralphie, and B.B. are going to be there, and according to Jimmy Joe, maybe the girls; Carrie Vitelli, Donna Murphy, and maybe Eileen Moran who's in 7th grade, but hangs out with Carrie and Donna.

Living right next to the hangout spot, I was the first one there. But here comes Whitey up the block, radio blaring "I Get Around" by the Beach Boys. Every other Beach Boy song that's been out has been about surfing or cars, two things that aren't really big on the block. Oh, some kids that go to Rockaway for the summer have surfed, and once in a while some teenagers manage to get a car somehow, but it's not like it's a way of life or anything. But when "I Get Around" came out last month, it was the first song by the Beach Boys that anybody really dug. The song is about hanging out. That's something we know plenty about.

"My buddies and me are getting real well known, the

bad guys know us and they leave us alone."
Don't think that's any easy thing, either.

"Round, round, round, round, I get around"
The other direction from up the hill comes Jimmy Joe, with Ralphie and B.B. right behind him. Now there's five of us. And the first few minutes are always spent talking about the same thing: "Waddya feel like doing?" And of course nobody knows, but before you know it there's a deck of cards out, a couple of guys are playing poker, a spaldeen comes out of somebody's pocket and a couple of guys are playing king/ queen and somebody else is manning the radio constantly changing the stations, playing as many good songs without commercials as possible.

Down the street, I see the girls coming up the hill. With them, though, is Bobby Bailey. Bobby is in our class, but he was left back. He was one of the troublemakers in the class ahead of us, now he's one of the troublemakers in ours. But he's never been much of a problem to me or Whitey really. He hangs out mostly on his block, down at Review Place. He likes to fight. And he really likes Donna Murphy.

Donna, Carrie, and Eileen slowly walk up the hill in a deliberate heel-to-toe kind of "taking their time" strut. Bobby in his slicked back, jet-black Irish wavy hair is telling them some sort of story and the girls are eating it up. I know Jimmy Joe likes Donna and he's paying particular attention to Bobby, even though he's right in the middle of king/queen.

"Game!" Jimmy Joe says to B.B. just as the group arrives.

"Yeah, game." BB agrees.

No big hellos. The girls take their places on the steps, facing each other, Carrie on the top step back to the wall, Donna opposite her, and Eileen one step down, looking up to them. They always seem to just talk among themselves, never really being part of what the guys are doing. Bobby stands at the bottom of the stairs looking up at them like a performer with his audience sitting in the stands.

I think Bobby's a show off. Ever since he sang that Nat King Cole song in front of the class, mimicking Nat King

Cole's facial expressions. Now he's standing there, singing along with the radio, the chorus to "Be My Baby" with his eyes closed, knowing everybody's got their eyes on him, especially the three girls. Most guys who like to sing don't like to fight. Bobby likes both. Thankfully, the song ends, and a commercial for funny cars at Raceway Park comes on.

"Hey, who wants to get some beers, man." Bobby says above the sound effects for Jungle Jim Lieberman's Little Red Wagon.

What a jerk. "Keep it down, Bobby." I tell him. "This is my building."

Bobby gets the picture. One of the reasons he's up here is to get away from the nosy neighbors in his building. He knows that my nosy neighbors will be just as bad. Everybody's so much braver when the people looking out their windows don't know you.

And in a much lower voice, Bobby comes up with a compromise. "Well, let's get some beers and go up to Pigeon Park."

He's really trying to be a big shot. First of all, it's a school night. Who the heck is going to drink on a school night. You have to go home earlier than on the weekend, and the chance of getting caught is much worse. Plus, this is like the first time Bobby has hung out with us at our usual hangout and he's trying to get the group to go somewhere else. We just got the right to call this our hangout. Last spring, we couldn't even sit here because the older guys were here everyday. It's only because they decided to hang out in the park that we're even here at all. And if we're not here, even for an hour, you can bet the little kids like Tony Pisani and Frankie Ryan will be hanging out here, probably causing more trouble than we would have, and pissing off everybody within firecracker or bottle-busting noise range.

"I don't want to go up there. There's nothing to do," I say, knowing full well that's not a good enough reason and is a lie. There's plenty to do up there. There's a basketball court and swings and even a nice hill with big boulders to sit on where you can look out on the Reservoir, which is huge, and

167

quite pretty actually. But I don't want to go up there. I don't want to drink.

I can see by the faces of the girls that the plan sounds like a good one to them. And I just know that means, that everyone else is going to fall into place right behind them. I don't mind hanging out with guys who are drinking, even though I'm not going to drink. I'm not chicken. But Pigeon Park is a little bit dangerous. Not that there's danger for us. Just the opposite. Pigeon Park, although just three blocks away, is a hangout for Jewish kids. And beer plus Bobby Bailey and some Jewish kids that don't look like us, equals trouble. And the hassles won't be other people hassling us; it'll be us hassling them. Or at least Bobby Bailey hassling.

Pigeon Park isn't even the real name of the park even though everybody in the neighborhood calls it that. The real name is Fort Independence Park, but I've never ever heard anybody ever call it that. The kids who hang out in Pigeon are almost all Jewish. That means that they go to different grocery stores, play different games, do different things, go to different schools, dress differently, and even look different than we do. And if for no other reason, that's why some guys from our neighborhood go up there just looking for trouble. Funny, but even the only guy from our neighborhood who is Jewish, named Lenny Rabinowitz, and who is just as tough and crazy as any little mick and ginney, goes up there looking for trouble.

It's not a Jew-hating thing. It's just that they're up there and we're down here. They go to public schools and we go to Catholic schools. They study; we don't.

"Well, I'm going to get some beer. Who wants to come?" Bobby says from the bottom step that leads down into the alley, looking up at all of us. The girls look at each other and give little eye movements and nods and eyebrows dance, and then Donna announces, "We'll go with ya." Once Jimmy Joe hears that, he says, "I'll go," which automatically means BB and Ralphie will be right behind.

"I'll go."

"I'll go," they echo.

"I'm going to hang out here and see if anybody else

168

comes out," I say, coming up with a legitimate-sounding reason. You never know who might show up and with what kind of activity. You could be just sitting there and any kind of thing can happen. One time Fitzy Fitzgerald came running out of the basement of my building chasing a rat, screaming his head off. "A rat, a rat, get it, get it, get it!" he's yelling with an empty quart bottle of Rheingold cocked in his arm, which he was probably downing in my basement before this poor miserable rat happened upon the scene to eat some corn chip crumbs. So Fitzy is chasing this rat, and here comes the number 38 bus storming down the hill full tilt, and he isn't going to stop for any rat, and the rat, running out of options, decides to take on the bus rather than the screaming Fitzgerald. He almost made it, but got nailed by the rear tire of the 38, in just such a perfect way that the front got squished first, and the back part kind of exploded like a bursting water balloon full of rat guts across the road, with a huge popping sound. Fitzy was the happiest I have ever seen him. He jumped in the air, celebrating the exploding rat like the Yankees won the World Series with a Mickey Mantle home run in the bottom of the ninth of game 7.

"Yeah, I think I'll just hang out here too," Whitey says.

"Well, let's go!" Bobby says, "I'll go get somebody to buy us some brews down at the bar."

I don't know. I'd just rather sit here on the stoop than go up to Pigeon. I waited a long time to be able to hang here if I wanted, and I don't want to give it up just yet.

"See you guys," I say as the whole group walks away. Ralphie was the only one who turned around to give a little wave.

"Maybe we'll go up there later," I say to Whitey.

"Yeah, maybe."

"I Get Around" came on the radio again on the WABC superhit replay, that's when they play hottest song two times in a row...

"I'm getting bugged driving up and down this same old strip, I gotta find a place where the kids are hip."

So what if we don't have cars, we know what the song is about.

169

"Hey, look, here comes your brother!" I say to Whitey. I can see Whitey's brother Alfie riding up the steep hill on an old truck bike, the kind with the really fat balloon tires, and even has shock absorbers and a big basket on front.

"Where the hell did he find that?" Whitey says in amazement. "That was my brother Brian's bike when we lived in Inwood." Alfie is riding up the hill making it look easy. Even kids with English racer 3-speeds have a hard time going up the hill, but Alfie is cruising, riding right up the middle of the street. He reaches the top, right opposite where the stoop we're sitting is at.

"Hey guys!" he yells over to us, "Why don't you do something instead of just sitting there?" Alfie is now making a big circle at the top of the hill, and he's looking way down to the bottom. At something, but I don't know what.

"Yeah, we're gonna," Whitey says, as we both watch Alfie in his peculiar pattern.

"Don't think too hard, you might hurt yourself," Alfie says, and just as he finishes, he makes a sharp turn and pedals full speed down the hill, roaring down as fast as anybody could possibly go in a truck bike, which you never see anybody do, because at the bottom of the hill, around a big curve, there's a traffic light and a very busy intersection and you'd get killed if you tried to go through that light. But Alfie just tore ass right down, not giving a damn about that light, and zips right through.

"Man, is he nuts?" I ask Whitey.

"Yup. It runs in the family," Whitey says to the final fade out of *"round round round round I get around..."*

Well, nothing is happening. We're not even playing cards or any kind of game with a spaldeen. Just kind of sitting there, listening to the radio, watching the cars go by.

"Wanna go down to the pizza place?" Whitey asks me.

"Nah, I just ate dinner."

"So?"

"So, I'm full. Plus I don't have any money."

"Neither do I," Whitey adds, recognizing defeat.

And I think it might be time for me to admit some defeat too. "Wanna go up to Pigeon and see what those guys are

170

doing?"

Whitey looks as thrilled as I am. "Yeah, what the heck."

To get to Pigeon Park, we have to walk up a huge set of steps that cut through a block. We call them the city steps. Going up those steps is kind of a natural barrier. Nobody goes up them unless you really have to. And I guess the people who live up there don't come down them unless they really have to. Once you're up the steps, you only have to walk a block, past some really old apartment buildings that look even older than my building. The first story is actually made out of stone. And I don't even know anybody that lives in there. Yet, five blocks in the other direction from my house, I'll bet you I know at least three people in every apartment building. This is the beginning of where the Jewish people live.

Pigeon Park is right next to a huge reservoir. It's as big as the biggest lake I've ever seen in my life. There's a barbed-wire fence that goes all the way around it.

It's just beginning to get dark now. We go through the entrance of the park and just up a little hill, and there's the gang sitting on one of the big boulders. I can see Bobby's holding a can inside of a little brown bag, and next to him another brown bag that would hold a six pack perfectly. We walk up the hill and join in the hanging out.

"If you want a beer you have to chip in," Bobby says, immediately setting down his ground rules.

"Nah," Whitey and I say. "We're just gonna hang out for a while," I add as we both find a comfortable spot on the car-sized boulder. It's actually a very nice spot. It overlooks the reservoir, and there are sea gulls flying around in the twilight sky, which is kind of reddish in the distance. And just to the other side, you can see a half court game of basketball with some older kids, getting in the last few minutes of a game before it's too dark.

I can see two fresh, empty cans of Schaeffer at the bottom of the hill. I'll bet Bobby's on his third already, since nobody else seems to be drinking. But I get the feeling we interrupted something because everybody's a little too quiet.

"Alright, let's keep going, whose turn is it?" Bobby

171

says, looking at the girls.

"It's our turn," Carrie chimes in.

"What are you guys doing?" I ask to the crowd.

"Twenty questions," Carrie says right to me. She hasn't looked at me like that in a long time. In fact, she's been ignoring me in class totally. I'm not sure anymore how I feel about her. She's been hanging out with some different kids or something I think. Older kids.

"Do you want to play?" Carrie says without an once of humor.

"Uh, I'll just watch."

"No. We have to know if you're in or out," Carrie insists.

"OK, I'll play."

"Whitey what about you?" asks Eileen.

"OK." Whitey goes along.

"Donna, you go," Carrie says.

Donna takes a deep breath and closes her eyes. She pauses about five seconds, holding her breath, and without opening her eyes, says, "Jimmy Joe, How big is your... thing?"

What the hell! All of a sudden I could feel tingles all over my body. I wanted to jump up and down and yell and laugh and point and cheer but I didn't. I sat there in total silence like everybody else did. All eyes now on Jimmy Joe waiting for him to answer. He has to. It's twenty questions. The girls can ask ten questions of the boys and everybody has to answer. And you can't lie. Oh, you can lie, but it better be a real-sounding one. Jimmy Joe looks very much like he's in a spelling bee, and he was just asked to spell supercalifragilisticexpialidocious.

He shakes his head, the way he does a lot, so that the long strands of blonde hair come way down into his face, and then he pushes the hair back behind his ear. He's thinking hard, biting his lip. And lets out the answer, "4 by 2."

Holy shit! I can't believe he answered! The girls are looking at each other like they just found out that Paul McCartney was coming to visit and they couldn't tell anybody. Carrie grabbed Donna's thigh and began to squeeze really hard.

Eileen put her hands to her chest. I don't know about the rest of the crowd, but I'll bet everyone is feeling the same thing I am. I feel excited, but real dirty. I know darn well we're not supposed to be talking about stuff like this with girls. I can't believe we're doing it. We shouldn't be doing it. It's wrong. But let's keep going!

"That was 20," Bobby announces.

Well, that was it. It's over. I can't believe it. The guys get 10, the girls get 10. The end. I wonder what we missed. I'll find out later. Right now everybody's in kind of a fast-talking recap, not mentioning exactly what was said, but talking about how shocked they were. When you-know-who-said-you-know-what.

And right in the middle of the excitement, a stranger appears. It's a guy about our age, with wild dark unkempt curly hair. I've never seen him before, and he doesn't look like somebody I'd know. He's one of the Pigeon Park Jewish guys. We all know it. And he knows we don't belong in his park. But he walked all the way up the hill to our group. This guy is either really brave or really stupid.

He says to no one, "Anybody got an extra beer they want to sell?"

Bobby gets up slowly with his big brown bag in hand. "Who are you?"

"I'm Howie," the stranger says.

"Howie who?" Bobby follows up.

"Howie Bash."

"Howie Bash!!!" Bobby laughs. "Howie Bash!!!"

I don't like the looks of this. This Howie guy may have come up here for a lot of reasons, but this was the one thing he didn't want to happen. Bobby Bailey, drunk on three beers, all hopped up on sexy girl talk, and in a big show-off kind of mood. And a Jewish guy named Bash shows up.

"Bash, huh? Yeah, you can have a beer, Bash. Hey, beer bash!" Bobby says laughing.

I hope Howie knows what's coming, because we sure as hell do.

Bobby reaches into his bag. "You can have a beer," he

173

says as he takes a can and opens it with a church key and hands it to him. And as Howie reaches for it, looking at the can, Bobby lets loose with a roundhouse sucker punch, "And you can have a BASH!" *thwack*

Right at the side of Howie's face, spraying beer over all of us. Howie goes down like a ton of bricks. Once he realizes what happened, he yells, "You son of a bitch. David! Lenny! HELP!"

The older guys playing half court stop, and tear ass through the hole in the fence after us.

Bobby's the first to yell, "Let's get out of here!"

And we run, girls and all, down the hill, down the block, down the city steps, and back to the stoop. Thank God they didn't follow us all the way down.

We all walked down the steps past the stoop, down the alley, that goes to the empty lot behind my building and sat on the steps back there.

Everybody was laughing about everything. What led up to the moment, the moment, and what happened afterwards. But nobody, including me, said to Bobby what was going through my head...*why did you do something so stupid, you asshole.* Maybe I was the only one thinking it.

Believe me, I've got nothing against fighting. Sometimes you have to fight. But what Bobby did was bullshit. Pure show-off stuff. And sucker punching is the lowest thing possible.

Once I got my breath back, I knew it was time to get away from these guys. I'll leave and they'll probably think I'm afraid that the older Jewish kids will find us, but that's not the reason. They can think whatever the hell they want. I just feel like this group is not my kind of people.

"I'm going. See ya," I announce to no one in particular. And get up to go.

Whitey looks at me, and doesn't hesitate.

"Yeah, me too. See ya."

A few "see ya's" are muttered from the gang as Whitey and I walk up the alley to the street.

We walk down the block without saying a word, but

174

keeping an eye out for big Jewish kids on the hunt for two "crisscross Catholics," as they call us. Whitey says, "That was a real pussy move. I hope Howie Bash finds Bobby alone one day."

"Yeah, me too."

It was late, it was a school night, it was time to go home and sleep.

Bobby Bailey's an asshole.

I knew it was going to be a big party. But I didn't think it would be like this. Since my cousins Jimmy and Elizabeth are close in age, they have lots of friends the same age. So many friends that Aunt Grace made an arrangement with a next door neighbor to have two parties instead of one. The teens could have their party, just down the hall, in the neighbor's apartment, while relatives got together in Aunt Grace and Uncle Cornelius' place. Graduation from high school wouldn't be for a couple of weeks for Jimmy and Elizabeth, so the party was a little bit early. Probably the first of the season by the number of people who turned out.

Aunt Grace's kitchen is really just a kitchenette without even enough room for a small table, but she along with my mom, Aunt Louise, and Aunt Gina were screaming about stuff almost ready and stuff ready and stuff past ready. From the tiny steaming kitchen to the dining room table, expanded with the maximum number of leaves, just inside and outside the kitchen entrance are the four noisy sisters pushing, shouting marching orders, and shuffling dishes, bowls, plates, and trays filled with antipasto, artichoke hearts, radishes, breads, anchovies, cheeses, peppers, and olives into a feast of loud flavors. Hot, cold, sweet, sour, spicy, mushy. The works. There's a buzz of kisses, hugs, and shouts of kids running from aunts trying to squeeze cheeks and uncles trying to tickle with hairy moustached kisses.

There are little kids all over, most of whom I don't even know, and really old people who I think are great aunts and uncles. But I don't see anybody I want to hang with.

"Where's Jimmy and Elizabeth?" I ask Aunt Grace between passing plates of hot peppers and cheese. "5F! Down the hall!" she shouts. I find my sister sitting by the kitchen, laughing along with the chatter that the four sisters exchange. "Grace! Don't take out the roast beef yet, it's still breathing, for goodness sakes!" my mom shouts.
"Stop it, Angie! We like it rare! If you want a well-done piece I'll cut one off for you."
"Oh don't bother, just leave it in till it's warm, at least."
"Do you want to go see what the other party's like?" I ask my sister who's watching the kitchen action like it's a TV show. "Not now, I'm going to help out here," she says between guffaws and shoving cheese blocks in her mouth.
Down the hall. Just two doors away. 5F. I ring the bell, and it actually works. The door doesn't open, but I hear the words, "Who is it?
"It's Vinny," I say into the steel door.
I hear on the other side a male voice say, "Who's Vinny? Should I let him in?"
"Yeah, it's my cousin." I then hear a door chain and several locks come undone followed by the opening of the door. The apartment is filled with teenagers. Music blasting, laughter, chatter, and some dancing. There's a wall of four windows, wide open. Wide open. And the curtains are blowing in the wind. There's a heavy smell of Lysol in the air. "Vinny! How you doin', man?" my cousin Jimmy says as he shakes both my shoulders and at the same time shakes his Beatle haircut.
"Lizbeth... Vinny's here!" Elizabeth comes through the crowd holding two glasses. "Hi, Vinny! Where's Anne Marie?" she says, as she gives me a quick peck on the cheek, careful not to spill the drinks.
"She says she'll come over in a little while."
I recognize some of the faces from the St. Patrick's Day Parade. "Remember my girlfriend Mary?" Jimmy asks me. I nod yeah. "And this is Lisa and Packy and Vicki, and Sheila and Benny and Pappo and Bobby and Jake." Nods all the way around. I haven't seen Jimmy or anybody since March, and as long as I thought their hair looked then, it's longer and even

176

wilder now. And dirty. Jimmy's over by the tabletop Magnavox hi-fi stereo with a 45's box. He's going through carefully and gingerly placing them on an automatic 45 spindle. "Vinny, you ever hear of The Rolling Stones?"

"Yeah.

"Well, here's a song that The Beatles gave them."

Jimmy twists a couple of dials and the sound thumps out. It didn't sound like the Beatles at all. Especially the singing. Even my mother says, "those boys sing so nice" when talking about the Beatles. It sounded like a rough colored singer, with real fast twangy guitars. "This is their new single, "I Wanna Be Your Man" written by Lennon and McCartney," Jimmy informs me, and then notices I have a dumb look on my face. "You know... from The Beatles."

"Oh yeah" That must be John and Paul.

"John Lennon says it's his favorite band. It's the other side of 'Not fade away.' I'll play that in few minutes. That's by Buddy Holly. You ever hear of him?"

"Uh, no." I sheepishly admit. And to feel like I fit in I add, "You ever hear the Mouse? It's really cool."

"The Mouse? Soupy Sales? That's not real music," Jimmy says, laughing a little, in a way that tells me he's trying not to hurt my feelings.

I thought to myself... why not? It sounds something like the other stuff they play on the radio. It's silly I guess, but so is "Itsy Bitsy Teeny Weenie Yellow Polka Dot Bikini" and "Alley Oop" and "Charlie Brown" and "Yakkety Yak" and everybody knows they're cool.

"Soupy Sales is what they call a novelty song, Vinny. This is real music. You know, it means something," he shouts over the speakers as they blast a line that I think says something about his girlfriend being bigger than a Cadillac.

"Yeah, I guess so," I went along, even though I didn't really get the difference.

I hate that feeling when you feel like you don't understand what older kids or adults are saying. Like when you're little and they're spelling stuff out loud right in front of you and you can't spell yet. I think it's time to go back and get something to eat.

Back at the other party, everybody was eating off of paper plates on their laps. Somebody had put "Hootenany" on the TV and it was blaring a song by two guys called the Smothers Brothers, one playing the guitar and the other a big stand-up bass. My dad was sitting on the couch across from the TV, and I could tell these two country bumpkins were giving him a headache. "Hey, Vinny, put on channel 2," he yells over to me. So I switch to channel 2, where Jackie Gleason is in the middle of one of his Joe The Bartender routines with Crazy Guggenheim. My dad always cracks up at Crazy Guggenheim. And sometimes he even gets teary eyed when Crazy closes the scene with a sappy Irish song. I hope he doesn't in front of all these people.

We ate and ate and then ate some more. Every once in a while, Elizabeth or Jimmy would come in to pick up another batch of food or drink for the older kids.

It's around 9:30 now, and most of the people are leaving. But my mom wants to stay to help Aunt Grace clean up. Not what dad wants, but at least she lets him sit and watch "The Lawrence Welk Show" so he's not complaining too loud, or she'll have him in there scraping lasagna cheese off of plates. In a half hour, his favorite show "Gunsmoke" will be on. That's an hour show, so I know we'll be staying until at least 11:00. And I can't take another minute of Lawrence Welk's Tribute to the Gay '90s.

"I'm going to go over to Jimmy and Elizabeth's party," I announce to no one in particular as I head out the door and down the hall towards the loud music coming from behind the closed door. I walk up to it, and hear not only the thumping of loud rock and roll, but a good amount of squeals, laughs, and howls. My knock goes unnoticed for quite a while. I have to bang really hard. The door opens, and it's a friend of Jimmy's I don't know, with freckles, wild red hair, and even wilder red eyes. "The party for you is down the hall, kid," he says as he slams the door. I bang again. Jimmy answers this time. He sticks his head out, looks down the hall, and pulls me inside. "You can come in, but don't tell anybody what you see. Anybody."

"I won't, don't worry." And I won't either. If there's one thing I'm good at, it's keeping a secret. I learned that from dealing with my brother. No matter what it was, if he told me not to tell, I didn't. I didn't want to find out what would happen if I did.

Now it's pretty cold in here. All the windows are still wide open, and it's pretty cool outside. Now everybody's dancing, and it looks like those that aren't dancing are on the couch or in chairs, or on the floor making out. There's beer just about everywhere, and I see Jimmy disappear into a bedroom, closing the door behind him, and a friend of his stands guard in front of it. I can't believe what I'm seeing. This is a first. Oh I've seen drinking and making out and dancing and heard loud rock and roll before, but never this loud, or much, or heavy. Nobody even notices me as I slip through the gyrating bodies watching guys and girls smoosh together, and even hands feeling each other up like I've never seen before.

A hand reaches through the crowd and pulls me to the bedroom. It's Jimmy. "Vinny, come on." I knew this would be something incredible. If all that stuff was going on out there in the living room, I couldn't imagine what would be going on behind closed bedroom doors. It was almost completely dark, and I was hit with a weird smell of something that smelled like the incense from church. The windows again were wide open. In the room is Jimmy and his girlfriend Mary sitting on the bed. Another couple making out on the floor, and a girl I think I remember from St. Paddy's day sitting on a chair over by Mary. Jimmy introduces me, "Remember my girlfriend Mary, this is Sheila, and over there on the floor are Jake and Packy." They both manage a wave from their wrestling match. "Sit down," Jimmy suggests, so I do, on the floor.

"You ever get high, Vinny?"

"Well, I drank one rye and ginger one New Year's but, no, not really."

"Well you're going to tonight," Jimmy instructs me as he reaches into the inside pocket of his collarless suit coat jacket, pulling out a Marlboro box. He flips the top, and out roll three small black pills, then he takes out a weird cigarette. "You can take this black beauty pill, or smoke this grass, which is it?" Shit. Am I scared. No way am I going to take a pill. That's what drug addicts take. And pot? I've heard what that does and I don't want to try it. But then again, just a little wouldn't hurt. How could one stupid puff do anything. So, here goes. "I'll try the cigarette."

"It's not a cigarette," Jimmy laughs, "it's a joint," he says as he puts it in his mouth, pulls out his Zippo lighter, and lights it up, dragging on it like he was trying to suck every molecule out of the paper. The joint became a deep dark red, with a huge plume of smoke, and loud crackling noises like a campfire. It lit up Jimmy's face in a dark devilish red glow. He held it for Mary and she leaned over and did the same. Then Sheila came over for it. Now it's my turn. Jimmy held it out for me. Sheila and Mary were staring at me with faint smiles. Oh well, here goes. Wait till I tell Whitey. I'll be the first from the crowd to do this. I inched forward and grabbed it from Jimmy. I took one last look and pulled it closer to my lips and I'm sure I got cross-eyed as I watched it all the way to my mouth. It's in my mouth. Go. I suck in, deeply, and without wanting to, just cough the biggest cough I ever have blowing the hot ambers all over the rug, forcing Jimmy to jump up and try to put them out before anything gets burned, and sending Mary and Sheila into fits of laughter. I can't stop coughing and Jimmy's frantically patting the rug. "You idiot! Didn't you ever smoke before?" Actually no. Unless you count that time in the 1st grade, when I got caught and got the hell beat out of me. I haven't smoked since.

The joint was out, and Mary and Sheila finally stopped laughing. He takes it from me, and puts it back into the Marlboro box. "So much for that," Jimmy says relieved the place didn't burn down.

"Well, maybe I ought to go," I say, expecting to get kicked out of the room.

"No, not yet," Jimmy says. "Vinny, did you ever make out with a girl?"

"Sure. We play kiss-o-leerio all the time." Sheila and

Mary laugh uncontrollably again.

Jimmy continues, "No, really make out. Like this."
He turns to Mary, and starts kissing her, with both of their
mouths open, I guess tongues going in and out of each other's
mouth, and hands rubbing all over each other's back. They
stop, and Jimmy says, "Well, I mean like that?"

"No. Never." That was easy.

Mary reaches out for me and says, "Come here, Vinny,"
as she takes my hand and makes me sit next to her on the bed.
She and Jimmy get up, and then Sheila comes over and sits
right next to me. I don't think my heart ever pounded so fast in
my life. I couldn't talk if I wanted to. But I didn't have to.
Sheila, a high school senior, long blonde hair, bigger-than-av-
erage boobs, short skirt, freckles, sits next to me and places
one hand on my lap and the other on the back of my neck. I'm
paralyzed. I close my eyes, and suddenly feel lips against mine.
That taste of smoker's mouth mixed with Juicy Fruit gum. A
hot wet tongue shoots into my mouth, like a dog's licking the
inside of a can of dog food. Up down all around the inside of
my shocked mouth as she massages the back of my neck and
the inside of my leg. I've been excited before. I remember the
first time I ever got really horny, watching Betty Boop do the
hula topless, with the lei around her neck just barely covering
her nipples with her little Betty Boop boobies flopping around,
and I actually got my first boner, but compared to this... wow!
Not only do I have a boner, I know that if she continues for
another two seconds, it will be ....TOO LATE!!! I've got to
stop. NOW!. I turn my head, and stand. "Uh, I think I better
be going. Uh, I want to watch Gunsmoke."

Everything is a blur now. All I can think about is how
close I came to losing it. I couldn't concentrate on Gunsmoke.

The rest of the evening... the good-byes, the FDR north,
brushing my teeth, going to bed all seemed like a dream. Wow.
I was right there. In the middle of it all. I could've done whatever I wanted. I didn't. But I will. I can't wait till summer
vacation.

I can't even think about schoolwork. As little as I stud-

181

ied the past 8 years of grammar school, I'm studying even less now. I've already been accepted into Cardinal Hayes, so grades don't matter a bit. I usually get about a 90 average just by paying attention in class, and handing in the absolute minimum amount of homework, so I figure if I drop down a few notches, I'll get an 85 average. Not so bad. And I think Sister Fidelis can't wait till this year is over, either. She's pretty much given up on homework for us. Tests are a joke, and she hasn't called anybody a tramp or accused a boy of playing pocket billiards in weeks. She pretty much just assigns us stuff to read during class, and as long as we're pretty quiet, she doesn't care what we do. Most of the girls pass notes to each other, most of the boys read "Mad Magazine." A few kids read real books. Since me and Whitey are in the back, we put in ear pieces of our small Jap transistor radios, and listen to rock and roll and draw pictures of stuff. Whitey's actually not bad. Sometimes he draws naked girls, based of course on what he has seen in a magazine.

We're even getting away with stuff like we never have before. Whitey can do this thing where he can whistle through his teeth so it sounds like a bomb is falling, and the way he does it, you can't tell where it's coming from, and at the end of the long whistle, he makes a low rumbling bomb blast sound. It's best done when it's real quiet in the class, when, of course, the best comedic affect is reached.

Graduation is only a week away. I can't believe how anticlimactic this is. Finals done. Graduation pictures done. Autograph books done. Parties almost done. Most people know where they're going to high school. Except Whitey. He's still not sure. He's even talking about possibly going to DeWitt Clinton, a huge public school. He'd be the only one from our class going there. He's on the waiting list for Hayes, and if enough people change their mind he just might make it. Hayes is strict. A lot of kids call it a factory because it's so big. But I don't care, they've got all kinds of cool extra curricular activities, like art and music, and every varsity sport there is. They don't have a varsity hockey team, but they do have a hockey club that's just like a real team, and there aren't enough

182

schools to be a real varsity sport yet. They even have a rocket club where kids build rockets and shoot them off over by the Long Island Sound. And it's just a few blocks from Yankee Stadium. I'm hoping to get a job as a peanut vendor. I could start after school, and then continue during the summer. That would be the coolest. I'd get to actually go behind the scenes in Yankee Stadium. We did that one time by accident. Last summer me, Whitey, and Michael Vitelli went to a game and brought one of those big plastic horns that you blow into, and they make a really loud sound like a moose in heat. We bought them at Yankee Stadium the time before, so you can imagine how surprised we were when they wouldn't let us bring them into the ball park. So many kids were blowing their lungs out with those stupid horns that people were complaining, and they decided to ban them. So when we entered the park, they actually took them from us, checked them into a wooden locker they rolled to the gate, and gave us a ticket to claim them after the game. But, after the game to them, and after the game to us are always two different things. After the game is when we really have fun. We always walk around the seats to see if we find anything valuable, then down to the dugouts to see if we can talk somebody into giving us something, anything from the dugout or the field. And now I know to split as soon as you get something, so some little asshole can't make up a story on you. Sometimes we just stomp on mustard or ketchup packets to see how far they'll go. Even without the thrill of splattering somebody a deck or two below. Or just pop empty beer cups really loud if you stomp on them exactly right. So there we are, hanging around the stadium until the ushers chase us out. But we still have to claim our horns. We head over to the gate where we came in only to find that the portable locker with our precious horns isn't even there. Wow! That gives us something we never had before. An excuse! An excuse to explore Yankee Stadium in places where we're not supposed to go. So we start opening doors, going down steps, and through long halls. Unbelievably, there's nobody around. We turn a corner, and there's a closed door. No sign at all. Behind it we can hear voices. A room full of men chatting. Vitelli, who's only

183

a 6th grader, has a lot more nerve than me or Whitey, goes over to the door and puts his hand right on the doorknob.

"Oh my. Maybe the horns are in here!" Vitelli says, as if he wants somebody to over hear him. He opens the door, and we step inside to a room full of half-naked men. We didn't say a word. We just stood there in total awe. There, right in front of us, were the Kansas City Athletics, some even with their johnsons dangling. The only reason I knew it was the Athletics was I didn't see Mickey, or Yogi, or Maris, or anybody familiar except for one face. I didn't know who most of them are, but standing in his jock strap dead ahead was Rocky Colavito. Everybody knows Rocky Colavito. He's a hero in the Bronx, because he's the only Bronxite in the majors, and he's a home run hitter. We were in shock. Real baseball players, right there, in their underwear, jocks, or bare-ass naked, goofing, joking, talking, drying their hair with towels, packing bags, listening to WINS, and totally unaware that three kids just entered their domain. "Hey, you kids!" we hear from somewhere, and a guy wearing an usher outfit comes out of nowhere and grabs me and Vitelli by the arm. "You kids are in big trouble," he says as he drags us towards the door. Now the ball players are looking at us, and just before we're through the door and into trouble, Vitelli yells, "Hey, Rocky! Mantle says you're a sissy!" and we can hear a big round of laughter go up as we're pulled out and the door slams behind us, and the usher tries to scare the hell out of us.

"You kids can go to jail for this, you know."

Vitelli holds up his claim ticket, and says, "Hey, we're just looking to claim our property mister!"

The usher looks at the ticket. "Alright, come with me," he says, disappointed that he shouldn't scare the hell out of us. See, all you need is an excuse.

We should be reading our geography books, but I'm in the middle of "Spy vs. Spy" in "Mad." A note plops onto my desk. I can tell by the practically unreadable handwriting that it's from Whitey and it reads, "My brother Alfie is going to show us how to make a UFO tonight. Meet on the roof of my building at dark."

Wow! Alfie's a cool guy. Since he's been home, I hardly see him around at all. He hangs out in other neighborhoods. But every once in a while he pops out of nowhere with something weird to do. He even showed us how to sneak into the music concerts they have up at Manhattan College. All you have to do is put on a certain kind of apron, tied a certain way, and walk right through the ticket line, because that's how the guys who run the concessions there do it. We watched him do it, but me and Whitey haven't gotten up the nerve to do it ourselves. Yet.

I nod to Whitey that I'm definitely "in" for tonight. It doesn't get dark till 8:30 now, but since it's a Friday, I'll be able to stay out a little later. I can't for the life of me imagine how Alfie is going to make a UFO, but if he says he can, I guess he can.

Since Alfie's been around, the girls in our class have been talking about him. I even heard Carrie Vitelli say that she never saw anybody who could look cute in just a tee-shirt and a pair of cut-offs the way Alfie can. Even though Alfie's as old as a lot of the kids who hang out in the local bars, I don't think he hangs out in there. Whitey says he doesn't like to drink. But he sure rides that old bike all over the place, at all hours of the day and night. And he always does that weird circling thing at the top of the hill before he takes off like a bat out of hell down the hill and into the intersection. And now his hair is getting really long. Even longer than the Beatles. He looks more like the pictures I've seen of the Rolling Stones. They've got really long hair.

With the weather pretty warm now, and school almost over, I'm hardly ever at home. Everybody practically races home after school and gets into street clothes in five minutes, and then we're out playing until dinner, then home for a half hour, eat, and back out until it's time to go home, and on weekends that's really late. Like 10:00. I definitely see my friends more than I see my family at this time of year.

It's a lot safer going up to Whitey's roof than it is going up to mine. No Mr. McHugh. There's just one stairway that leads up to the roof, and the people who live down that end of the hall are old, and don't complain. Not that being old means people don't complain. Mr. McHugh is old, and he'll beat your brains in with a sawed-off baseball bat. I knock on Whitey's door at 7:30. He doesn't need to say "who is it?" He knows who's there. He just opens the door and steps outside. "Alfie's gonna meet us up there at 10:00. He gave me a list of things we have to get. Do you have any money?"

Fortunately, I took two dollars of change out of my safe. Since my brother moved out, I actually have money in there. My brother figured out how to jimmy open the cheap door and take money for cigarettes and stuff when he was low. "Yeah, I got a couple of bucks."

Whitey takes a crumpled piece of paper out of his dungaree pocket. "Here's what we need: 3 dry cleaner bags. Scotch tape. One box of birthday candles. One box plastic straws. 3 to 6 votive candles. And matches."

"That's the list to make a UFO?"

"That's what he says." "OK. Let's get going."

The hardest thing on the list would be the dry cleaning bags. There was a slight chance that Johnny Bazzicalupo might still be in the cleaners, since he's usually there late on Fridays.

Looking through the front window I could see a light in the back. I take a quarter out of my pocket and tap on the glass. Here comes Johnny from the back of the store.

"Hey Schmidt, waddyah want, we're closed."

"Johnny, could I have three bags?"

"What the hell you gonna do wid dem?"

"Ahh, it's a class project we're doing over the weekend, about ah, photosynthesis, and we need plastic bags."

"Wait here."

He walks back into the store and comes back with three bags that he obviously took out of the garbage, all crumpled up.

"Here you go, now get outta here."

"No they have to be new bags."

"What? You think I get these things for free?"

"We'll pay you."

"Alright alright." He goes a little bit further into the store and comes back with three new bags. "A nickel apiece."

I reach into my tight dungarees and pull out three nickels. "Thanks, Johnny."

He slams the door and locks it.

"What a gyp! 15 cents!" Whitey says.

"Yeah well at least we got them."

The tape, birthday candles and straws we could get down at the "5 and 10." That's actually "Woolworth's," but nobody calls it that. Everybody calls it the five and ten, or the five and dime. I don't know why; there's hardly anything in there for a nickel or a dime. It's been there forever. My mother says she used to shop there when she was a little girl when stuff really was a nickel and a dime. It still has that old fashioned wooden floor that creaks when you walk on it. The votive candles are all that's left. They're the big fat candles they burn in church. Like the kind up front where you put a dime in the slot and light a candle for a cause with a skinny wooden stick that you light from an already burning candle. The big candles in the five and ten are a quarter each. That'll bust our budget for sure. Then Whitey comes up with a big idea. "Let's go to the church, put in 60 cents, and take six candles. That won't be stealing, because people put in a dime for the candles anyway." That seemed like a good idea. I'd never want to steal from the church. That would definitely be a venial sin, and probably bad luck. But putting in a dime for each one would just mean that you're getting them at cost. Why not.

"Whitey, you're a genius."

It's weird going into the church on a Friday night. There's a few old ladies saying the rosary in the back, mumbling the way that they do. The mumbles echo through the almost empty church. We have to walk all the way up to the front where the candles are.

It's right below a huge statue of Jesus on the Cross. It's the kind where Jesus is wearing his flowing white robe on the cross, not like the one you have to kiss on Good Friday

187

where he's just wearing a loin cloth and is bleeding. And it looks like he's staring at us as we drop in the thin dimes, and take 6 candles, stuffing them into our pockets. Just as we're ready to turn around, I hear the unmistakable sound of a man's walking shoes on the hard marble floor, and the swooshing sound of a priest's robe. Shit. I whisper to Whitey. "Light a candle, quick."

"Well, Roberto and Vincenzo !" It's Father O'Shaughnessy, head of the altar boys.

"What brings you two here on a Friday night?"

I blurt out as I start to light two more candles.

"We're lighting candles Father, for er, ah, a safe summer."

Whitey's probably bleeding inside his mouth from biting his lip so hard.

"That's excellent. Don't forget to stop by to talk about the altar boy outing. We need some older boys to go along too!"

"Yes Father," we say in unison as Father O'Shaughnessy continues past us, and goes up to the altar to take care of some priestly equipment matters for the weekend.

We rush out, and just when we're almost all the way to Whitey's building, I realize something. "Oh crap, Whitey. We didn't put extra dimes in for the two candles we lit."

"Oh so what. I'm not going all the way back there now. Do it on Sunday." I guess that was alright. But deep down inside, I thought it could be thought of as stealing if something happened and I didn't drop those two dimes in the box. Oh well. Screw it. For now anyway.

I feel like I have the secret ingredients of a bomb or something. All these weird things, and I have no idea how the heck they are going to be made into some kind of UFO, but I believe Whitey's brother Alfie. He's always doing unusual things. But cool unusual things. Just seeing him circle with his bicycle at the top of the hill before he tears ass down lets me know that he's got to know what he's doing. Otherwise he'd be dead. He's always got a weird intensity about him.

And strange eyes that look right through you.

The wait until 10:00 was murder, but now it's half past and still no sign of Alfie. It's really scary being up here on the roof, just me and Whitey, in the dark. In the distance you can see the dome of Manhattan College glowing all white, like a monument in Washington. And the lights in the windows of the tall apartment buildings in Riverdale. And as the "el" goes up Broadway, the sparks from the wheels light up for blocks around, like a bolt of lightning. Especially off to the right where the train yard is, and as the trains line up for the night in the yard, and switch tracks, the wheels squeal and sparks shoot into the night, heard and seen for blocks and blocks. And way over to the right, is a big black hole of woods and park; Van Cortlandt Park, with just a ribbon of light cutting through from the highway. Red tail lights on the right, white lights on the left. And I know that in that darkness there are groups of teenagers from here to Woodlawn, in the dark, doing things that they can't do on the streets of their neighborhoods in the day time.

Six stories below, I can see a group of kids. It's hard to tell, but I'll bet it's Carrie, Donna, Jimmy Joe, Ralphie, and BB, because we told them we were making a UFO at 10:00 and launching it off the roof. They're gathered around the mailbox on the corner, with Carrie sitting on top. I can barely hear occasional laughs, yelps, and sounds from the transistor radio.

"Hey, Whitey, whistle down to them." Whitey walks over to the edge, and looks down.

"Man, I love it up here. Just think if somebody were to come over here and PUSH" and on the word PUSH he grabs me from behind and gives me a good jerk towards the edge of the roof, scaring the hell out of me, "you right over!"

"Hey, asshole, don't do that!"

"You're such a chicken," Whitey laughs, as he sticks his head over the wall and sticks two index fingers into the side of his mouth and blows a quick, loud whistle blast. I wish I could do that. I sure have tried. For hours. But no good. Just as the whistle is out, the whole group down below looks up to

189

us. And the one I figure to be Jimmy Joe yells, "Let's go!"

"Alright alright" Whitey shouts back.

"Is he gonna show up?" I say to Whitey.

"He'll be here." And just as the words leave his mouth, I hear the unmistakable sound of the stairway door slamming shut. "I hope that's him," I say, looking over into the darkness where the door is. I can hear the sound of soft shoes crunching the textured tar paper, and out of the dark comes Alfie. His long, thin, blonde hair blowing in the breeze as he comes towards us and says right away, "You got everything?"

Alfie looks even stranger than usual. I don't know why, but he does. I don't smell booze so I don't think he's drunk, but he looks something like that.

"Yeah everything" Whitey says, as I hand him the brown bag filled with the mysterious ingredients. Alfie takes the bag and walks over to the edge of the roof. He looks off into the distance in a strange stare. His head does a long wide arc as he looks across the valley that makes up our world, from left to right. From the distant glow of Manhattan where you can see the tip of the Empire State Building, to the 225th Street bridge, to the tall apartment buildings of Riverdale, to the park, he seems to be studying every light bulb and says softly, "The breeze could hurt us, but it could help too."

He takes the bag and starts to carefully remove each item. He takes the straws and sticks them together, one end into the other, making a straw stick around a yard long. Then he makes an "X" out of the two big pieces, taping them together where they cross. Then he makes another long straw stick, long enough to make a box around the "X." Then he takes the birthday candles, and begins taping them upright along the X and along the straws that form the box. Alfie is doing everything is a slow, ritualistic way. Not making a sound. This whole thing is weird. Once the frame of the straws is complete he takes the votive candles and places them inside the box that has been formed, but not attaching them to anything. "Are these from Church?" Alfie asks us.

"Yeah, but we paid for them." I say.

"That's really weird," Alfie says. "Church candles

burning to make a UFO that'll rise up to Heaven. Take the matches and light the votive candles while I get the bag ready." Alfie picks up the straw frame with the birthday candles attached, and starts to tape the dry cleaning bag carefully to the straws. We light the candles on the ground. "Here's the tricky part," Alfie says as he holds the contraption carefully. "I'm going to hold the bag over the candles, and slowly lower it, and you guys very, very carefully light the birthday candles, and don't let the bag get near a flame because it'll ruin the whole thing if the bag gets a hole in it."

As Alfie gets closer, his face has a strange glow, lit by the candles, and distorted through the dry cleaning bag. He looks like a ghost. "Now light the candles." He holds the bag over the votive candles that were laid out on the floor. And like magic, after a few moments, the bag starts to sort of inflate. "I get it!" I say. "The hot air from the votive candles will heat the air, and fill up the bag, and make it rise, and the birthday candles attached to the frame will keep the air hot once it starts to rise, and from a distance it'll look like a UFO!"

"Very good, Vinny." Alfie says. I felt good. Like a teacher or somebody told me I did a good job on an answer.

The bag is all filled out now, and you could see it wants to rise up. Alfie lifts the bag about knee high and says, "Be careful and light the birthday candles." So very, very carefully, Whitey and I light the candles. Once they are all lit, Alfie lowers the bag, getting maximum heat from all the candles. "OK, let's go," he announces. He can now just hold the bag by placing his hands on the top of the bag so it doesn't float away. He walks over to the edge of the roof. "The wind is blowing away from us. That's good," he says in a creepy kind of whisper. Whitey gives a whistle blast down to the gang, and they all look up. Instead of shouts, there's total silence as they see from a distance the lights we hold in front of us. "Here it goes," Alfie says as he lets go of the straw frame at the bottom of the bag. At first it just kind of floated there eerily, but then it actually started to rise up a little bit, and lo and behold, actually started to travel away from us, going up very slightly. And as it got higher, just a few feet higher than the roof we were on, and it got a distance of about 20 yards away, you could see that this thing did look really weird. Strange lights in the distance for sure. Floating on its own with the plastic bag reflecting the orange birthday candle flame in a bizarre pattern.

"I can't freaking believe it!" Whitey says, staring at it. Alfie has a strange smile on his face. This is cool. I'll bet there are people who see this thing and have no idea what they are looking at. All those apartment buildings have people in them who are always looking out the window. And if they happen to be looking over here, they're seeing something they can't understand. Strange lights in the distance? It must be a UFO? Maybe they'll even call the cops, or the Daily News, and it'll be in the paper tomorrow. But it's not going any higher now. In fact, it seems to be coming down slightly as it goes further away. More than slightly. Shit.

"Uh oh," Alfie says. "It looks like it's coming down." It sure is. And it's pretty far away. It made it to the highway. And it looks like it is going to land in the brush next to the highway. Yes. It does. We can see it slowly land in the brush. It's gone. "Uh oh," Alfie says again. "I thought this might happen."

I thought..."What might happen?" and then I realized what "this" was. Right at the point where it landed, there was a glow. And the glow started getting brighter and brighter. And the glow was now a full-blown, burning brush fire, right next to the Major Deegan Expressway. It's no UFO anymore. Now it's a very identifiable thing. A freaking fire right next to the highway.

And Alfie is laughing like a lunatic. I can't believe it. I think he must be high or something.

"Shit. Let's get out of here!" I say to the guys.

Alfie coolly turns to me and says, "Don't be stupid. This is the good part. Nobody knows it was us. Just enjoy the show."

I didn't want to, but I did. And I had a strange feeling doing it. I knew I was part of something wrong, something bad, yet I got a thrilling sensation watching it from all the way up here. The birthday candles turned into a raging brush fire. Traffic on the highway slowed with gawkers. Cars stopped on the side streets. People yelled out of windows. Kids ran down the block to look. And eventually, fire trucks came to douse the flames, followed by huge clouds of billowing white smoke that we could actually smell all the way up here.

It wasn't what I expected, but it was a thrill. Yeah, somebody could've gotten killed if the contraption had landed somewhere more dangerous. But it didn't.

Alfie didn't say a word during the entire flaming show. But once it was all over, he turned and said to us, "You kids just don't know how to have fun anymore." And then he went off into the darkness.

Whitey and I gathered up the stuff left over, dumped them in a garbage can in the basement and went off to find the gang so we could hear about how cool the whole thing was. But we couldn't find them. All that remained at the site of the fire was one fire truck.

"What happened here?" Whitey asks the lone fireman walking away from the blackened, smoking brush.

"Ah nothing, somebody on the highway threw a lit cigarette into the brush."

Crap. What good is it if there's no recognition?

It's weird but it feels like I'm never home. I see my friends more often than my family. But even weirder is the fact that I feel like I'm about to go somewhere I've never been before, and I know I'm not going anywhere soon. We sure as hell aren't leaving this one bedroom apartment that I've been living in for all of my thirteen years, and my parents have been living in for almost twenty years. Sure it's small, and it's dark, but it sure is cheap. Live in a small dark apartment and at least you get Christmas presents, and decent clothes and vacations.

But every morning, I know that school is just about over. One more week. Graduation on Saturday. And it's hot like summer now. There's no more homework, no more crazy lectures. Just killing time with Sister Fidelis looking more tired than ever, not caring what we do as long as we're relatively quiet and not bothering anybody physically. You know, grabbing girls' bra straps, or punching Mark Fay in the arm. We even have half days this week, so school is actually a good way to get together with everybody, and make plans for the rest of the day. Since nobody's home at my house after 5, it's a cool feeling being on my own. Then of course, since my parents know there's no homework, I'm out immediately after dinner. I can't stay out past 9 while there's still school, but next week I'll probably be able to stay out till 10 or 11 or maybe even later.

And just thinking about no more nuns makes me realize how different high school is going to be. Priests and Brothers are no picnic, but it'll be more....grown up. Sometimes I think the nuns get so crazed during class because they can't figure out math and science problems either, and they're afraid the students are going to find out. I think most of us are finding out about a lot of things.

This Saturday after graduation, we're having a party for relatives. I'll probably get some cash. It's a double party, being that my sister is graduating from high school, so it'll be a big one. But even though, all I can think about is going to other parties at other kid's homes. Yeah, relatives will be over; but these past few weeks, our class is more together than ever. I hear even Jerome Mullooly is inviting kids over. He's the one who isn't allowed to watch The Three Stooges, and his family kneels down and prays together every night. I'm sure some kids are probably going to be drinking and maybe even sniffing Carbona, so I'm almost afraid to think what might happen at some of these parties. But I don't care that much. Something else that's amazing is how all of a sudden girls that I've known since the 1st grade all of a sudden look kind of good. And some of them even have boobies. Oh sure, some are members of the I.B.T.C. (the ittie bittie tittie committee), but some girls have got real boobs. (I think) We always hear from Carrie and Donna about how some girls with boobies bigger than theirs "stuff," but they all can't. I mean, Ann Cunningham has been in my class since the first grade, and I don't think I've said five words to her in eight years. But one day a few weeks ago and BOOM. I noticed that underneath that jumper and that white blouse were extra large boobs. And no way are they tissue paper. They are big, bouncy, boobies that must've sprouted overnight, and must be held up by over-the-shoulder-boulder-holders. And I'm not the only boy who noticed, either. She's been talked to, and about, by every boy in the class. And besides her sudden giant growths, other females previously bypassed have gained some attributes as well. Irene Esposito, Linda Leary, Eilleen Tessitore have all sprung nice-sized summer melons, and resigned from the I.B.T.C. for good. And what better place to discover new classmates with new body parts than at a party dancing slow to "In the Still of the Night."

The other thing about the last week of school is that it's the last week for doing stuff with a lot of other kids. Because once school is over, lots of kids disappear. Some go away to Rockaway or the Catskills for the entire summer, and some go to day camp. So this last week is the last chance to play a game of baseball, where you need at least 18 guys to show up for a game. That's why during the summer, other games become so important. Like Wiffle ball. You only need a few guys to get something going. And with so many classmates gone, it also means you have to hang out with kids who aren't your own age because there just aren't as many kids around. Some kids like to hang out with younger kids so you can be better than them at sports. But me and Whitey like to hang out with older kids. You learn more.

So I'm going to enjoy this week the best I can because Saturday it ends for good. Graduation means the end of a lot of things. No more nuns. No more being treated like a little kid. No more of the same kids year in, year out. This is going to be the summer of a lifetime.

I don't have to sneak notes in class anymore. In fact, I don't even have to whisper.

"Hey, Whitey," I say loud enough to be heard several seats in front of me. Whitey takes his nose out of a "Sad Sack" comic and looks back at me. "What do you want to do after

195

school?"

Whitey gets a quizzical look on his face, and scratches the top of his head. "I don't know. Screw some girls?" Linda Leary, who sits right behind him, picks up her handy wooden ruler and cracks him over the head with it. It doesn't really hurt, but it makes a heck of a sound. "Shelley, don't be such a pig in public," she scolds him.

"Owwww, that hurt, " he says in mock pain, looking for sympathy from her. He looks over to me and says, "I don't know, let's just hang out on the stumps."

Well, so much for big plans. That's what we almost always do. Hang out by the stumps next to my building. Yeah, it's a cool spot, but it's what we always do. "Alright, see if anybody else wants to go," I suggest to Whitey.

So Whitey starts tossing notes and talking to other kids. And as if it was a big deal, they'll all say yeah, and we'll all wind up sitting next to the stumps at the top of the steps that lead to the alley next to my building. There will be a radio tuned in to WABeatleC or WINS or WMCA, and a deck of cards, and cigarettes, and bubble gum, and a spaldeen, and some girls and guys, and we'll hang out. And something will happen. Nobody knows what, but as the weeks go by, and more and more boys start getting high, and more and more girls start getting boobs, and the days get hotter, there seems to be more and more things happening. Guys and girls make out more, but guys seem to be getting into fights more. And since none of the guys like to fight their friends, they seem to be picking fights with kids outside our group. Doesn't matter who they are. But if we don't know them, and they look different than we do, there's a good chance that Bobby Bailey or Tommy Kowalzyck, or a new kid on the block, Paul Kilker, is going to pick a fight. And I don't like it. But who am I to stop them?

I'm kind of pissed off because my mother told me that my cousins Jimmy and Walter aren't coming to our graduation party. Elizabeth is, but the boys aren't because they have to go somewhere that night. I doubt it. But to tell you the truth, probably when I'm graduating from Cardinal Hayes High

School in 1968, the last thing I'd want to do is go to an 8th grader's graduation party. I'm glad that Elizabeth is coming, but that's because she likes my sister, and it is her party too. And I've got so many things to do that day, I don't plan on being there the whole time either. So screw Jimmy. And Walter too.

Why is it that graduation is on a Saturday, then you still have school next week? It is just half days until Wednesday, but still why can't they let you just make a clean break? And they don't even give you a real diploma. They say it's because if somebody failed, they don't want them to be embarrassed, not getting a diploma when everybody else does, and have kids crying their eyes out when they get surprised with a blank piece of paper while other kids are throwing their hats in the air after reading their diplomas. Bull. It's because if they hand you that diploma, you could just turn around and yell "Drop dead, Sister Fidelis!" and run down the aisle giving every nun the finger, and maybe even moon them if you wanted. You've got the diploma, who cares! And what better forum for revenge on the nuns while all the parents are sitting there thinking we're all just a nice bunch of little future nuns and priests all dressed up in our caps and gowns, when most of us are ready to go berserk. But we can't really. Those nuns are no dummies. Hold onto the diploma until Wednesday. The very last day. You've got to be able to hold something over our heads, or else. They know it, and we know it. And I can't believe tomorrow is graduation. Tomorrow will be great. And tonight won't be so bad either.

Whitey turns around with his index finger over his mouth and goes "ssshhhhh" as he plops a folded note onto my desk. I open it up, and there's a drawing of a plump kid not looking unlike Whitey at all, holding up a quart of Rheingold and burping. The balloon above his head reads, "Big party tonight! In the stands!!!"

Wow. The stands. That's where the big kids hang out. At the Van Cortlandt Park football field there's a huge concrete grandstand on one side. And that is where you go after

197

you realize that you can't hang out on your block anymore. Because you start doing stuff that goes beyond Mr. Santirocco sticking his head out the window and yelling, "Hey you kids! Shut up!" Now it's more than likely Mr. Santirocco, or Mrs. Ryan, or Mrs. Kwykelski would stick their head out the window and just gasp and get on the phone to the 5-0 (that's the 50th precinct). Kids drinking, smoking, sniffing, or hands down pants of girlfriends or up shirts or who the hell knows what might be going on. So not so much in the best interest of Mr. Santirocco or Mrs. Ryan or Mrs. Kwykelski, kids just graduate to the park for their own benefit. And tonight, it looks like we're graduating.

You could tell by the number of folded-up pieces of paper being tossed from one desk to the next that word was getting around fast. Of course, you already know which kids wouldn't show up. You could pretty much guess that if by now they haven't walked by the stumps where we hang out, or if we didn't see them hanging out in the other neighborhood hideaways, like next to the railroad tracks under the bridge, or in the fort by the cow path, or at the seesaws or park benches at least once, no way are they going to show up at the stands tonight. It's not the kind of place you show up on your first night of hanging out. Even the most gifted of baseball players rarely goes right up to the majors. They make a big deal out of Ed Kranepool doing it on the Mets. He went right from high school right here in New York to playing for the Mets. But that's because it's the Mets. Believe me, any other team in the majors would've sent him riding busses and eating Spam out of the can in the minors just so his head wouldn't be too big. But the Mets stink so bad, a kid with talent like Kranepool might as well take over for the broken down war-horses the Mets have playing for them. Maybe in a few years some of the young guys will turn in to something. At least that's what my dad says.

A kid can't just show up in the stands. There are big kids there. And not just high school kids, either. Some of them don't even go to school. Some have full-time jobs. My brother used to hang out there when he dropped out of school, and worked full time, but since he got married and has a baby on the way he doesn't seem to hang out anymore. That's good for me. I just know that if he was up there, he'd kick my ass for being there. But since he's not there, people know that I'm his kid brother, and that's worth plenty. They won't be bothering me. But if the older guys don't know you, or have seen you around and don't like you, or find out that you're related to someone who they don't like, it could mean real trouble. Big trouble.

I never thought so much about clothes in my life. I've got stuff in my drawers that I just won't wear anymore. Pants can't be baggy. I won't wear them. Lucky for me my mother's a good sewer, and if the pants are real baggy, she throws them onto her Singer sewing machine and makes them tighter. Sneakers are OK for everyday playing, but at night you've got to have something cool. Like pointy shoes with big heels. But the hardest part of looking cool is hair. I know my cousin Jimmy and his friends downtown almost all have the floppy, combed forward look that The Beatles have, but around here, although some guys still have the slicked-back Elvis-Dion-Fabian look, most guys have more of the "Beach Boys" parted-on-the-side, longer-on-top, hanging-in- the-eyes no grease kind of look. Still. I don't know how Whitey's brother Alfie gets along with the usual guys who hang out, because there's nobody else around here that has hair like him: wild. Except maybe for the Jewish kids from up by Pigeon Park, but everybody knows what happens to them. So tonight, I'll be wearing my tight black pants and pointy shoes, but won't have the floppy Beatles look or the slicked-back Elvis look. Something in-between. And without asking, I just know that Whitey will have almost the same look, as will Bobby Bailey, Ralphie, Jimmy Joe, BB, Paul Kilker, and any other guy who wants to fit in to the crowd that hangs in the stands and not hear "Hey, look at the faggot" or "What are you supposed to be? A fuckin' Beatle" because shortly after you hear something like that, you can kiss your ass good-bye.

199

Whitey's elevator is broken again, and as I walk up the six flights, I can hear the sounds of an argument get louder and louder. There's no need to put my ear to Whitey's cold steel door. It's obvious that his father is not in Florida, but very much at home, drunk and not in a good mood. I can hear his mother saying, "Get away from me. Don't you dare raise a hand to me." His dad is barely coherent, saying something about how he doesn't want to come home from work to a filthy bathroom and who the hell is taking care of this goddamned dump anyway? I'm not sure if I should knock. Luckily I don't have to. The door opens, and Whitey comes out. "Let's get out of here," he says as he leads me down the six flights three steps at a time. I don't ask about what I heard, and Whitey doesn't offer as we make our way down the street towards the park and our initiation into what could be our future. I don't even ask why his father isn't in Florida yet.

"They're packing to go upstate for the summer," Whitey says matter of factly.

"Are they leaving without you?" I ask, not able to imagine my parents doing something like that.

"Yeah. Tonight." Whitey confesses. "I'm glad. At least it'll be quiet for a while. My brother'll be in charge."

I didn't even want to know any more details for the rest of the walk. A block before the park is Review Place. A small street with buildings even older than mine or Whitey's. The kids on the street here, whether really small kids just learning how to play jacks or Chinese school, or kids just a step or two away from hanging out in the stands, always seem a little dirtier and more ragtag than the kids on my block. And the kids on my block aren't exactly Sears Catalog either, believe me. It really reminds of that movie "Dead End" on this block.

As we get closer, I can see Bobby Bailey and Tommy Kowalzyck leaning up against the building, cupping their cigarettes so they're hard to see. Bobby's really got nerve because the building he's leaning up against is his building. "Hi, Bobby, hi Tommy. Going to the stands?" I ask. Bobby and Kowalzyck both give that big head-nod up, without saying hello, and blow smoke out of their noses.

"Yeah, we're going, but we've got to do something before we go," Bobby says while his eyes scan the street and the windows above for big eared spies.

"Like what?" Whitey asks.

"Like get some beer. For nothing," Kowalzyck says with smoke billowing out of his mouth.

Oh shit. We aren't even through the park gates yet, and we're already planning something that at the very least can get us whacked in the shins with police billy clubs. "Oh, and how's that going to happen?" I ask.

"Clooney's going to put 12 cases of Rheingold out in the back garbage of Connelly's in a half hour. We're going to get them and bring them to the stands," Bobby informs us.

It makes sense. Clooney is in high school, and he's a real drinker. He works in Connelly's grocery store, and at the back door, they usually have a huge pile of garbage consisting of broken-up fruit crates, and cardboard boxes, and all kinds of grocery store garbage. Old man Connelly has had that store for forty years, and he's about 80 years old, and needless to say, doesn't keep very good inventory. It would be easy to hide 12 cases in there if you did it right. At least we're not going to rob a beer truck or something.

"How are we going to get the beer to the stands?" Whitey asks.

"We're each going to grab three cases and walk up Broadway," Bobby says, like he's revealing a big, thought-out plot.

Going right up Broadway probably is the best way. It's underneath the ""el," and for some reason you just feel like you're not being seen with all that traffic and the cover of the "el" overhead with its dark steel rattling.

So after Kowalzyck, Bobby, and Whitey smoke a half pack of cigarettes, and we talk about Ann Cunningham's boobs, Mickey Mantle's chance of hitting more homers that Maris this year, and what girls probably go all the way, the half hour is up, and it's time to pick up 12 cases of beer, and either be a hero to a stadium filled with kids, or get the shit beat out of me by an overweight cop, my mother, and my father, and in that order.

"Let's go," Bobby says as he snuffs out his cigarette against the brick wall and leads us to the garbage pile that is our destiny. The taps on the heels of his shoes are like the street beat of a marching band as we march off to war.

The entrance to Connelly's is on 238th Street. But around the corner on Broadway, there's a rear door to the deli where every night all the garbage is placed. There aren't any store fronts adjacent to the deli door there, so it's pretty out of the way, which is why Connelly likes to put the garbage there I guess.

Whitey and me are right behind Bobby and Kowalzyck, and I can tell by the pink color of Whitey's face that he's just as nervous as I am. We walk right past the big stinky pile of garbage, smelling of rotten vegetables and wet cardboard that juts out five feet into the sidewalk piled almost up to the top of the doorway, and almost down to the next corner. Bobby and Kowalzyck stop. We almost knock them over. "Shheeesh, what are you guys doing?" I whisper to the two idiot ring leaders.

Bobby has this way of acting much older than his 14 years. He can even raise one eyebrow really high, and lower the other one while he takes a long drag on his Marlboro like some kind of little Ben Casey telling us that he has to perform open heart surgery. "Wwooooooooosht" is the sucking sound he makes while doing the eyebrow thing, and snapping his tongue at the end of his long draw on his cigarette. "Let's just stand here for a minute, and make sure the coast is clear."

Bobby keeps his eyebrows in that cockeyed position as his eyes scan from one side of the street to the other, and up to the "el" right above us without turning his head. "Let's go." And like Sergeant Saunders in "Combat," he leads us into battle. His taps are even louder with the force of his quick-paced walk, to the garbage pile and right face! Into the pile he goes, with Kowalzyck, me and Whitey right at this heels. Now it really stinks. Bobby quietly pushes aside some fruit crates filled with smelly rags and rotten fruit and believe it or not, there are two towers of Rheingold beer carefully camouflaged in the middle of this putrid mess. Bobby picks up three cases, turns and is gone up Broadway. "Crap, hurry up!" I say, knowing that time is of the essence now. It's dark out and the "el" is rumbling by, but there are many, many ways for me to get busted along with the other guys, especially since I'm last in line. Kowalzyck grabs his stack of three and splits. Whitey reaches in, grabs three, turns around and says, "Take these and go," as he hands them off to me, and not being one to argue, I'm off. Bobby and Kowalzyck are a half block ahead of me already. Once we get to the park we'll be home free, and it's just a block and a half away.

I turn around and Whitey is behind me, laughing uncontrollably as he hurries to catch up with me.

I'm not laughing at all. All I can think about is Mr. Connelly, running up Broadway with Prince the German shepherd grocery store dog chasing us, or a cop car cruising by seeing two 13 year olds with peg leg pants and Beatle boots running with 12 cases of beer. But Whitey is laughing like he's having the time of his life. "Whitey, are you nuts?"

"Aw shit, if you don't think this is fun, it ain't worth doing," He says between chortles.

The park entrance is across the street. Once we're in the cover of the park's darkness we're home free. And we are. The park is pitch black, thanks to kids busting the overhead lamps with baseball bats. The cover of darkness is essential. They've stopped trying to replace the lamps because they just get smashed that same night. Just ahead I can see two dark red tips of cigarettes being sucked and glowing. Bobby and Kowalzyck are sitting on their loot, enjoying a smoke like two pirates on their treasure chests.

"What kept you guys? Let's go," Bobby says as he stands with his cigarette dangling from his mouth, lifting his three cases and leading our parade of purloined Rheingold.

We did it. And just beyond that dark cast-iron gate is the "stands." I can already hear the deep voices of grown-up guys, not the school yard shrieks of kids playing "what's in the ice box?" or "red rover" or "freeze tag" but the husky, hearty laughs of teenagers. And the laughs of teenage girls right along with them. Not giggly little grammar school girls. Boy, are we going to make an impression, marching Beatle booted with 12 cases of free beer to high school kids, high school drop-outs, and even some college kids.

The giant concrete stands stretch the entire length of the football field. And there must be a half-dozen different groups of kids hanging out, each with their own radios blaring, cigarettes glowing, beer and wine flowing. The closer to the entrance gate, the younger the bunch. The really old kids are all the way at the end.

I 've heard stories about what goes on down that end. Guys having sex right there in the open with their girls, pot smoking, and I even heard that people take hard drugs down there. With needles. And every once in a while, a cop car comes into the park with all the lights out, trying to sneak up on them in the dark. But from the top of the stands, you can see anything approaching and there's plenty of time to run across the football field and the baseball field, down to the railroad tracks, and into an infinite number of hiding places or escape routes. I think there are even guys who hang out up there who have done stick-ups at liquor stores and gas stations. I don't think I'll be going down that end this evening.

Kowalzyck and Bobby have been here before. I know that I'll probably know everybody in the group from hanging out, or from class, but still I'm nervous being that this is my first time in the stands. If somebody is drunk, and doesn't like my shoes, or my brother, or is just in the mood for a fight, and he thinks I'm just about the right size to beat up, it could mean trouble.

"Ho ho ho, Merry Christmas, everybody!" Bobby yells to the first group of kids about halfway up.

"Whoah, yeah!" "Alright!" "Hallelujah" and all kinds of shouts of joy come out of the darkness followed by the sounds of sneakers, and heels with taps as they stampede towards us. The commotion has spread to the next group over, and about half of that group jumps up and is on the way over to check us out. In fact, each group all the way down sends over a scout or two to check out what the youngest kids are up to. The only group that doesn't look like they can be bothered is the one all the way down at the end.

We're heroes. My first time here and what an entrance. Cardboard six packs are being ripped apart, and cans of Rheingold are being opened so fiercely it sounds like lady fingers firecrackers exploding. The twelve cases are in two towers of six, and instead of 3 or 4 bunches of kids hanging out, there's now one big party going on around the twin can towers. The three or four radios that just a few minutes earlier were competing for dominance are now all tuned to the Good Guys on WMCA blasting the raspy vocals of The Beatles singing "Twist and Shout".

I look around and see kids from my class. Mostly from Review Place. There's Kevin Flynn and Paul Donnegan, and Mary Alice McElwain, and Eileen Tessitore. There are even a few of the tougher kids from the 7th grade like Frankie Meeney, and Billy Cuddy. But mostly everybody is in high school. Even some seniors. And the four of us are being treated like returning war heroes. All kinds of "thanks man" "good job" "atta way" and pats on the back, but most of all, recognition. I'm no longer a little 8th grade putz. Carry 3 cases of free beer into the park, and you are definitely one of the gang.

What a night. These kids know how to have fun. Not little-kid fun, but real fun. Everybody laughs like crazy when Bobby Bailey, who has been smoking and drinking nonstop goes down to the track to take a leak and starts throwing his guts up. And Billy Cuddy is so drunk, he fell down a flight of concrete steps. That would've been a lot funnier if he didn't bleed so much. But he's fine. Really.

I have to take a piss myself and decide to go a little bit away from the crowd, around the corner of the stadium. I'm far enough way so that can I can have some privacy, and right in the middle of the "y" as I squirt my name in the dirt, I'm tapped on the shoulder. I immediately shove my thing back into my BVDs, fully expecting to see Whitey standing there with a goofy look on his face and maybe a six pack cardboard box on his head, but instead, see two very mean, very Puerto Rican-looking guys probably 21 years old. Crap. What now?

205

Before I could do anything the shorter stockier of the two reaches out to grab me, and demands, "Give me your money." I don't know how I did it, maybe from the years of training avoiding grabs from people playing "ringo- leaveo" but even though he grabbed my arm, I managed to squirm my way out of his grip, and tear ass out of there. They chased me down the length of the wall, but didn't turn the corner with me. I ran around that corner screaming for help. "Two Puerto Ricans tried to kill me!"

"What! Where? How? Let's go!"

About 20 guys run across the football field, the base-ball field, and through a hole in a chain-link fence towards two dark figures running full speed down the path. "Get the fucking spics!" I hear Bobby Bailey yell as he leads the charge with 3 or 4 guys right with him. "That's them," I yell, wanting instant justice. Just as the wedge of guys is about to grab the two dark strangers, they turn around, and SPROING, even in the dark-ness you could see two switch blades as the two hold their ground, fending off a group of drunken teenagers seeking revenge.

"Back off, motherfuckers!" one of the PRs yells. Our group is frozen. For a moment. Then out of the middle of the pack a quart bottle of Rheingold comes flying through the dark-ness, spinning end over end in slow motion, spilling beer with each spin and THWACK, hits one of the crooks right in his face dead square, exploding in a burst of beer, glass, and then blood. The other guy runs and doesn't turn back, and is lost in the railroad track brush. The other guy falls like a sack of potatoes onto the path, his knife next to him. He's uncon-scious. Our gang is silent. I have the same kind of feeling I had the first time I actually hit a pigeon with a rock after trying to hit one hundreds of times. The pigeon fell off the ledge and hit the ground. It just laid there, motionless. I was in shock. Oh dear God, please. I'll never do this again. Please let it live. It did. It got up and flew away. I kept my part of the bargain.

Bobby walks over to the bloody bad guy, and screams, "Fuck you, you fuckin' motherfucker!" We all watch him in silence. Bobby looks like he's ready to explode. Fists clenched.

206

Arms shaking. He reaches down and picks up the switch blade. "You fuckin' motherfucker!" Bobby holds the knife with white knuckles and reaches down to the guy, who's just starting to moan as he comes to, and grabs the guy's hair, holding his head back, exposing the full length of his white neck in the darkness. I'm paralyzed. The world has stopped. Next to my ear I hear a blood-curdling "NOOOOOOOO" as Whitey lunges towards Bobby, tackling him, and wrestling the knife from him. Whitey picks up the knife and tosses it with all his might into the marshy brush of the railroad tracks. "Shelley, what the hell is the matter with you?" Bobby screams at Whitey. Whitey doesn't say a word. The Puerto Rican guy is coming to. Whitey goes over and helps him up. Me and a couple of other guys go over and help him too. Once he realizes where he is, and sees the blood, he just silently backs away from us, and also disappears into the railroad marshes.

We all turn around and walk back to the stands. Nobody's laughing now. Especially not Bobby. Or Whitey.

Back at the stands, the small group that was around our Rheingold shrine has grown into a huge gathering of 40 or 50. And the twin towers of beer are gone. All that remains is cardboard. But the beer is in full evidence all around, with just about everybody in the group stewed to the gills.

"Hey you assholes!" a voice from the darkness yells, approaching our free beer blast. Mike Clooney, the deli worker risking his job for the sake of seeing every teenager in the neighborhood bombed thanks to him, is off work, and carrying 4 cases of Schaeffer, and right next to him is Fitzy Fitzgerald, also with 4 cases of Schaeffer. I'll bet they didn't buy them, either.

"Where the hell is the beer we put out?" Clooney wants to know as he walks up the steps to the middle of the pack.

"Can't you smell it?" Bobby yells.

"All I smell is piss!" Clooney responds.

"You got that right!" Bobby shouts back, cracking himself up in a fit of laughter.

I like Clooney all right. He's not really mean, although once in a while when he tries to outdo Fitzgerald's depraved sense of humor, he can be dangerous. And that's when they're sober.

Fitzgerald never lets me and Whitey forget that time in the basement when he tricked me and Whitey into thinking we were going to see Tina Robustelli naked, and wound up getting bombed with water balloons. So I think I'll just stay in the background. And come to think of it, where is Whitey?

Up at the very top of the stands, you can look over a wall that looks out across Broadway. You can see the "el" and Manhattan College and the skyscrapers of Riverdale. Whitey's up there by himself. Staring off into night. As a train goes by just in front of us, the sound is deafening, and the sparks illuminate Whitey's face like many bolts of lightning.

"You're not drinking anymore?" I ask Whitey.

"Nah."

"Me neither."

Whitey isn't even looking at me. And a whole minute goes by before he talks.

"I almost killed that guy," Whitey says in a whisper.

"Shit, you threw the bottle?"

"Yeah. It scared the hell out of me."

"Me too."

"I wanted to kill Bobby."

"Me too." I say. I think Whitey's crying a little. Crap, that's all I need. Maybe he isn't.

"You've got to admit, though," Whitey says, more like himself, "that was a hell of a shot."

The party atmosphere is turning crazy. Fitzgerald is jumping up and down and screaming about collecting bottles, and going on a rampage through Riverdale. That's all I need to top off my evening. I think I've seen one bottle too many whipping through the air already tonight.

Whitey and I quietly head out of the park, and back through the neighborhood to the stumps. It's late now. About midnight. There's hardly any traffic and not a soul around. The alley where we spend so much of our time playing ball, and cards, and reading Playboys looks dark and scary. Whitey's got a small transistor radio, and it's on real low. We're not even talking. Just listening. And just above us a window opens. I know it has to be Mr. Santirocco.

"Hey, you kids, get the hell out of here before I call the cops."

Whitey and I look at each other. "You want to go home?" I ask Whitey.

"Not really. But I guess I ought to."

"Yeah, me too," I agree, admitting defeat. We didn't have the kind of night we had hoped for, but tomorrow is graduation. So we both go to our sleeping homes.

Fortunately, I didn't get in any trouble. I'll hear about Whitey in the morning.

"Get the hell out of bed this instant," my mother screams right into my ear, accompanied by the worst most brutal of all wake-up procedures. "The Poke." Please, anything but the poke. Pour ice water on my head, put roaches down my shorts, put an M-80 under my pillow, but please oh please don't POKE! Oh no... here it comes!

"I said NOW! (POKE) I just ironed your shirt for you. (POKE) Everything is ready, you've got to eat something (POKE POKE) I've got to make the bed. Go take a shower. Don't mess up the bathroom I just cleaned it (POKE POKE). And put all that crap on the chest 'o drawers away" (POKE POKE POKE).

"All right, all right, I'm up. Stop poking."

"You get out of bed, the poking stops."

I look over to the other side of the room, and my sister's bed is already made. Her privacy blanket that she drapes across the bed is neatly folded on the bed. And I just know she's sitting in the kitchen, probably eating some Entenmman's coffee cake, or worse yet, the chocolate-covered donuts. How they get away with calling that a breakfast "food" I'll never know. There's about an inch of chocolate on those donuts, and when you bite into it, it cracks just like you're biting into an Easter bunny or something.

My sister always gets up real early to get ready. That's

209

one way to get at least a little bit of privacy around here. She's been marking the days left until she goes away to college on a calendar. I can't wait either. Finally my own room. My parents will stay on the Castro in the living room, and I'll have my own freaking room. Maybe I'll even be able to get my own desk, if we get rid of something in here. There's not an inch of space that's not used. Dressers, shelves, bunk beds, a cart with a TV that you have to move around if you want to get into a closet or a drawer. My old toy box, which is this massive plywood box that my father built, is now filled with canned Italian tomatoes, toilet paper, paper towels, cans of vegetables, soup, and juice, and anything else that was marked for clearance in Safeway at a ridiculously low price.

One entire wall is a huge closet, with sliding doors, and a cabinet on top that goes right up to the ceiling that my father also built. There's stuff in there that no one has been able to look at for years, unless you spend about a half-hour on a ladder, and take everything out.

It's easy to dress for graduation. The same white shirt, blue tie with the embroidered "PS" centered on the front that's starting to unravel, and blue pants. Same outfit I've worn for eight years. But at least I have peg leg pants. And cool Beatle boots with taps on the heels.

"You're not wearing those stupid Bee-UL boots." I don't know why, but both my parents have a hard time saying the word "Beatle." It comes out "BEEE-ULLLL."

"Yes, I am. It's allowed!"

"I said no! Everyone's going to look so beautiful in their caps and gowns, and there you go sounding like a tap dancer doing a ball and chain down the church aisle. NO!"

"Everyone's got them! I'm telling you, I'll look stupid if I DON'T wear them!"

Oh, why can't she understand? It's bad enough to be wearing the stupid school uniform, and the gown, and the dumb hat! I've got to wear the boots with the taps on the heels.

"I don't care, you're not wearing them, now put on your old school shoes!"

She hit the nail right on the head. The OLD school

shoes. The ones I used to wear. Before I was cool. Before I was in a room where people smoked grass. Before The Beatles got off the plane in New York wearing Beatle boots.

"They don't fit!" I lied.

"Alright, put on those damn stupid Bee-ull boots!"

I don't know why, but I feel embarrassed. Not embarrassed because I'm wearing this stupid mortar and tassel on my head, or a long gown. But embarrassed to be in the back seat of a car, driving down my street with my family. It's weird. I'm actually afraid somebody is going to see me with my family... like I'm not supposed to be seen with them outside my apartment. I don't get it. I certainly love my parents, even my brother and my sister. And I don't feel weird when we're at home, or we have company, or even if we're driving somewhere that's out of the neighborhood where nobody knows me. But coming down this stupid street, West 238th Street, Bronx 63, New York, for some reason, I don't want people who I don't even hang out with, to see me in this car with my own family. It's like I'm afraid that if they see me with them, they might think that I'm like them. Not like me. Maybe it's just that we drive a red-and-white 1948 Ford Country Squire station wagon with really noisy springs.

Even getting out of the car at the Church parking lot, I feel uncomfortable. So, "See ya!" I say to my own flesh and blood, as I dart over to a group of friends, also avoiding their families. Except for the sissy kids like Mark Fay. He's yukking it up with his parents, and Sister Annunciata, who we had in 3rd grade. God, I hope she doesn't come over here.

And now the time has come. Sister Fidelis rings the hand-held bell, just like at recess, and we automatically know to line up in silence. I just pray to God Almighty this is the last time I'll ever have to do this, and that nobody I know who's already in high school walks by. Amen.

Presentation Church is right next to Presentation School. The church and the school are almost interchangeable. Both boxy rectangles made of red brick and cinder blocks. They were both opened a long time ago, around 1950. They're named

211

after The Presentation of Mary in the Temple, whatever that means. There are some kids in the neighborhood who aren't Catholic and don't go to Presentation. And they think we're rich or something because we don't go to public school. What they don't realize is that it's free to go to our school. Oh, your parents do have to put money in collection basket at church every Sunday, but that's it. And it doesn't even have to be a certain amount. I guess that's why every classroom is filled to the rafters with all kinds of kids. I know for a fact that some kids live in huge private houses with yards and big cherry trees, and grapevines, and even have two-car garages. But I also know that there's a Chinese family named the Hands, and they lived in a house that had a dirt floor until just a couple of years ago. And their parent's used to grow vegetables in the backyard, and sometimes even went through the garbage looking for stuff. It's true that they moved and now live in a nice private home, but my mother says that's because their father has a Chinese laundry where he works 16 hours a day and probably doesn't pay any taxes. But most of the kids live in roach infested pre-war absentee landlord, radiator banging, fire escape sitting, plaster peeling, paint chipping, stopped up plumbing, elevator not working, tiny little boxes just like we do.

We're all lined up outside the Church in our usual size places. I can hear the organ music playing happy music. Not the dreary stuff they usually play on normal Sundays or at funerals. The nuns are all whispering to each other, pointing, nodding, and then taking off into the Church to relay the message to someone else. And bellowing out of the Church comes the first notes of "Pomp and Circumstance." Sister Fidelis takes a stand directly in front of our whole class. She holds up both hands shoulder high, with her palms facing us just like the statue of Jesus that fell on Robert Damrow's head. And for the first time, I can sense a feeling of desperation from her. She's looking at us in a different way. As if she's helpless, and she actually needs us, as she says, "Class, please behave, please." She lowers her hands and just looks at us. It seemed to me to be the first time that she ever asked us for something in such a way. She tried to make eye contact with as many kids as she could.

When her eyes met mine, I felt for the first time that she was actually a person. And this person was asking us... no... me, to help her out. To behave. And for the first time, I think we all understood and would actually give it a shot.

The Church feels different today. I've never seen it so packed with really dressed-up people, except for weddings. Funerals have people who are dressed up, but there's usually only about five rows of them. Then there's always about six old ladies in the last row of the church who don't pray along with the funeral mass, but mumble the rosary the whole time. And, it's always the same six old ladies. They don't say the rosary together, either. They just mumble along, creating a jumbled, echoing holy sound like a bunch of monks or something.

I could tell everybody else felt that today was different. Whitey wasn't slouched over, shuffling along. His head was erect. Chest out. Chin up. Even Deborah Laturza, who so many times was disgraced in class for being fat, smelly, stupid and weird, looked dignified, except for the tiny oatmeal stain on her gown that probably nobody else noticed. For the first time in all the eight years of grammar school, I felt like we were a group. A class. We made it.

Miss Schmelzer played the church organ like a real professional. There was a group of kids from other classes who sang the songs up front, and they sounded like they rehearsed and everything.

And I could see parents with tears in their eyes. Fathers in poorly fitting brown suits and stained ties standing tall, and winking at their kids when they caught their eye. Grandmas and grandpas wiping tears from eyes. Even little brothers and sisters looking in awe. For the first time I realized we were actually accomplishing something in our lives. Some of the people watching probably never even graduated from grammar school. And for some of the kids graduating, this just might be the greatest achievement in their academic life.

We've had ceremonies like this before, I guess. First Holy Communion in the 2nd grade was similar, but to tell you the truth, we were all pretty much scared to death in the 2nd grade, and in the 4th grade for Confirmation. We did just about anything they told us to do. But since about the 6th grade, kids started to realize that making fart noises, or spitting paper wads, or tying somebody's shoelaces together was not only fun, but worth the risk of getting caught. The thrill of making the right people laugh outweighed the danger of getting caught. So by the 8th grade, the majority of kids figure, "What the hell. Let's have some fun. Screw it. So what if I get in a little trouble. There's stuff that needs to be done."

But today, it seems like everybody is behaving because they want to. Man, this is going to be a weird summer.

The great thing about getting older is almost everybody understands that the best present one can give is cash. There's an awkward time of cheap, ugly clothes that comes immediately after the time your relatives aren't sure if giving toys is too babyish. But once they see you wearing peg leg pants, and listening to rock and roll, they know there's nothing left to do but give cash. Besides, it's a lot easier. Of course, there's always one relative who insists on giving you a made-in-Hong Kong dress shirt in that weird crispy cellophane on the $1.99 table at S. Klein or worse yet, John's Bargain Store.

John's Bargain Stores are all over the city and they have the cheapest junk imaginable. Everything is on tables with no rhyme or reason, like this corner is for men's underwear that falls apart after one wash, and this wall over here is for toys that are so cheap they'd break the first time you threw one at your friend's little brother. Stuff is just scattered throughout the store on tables that have these handmade signs painted with red and black paint. In fact, at the back of the store, there's a table with plastic jars of black and red paint and thick paint brushes where the workers actually make the signs by hand. I wonder if that's the kind of job you get if you go to art school? Unless you're really, really cheap, you don't buy anything there except the absolute most basic things like, rubber bands, hangers, and water pistols. But there's not a time when we go down to 231st Street when we go in that store to look at what kind of bargains they have that day. And it's only the last couple of years that I know what junk really is that I refuse to wear the clothes they sell. I remember my mom getting pissed off at me the first time I said I wouldn't wear the plaid shorts that were on sale for 99 cents.

And now, even my parents get ticked when Aunt Gina gives me a shirt that came from John's Bargain Store. She'll even put it in a Gimbel's box to trick us, but there's no mistaking those crappy shirts in those crispy cellophane wrappers with straight pins every two inches.

But thank goodness everybody else hands me an envelope with cash. A couple of relatives even give me those smaller envelopes that are the exact same size as paper money, and have cards that aren't really cards, but just holders for bills, with an oval cutout that shows you which dead president you got as soon as you open it. No phony poems like, *On this very special day, you are finally on your way! Graduation time is here, for someone we hold near and dear!* Just open the card and there are the words we want to see: "Legal Tender."

And the coolest thing is usually when an Uncle, who's been sitting in the kitchen drinking milk glasses of whiskey, shakes your hand and sneaks a 10 dollar bill into your palm, usually mumbling something like, "Go and have some fun, kid."

Lucky for me, my sister is the one who is getting most of the attention from everybody, since she graduated from high school, but I'm getting just as many envelopes, without as much work. And once everybody has dropped off the cash, and stuffed their faces, I know it's time for the real fun to start. Open-house graduation party time.

Get a bunch of guys together at a meeting place, like today's flagpoles in the park, all dressed up in their coolest clothes, taps on their pointy big-heeled shoes, Brylcream in their hair, and there's bound to be trouble. I just know it. Guys really like to show off, especially when they're dressed up and they know everybody's looking.

Whitey's standing in front of his stoop waiting for me. That's good. Not just because I don't like going up to the top

215

floor of his building, but lately, you never know what's going on in his house.

Me and Whitey are probably the only two kids without Brylcream in their hair. Except for the few who actually still have crew cuts. We both have that look that The Beach Boys have. No grease, long in front, almost in the eyes, and always having to push it out of your eyes. I think the only person with a Beatles haircut in the whole neighborhood is Whitey's brother Alfie. Almost everybody else has the usual Ricky Nelson, Elvis after the Army, Jeff Stone on The Donna Reed Show, greased-back look. There are still a few of the really greasy pompadour pre-Army-Elvis guys around, but they're the older high school dropout guys. There are fewer and fewer of them around. In fact most of them are actually getting married, work in gas stations or down at the Kingsbridge chain link fence company, and have big beer bellies.

The fact that we're meeting at the flagpoles is also a clue that this is going to be a memorable night. The flagpoles are usually where you meet for a fight, or to go drinking, or to meet on Halloween night and decide exactly what kind of terror we intend to inflict on passing busses, kids younger than us, and groups of people more than a half block away that look like they don't have anyone who can catch us.

"You think the guys are drinking tonight?" I ask Whitey without even saying hello, as he jumps down from his perch on the concrete wall connected to the picket fence around the front courtyard of his building.

"Absolutely. That's got to be why we're meeting at the flagpoles, otherwise, we'd just meet on Review."

Review is the corner of Review Place and 238th Street. That would be the most central location of the neighborhood in public view. But the flagpoles, about two blocks away in the park, are the most central location not in public view. Whitey's right.

"Are you drinking tonight?" Whitey asks me as we automatically cross the street where we always do, taking the same route we take to school everyday.

"Nah. My parent's will be looking out for it tonight.

When my brother graduated from 8th grade, he puked in the Madonna flower pot that my mother keeps artificial flowers in on top of the TV in the living room. Plus doing the twist with beer in your stomach isn't such a good idea."

"I don't think I'll drink, either," Whitey says as we cross from in front of the Church where we graduated that very afternoon, into the park directly across the streets, where the flagpoles are. I can already see a crowd of 10 or 15 guys near the poles. And I can see some of them holding the brown paper bags that a six pack of beer fits perfectly inside of. Ten or fifteen guys is practically every boy in our entire class. There are about thirty five girls in our class. We used to be more even, but the past couple of years, more guys seemed to either get left back or moved, or got kicked out.

It looks like just about all of the boys are here. The guys you'd expect, of course, Bobby Bailey, Kowalzyck, Jimmy Joe, Ralphie, BB, each of whom have a brown paper bag, but then there are some surprises, like Jerome Mullooly, and Mark Fay, and Robert Damrow, who usually aren't even allowed to come out day or night. And guys like Gerard Adams, and Joey Trotta, who are the big jocks in class, and don't like hanging out unless it's for a serious game of basketball, baseball or football. Then there are the other guys like Brian McCabe, Tommy Manton, and Tony DiNardo, who hang out once in a while, but actually study, and seem to take school work seriously. From a distance it looks as though it's one big happy family, but as we get closer it's obvious that the beer drinkers are in one group, the jocks in another, the fags in another, and the smart guys in another. Screw it. Me and Whitey will bounce around. That's the way we like it.

There aren't any girls here. They're probably all at the first party, at Irene Esposito's house. But I'll bet there's one or two, like maybe Cathy Vitelli and Donna Murphy, who are in the basement of their building having a couple of sips of Rheingold right now. I hope there's even more than that, because everybody knows what happens when girls drink. At least I hear everybody knows.

Somehow, without an announcement, everybody leaves

together, all in one big group, beer cans and bags left behind, except for the odd can or two stuffed into a suit jacket inside pocket, off to enjoy the night we've been waiting for. Oh, we've all been to parties before. I've had some kids over a few times just as a couple of other kids have, and we've met places like forts to hang out in groups, but you pretty much knew what to expect at those. But tonight is different. For some reason, parents let kids come over that on other days of the year, they'd be yelling at their sons and daughters if they were seen on a street corner with them. I can't believe that Irene Esposito, who lives in a brand new apartment building on the 25th floor, with an indoor parking garage, fancy elevators and a master antenna on the roof, is going to let all of us into her home with her parents there, and maybe even some relatives. And Joanne Martorana too. Her parents don't let her out of the house at all unless it involves some kind of church or school related activity, and we're invited there too. I don't know what it is about big events like this that makes parents all of a sudden let kids do things that they don't let them do for years. But to tell you the truth, we look like a pretty neat bunch all dressed up. You couldn't tell from just looking at us that some of the guys downed a few cans of Rheingold, and are probably going to drink a lot more before the night is over and punch or throw something somewhere. And that a few more of us would do anything to get somebody's daughter into an alley or darkened doorway or up on a roof and see how far she'd go. As if that might happen. Yet some others in this group are probably making mental notes of everything that's going on to squeal to nuns, priests or parents at a later date. But we're all marching up 238th Street like some kind of peg legged marching band, celebrating the end of eight years of confinement, mental torture, and threats known as grammar school. *"Behave or I'll put this liquid on you and it will turn you into a frog!"* *"Memorize your multiplication tables or I'll put you down in the dungeon with the spanking machine!"* *"If you eat meat on Friday, that's a mortal sin, and you'll burn in hell forever!"* *"Touching yourself when you go to the bathroom is a filthy, disgusting animal act AND it's a sin!"* *"Only Catholics go to heaven;*

218

so if one of your parents is not a Catholic, or was excommunicated because they were divorced, they cannot enter heaven and you will be separated for all eternity." *"Viva Las Vegas is rated C on the Legion of Decency list, which means condemned, which means if you see it, it's a mortal sin!"* Will we keep hearing these threats and warnings forever? Maybe. But at least now, I think I can tell when I'm being lied to. Sometimes.

The one thing that worries me about going to Irene Esposito's house is that the building she lives in is right next to the area with all the Jewish kids we call J.T. I just hope we don't run into any Jewish kids with Beatle haircuts, because I know that will mean trouble. Especially with a group this big. The bigger that crowd, the bigger the show-off Bobby Bailey has to be, especially with somebody he's sure he can take.

All 12 of us are jammed into one space-age automatic elevator going up to the 25th floor. Whitey's right next to me and I see him reaching down and pinching Bobby Bailey's ass. "Whoahly shit! If I find the fag who did that, I'll kill him!" Bobby screams, unable to even turn his head around in the smooshed crowd.

"I think Mark Fay did it!" Whitey yells back to Bobby.

"No I didn't, I swear!" Fay shoots back. It's the loudest I ever heard Fay get in all his life. Pinching a drunken Bobby Bailey on the ass is not something you want to be associated with. "I didn't, I didn't, I swear I didn't!" he reiterates, coming pretty close to sobbing like a little girl.

The door opens and about half of us fall out onto the floor of the 25th floor in a roar of laughter that makes us all forget about Fay's whining. Time to straighten up, dust ourselves off, and enter Irene Esposito's luxury high-rise apartment.

Not a doorbell, but a buzzer. And built into the door is a tiny lens, no bigger than a dime, where the person behind the door can look through and see who's at the door without opening anything up. My door has a little round door about the size of a coaster that's been painted shut for years. We just yell "who is it?" real loud. You wouldn't know there was a party

219

going in this house. No music, screaming, laughs or chatter. I can see that someone is peering at us through the peephole. Then the familiar sound of the chain undone, and three locks being opened. Then the surprised look of an Italian looking middle aged mom who reminds me of Jackie Kennedy with her haircut, and nice thin figure. She's even wearing a dark blue narrow dress with brass buttons, and gold earrings that dangle. She looks nervous like Jackie Kennedy too. Like the time she was on TV, explaining how the wall paper in the white house was over a hundred years old, and they even had their own full time furniture re-upholsterer who did nothing but re-stuff old chairs and couches. Why didn't they just go to Castro Convertibles like everybody else?

"Oh, you must be Irene's classmates. Come inside," she says, waving her hand in a graceful sweep, like a model on "The Price Is Right" pointing to a Hotpoint washer-dryer, motioning for us to enter. The gang is as quiet as first station at Stations of the Cross. Mrs. Esposito isn't like any of the moms I've met. She's got an air of richness about her, like the people the Three Stooges wind up having a huge pie fight with.

I remember before this building was even here, there was an old abandoned, empty house on a big old lot. We used to call it the "haunted house." It was the only one around. It was scary to go in it even on a nice summer afternoon. It stunk really bad, like piss and puke and worse, and there were old mattresses and empty beer cans and wine bottles all over the place. At night, we wouldn't even go near it. The older kids used to go in there real late, and I can imagine what kinds of things happened. I heard there was even a murder in there one winter when they found a bum dead. But now it's a 25-story apartment building. The nicest one in the neighborhood. They even have terraces. Imagine what kind of damage you could do throwing stuff off a 25th-story balcony.

The carpeting is that really thick stuff you could use a rake on. The wallpaper is silver, with black-velvet designs. And instead of just bare light bulb fixtures like we have in our house, with a glow-in-the-dark traffic light hanging on a string, there are fancy chandeliers all over the place. Each one having

220

their own wall switch. We don't have a wall switch in our entire apartment that works. There are framed paintings in the hall of fancy balls with people in white wigs dancing, like a bunch of George Washingtons. We actually walk past a doorway with a velvet rope across it. I think it must be the living room. It's got white furniture. White coffee table. White end tables. White telephone. White curtains. Even a white rug. The couch and stuffed chair are white, except they're covered with clear plastic covers. And no TV. It looks like a showroom at Gimbels. Past that room is a fancy dining room with the biggest chandelier yet. We keep going. I can't believe how many rooms they have. Finally we arrive in a room about the size of my whole apartment, with brand new everything. Console stereo, TV, bar, even an undersized pool table. On one side of the room are about 10 girls from class, giggling and whispering to each other. This is it. The big party. The stereo has on some really corny cha cha record. That's been what older people are doing at parties instead of the twist. The cha cha.

"Come on now children, let's mingle a little," Mrs. Esposito announces. Children? Oh great. I already want to go home.

"Thanks, Mrs. Esposito! What a lovely home you have!" Bobby Bailey of all people, says. He reminds me of that Eddie Haskell guy on "Leave It To Beaver" when grown ups are around.

"Well, I see you have some real gentlemen for classmates, girls!" Mrs. Esposito says. Yeah. If she knew Bobby already downed two quarts of Rheingold, and threw up once, she wouldn't think he's such a little gentleman. I don't know how he manages to act sober.

"Now you just do whatever you want now. You don't need me to chaperone! Have fun!" Mrs. Esposito says as she turns to leave us.

"Mrs. Esposito?" a voice calls out just before she's out of the room. Whitey of course. "Can we put on the radio instead of records?" he asks.

"Yes, you may," she says and she's gone, closing the

221

sliding door behind her.

"Good thinking, Whitey." I tell him as he walks over to the coffin sized stereo, color TV, bar, console, and begins to study the knobs. And with a few flicks of switches and turns of knobs, the sounds of The Beatles' "I Saw Her Standing There" is playing halfway in.

Crossing the room? Holding hands? There it is. All right out in the open. No denying it. No pretending like we don't even know the girls are on the other side of the room giggling and whispering about us. Playing kiss-o-leereo is one thing. That's a game played at night when there's nobody around when you find a girl in a hiding place. That has to be the trickiest game of them all. Ringo-levio almost always leads to a fight between two guys, when somebody grabs somebody else a little too hard, or gets a little too protective of his teammates. Most games have moons up as a final consequence, and that can lead to humiliation, and of course a sore butt, and again a fist fight. But kiss-o-leereo required the greatest skill. The girls go out to hide, and the guys have to go out and find them. Whoever a guy finds first he has to kiss. So the game is actually totally controlled by the girls. If they're good at hiding, whether it's the nice weather version, and you're out in the park or down by the railroad tracks, they can see which boys are getting close. If they want the boy to find them, they'll make themselves a little more noticeable, and the boy thinks he's found her on his own. Not likely. Because if a girl is smart, and I've never met one that wasn't smart in this game, she's caught only when she wants to get caught. So, if there's a girl who you DON'T want to kiss, but she wants you to find her, I'm afraid you'll be making out with her. The girl also controls the intensity of the kiss. If she likes you, you can bet you'll be pressing lips and going around and around in circles with eyes closed in a swirling dizzy haze of bubble gum, Prell shampoo, and tobacco breath. Why is it that every girl who plays kiss-o-leereo, chews lots of bubble gum, smokes Marlboros and uses Prell? And there's nothing, but nothing worse than making out with somebody you don't like. But when you play the game right, and it is somebody you like,

222

and you're going through a dark stone-walled passage in a cellar of a 50 year old apartment building, stepping over old, broken baby carriages and piles of plaster, pushing past dangling wires, and you turn around a dark corner, and see the girl you were hoping you were clever, and lucky enough to find (yeah right) standing in an old dumbwaiter door, where people lowered their garbage for 50 years until it got to easy for teenagers to break into apartments, and now it's the scene for total seclusion where a boy and girl can kiss in private. Ah, the beauty of it. It may have been the passage for trash, but once your eyes meet with the realization that there's no one in the world who will find you, and there's just one reason two people would be in this spot, and you get closer and closer, shaking as you place your hands on her arms, pushing yourself closer and closer, until you're both a little cross eyed and close your eyes, and are hit with the intoxicating smells of gum, smoke and shampoo, and BAM, you're in paradise.

But HERE? In Irene Esposito's 25th floor luxury apartment, with parents right behind a folding, sliding door? Actually walk across the room in clear view of everyone, and ask ONE PARTICULAR girl to dance? That takes nerve. Because everybody knows that dancing is just the beginning. I believe the rules of romance are: 1) dance   2) hold hands 3) make out 4) feel up 5) go to bed 6) get pregnant   7) get married 8) have kids 9) die. How can I face up to such a thing? Maybe after six or seven bottles of 16-ounce Coke...

"W-A-BEATLE-C Super hit replay replay replay..." The radio jingle goes. That means "I Saw Her Standing There" will be played again. And there it is: "Fah!" There's a line in there about a girl being 17. The 17 year old girls I know are real mature. But the 13 year old girls standing across the room here sure aren't. Oh, they look like they could actually have sex someday. They all have boobies ranging from the bee stings on Marion Kennerly, to the bouncy milk balloons that Anne Cunningham has been hiding for the past year. But guaranteed... they all have had their periods. And that means they could have sex and even have a baby. Fitzy Fitzgerald says, "Old enough to wear the rag, old enough to bear the bag." And

after days of hinting that I had absolutely no idea what the hell that line meant, I finally found out from Whitey, after he asked his brother Alfie. Fitzy's a jerk.

"You gonna ask somebody to dance?" I ask Whitey, hoping he will, so I can be right behind him.

"Yeah. I'm going to ask Anne Cunningham if I like the next song."

Daring. Anne Cunningham doesn't hang out with us. Oh yeah, she's been in our class since 1st grade, but nobody really noticed her until this year when all of a sudden it seems her uniform blouse was pushed out further than anything we'd ever seen before. And she wasn't fat, either. And to suddenly ask her to dance in front of the girls who have hung out with us, would be daring. Everybody would know why she is suddenly getting all the attention. Why all the boys now sneak a peak at the girl who sat quietly and undisturbed behind thick glasses and got a 98 average for seven years straight, and never got noticed once.

But wait. There goes Bobby Bailey. Boldly crossing the no-man's land to the other side, making a bee-line for Anne Cunningham and her breasts. I can see Carrie Vitelli and Donna Murphy sticking out their lower jaws and scowling. Carrie and Donna have hung out with us guys for a couple of years. They've even made out with most of us at one time or another during kiss-o-leereo or spin the bottle, and here's Anne Cunningham getting the first dance at the first real graduation party.

"Well, so much for that idea," Whitey says to me, punctuated by a nice round Coke burp.

I don't think I could ask Anne Cunningham to dance. I'd feel too embarrassed because I just know that the only reason I'd be asking her was because I wanted to get close to those boobs. And that's just about what I'd be staring at since she towers over me. So what the heck. I've had three Cokes. "Fun Fun Fun" by The Beach Boys is on the radio, and it's graduation night.

"I'm going to ask Carrie to dance. You ask Donna," I instruct Whitey.

"Let's go." Whitey says downing the eight ounces of Coke left in the bottle and letting out a belch for the road.

It's not easy walking across the room towards a girl you kind of like, and aren't sure what to do about it, but it is a party and dancing is what we're supposed to do.

Carrie sees me coming, and pretends she doesn't.

"Wanna dance?" I force the words out of my throat, over my tongue and out my mouth.

"OK." I see Whitey has done the same. And we're off in a twisting frenzy. Round and around, and a up and a down we go again is exactly right. Twisting looks like fun when you see other people doing it, but it's really uncomfortable to do. We're dancing about a foot from each other, and yet, not even looking into each other's eyes. I'm noticing the ceiling, the black-and-white square boxes of the linoleum, and how Anne Cunningham's boobs can't be contained by her industrial-strength- over-the-shoulder- boulder-holder, but not a glance into Carrie's eyes. I'm nervous as hell caught up in a fast and furious twist-a-thon, and I can't go on. What a cramp! Right in my lower stomach area. I have to stop. I might throw up or something.

"I've got to stop, Carrie. Sorry."

"Fine," she says in that little bitchy kind of way.

I can't tell her I've got a stomach cramp from doing the twist. That's the lowest rung on the ladder to sex and I can't even do that. I think I'd better sit down for a while and watch.

I'm amazed at what's going on now. Everyone is dancing with everyone. And Bobby Bailey is putting on a twisting clinic. Mrs. Esposito comes in and even she starts dancing with Bobby. And for the first time in my life, I get a sexy kind of urge for someone's mom. She's doing the twist in a slow, rocking kind of way. Not the frenetic go-go girl kind of twist we see on TV and try to imitate. But a wiggly, squirmy kind of dance that has me getting a little too excited in the worst kind of way. The kind of way that shows. I cross my legs for the rest of this dancing display by Mrs. Esposito. Now I know why Betty Boop gave me those feelings that made me rub against the arm of the sofa.

All the boys want to dance with Mrs. Esposito. I don't. I'm afraid to. I don't want to dance with a grown-up. I thought tonight was OUR night. Our night to put the past behind us, and maybe get to know the girls who up until recently were just boring, smart, tattle-taling, spelling-bee winning, crying, whispering, giggling, neat, clean, obedient, book- reading, pains in the ass. That is except for Tina the class tramp, who supposedly screws older boys, among other things. And the couple of girls in the class, like Carrie and Donna, who hang out with us and get lousy grades just like most of the boys.

But suddenly this party has turned into a grown-up affair. Both of Irene Esposito's parents are turning everybody into a twisting, cha-cha, rumba, limo, mumbo jumbo bunch of jerks. Aunts, uncles, next door neighbors, all grabbing boys and girls, and putting on "The Girl From Ipanema" and "The Baby Elephant Walk" and "The Alley Cat" doing the dumbest dance steps you ever saw. I can't believe my eyes, but even Mr. two-quarts-of-Rheingold Bobby Bailey is doing it with them. And Carrie, Donna, Anne Cunningham AND her boobs and just about everybody. Except me and Whitey.

"I can't believe this. The freakin' alley cat?" Whitey says to himself in a Coca-Cola induced daze.

"This is worse than the Holy Name Society's St. Patrick Day Dance." I add. "At least at that everybody gets polluted and dances a jig. Let's sneak out before they make us do the 'Hokey Pokey.' "

"Roger," Whitey says, putting down his 16 ounce bottle of Coke. "Let's vamoose."

I thought we'd have to sneak out, but nobody has any idea that we're leaving. The folding door is open, so we just slip out the door, past the waltzing George Washingtons and the roped-off living room, and out the front door.

"Think anybody's still at your house?" Whitey asks me, knowing that's the last place we want to wind up.

"Yeah. Probably," I admit in defeat. "Let's go."

Across Orloff Avenue we go, past another luxury building that used to be a cool lot. In that lot, Whitey pushed Ralphie into a giant hole filled with muddy water that is now an indoor

226

swimming pool. I can't believe there's a building in our neighborhood with indoor parking and an indoor pool! Little did Whitey know that the 8 foot-deep mud hole was loaded with dangerous cables, and old fence and rusty pipes, and that Ralphie can't swim. Whitey had to jump in and save him. Fortunately, Ralphie didn't tell on him. It's funny how kids don't tell on kids from the block, even if they do awful things. There's a girl two grades behind us who is blind in one eye. It's just a gray blob now. When it happened she told her parents, the doctors, teachers, in fact everybody, that a car went by, and kicked up a pebble that went right into her eye. But I know for a fact that a kid in her class had a BB gun, and was fooling around shooting at kids, and got her in the eye. He made her swear, while she was on the sidewalk crying and screaming in pain that she better not tell on him. She hasn't yet. I haven't either. Nobody has.

Across the street from that luxury building is another one. When that was a lot, we used to dig huge holes and put very thin, but strong branches across it in a grid form. Then we'd cover the branches with newspaper, leaves, and brush, topped off by some dirt, creating a "trap." To tell you the truth, I'm not sure if anybody ever fell into one, but we would spend two entire days perfecting it. I don't know why, but I don't know any kids from those two buildings.

Orloff leads over to our street, 238th. There aren't any new buildings on this block.

I look down the street to the intersection of 238th and Orloff about two street lights away, and circling around the top of the hill is Whitey's brother Alfie.

"Hey there's your brother, let's ask him what he's doing!" I urge Whitey.

"I don't want to talk to him."

"Why not?"

"Oh, the usual stuff at home. My parents went upstate, me and Alfie and Brian are alone for a week."

"Oh, come on!" I insist.

I leave Whitey behind and go over to Alfie on an old balloon tire truck bike. He's circling around, with his long hair blowing in the wind as he stands on the peddles. He hardly ever sits on the seat. He's either peddling real hard up a hill, or down a hill, or on flat surfaces going as fast as possible. I have no idea where he goes, but he's always going somewhere. Maybe somewhere where the kids look and act like him. Because there's nobody in this neighborhood who has long hair like that, with paperback books sticking out of his back pocket, and old worn-out sneakers with holes in them, no socks, and toes sticking out.

"Hey Alfie, what are you doing when you circle around up here?"

I startled him. He jerks the handlebars, and almost loses his balance.

"You're Schmidt, right?"

"Yeah, Whitey's best friend."

"Tell Whitey not to listen to Brian. Or me. Or anybody."

I'm not sure what that's supposed to mean. Alfie always has a serious look on his face.

"OK. What are you doing circling like this?"

"Look down at the window, above Snookey's neon sign, second pane from the top, third pane from the left. You can see the traffic light in it."

And with that he was gone. Full extension. Standing up, pedaling with all his might, down a treacherous hill with a curve just before you hit bottom. So that's it. A reflection in the window to see the traffic light around the corner. Wow.

"Hey, Whitey! I know what he's doing! Whitey?"

Whitey was gone. Nowhere in sight. Shit. Where the hell did he go?

It's too late and too close to Mr. Santirocco's window to yell for him. He could have gone in any of about five directions from this point. He could have slipped past me, and gone down the hill towards his building, but I think I would've seen him. He could've turned around and gone back down Orloff where we just came from or gone up the city steps to J.T. Something tells me Whitey has gone to J.T. He won't bump into anybody he knows up there.

I'm guessing that seeing his brother Alfie must've pissed him off for some reason. Whitey's my best friend, but I have no idea what's really going on at home. Or any body's home. Once in a while you might see somebody's father or mother look drunk, or hear yells behind a closed door, or see somebody show up with a black eye, and know that if they were in a fight, win or lose, they would've been bragging about it. But except for my own family, and being over a relative's house, I have no idea what goes on in anybody else's home. Nobody asks and nobody tells.

I've never walked up here by Pigeon Park alone at night before. I've got to admit, I feel pretty brave walking around with a few of my friends with me, but alone, not so brave at all. You don't see many people hanging out on stoops up here in the Jewish neighborhood at night, unlike my block, where there's almost always some old skinny Irishman in a pork pie hat sneaking a cigarette or a half pint of booze.

There are a lot fewer stores up in this part of the neighborhood. And for some reason, absolutely no bars. I think the only place Whitey might be is in Pigeon Park.

Pigeon Park's lights aren't all busted out like down in Van Corlandt Park, our hangout. And from outside the wrought-iron gate, I can see Whitey sitting on the boulder on the top of the hill where we've sat in the daytime before. There aren't any other kids hanging out in the park. Just Whitey, sitting up on that rock. Drinking from a small bottle.

Walking into the park, I have a strange, nervous feeling. Almost like walking up to a girl that you're going to dance with. And I realize why. I have to talk to Whitey about something emotional. This is a first. I feel like a jerk, but I can't just leave him there.

"Hey, Whitey. What happened with you?" I say as I walk up the grassy hill to Whitey's rock.

"Nothing. I didn't want Alfie to see me."

"Oh. What are you drinking?"

"It's Gypsy Rose wine. Want some?"

"OK."

I didn't want to drink tonight. I know my parents will

be looking for it.

"Do you have any Sen-Sen?" I ask Whitey.

"Yeah," he says handing me the small bottle of wine and the small purple box of the liquor-masking gum.

I had heard about Gypsy Rose wine. It was cheap and wasn't easy to swallow like rum and Coke. I kept my lips tight, put the bottle to my mouth, and sipped a small amount. It was syrupy, sweet, and burned my tongue, but I swallowed.

"How can you drink this stuff?"

"You get used to it," Whitey said as he took the bottle back and finished off the last gulp.

This spot is pretty at night. You can look out over the huge reservoir, and it looks just like an upstate lake, with the apartment houses in the distance sparkling off the water. I feel awkward. Not knowing what to say. Should I ask Whitey about keeping his drinking secret from me? Why doesn't he want to see Alfie? Why are his parents upstate without the three kids? What's he doing up here, and why didn't he just wait for me?

"My father's real sick. He's in the hospital," Whitey says staring off into the distance. "My mother's upstate at her sister's near the hospital. He's got something wrong with his liver and internal bleeding."

"Oh."

I don't know what to say. What can you say to someone with such problems? I've never had to talk to someone about something like this before.

"My brother Alfie and Brian had a fight tonight. Brian was drunk, and Alfie was high on pot or pills or something, my brother said. Brian called him a drug addict. I hate both of them. I don't want to go home."

There's no way I can ask him to my house. With my parents in the living room on the Castro convertible, and my sister in the bedroom trying her best to hide from me, there's nowhere for him to sleep. Crap.

"Let's just stay out." I suggest.

"Yeah. That's cool. Maybe we can go to the pool hall, or take the subway down to Times Square or something?"

"Maybe," I say. Knowing that going downtown is out of the question. Too dangerous. I think we should stick to the neighborhood. Our park.

"Let's see if anybody's in the stands?" I hope Whitey agrees.

"OK."

So down the hill and out of Pigeon, back to our own turf. We'll be safe there. It's a long walk. A quiet walk.

It's like we never left. The stands are packed tonight just like they were last night, except the kids from our graduating class who are probably playing spin the bottle, or doing the hokey pokey with Aunt Katie and Uncle Mike at family celebrations. People are in exactly the same spots, going from left to right, youngest to oldest. And since there's not a twin tower of free beer like we provided last night, the groups are even more separated.

I have a feeling it could be a little more difficult for us to fit into a crowd this time. First of all, we're dressed up. Second of all, it doesn't look like anybody from our class is here. Younger and older, but none from our class.

From down below on the ash track, you can see the groups, but it's hard to see faces, and I don't think anyone has noticed us yet. "What do you want to do?" I ask Whitey. If it was up to me, I think I'd rather just hang out in front of my building on the front stoop. That way I could tell my parents I'm just out front, and they'd let me stay there as long as I wanted.

"Let's see if Clooney and them guys'll let us have some beer," Whitey says, already walking past me, and bounding up the big concrete block steps.

Over to the left I can see the younger kids, led by Paul Donnegan, a little shrimp of a kid who's probably the best athlete Presentation has ever seen. An unbelievable shortstop, outstanding quarterback, incredible jumping, shooting guard, barely five feet tall, already smoking two packs of Marlboros a day, and downing two six packs on the weekends. And he's not even out of seventh grade yet.

Over from them are the guys who are a little older than

we are. Clooney, Fitzgerald, and a few others who I don't know too well. Whitey heads right for them.

"Hey guys, got an extra beer?" Whitey says as if he's one of them.

"Sorry, Shelley, the prom ended an hour ago. What the hell are you supposed to be a freaking fag undertaker?" Clooney says between swallows of beer, drags on a cigarette, and big laughs. Fitzgerald and the other guys crack up.

"Well, can I?" Whitey asks, ignoring their guffaws.

Clooney, in a fit of generosity, reaches into his cardboard box with melting ice leaking down the steps, grabs a can of Rheingold and hands it to Whitey. "Choke, on it Shelley. You want one, Schmidt?"

"No thanks."

Whitey takes his Rheingold, picks a can opener up off the floor, opens it, and starts to chug. Really chug. Chug chug chug chug. "Holy shit, Shelley!" Clooney says, admiring Whitey's style.

Whitey is going to down the entire can in one gulp. I've seen Whitey down sodas like that, but never beer. Not many people can do it. It actually requires opening up your throat, and dumping the liquid down. Not swallowing. Dumping. The whole gang is watching Whitey in silent awe. A lot of guys don't even really like beer. I know for a fact some guys brag about drinking a six pack or more and actually dump their beer when they go to take a leak. They even fake getting drunk. No denying what Whitey's doing.

"Not bad, Shelley," Clooney proclaims for all to hear, "I've only got four beers left, but you can have one more for that fine display."

"Thanks. This one I'm just gonna drink normal," Whitey says in a real low key "I belong" kind of way.

Early in the evening, you could sit down on the concrete steps, but this late in the evening, there's so much melted ice, spilled beer, and piss runoff from up top, you don't dare take a seat. There's a radio, of course, tuned to Murray the K. He's off into one of his gibberish tirades. Some of the guys in the neighborhood can understand it and even do it. I can't. It has something to do with adding "eee-a-zize" and "oh-a-ziz" sounds in the middle of words, but I don't get it. There's a whole lot of things that Murray the K does that kids imitate. The whole A-VAY thing, and gibberish, and saying "cool, baby"or "daddy-oh" or "crazy man" or other slang terms, and talking about watching "submarine races" down by the water, and listening to the Beatles. Even wearing that goofy hat. That's the one thing I really don't get. He wears this hat that's like the kind of hat Bing Crosby or Frank Sinatra wear when they're golfing on TV. And he kind of dresses like that too. He wears a lot of those "shirt-jax" that you don't tuck into your pants, and sweaters like Andy Williams wears on his TV show. Square. But he's got every kid in NY it seems talking like him, and listening to The Beatles. I wonder if he'd be as popular if everybody knew what he looked like.

"Shelley, how come you're drinking beer over here with us when your brother's down there?" Fitzy Fitzgerald asks, pointing to the dark end of the stands where college aged kids and older hang.

"Really?" Whitey says, with surprise and fear in his voice.

"Yeah, he's probably down there shooting up," Fitzy Fitzgerald shoots back.

Whitey's head jerks towards Fitzgerald. "What the fuck are you saying?"

"Fuck you, Shelley."

"No Fuck YOU, Fitzgerald," Whitey screams into Fitzy's face.

"Calm down, guys," Clooney says, "and shut the fuck up, Fitzy. We're all white here."

Both Whitey and Fitzgerald back off. "Look, Shelley, those guys down there do drugs, and that's why the cops have been coming through here lately, and your brother Alfie does hang out with those guys sometimes." I can tell Whitey is still agitated.

"Yeah, not all the time, sometimes." Whitey adds.

And shit. As if on cue. An unmarked car with no headlights on pulls onto the track, right next to us. Two guys in baggy suits get out with flashlights. "All right, guys, don't worry, but don't go anywhere, either." One of the undercover cops yells up to us.

This is it. Oh my god. If they bust us for something I am dead. Freaking cops.

They're both slowly walking up the steps with their flashlights scanning the wet mix of water, beer, and piss. "OK, good work, gentleman. You're just drinking beer, right?"

"Yes, Officer." Clooney responds.

"Keep it that way," the cop says, as they both walk past us and start to walk toward the dark end of the stands where the older kids are. And in the distance, I can see a quiet mad scramble of bodies gathering things and running like hell. And I also see a long-haired dark figure tearing ass, standing on his pedals, biking into the dark of the park.

"Shit! Let's go!" one cop yells to the other as they awkwardly run towards the fleeing kids. By the time they're halfway there, the kids are all gone, into the darkness of the rest of the park.

The cops walk back towards us and pause to say something. "You kids drink beer and wine we won't bother you. But smoke that shit, or pop pills or whatever, and your ass is going to jail. Understand?"

A weak, mumbled chorus of "Yes, Officers" follows.

"Shit, that was close," Clooney says gulping the last bit of Rheingold in his can.

I knew just how close. I think Whitey knows too.

"Anybody hungry? I'm going to go over to White Towers and get some burgers," I say to our shell-shocked group.

Everybody there kicks in a buck or a few quarters each. So I'm off to White Towers.

"Want to walk me, Whitey?"

"Sure."

Fitzgerald yells at us as we head down the stairs, "Don't take off with our money, you little pricks."

White Tower is across the street from the park, right at the very very end of the Broadway "el" at 242nd Street. It's always crowded around here, even late at night like it is now.

People are getting off buses coming down from Yonkers, and getting onto the "el" and visa-versa. If you stand just north of the "el" and look south, it looks dark and dreary and crowded with the "el" over the street and the pillars taking up most of the street. But if you look north from the "el", towards Yonkers, it looks open and green. There's about a block of stores at the end of the "el". The kind of stores that only people passing through would go to. When you're just passing through, like when you just rode 55 minutes from the South Ferry on the dank, stinky iron horse, and you get off, and finally out into the fresh air, any store looks good. Even the dirty Lou's Candy Store or the raunchy Terminal Bar. There are no less than four bars on this one block. At night, a couple of them cater to the Catholic kids from Manhattan College which is just up the hill, but for the most part these bars usually have several serious drinkers on stools. The boilermaker- at-nine-in-the-morning variety. This is also one of the few places in the neighborhood where you see colored people. Colored bus drivers and subway motormen who are at the end of their run stop in the deli for a coffee, and the candy store for a pack of Cools and a Daily News. I wonder where they live. Probably down in Harlem, I guess.

The White Tower used to be called White Castle. It's a bright white enamel building with spotlights on it that make it visible the whole length of Broadway. And it's painted like it's supposed to look like a castle with those turrets on the top. It's open 24 hours a day, and right now, nearly midnight, it's the only place open that isn't a bar.

The inside of the place is all stainless steel and there's even a drain in the middle of the white-tiled floor. I was in here early one morning, and they were just hosing the whole place down. Walls, booths, the floor, and just blasting everything into the drain. Just like the monkey cage in the Bronx Zoo.

Sitting at the counter is a strange group of people that I'm sure don't live around here. There's a little old Puerto Rican man wearing a hat that's made out of a brown paper bag. He's wearing a jump suit that says "Art Steel" on a patch over

235

his heart. That's where they make desks and file cabinets in a big factory down on 234th Street. They also sponsor a little league team and they're called "Art Steel." That's one of the cooler Little League names. There's also "Stella D ' Oro" which is OK, and "North Side Savings"; but I've been on the two worst names, "Williams Funeral Home" and "Pig 'N Whistle." It's not easy to have pride in your team with those two names screaming across your back.

There's a big, burly, hairy, Irish-looking guy at the end of the counter. And close to the door where we are, there's a colored lady in a really tight dress, with her boobs pushed out of the front, those fishnet stockings and really high high heels. She must've just come from a party or something.

Whitey nudges me and whispers into my ear, "That's a hooker."

"Really?" I respond with a look of shock. I am shocked. I don't know what a hooker is.

Whitey looks at me like he knows I don't know, and says, "You know, a who-ah." I know what a who-ah is.

The Irish guy at the end is waving at the small Greek behind the counter with the pencil behind his ear and the ciga- rette in his mouth. "Here's what I want. I want half-cooked bacon on white bread with lots of butter." The bearded drunk yells across the store in a cigarette- and-whiskey gravely brogue.

"OK, OK, comin' right up," the short order cook says with his cigarette still dangling, writing onto his note pad.

"OK, kids, what you want?" he barks at us through his filtered cigarette. I know we collected about 6 dollars.

"Five regular burgers with everything, and five french fries."

"Here or to go?"

"To go, but can I have a small Coke for here?" I ask.

You can see why they have to hose this place down. You can taste the grease in the air, and the floor is a sticky mess.

He brings me a glass filled with Coke, and on the top of the dark bubbly stuff is a thick film. "Excuse me, sir?" He comes over. "What's this in my Coke?"

The Greek takes the glass, holds it about two inches from his nose, closes one eye, puts it back down in front of me, and says, "It's grease... or something else. I didn't do the dishes," and turns back to his sizzling grill. Oh well. The grease I don't mind, it's the something else that bothers me.

The colored lady puts a dollar down on the counter and gets up. She leans over to me, and gives me a little motion with her index finger for me to come closer. I'm scared as hell, but I do. An aroma of syrupy perfume cuts through the grease and hits me hard making me a little dizzy. I can also smell something exotic, like the incense in church. This is the closest I've ever been to a colored lady. Her skin is jet black, and her teeth as white as a brand new baseball, and she's absolutely gorgeous. She's got a sexy wet smile and says to me in not quite a whisper, "Don't take that shit from him, ask for a clean glass." She winks at me and pushes open the door out onto Broadway, then down towards the "el."

I feel funny. I can still smell her. And that smile she gave me makes me almost feel like she wanted to kiss me. "Man, she was sexy!" Whitey says, nudging me with a sharp finger. "She must be a who-ah," he adds, still poking me.

"Sir, excuse me. May I please have a clean glass?" I say across the counter to the Greek as he slops the soft butter onto two pieces of white Fink bread. All the luncheonettes and diners use Fink bread. You only see Fink bread in places like that. Fink has trucks all over the city, and on the side it says in huge letters "Fink Means Good Bread." Go figure.

"Sure kid," the counter man says not even pissed off. Wow. That was easy.

He delivers the clean Coke, and a bag filled with sliders and fries. "May we have extra ketchup please?"

"Sure kid."

On the way out, the Puerto Rican guy smiled at me, and held up his glass of Coke like he was toasting us. It sure is different out, late at night.

"OK, I've got 4 sliders and 4 french fries in here, take what you want," I say to the four guys left. Whitey and I take the other burger and fries. The crowd has really thinned out.

And the real old kids all the way at the end of the stands are gone. The younger crowd is gone too. Just our group of six, and another group about 10 yards over. It's not as much fun as last night when there was plenty of free beer and everybody gathered around like one big happy gang.

"Can I have another beer, Mike?" Whitey asks Clooney between chews of the little square burger with holes.

"No more brewskies, Shelley. Last gulp right here," Clooney says as he downs the last bit of his Rheingold backwater.

Minutes went by just staring at the lights above the Major Deegan Expressway in the distance with the sounds of late-night DJ's on the radio. I don't even know who these guys on the radio are. The food is gone, the beer is gone, the laughs are gone. And way in the distance, there's a flash of lightning, followed several seconds later by a low rumble of thunder.

"I think it's going to rain," Whitey says, studying the distant sky and looking at the moon, getting totally covered by clouds.

"Yeah."

Another streak of lightning in the distant sky, but this time the thunder is a few seconds closer to the flash.

"It's coming this way," Whitey says. "Let's go somewhere."

"Where?" I ask him, knowing we don't have any money left to sit at the counter of White Tower.

"Let's start walking."

"OK."

"See you guys," we both say to the drunken foursome staring off into the distance.

We walk through the pitch-black park, thanks to another wave of anti-park light vandals, with the lightning and thunder closing in.

"Let's just walk towards home, and if we have to, we can just duck into a doorway or even hang out in the alley that leads into my cellar that's covered," I say to Whitey, thinking it sounds like our only alternative.

238

"Yeah, I guess," Whitey says like he could care less.

We make it all the way to the entrance to my cellar when the sky opens up. It's pouring rain. We grab a couple of milk crates from the deli next to the alley where we can sit and hide from the rain, and watch it pour. It's raining so hard that there are rivers coming down the gutter, shooting down the steep hill of 238th Street, with chunks of garbage coming down. The streets and sidewalks being washed clean in a much-needed late-night June thunderstorm. There was a lot of dog crap and garbage around, so this is perfect. And since the rain and thunder are making such a racket, we don't have to be quite so quiet here. Actually, this is the most fun I've had all day. Just sitting here with Whitey, watching the storm take away the smells and garbage down the hill and into the sewers. And guaranteed there will be a lot more sewer balls after this storm. The rain is letting up now. Just a nice steady sprinkle. Now comes my favorite time. Just after a storm, when there's actually a fresh smell on the street of clean, gleaming concrete and brick. You can smell it as soon as it stops. Nothing like it. Just clean, scrubbed, brick and concrete. Even the tops of the garbage cans look clean. It's great just to sit here on a wooden Borden's crate and look out on good old 238th Street and enjoy the smells. It's kind of like being out in the country right now. Quiet. Clean. You can even hear crickets.

The street actually glistens. The water running down the gutter actually looks clear, like you could drink it. An old Chinaman pushes his shopping cart up the street, and the slight sound of his squeaking wheels fills the air from the bottom of the hill, all the way to the top.

"It's cool to just sit here this late," Whitey says, and just as soon as the words leave his lips, a lightning bug zips by us. Whitey snaps his fist out and snatches in a flash. He slowly turns his fist, and ever so slightly opens the opening by his thumb, creating a little space where you can see what's going on inside there. The lightning bug fills the darkness of his fist like the sparks of a subway car going through a tunnel. After three or four lights, he slowly opens his fist and the bug flies away.

239

"Have you heard anything from Hayes?" I ask Whitey, knowing that my orientation at the huge boy's high school is just 4 weeks away, and if kids who are on the waiting list are going to be accepted, they'd be finding out real soon.

"Nah. Not yet. I think going to Clinton would be fun. I could walk there."

Clinton's a big public high school for boys. But it's kind of crazy there. I hear that the halls and the area outside the school are wild. You can do whatever you want. They don't hardly even take attendance and collecting homework is nearly unheard of.

The only sounds are an occasional car going up the hill, a couple of drunks going home, or somebody coming home from a late-shift job. I'd hate to do that. That's my brother's shift.

Just as the number 38 bus gears scream past us going up the steep hill, I thought I heard a muffled crash of some kind, coming from somewhere. There's a big curve on the hill here, with my building on this side, a row of stores connected to it, and across the street, and just down a little bit, Whitey's building that actually turns with the street. There's a lot of sound bouncing around.

"Did you hear something?" Whitey says looking over towards the courtyard in front of his building, which you can't really see inside of from where we are across the street, and just up a little bit.

"I don't know, maybe."

Now it's my turn, I reach out and grab a lightning bug. A big one.

"Got one!" This is a first for me. To just snatch one out of the air. I'm amazed at how bright its light is inside my hollowed-out fist.

Whitey gets up and starts to walk over towards his building without saying a word. I don't think anything of it, still entranced with my trapped firefly.

"Vinny. Come here. What's this?" It's Whitey's voice. But it sounds weird. Like when somebody gets taken over by a Martian by getting drilled in the back of his head in that movie

"Invaders From Mars."

I look over and he's standing at the top of the stairs not moving. And not speaking anymore. I let my captive bug go, and jog across the street to see what's over there. I walk up the four short steps that lead into the courtyard, and before I can say something to Whitey, I see something a hundred times weirder than anything I've ever seen in any horror movie. In the middle of the courtyard, there's a huge pool of blood, and in the middle of it, is a gurgling mass of red-and-white flesh, moaning and barely moving. White boards from the picket fence that line the garden are splintered and sticking out of this giant mess of twisted muscle and red matter. My mind is racing. Exploding.

What the hell happened? Somebody must've jumped off the roof. I turn around to Whitey, and he's just frozen. Staring at it. And all he is saying is, "Who is it? Who is it? Who is it?" Slowly. Over and over.

"Holy shit!" I yell as I turn around and try and think of somewhere to call the cops. Just down the block is a bar. Grecco's. I tear ass down there. I can't get enough air. I've never run faster in my life. I burst in the door. There's just a few guys at the bar watching TV. "Call the cops call the cops call the cops! Somebody jumped off the roof of 137! Call the cops! Call the cops!"

I don't know what I must've looked like, but the bartender looked at me all scared too. He knows I'm not pulling some practical joke. "Tony, call the cops," the bartender yells as he jumps the bar. "Show me, kid."

We run up the hill. I know this bartender a little. He's an older guy, but I think he lives in Whitey's building. He probably knows Whitey. We get to the courtyard. Whitey's still standing there. In the same spot frozen, muttering over and over again, "Who is it? Who is it?" The bartender screams in holy bloody terror at the sight of the disfigured body moving even less now than it was before, and making bubbling noises and deep groans and rattles in the thick red liquid.

"Oh my God! No God. No God! No." There's nothing he can do but look. It's helpless. The bartender is panicked. He goes up to Whitey and grabs him by the shoulders and screams, "It's your brother, Whitey! It's Brian. It's Brian. It's your brother!"

My whole body tingled like I was plugged into the wall socket. Now I was frozen. This is no horror movie. This is real. I turned and ran as fast as I could, up the hill, and into my house. Everybody's asleep. I sneak past my parents on the Castro in the living room, and into the bedroom. I'm crying. Sobbing. I start to take off my clothes. My sister slowly opens the curtain across the bunk bed and looks at me. "What's the matter?"

"Whitey's brother just jumped off the roof of his building or something, and I think he's dead and me and Whitey found him and called the cops."

"Oh, my God! Do you want to tell mommy?"

"No. Not now. I want to go to sleep."

The window was open and the streets were filled with sirens. Cop cars. Ambulances. And loud voices just out of view from my window. I'll never sleep tonight. Shit. Am I scared.

I try to close my eyes, but every time I do, I hear Whitey's voice calling me over from across the street. But over his voice I see the body, pierced with white picket fence in that deep pool of blood, gurgling it's last breath of life, not able to say "help me" or "shit", just moan and attempt to get up. Then I see Whitey's face. Now I know. He was standing there in shock. He knew. He knew.

More sirens. More voices in the distance. Occasionally an angry yell. Even though it's a warm night, I close the window at the foot of my bed. I can't see what's going on up the hill. Just the spinning red lights going across the buildings.

What about Whitey? What is he going through right now? I can't do anything but quietly sob and say Hail Marys. Over and over and over and over and over.

"What's this window doing closed? It's stifling in here. Get up, it's almost 10," my mother rattles off, opening the window, poking me once in the ribs, exiting the room dressed in her flowery house coat, and curlers still in her hair.

The instant I wake up I momentarily, for a split second, forget about what happened last night. Now I remember. It's Sunday. I'll probably have to go to the one o'clock mass with my family. My sister's little cubbyhole curtain is already down, and her bed made perfectly. How can I walk down the street to church? I'd have to walk right by the building. I don't want to. I don't ever want to look at it again. I've got to find out what happened. Could Brian Shelley really have killed himself? Why? He couldn't have been thrown off, no matter how drunk he was. He's too big and he's got a gun. I better tell my parents what happened.

My father's shaving over the bathroom sink, and my mother's behind him taking curlers out of her hair. I've got to be cool. I've got to just tell them. I stand next to the tiny bathroom.

"Last night I was there when..." I can't go any further. The sounds and images take over inside my head. I'm crying like a little girl. Uncontrollably. I can see my father shocked. Holding up his safety razor, only half shaved.

My mom is scared. She runs over to me and hugs me. "What's wrong? What happened?"

Through the crying and heavy heaves, I manage to get the words out.

"I was out late, and me and Whitey found Whitey's brother dying. He fell or jumped off the roof of his building."

"137?" my father asks, referring to the address of the building.

"Yeah."

"Oh, my God? How awful. How terrible," my mom says, hugging me. My dad is down on one knee rubbing my head. I'm crying even harder. I can see tears in my mom's eyes. But with them next to me like this I feel really protected. I suddenly have a sensation like everything will be alright. I can't remember the last time I was hugged and had my head rubbed that I wasn't embarrassed.

"What about Whitey?" my mother asks.

"I don't know," I say, ending the waterfalls.

"I'll call Mrs. Stanley. She lives in 137," mom says as she digs out her phone book, and dials the number on the black phone that sits on the living room end table.

"Hello, Theresa? This is Joey Schmidt's mother, Angie."

"Yes, I heard..."

"Oh my God..."

"How awful..."

"God have mercy..."

"Yes..."

"Yes..."

"With Whitey, yes..."

"Thank you."

She hangs up the phone.

My mother has to sit down. Now she looks like she's going to lose it.

"Brian came home drunk. He forgot his keys. He tried to lower himself from the roof with a clothesline and go into the bedroom window and the rope snapped."

Holy shit. Me and Whitey were right across the street. Whitey had keys. If only he saw us... oh my God. We were right across the street. Oh, my God. Poor Whitey. I'm not going to tell anybody. I couldn't.

We got ready for mass. My dad drove around the other way so I wouldn't have to go by 137. During the homily they mentioned Brian Shelley in the middle of mentioning about four other people having passed away. Luckily, I didn't see anybody I knew. I didn't want to see anybody.

Mass ends and me, my sister, my mom and my dad pile back into the wagon. dad pulls out of the parking lot, using a different exit than usual. I can tell he's going to go around the block again so we don't have to pass the building.

"Who wants to go to Rye Playland?" my mom says enthusiastically. I can see my dad roll his eyes up to heaven. Rye Beach Playland is great. It's got the best fun house I've ever been in, called the Magic Carpet Ride.

"Yeah, let's go!" I chime in.

I can see my sister is siding with my dad, not looking too thrilled with the idea.

But my mom is pushing full steam ahead. "Let's go home and change, pack a lunch, and hit the road!" she says like Judy Garland laying out a plan to Mickey Rooney and the rest of the Andy Hardy gang. And when my mom says "go" we go.

Yeah, I know she's doing it because they feel sorry for me, having seen something more horrible than they even show on TV, or for that matter even in the movies. If somebody's been killed by falling off a roof, all you see is a guy flying through the air and then landing all in one piece. You don't see a deep pool of thick blood, and blood and guts all over the place, and gurgling.

There's no doubt that was the most disgusting and sad thing I've ever seen, but I've seen other bad things too. One time they found the Chinese cook from Grecco's dead in his apartment after 3 days in the middle of the summer. I didn't see him, but I was right outside the apartment. I'll never forget the smell. That end of the hall still has traces of the odor, two years later.

And I know guys whose family members have been killed. Tommy Kowalzyck's brother was climbing a high-tension wire down by the river, and got blown up by electricity. Dead. A guy from my class, Willy Fricker's brother, Freddy, fell out of a chestnut tree and landed on his head. Dead. Eddie Ford was driving a car real fast around a traffic circle, the car flipped over and his best friend Phil Rutigliano's head was crushed. Dead. A kid in the 4th grade, who was funny and liked by everybody, named Gerard Murphy, was hit by a car right in front of his building. Dead. But I didn't see any of those.

So if my parents are being nice to me because they feel sorry for me, that's fine. Rye Beach Playland would be great. It's a lot closer to us than Rockaway, or Palisades, or Coney Island. It only takes about a half hour to get there. It's not as big as the other amusement parks, but my mom says the other ones have gone "honky tonk" whatever that means. The lines aren't as big there, and there are some things that are real old-fashioned at Rye that have long been torn down at other amusement parks. They have a real steeplechase there. That's kind of like a merry-go-round for older kids. There are these merry-go-round type horses, but they aren't made up to look like fairy-tale horses. They're made up to look like racehorses. With fancy saddles, blinders, numbers and everything. And they're all on different tracks so that they're not all going the same speed when they go around the track. And they go real fast. If you fell off, you could get seriously injured. You have to be over five feet to ride on it. It's measured by standing next to a wooden jockey. And come to think of it, I think this may be the first time I'm here that I am over five feet.

There's a long tree-lined road that leads to the amusement park called Playland Parkway. Unlike Rockaway, where it's right on a city block, just a block away from the "el.". And to get into the parking lot, you go through these big sand colored concrete arches.

I can hear the clickety clickety click of the "Dragon" roller coaster going up the hill. Dad pays the 75 cents parking, and the screams begin as the coaster is let loose on the scary ride. I must say, I don't have to try too hard to forget about what happened to me yesterday. I just wish Whitey was here with me. My sister hates rides.

Mom and dad and my sister all hate rides. There's a shady picnic area next to the steeplechase, and that's where I'm supposed to meet them after I've gone on the rides. I have a whole book of tickets, good for about 4 good rides or 8 bad ones. But the first ride I want to check out is the Magic Carpet Ride. The Magic Carpet is the highlight of this fun house and it's the last thing. In fact, the Magic Carpet dumps you right out to the main midway next to the entrance to the ride. The magic carpet itself is a really long carpet, that goes over bumpy rollers like a giant, stained conveyor belt. I've never actually seen anybody throw up on it, but those stains are the proof. Most of the fun house is pitch dark. Some young kids can't even get into the place, because the first thing you have to do is walk up moving steps. It's not so easy, either. Then you go through some really narrow dark halls, occasionally blasted by smelly air blasts out of the walls or floors, when you come into the crooked room. For some reason, it looks pretty straight, but if you don't hold onto the railings in the room, you go flying.

It's fun to let go, though. But I always rush through everything because I want to experience the Magic Carpet ride.

But just as I'm ready to plop into the bench that will deposit me onto the Magic Carpet ride with the pull of a big black lever, the old guy at the controls says, "You alone, kid?"

"Yeah." And without asking me for permission, pushes some 10 year old fat girl next to me on the bench, and KERPLUNK here I go on the Magic Carpet ride, right next to a chubby ten year old girl I don't even know. I just sat there. Not floating on a magic carpet over Calcutta, like I did the last time I was here with Whitey, but just sitting on a moving, dirty, smelly rug, down an incline. And onto the floor. Thank God nobody saw me.

I can see my family eating on the picnic tables across the way. They don't notice that I'm out. Rather than use another four tickets on two good rides in a row, I decide to go through one of those sit-in-the-car-and-go-through-some-spooky-stuff ones, called "Spook Town."

There's only a couple of people on line, and fortunately, the teenage operator lets me get in the car alone. These things are never really scary. The first thing that happens is you crash through two doors, and head into the darkness. Pieces of thread hang overhead and brush across your face, like you're supposed to be going through cobwebs. And when you hit a certain spot on the track, lights pop on, and for a couple of seconds or so, you see something like a monster or a witch. Even when I was a kid, going through with my sister, this never scared me, even though she would scream. A flash of light... a witch. Flash... Frankenstein. Flash... a bloody vampire. Flash... a coffin opens. Flash... a vampire with a stake in his heart, and blood pouring out. Flash... blood. Blood. I don't see stupid rubber masks anymore. I see blood. I see Brian Shelley drowning in blood. Pieces of picket fence sticking through him. I hear girls scream around the bend. I hear myself sobbing last night. I think I might be crying now. I close my eyes. The sounds are stupid: cars on a track, car horns, fake chains rattle, bad recordings of screams and howls. But I don't want to look.

The door crashes through the last dark door, and I'm into the blinding light of day. I'm in a lousy mood now. I don't think the teenage operator saw me crying. I want to go home. I want to call Whitey.

I go into a bathroom and wash my face. My family is still eating spiced ham sandwiches and drinking Dixie cups of grape Kool Aid. "Can we go home?" I ask the group. They all take turns looking at each other, and at me.

My mom is the first to speak. "Did you use all your tickets?"

"No. I'll save them."

I really feel like a sissy. I should just be having a blast. But I can't.

"If you want to go now we can," mom says in a very quiet voice.

Moms somehow know things that nobody else would pick up on. Without words.

"Yeah."

We pack up, and for the first time since I think about first Holy Communion, my dad held my hand for a few steps on the way to the car. I don't care who's watching. It felt good.

On the way back to the Bronx, my mom tuned in WNEW, with all the old- fashioned music. Hearing her sing about some little brown jug was good. My dad didn't drive past 137 again. But I am going to call Whitey. I am. I swear.

It's early Sunday evening, yet I don't see anybody hanging out on top of the hill next to my building. Usually there's at least somebody there. Just as well, we look pretty goofy carrying all this stuff back from the car.

As soon as I'm home, all I can see is that heavy black phone. I want to call Whitey, but I'm afraid. I'm afraid to talk about anything. How can we ever talk about anything, know-

248

ing full well what we both saw? We both saw it. How can we not talk about it?

BRIIIINNNNNNGGGGG. It's the phone. What if it's Whitey? I'm afraid. I go to the bathroom and close the door. My mother picks it up. I open the door a bit to listen.

"Hello... Yes, Theresa... Tomorrow... 10am... Yes thank you... He's doing fine, thank you... Yes, we understand... Thank you... Good-bye." She hangs up the phone. "Vinny, come out here."

I open the door slowly and brace myself, staring straight ahead. I'm not going to cry.

My mom walks over to me, ever so softly.

"Vinny. That was Mrs. Stanley on the phone. The wake starts tomorrow and the funeral is the next day."

I'm not going to cry.

"You don't have to go. I think they'd understand."

"I'll go."

I see my dad and Anne Marie standing outside the kitchen. They're watching us. I turn around and go back into the bathroom. I look in the mirror. No tears. Not a trace.

At least I was able to sleep. I hate getting up early in the summer. The morning sun actually woke me up. It's real early. My sister is still hidden behind her privacy blanket. Our window faces west. The morning sun is golden, and makes the brick on the buildings on the other side of the highway look real peaceful. Pretty. Hardly any traffic on the highway. Nobody on the street. The "el" is moving slowly. Lumbering out of the station heading uptown to the last stop, and maybe into the yard. It's a beautiful summer day. No school. No rain. I wonder what time the wake starts.

I've been to wakes before. My Uncle Klaus died, and his wife, my Aunt Louise, had a nervous breakdown right then and there. She tried to jump into the coffin. I went to another one for one of my father's Aunts, but it was uneventful. I sat in the back and didn't go up to see the body. When you do that, you have to kneel down on the little kneeler and that puts your face right even with the face of the dead person. God. I hope the coffin isn't open today.

249

It's almost time to go. My parents are at work. My sister is out doing something with her friends. I'm going to walk to Williams Funeral Home. All this time I saw the name Williams Funeral Home on those Little League uniforms, and it never really dawned on me that I'd actually be going in there to a wake of someone I knew.

There's the whole gang out in front. Bobby Bailey, Kowalzyck, Ralphie, BB, Jimmy Joe, Carrie and Donna. They're all talking and even laughing a little. Everybody's dressed up. I hope I don't cry. And I hope they don't try to make me laugh or something.

"Hi, guys," I say, walking right next to but not into the crowd. But I get a strange, aloof reaction. Everyone gets stone-faced, almost scared once they see me. I hear a few mutterings of "Hi, Vinny." I go right past them into the funeral home.

There's a board with the different names of the different wakes. There are four. Brian Shelley is listed in the Cardinal Spellman room. And there it is. That doorway right there. And I have to go in. And not cry.

There's quite a crowd in the room. It seems like everybody's talking and mostly standing around. There are even a few laughs heard around the various groups of young and old. One group is old ladies, another old men, another is guys in their 20s and late teens, and a whole group of guys in police uniforms. Up front is the coffin. It's open.

The room smells like roses. There are tons of them. Up front, I can see Whitey talking to the group of cops off to the side. He's wearing a dark, baggy suit, a fat black tie, and clunky shoes. They must be new clothes. He wouldn't be caught dead in those clothes ordinarily.

I'm afraid to go over to him. But I know I have to. I see his brother Alfie over in another group of guys. My legs don't want to do it, but I cross the back of the room so I don't have to go to the other side up front, and pass the open casket, and walk towards Whitey's group. I dread the moment when our eyes meet and we both face the realization of what we've experienced. I don't want to break down.

I stand a few feet away. Whitey looks over and sees

me. I walk over.

"Hi, Whitey."

"Hi,Vinny," Whitey says, like he hardly even knows me. Then he turns back to the cops he was talking to. He's ignoring me. Holy shit. I never expected this. Now what do I do? What the hell is going on? I look around, and everybody is engaged in conversation. Everybody but me has a group. There's nowhere for me to go... except up to the open casket. There it is. The American flag draped over it, and the top part open.

I walk over to the kneeler and kneel. And there it is. It looks totally fake. It doesn't look at all human. It looks like a dummy with makeup. All wax and unreal. You can see where they stuck in the eyebrows, and drew lines on the forehead. And it has a slight smile. That's not even a person in there. I couldn't cry even if I wanted to. I look over and Whitey's actually laughing with the cops, the center of attention. And here I am with this wax creature. I close my eyes and say 10 Hail Marys super fast. I get up and walk over to Whitey. He looks at me. I look at him.

"See ya later, Whitey."

"Yeah. See ya."

Now I feel like crying.

I don't even feel like hanging out with the kids outside the funeral home. I've seen what I had to see. Tomorrow is the funeral mass. Walking up Broadway always looks like a rainy day. The street is forever in the shade from the "el" overhead, and every few minutes the roar of the train drowns out everything. But really what it creates is silence. There's a wave of silence from Dyckman Street all the way up to 242nd Street, under every train, from the people below, in mid sentence who instinctively know that it's futile to try and talk with the "el" overhead. Without saying "excuse me" or "hold on" or even "oh, here's that damn train", people just pause for a moment, take a deep breath, and maybe think about something else. And maybe in that five seconds that the train makes you shut your yap, your brain just might make you think a little harder about what you were going to say, and just maybe in

251

those five seconds, you'll change your mind, or think twice, or just plain drop it. Sometimes it can even stop you thinking.

We don't have to go to school today or tomorrow. But Wednesday we pick up our real diplomas. The rest of school is in session for half days. It's a funny feeling being on the outside of the school looking in, while there are teachers and kids in the classrooms. There are handmade construction paper flags still on the windows left over from Memorial Day. I can see Miss O'Boyle standing in front of the second grade class pointing her finger at them. She's probably warning them about how tough third grade is going to be, and how they better listen to their parents over the summer, especially when they're near the water because they could easily get a cramp and drown. Above the second grade is our empty classroom, but I can see the overhead lights on. For some dumb reason, I feel like going in, and seeing what's going on in the class.

From the cinder-block wall stairwell I can hear voices echoing from other classrooms. Not the regimented "5-10-15-20" multiplication chants, but just the low chatter of kids playing "Candyland" or "Chutes and Ladders" or "Monopoly" in the older grades, waiting for Wednesday to hit. The door to the 8th grade is open. I want to see what's going on in there. I don't know why, but I do. I stand next to the doorway and lean in to see. And there's Sister Fidelis sitting at her desk doing work. I pull my head back. She didn't notice me. I could just walk back down the stairs and she'd never know, but for some reason, I want her to see me.

"Hello, Sister."

She looks up from her work, a little bit startled.

"Well hello, Vincent. Come in."

"I was walking by and thought I'd drop in."

This is a bad idea. I don't know what to say. I've never talked to her before by myself like this.

"I see you're dressed up on your day off. Where have you been?"

"A wake."

"Whose?"

"Whitey Shelley's brother."

252

"You mean Robert Shelley's brother. Yes. A terrible tragedy. What's his name?

"Robert."

"I know that; what's his brother's name?"

Boy am I dumb.

"Brian."

"God rest his soul. Vincent?"

"Yes, Sister?"

I think this is why I came here. Sister Fidelis will have something important to say to me about life, death, God, high school. I just know it. All these eight years of fears and threats and humiliations will make sense. All those things she and the other nuns did were part of ruling a mob of wild kids who needed to be kept in line. Even me. If I could get away with more, I would. I scare pretty easily. But some kids don't. More harsh measures are needed. But under the many layers of heavy black linen is a knowing heart.

She reaches over to the desk drawer on the far side of the desk, by the window and pulls it open. She pulls out the miserable excuse for a sling shot that Whitey brought in to class as a substitute, and hands it to me.

"Always remember to avoid the near occasions of sin. You may return this to Robert. See you on Wednesday."

I didn't even say good-bye. The "near occasion of sin"? What is that? That was all I could think of all the way home. I got my Baltimore Catechism and thumbed through it. And there it was, number 76: *"What are the near occasions of sin? The near occasions of sin are all persons, places, or things that may easily lead us into sin."* That could definitely limit your chances for a good summer.

I've been an altar boy at probably a fifty funerals. In fact, that's the second-best thing an altar boy can do. First, of course, is a wedding. It's understood you'll get a tip. But those are usually on a weekend anyway, so that can be a drag. But funerals generally are on weekdays at 10 or 11 in the morning which means you can leave class. And if you dilly dally enough afterwards, you could skip all morning and not have to come back until after lunch.

I must admit, though, we used to fool around a lot at funerals. All you have to do is see somebody like Georgie Lannen go cross-eyed for a second and you're trying not to explode with laughter. You really forget that you're at a funeral, and there's a dead person in that box, and people who loved him are sitting around crying. I remember one look from a man, though. One look from a man with tears in his eyes, who looked at me after I broke into a smile upon seeing something that could only be thought of as funny at a funeral. I took funerals more seriously after that.

But I don't think I'll ever be at a more serious funeral than the one today. I'm not going to the wake to see the last service there. I'm going right to the church for the 11:00 service.

From all the way down the block, I could see this was a funeral unlike any I had ever seen. Bunches of limos. Police cars. Black official-looking sedans. Even police motorcycles. Tons of people, and cops in their dress gear, hats, and white gloves. There were even cops that weren't from New York. I didn't want to walk in the main entrance. I don't feel like I belong here. I walk around the rear of the church, hoping to go in a side entrance. The door is open, and from the auditorium just below I hear a high-pitched blast from a musical instrument. I walk down the steps, and peek through the glass widow. There's a bag-pipe band there, in full dress, with pipes, drums and everything. I see on the front of the big bass drum "New York City Police Department Emerald Society." The same Emerald Society that starts off the Saint Patrick's Day Parade every year. In fact, the guy who is the leader of the band, with the huge round furry hat, and the big silver stick, who must be six and a half feet tall is there. When you see him coming up 5th Avenue, a hush goes over the crowd. People stop their yammering and stare at him. Then they break into a hard, steady applause. No screaming or yelling or whistling. Just a serious applause, like they do for the President after a big speech.

I enter the church and it's almost filled. It's dead quiet. I take a seat in the back, next to one of the old ladies who mutters the rosary at every funeral for the past 50 years. And as if silence couldn't get any more quiet, it does. The doors at the rear open, and the sun pours in, making it hard to see what's entering the church in the glare. The organ starts, the people rise, the casket is being carried by six cops with hats and white gloves. And right behind them is Whitey's mom, and his dad in a wheelchair, and then Whitey's brother Alfie, in a tie and jacket, and Whitey in his baggy suit. Alfie's hair looks really long compared to the jar-head look of the cops, and Whitey's hair looks different. Like Brian used to wear it. You can tell he's been crying a lot.

They don't look at anybody in the church. Eyes to the ground. Slow, shuffling steps on the hard marble floor. Everybody slowly takes their seat. The casket is placed on a wheeled chrome cart in the aisle. Right next to it is Whitey's father, also on a wheeled chrome cart of sorts, his wheelchair.

As the mass begins, I don't hear words. I hears sounds. My mind hears the sounds from that night. Just three days ago. Moans and groans and screams and crying. And this is the end. After all the masses, and tests, and lectures, and lessons, and warnings, and memorizing prayers, and reading psalms, and burning letters, and kissing crosses, and stations of the cross, and studying why God made us, this is the way we end. No wonder the nuns and priests are so persistent with their fears. Death is awful. But with all the terror they put before us, I had no idea it could be this awful.

The priest stops. Silence. And suddenly from the rear comes the piercing wail of the New York Police Department Emerald Society's pipes playing "Amazing Grace." The old lady next to me stops muttering her rosary. No one's crying now. Just staring in awe at the power and majesty of the band, in their dress kilts, and deadly serious expressions as they march up the aisle, past the coffin and out the side entrance. Just an inkling of the power that awaits us all when we're up there in the box, making our final stop into the place where we'll spend eternity. That's why the nuns and priests are so intense. Get ready. The end is near. And you better be ready.

The service is over. And like they came in, the group

goes out. As Whitey goes past me, even though he's a whole section away, I could swear he saw me, but turned quickly away as if he didn't. And then they were gone. I stayed in the church as it emptied, and could hear one more playing of "Amazing Grace" as everyone piled into limos and sedans, and took off for the cemetery. The lady next to me stopped saying her rosary and left. Mrs. Carroll, the church worker, starts taking away the candles and the other funeral mass extras. The altar boys come walking out of the sacristy with their cassocks on hangers. The big one says to the little one, "... we'll just say we're late because Mrs. Carrol made us clean up the sacristy. How much money you got?" And out they went. I didn't go to the burial. How would I get there? I don't think I could take it.

I always thought that the day I actually picked up my diploma would be the happiest of my life. For eight long years, not being able to wait for the end of the morning, day, week, dreading Monday, thinking of new ways to describe an illness that could keep me home. How I looked forward to Columbus Day, Halloween followed by All Souls day, Thanksgiving's four-day weekend, Christmas vacation, mid-term break, spring break, and then the time of year that made life worth living: summer. And how I dreaded that last buzz cut before first day of school back from summer, and the smell of new bookbag vinyl "back-to-school" specials at John's Bargain Store.

But picking up my diploma today is not the most joyful thing of all time. I want it. I'm glad to get it. But I've got other things on my mind. I still can't stop thinking about you know what. And after the wake yesterday, I can't help but worry about Whitey. He acted and looked real weird. He was putting on a fake front, wearing that square suit and wing tips, slicking back his hair and yukking it up with Brian's cop buddies. He acted like he didn't know me. Or like me.

I also expected some kind of class celebration or ceremony today. Yeah, we had a full-tilt graduation over the weekend, but all we received were fake diplomas. Today is the real day. But looking into the classroom, I see there's no ceremony. There's not even a class. It turns out that you just

256

show up, get your manila envelope, and leave. That's it. Bye bye.

Mark Fay and Louis Zummo, the two biggest sissy tattletales in the class, are in front of me at Sister Fidelis' desk. Each one has a wrapped gift box for her. Shit. I usually do have a gift for the teacher at the end of the year. It's always a leftover from Christmas that my mother received from somebody and stashed away for just such an occasion, like a stinky round box of powder with a big puffy applicator. I forgot.

"Thank you, Sister Fidelis. You've been my favorite teacher ever, all year," Mark Fay chirps.

"Thank you, Mark, and good luck to you at Cathedral. I hope you stick to your parent's dream for you."

Oh boy. Cathedral is the high school where guys go who want to be priests. And Mark's parents have decided HE'S gonna be the priest in the family.

Mark picks up his envelope and goes past me. "Good morning, Vincent."

Who says "Good morning"? Only old farts say that.

"Thank you so much for being a wonderful teacher," Louis says, outchirping Mark, "I'm so sorry to be leaving Presentation."

Sorry to be leaving? Why? 8 years of this isn't enough?

"Thank you, Louis, and I look forward to seeing you throughout the summer."

Oh my God! Don't tell me some people have to come back for something! I hope I ain't one of them.

"I'm looking forward to it! I love gardening!"

Sheesh. He's going to do the yard work at the convent. What a sap. The only time I ever did that was back in 6th grade, and I thought it would be a gas to collect all the crickets I could find in the yard, and dump them into the mail slot of the convent's front door. But not smart enough to take Whitey's throat clearing as a signal, I didn't see the principal standing behind me. I was snagged. I can't believe she didn't smack me in the face. All she did was yell at me a little, after I told her through chattering teeth and my imitation of Jackie Gleason's "homina homina homina" that I was just gathering

257

up crickets for disposal... isn't THIS a garbage chute?

Louis grabs his envelope, and again, "Good morning, Vincent" as he leaves.

"Good morning, Sister."

"Vincent, remember what I told you yesterday?"

"Yes, Sister."

"Good. And good luck in high school, college, marriage, and death."

"Thank you, Sister."

I turned around in shock. Let me out of here.

"Vincent!"

"Yes, Sister!" I whipped around thinking she had something even more incredible to tell me. Like when the end of the world is or something.

"You forgot something."

I forgot my diploma.

I grabbed it, turned around and jumped down the stairs three by three. It's a gorgeous day. Grammar school is over. No more nuns. No more uniforms. Summer vacation is here. I've got to find Whitey.

I'm afraid to call for Whitey. I don't even like walking past his building. In fact, there's some construction going on there. I can't help but get a closer look. Maybe from just across the street.

They're tearing the rest of the picket fence down. If that fence wasn't there, and he fell just to the right a little bit, and landed in the bushes, maybe he would've survived. One of the Walsh brothers fell off the roof of my building, but grabbed onto a few clotheslines on the way down and he lived. Mondoo Moran fell five stories down a dumbwaiter shaft, but he lived because he fell into a pile of garbage at the bottom. If only Whitey had gone home earlier, he could've let Brian in. God. If I'm thinking about this stuff, I can imagine what's going through Whitey's mind.

I can't cross the street and go into that courtyard. I think I'll just go home and call Whitey. To think Whitey's lived on the top floor all these years, right in the front of the building with that great view, and this is what happens.

I take a gander up the building, floor by floor, to look at Whitey's windows, where Brian tried to get into, and just as I finally make it to the top, there he is. There's Whitey. He's been watching the workers in the courtyard and been watching me. But as soon as he sees that I see him, he ducks back inside without a "Hey, Vinny" or a wave, or even the laziest of the hello signs reserved for acquaintances you're either too familiar with or just don't care about, the head nod. Shit. I better go up. But I'm not going through that courtyard. I walk to the alley next to the building and into the cellar. This cellar is smaller than mine; but if it's possible, dirtier, darker and smellier. His elevator has a round, glass, cracked window. It would be broken through except for the chicken wire that holds it together. The ride from 'B" to "6" sure seems long. I just stare at the numbers above the door that don't light up and watch the floors go by until it jerks to a stop. I know it's the sixth floor because somebody wrote a six on the wall with a magic marker.

I walk over to Whitey's dark brown metal door right next to the stairwell. This is the first time since the accident that I'm here, and I'm drawn to the stairwell. I look down. And it looks deeper than I remember it. I remember the things we dropped down here for fun to see how they would splatter. Like watermelon.

It's now or never. I knock on Whitey's door. No answer. I knock harder. No answer. I bang two times. I hear the chain and the locks open. The door opens a crack. It's Alfie.

"Hi, Vinny. Whitey's taking a nap."

"Oh. OK. I'll try later. Bye."

The door closes and I hear the chain and locks again. I think I'll walk down the stairs. Maybe I'll see if anybody's hanging around the park. It's a nice day. It's summer vacation. And since most of the families haven't gone away on vacation yet, there's probably even enough guys for a full baseball game. I'll go home and get my mitt just in case.

I wonder why Whitey doesn't want to see me?

It's amazing how so many kids get to go away for the summer. There's no way we could pull off something like that with both of my parents working. Almost everybody that goes away for the summer goes to Rockaway Beach. I guess that's because the subway actually goes there. Dads can still get to work, although instead of a half-hour ride on the subway from the Bronx, it's close to two hours on the subway from Rockaway, and it's the line with the oldest cars. The motorman actually rides between the cars to open and close the doors. The seats are made of this stuff called cane. They're real bouncy, and look like bamboo or something. In the summer, they have these huge fans that slowly spin overhead. If you're any taller than about six foot two, you have to be real careful because you could get your head chopped off. There's no cage or anything over them. But they turn very slowly. As if it's supposed to make you feel cooler because you see the fan spinning. The train even sounds different from the subway trains on the Broadway/IRT. These trains start off real slow, and go *"hum hum hummmmmmmm hum hum hummmmmmm hum hum hummmmmmmm hum hum hummmmmmm hum hum hum hum hum hum hum hummmmmmmmmm"* until all the little hums are joined together in one long humming until the next screech of steel on steel at the next station.

The ride from the Bronx to Rockaway is a real adventure. You start out right in your own neighborhood at your local "el" station. (Ours is 238th Street on the Broadway IRT.) From there you go to 168th Street, where you take an elevator that has an elevator operator in it. That elevator is always jam packed with subway riders, and in the summer, everybody is a sweaty mess. They jam into that elevator car like it's the last one of the day, and if you thought the subway was crowded and smelly, you can imagine what this elevator is like. This elevator operator job has to be one of the worst in the world. The ride is a really long one, with no stops along the way. You go up up up, and then when you get to the top, you're at another subway line. The "A" train. You take the "A" train which thankfully is an express, and that takes you all the way to Rockaway... through Harlem, all the way downtown, and through a tunnel into Brooklyn.... you go through Brooklyn for a long time, with station after station of street names I'm not at all familiar with. Streets where I don't know anybody from the area, and just when you don't think you can't take the constant *hum hum hummmmmms* anymore, all of a sudden you're out of the tunnel. Then it's really like you're in another world. The train goes across water on a long rickety wooden bridge that goes so close to people's homes you can see them through the windows. But not like in my neighborhood where the houses next to the "el" are apartment houses; these are private houses. Some of them are actually on stilts in the water. But even though they are actual houses, and not apartment buildings, they look just as crappy as any other apartments next to the "el" along Broadway in the Bronx, with tattered drapes hanging out windows, and broken window panes, and old sad eyed people looking at us as we rush by. And after a couple of miles of dark, smelly water, with rotting piers and old tires tied to motorboats, in the distance you can see the top of the roller coaster. And once you get across a huge bay, you can see the ocean down any of the streets that lead straight down to the beach.

And fathers from all over the Bronx, Manhattan and Brooklyn make this journey everyday. Traveling the the awful trek so that their families can enjoy the summer at Rockaway Beach crowded into tiny linoleum lined boxes called bungalows; filled with furniture thrown out from New York City homes and apartments a generation ago.

That is why it's important to get a baseball game going this week, this day. Because any day now, the Frasers, the Callahans, the Finnerans, the Monahans, the Esslingers, and thousands of other families across NY will start their summer trek, and will fill their cardboard suitcases and cardboard boxes, and make their great migration to the ocean. With that they leave behind the kids in the neighborhood who don't go away for the summer. Like me and Whitey.

I've got my "Ralph Terry" model glove that we got with S & H Green Stamps last year. Hopefully, other kids in the neighborhood are thinking the same way I am, and there will be a bunch of them over in the park, waiting to choose up sides for a "real" game...at least nine guys on a team. Because once summer really hits, and there are fewer guys around, we're lucky to play with 4, or even 3 on a team. Then you're only allowed to play on one side of the field. It gets really weird if there's only three on a team. Since most guys bat righty, you only put guys at short, third, and left, but then you make third base first. Of course you have to bat fungo. It gets really hairy when you have a guy at second or third. If there's a play at second, the shortstop has to cover the bag, but if there's a play at third or home, all you have to do is throw the ball to first and beat the runner. No steals. No leads off base. It's always interesting to see the negotiating that goes on once a situation comes up that's a little out of the ordinary. "Waddyuh mean that's a double play because the infield fly rule was in effect and the runner on second was off the base?!!"

Normally, I'd stop by Whitey's to call for him because he's on the way to the park. Not today. Not now. Just me and Ralph Terry. Through the fences and trees at the entrance of the park, I can see a bunch of guys at the baseball diamond. Looks like there could be enough for a real game with pitching and everything. A whole mob.

And there is. Guys of all ages. Some of the younger really good players like Paul Donnegan and even some high school kids. Robbie McDougal even plays for Manhattan Prep. A varsity pitcher yet. Whoever gets him wins. And Hector Lopez, the second Puerto Rican kid in history to hang out in the neighborhood, is here too. He goes to public school, but he's one of the best players around. And the fact that he has the same name as a real Yankee player makes him that much more desirable to have on your team. I don't really know him that well. He lives down on Review Place and hangs out with Donnegan and those guys, but he seems really funny. Even while playing in a game, he kids around and makes everybody laugh, even though he's real good. There's never a routine play with Hector. A flip behind the back or bouncing a short pop off his head and catching it is his style. That's a lot differ-ent from Robbie McDougal, who even takes these choose-up games as serious as a knife fight. I'd rather be on Hector's side.

It's hard to believe that this mess of kids fooling and running around, playing pepper with cigarettes hanging off their lips, running around with cups on the outside of their pants, is going to gel into a game of baseball. But before you know it, McDougal and Joey Trotta, the two best players, are choosing. I'm not the last one picked, but I'm pretty close to it. Fortunately, because I throw lefty, there's no way I'm going to be catcher. Everybody knows that lefties can't play catcher. Even in choose-up games in the park. So some poor slob will have to crouch back there with a leftover Little League mask that somebody stole when the Dodgers were still in Brooklyn and that's it. It's usually Whitey back there.

Once things got organized, I began to realize that this was probably the best game I've ever been in. Sure, they stuck me out in right field, where the ball hardly ever goes, but with McDougal and Trotta pitching, it's like a real game. I mean a real game. With balls and strikes, and close plays, and low scoring. Not the usual fungo free-for-alls that most of us play with guys like Joey Trotta just pumping the ball over the outfield fence for home runs every time up. And that isn't easy. It's got to be 300 feet down the line, and Yankee Stadium is 301 at the left field foul pole. But even Joey is grunting and missing McDougal's fast ball, and looking as bad as I probably will against his curve. I know I'm not that good at baseball. I can field well, and have an excellent arm, but I can't hit if my life depended on it. And seeing McDougal out there, any fantasies I've had about playing baseball at a big school like Cardinal Hayes next year are just about done. In fact, I'm scared shitless knowing that I have to bat against him next inning.

It's zip to zip. I'm up next. I watch Kevin Flynn swing at three fast balls. Sit down Flynn. I've played a lot of games in my life. Tackle football on concrete, hurling, ice hockey, pin darts, slingshot wars, but I've never been as scared playing anything as I am right now. McDougal looks like he doesn't even know me. I'd feel a little better if we had helmets like they do in Little League, but that's too sissy. It's just me and an old Louisville slugger that I got on Bat Day. The Mickey Mantle model. All I know is I don't want to look like a fag. Everybody on the field is staring at me as I approach the plate. This isn't lob ball. This is real hard ball. But I'm determined. I'm not going to be scared. Not in front of all these guys. I look out to McDougal. He's not trying to look mean or friendly. Just blank. Just pitching. I'm set. I'm not bailing out. I'm going to hit this damn ball if it kills me. All six foot two of McDougal goes into that big major league Juan Marichal wind-up. Leg up over his head, arms twisting around, swoosh, here it comes. Shit, I've never seen a ball this fast coming at me in my life. It's coming right at me. I hope it's a curve ball. It isn't. I'm frozen. THWACK. Holy shit. I never thought it was possible to have that much pain on the meat of my upper arm, just below my shoulder.

"You asshole, why didn't you get out of the way?!!" McDougal shouts at me. Shit. I thought I'd be an asshole if I did. I don't think I'm actually crying. Yes, I am writhing and wincing with pain. But I'm not crying. At least it didn't hit me in the temple, the adam's apple or the mouth. But that's it. I'm done for today. "I think I better quit, guys."

"You jerk, you should've jumped out of the way," McDougal adds more insult to my injury. I can see Hector at short stop, laughing hysterically behind his glove. I pick up my Ralph Terry and my bat, and head away from the field. I can't believe how much my arm still hurts. The game continues without me. Of course. It shouldn't be any other way. Somebody goes down, so what? The world's supposed to stop or something? There's always somebody else on the sidelines ready to jump in.

Just beyond the outfield fence, there's a place to sit on a railing and watch the game from afar without being noticed. Not only is McDougal striking almost everybody out, he's hitting the ball against the outfield fence or through a gap every time up. After a while as the pain is starting to fade, I hear somebody over by the railroad tracks walking down through the brush to the tracks. I catch a glimpse of what I think is

Whitey with somebody else.

The game doesn't interest me as much as this. I sneak over to the hill that leads down to the tracks. It looks like the two guys were going to the part of the tracks that are under the bridge. I head over to where I can spy on them. Could it be Whitey? Who could he be with? And why would they be going under the bridge?

It is Whitey. And he's with Sean Symington. The same Sean Symington who practically beat up me, my cousin, and Whitey at my brother's wedding. Symington the hitter. From where I am hiding, which is pretty far away, I can tell one thing about them. They're under the bridge for the one of two reasons all kids go under there. One, to throw rocks at pigeons, or two, to sniff glue. They're not throwing rocks. I don't want to see what they're doing. I sneak back up the hill, trying not to make noise on the dead leaves and rusted Rheingold cans. Whitey and Sean Symington? I walk home in a daze. By the time I get home, put a baseball in my glove, a rubber band around it, and under my bed, I remember that my arm hurts like hell.

Whitey's brother Alfie got a job at the deli down at 238th Street and Broadway. He works behind the counter and he is one odd duck back there. The owner of the deli is an old Nazi named Hans Engelman. I say Nazi because he really was a German soldier in WW II. Everybody knows it, and nobody cares. Hans looks like a stocky, barrel-chested Bela Lugosi. And he's just as charming as Count Dracula when there are customers in the store and just as mean as Dracula the Vampire if you mess around in his store. Besides Hans, there's this other deli clerk named Frank. He looks exactly, and I mean exactly, like Arnold Stang, the guy in the Chunky commercials. He even sounds like him. Hans has a strict dress code. White shirt with the big white apron that goes up to your chest, and a bow tie you get out of a cigar box in the back. The sight of Alfie in that outfit is something to see between Hans and Frank. There those two are and there's Alfie with his long blonde hair, white shirt, bow tie, ratty dungarees and holey

Converse sneakers. Hans is really particular about his workers. He fires guys all the time. He once fired somebody for saying "shoot" (instead of shit) when he was frustrated with a pushy customer. So for Alfie to work there, looking the way he does, must mean he's a really good worker.

I'm kind of afraid to go into the deli to see Alfie. I want to talk to him but I feel really dumb. What am I supposed to say, "Why's Whitey hanging out with Sean Symington?" What, am I queer? Screw him if he wants to hang out with Symington. I used to hang out with Tommy Kowalzyck all the time before me and Whitey became best friends. But for some reason, this seems different.

I know Alfie's working now, he works 2 to 10 at night. I usually see him riding his bike someplace after 10 with his apron still on, flapping away. I already had dinner, and I can see the deli dinner rush is over as I peek through the space between the Bert and Harry Piels cardboard display in the front window without being seen. Hans is gone for the day, but Frank is still there, waiting on a really old lady with a huge shopping bag filled with Rheingold quart empties. I take a step to the right, and I can see Alfie, in the hall that leads to the back of the store. He's got a mop in a wringer, and he's really exerting himself, getting every last bit of dirty water out of that mop. I can see Frank's now taking six new quarts of Rheingold and carefully placing them back into the double shopping bag for the old, over-rouged lady. I wait for her to hobble to the door, as I pull it open for her. "Thank you, young man," she says, leaving a trail of some kind of overpowering perfume in her wake.

I walk over to the wooden refrigerator door and take out a 16 ounce Coke. Alfie doesn't see me. He must be in the back mopping. I go over to the counter and Frank takes his head out of the "Daily News."

"17 cents junior."

I hand over a quarter and Frank rings it up on the cash register, whisks out my 8 cents change, bangs the nickel on the counter so it flips chest high, snatches it out of the air and slams it down. "You want that opened?"

266

"Yes please."

"Yes please? Manners and everything? Good for you, junior." He picks up a bottle opener and flips off the top, sending it over his head, picks up an old coffee can from under the counter, holds it out and PLUNK. Bull's-eye. What a show. I almost forgot why I was really there. "Is Alfie around?"

"Sure junior. Say, you ain't his kid brother are ya?"

"No. Just a friend."

"Just a friend, OK junior, hold on." Frank walks over to the wooden refrigerator door and opens it. "Hey, Alfie, come on out, there's somebody to see ya."

Alfie walks out from the hall that leads to the back, wiping his hands on a clean towel. He's got a puzzled "what-the-hell-are-you- doing-here?" look on his face.

"Oh, Vinny. Come on back here."

I follow Alfie down the narrow hall. There are shelves from the floor to the ceiling filled with all kinds of things; toilet paper, cans of peas, rolls of butcher paper. It leads to a kitchen, back room area. It's a lot darker than the brightly lit front of the deli, but the huge stainless steel stove/oven gleams. The linoleum is worn clear to the floor in some places, like in front of the stove and next to the table where somebody has been peeling a sack of potatoes, but everything is spotless and smells like it was just cleaned with Lysol. And there's a delicious smell of roast beef cooking.

"Hold on a second," Alfie says as he grabs together the bottom part of his apron, making it like a pot holder, opens the oven, and pulls out a tray with a picture-post-card perfect roast beef. He places it on top of the stove. "It has to cool off for a while."

"You actually make the roast beef here?"

"Yeah, we make everything, potato salad, meat cakes, cole slaw, soup, stew."

"Wow." I was impressed.

I watch Alfie as he takes care of cleaning up his work as he goes. I'm not going to say anything about seeing Brian's death. I can't. I just want to talk about Whitey, but not even that really. I don't know why I even came in here.

267

"Funny you should show up, Vinny, I've been wanting to talk to you. Have you noticed Whitey acting... different... lately?"

I was taken aback. "Well, to tell you the truth, I haven't really seen him at all lately."

Alfie pulled over a wooden stool and took a seat. I could tell he was thinking.

"Were you with him today?"

"No, I was playing baseball, then I saw him with Sean Symington."

"Where were they?"

Now it was my turn to think. Should I tell Alfie I saw Whitey going under the bridge? Would that be ratting on him?

"Where were they going?" Alfie asked me again.

"They were down by the second bridge, at the tracks."

I could see Alfie was now upset. He reached up, began rubbing his forehead like he was trying to push down a painful bump. I could tell Alfie knew just what that meant.

"Thanks, Vinny."

I walked out, not knowing if I did the right thing. I hope I don't bump into Whitey on the way home.

I haven't seen Symington around in ages. He mostly hangs out in Bailey Park. That's a playground that's about five blocks down Bailey Avenue. Five blocks may not seem like much, but it's practically a whole different neighborhood. A lot of kids near the park go to public school, or to St. John's which is the next parish over. St. John's is a lot bigger than Presentation, and it seems like they have more really bad kids than we do. It was down by St. John's that I experienced something that I'll probably never forget.

You see fights on TV all the time. And every time you see a punch, there's a loud THWACK you hear that goes along with every punch. I've seen plenty of fights on the street or in the school yard, and never once did I hear such a sound. Until one day down by St. John's. We were coming back from Fieldstone where we go to get chestnuts every fall. Why do we get chestnuts? I'm not really sure. Except that I know come fall, we take our boxes up to Fieldstone Road and throw thick sticks up into the majestic chestnut trees that line the median. Fieldstone Road is the richest street in Riverdale. Every house a mansion or some huge United Nations residence. But that's where the chestnuts are. And with all those big front yards, and trees, and even a little park with a pond in it, you never see any kids around up there, or even just people walking down the streets. If we knew one kid with a yard like that, the entire neighborhood would be over everyday.

But to get up to Fieldstone Road, you have to walk through a few other neighborhoods that have kids on the street. Kids we don't know. And one of those neighborhoods is St. John's Parish. It's the heart of Kingsbridge. Sort of the "downtown" of our area. There are lots more stores and not as many trees or parks as my neighborhood.

On the way back from one very fruitful chestnut gathering expedition, we were hauling our boxes of chestnuts down the long city steps that cut through Ewin Park, down the steep hill that separates the lower class of Kingsbridge from the upper class of Riverdale. Ewin Park is kind of a no-man's land between the two. It was my mistake for lagging behind the others, but I was. And two really big kids I didn't know appeared out of nowhere and blocked me on the step landing. I didn't want to yell "help." I would've sounded like a sissy.

"Waddyuh got in the box?" the really big, fat, frecklefaced, bucktoothed crew cutted one asked.

"Chestnuts." I said flatly, knowing that I was in deep shit, trying to figure out if it was going to be fight or flight. I could see Whitey, Jimmy Joe, and Ralphie down the bottom of the steps, goofing around with their biggest chestnut haul ever, oblivious to the fact that I was about to get my ass kicked.

"Fuck chestnuts," The smaller gap-toothed dirty little mick with long bangs covering his eyes said, as he smacked the box I was holding down, sending my entire batch tumbling down the stairs. And without another word, as I was watching the shiny brown objects bounce away, THWACK. That sound. That sound of a punch you hear on TV and in the movies. That's why you don't hear it when you watch a fight! You only hear it if it's you. You hear it in YOUR head. And much to my surprise, another thing I see on TV came true. When Popeye hits Bluto with his last punch of the fight that sends Bluto into oblivion, you always see stars spinning around Bluto's head. Well, wouldn't you know it. Now I see stars too! And all in one split second. Next thing I know I'm down on the ground, holding my mouth in pain. Lots of blood. It's my lip. Glad I always carry a handkerchief.

I see the two assholes who sucker-punched me running up to the top of the steps, and out of the park. And my friends FINALLY running up to me.

It was that beautiful fall day not far from St. John's that I learned about the sound that punches make, seeing stars, and getting hit really hard in the face when you don't expect it.

That was two years ago. Symington hangs out around St. John's mostly with kids younger and smaller than him. But I know that lately he's been hanging around our block a lot and at Van Cortlandt Park. He's not just a hitter anymore. He's not just into punching out people he doesn't like. He's into a new kick... vandalism. Breaking windows, tearing up shrubbery, spray painting on walls, smashing car windshields. But I get the feeling he likes seeing other kids following him or even doing the damage for him. It seems like the worst kids always want others to do what they're doing. Even more so.

I haven't seen Whitey in days. It doesn't seem possible, but it's happened. And now, there are a lot of kids gone away for the summer. Off to Rockaway. I can walk by Whitey's building now. There's a chain-link fence where the picket fence used to be. There's almost always kids hanging out down on Review Place. Not many of those kids go away for the summer. So what if they're all a little bit younger than I am? They're pretty good at organizing games. Short-handed baseball and Wiffle ball are the two best.

The deli where Alfie works is right across the street from where the Review guys hang out. That's where they go for sodas and stuff usually. After dark, the guys are good at getting a Ringo-Leeveo or Black Joe together. It's fun playing in that empty lot with all its trees and junk you can hide around. And it's right next to the railroad tracks. It's a good alternative to hanging out on my block.

I've always been smallish for my age. And there have always been older kids that played with Ringo-Leeveo or Black Joe up on my block. But most of the guys on Review are around my size. And it seems like the small ones are all incredibly fast, like Paul Donnegan. But I kind of feel like one of the better players.

"I'm gonna get a soda," Paul says as he passes me by, as I just show up for the day. I figure, what the heck, so I go with him across the street to the deli. Alfie's behind the counter.

"Paul, Vinny," Alfie says without looking up from scooping potato salad out of a big bowl into the tray under the glass counter. Paul buys his 16 ounce bottle of Coke. I do the same. Just as Alfie is handing me my 8 cents change, he looks me in the eye. It's a piercing look. I feel like he's going to yell at me or something. "Have you seen Whitey around?" he asks me dead serious like.

"Nope." Alfie goes back to his salad scooping. Paul's a few strides ahead of me. Out the door and across the street we go.

I wonder if Alfie has seen Whitey around? I wonder if Whitey's really hanging out with Symington and those guys all the time? I wonder what he's doing? Maybe I'll get a good idea tonight. There's supposed to be a big party in the stands, and I hear that everybody knows there's going to be free beer. I'm sure Symington will make a point of being there.

But this afternoon is a special day. Opening day of Wiffle-ball season. For the past nine months the empty lot by the railroad tracks, next to what we call "the cow path" which is just an old dirt short cut to the school, has been a garbage-strewn dump. But today, with great cooperation from every kid on the block, every bit of glass, old tin can, and crap of every shape and size is being picked up, put into an old wheel-barrow and dumped down by the railroad tracks. It exposes a large dirt-and-grass patch, perfect for Wiffle ball. And with a few old hammers and nails, Paul Donnegan and Hector Lopez

271

are fixing up a wooden fence that is looking more and more like the outfield fence of a baseball field. Petey McFarland comes out of the alley onto the lot, er field, with a rubber barrel. Hector, who I think is actually the organizer of this whole thing, is ecstatic. "Let's go," he yells.

Being from up the block and a grade or two ahead of most guys, and not really part of this usual gang, I'm just along for the ride. A follower.

And off we are, all 8 or so of us, out of the lot, across the cow path, down the garbage-covered hill to the railroad tracks. And all of us running and screaming towards the back of the Stella D'Oro cookie factory. You have to be careful where you're running because the ties are in swampy water. And sitting next to a loading dock is a big round rail road car. Not a boxcar, but a roundish tanker. I still can't figure out what's going on, but everybody, especially Hector, is real excited. Bigger than going to get chestnuts. Hector has the rubber barrel and he jumps under the loading platform, disappearing. "Si si si! Bingo!" And up pops Hector through a hole in the platform, his hair and face totally white with.... I don't know. But it's like a cartoon. "Fill 'em up!" he yells.

"What the hell is that stuff?" I ask Petey, who being a little chubby is holding up the rear with me.

"Flour! Over-spill flour. Tons of it." And there it is. Tons of pure white flour under the loading dock. What happens is the freighter car pulls up here filled with flour for the cookie factory, and some big hose is connected to the tanker, and sucks all the flour out of it. But a lot spills and winds up on the ground. And what better way to paint a batter's box, foul lines, bases, and each other, than with tons of found flour. Which is what we did for the next couple of hours, until the field looked like a perfect baseball field, and we all looked like white, dusty, laughing, ghosts from head to toe. Creating the best Wiffle-ball field in the Bronx or maybe the whole stinking world. And after the singing of a serious National Anthem, heads down, hands over hearts, and "play ball", the summer began. With or without Whitey Shelley.

We were practically black and blue from trying to smack the flour out of our hair and clothes. Luckily, I got home before my sister or my parents, and was able to take a shower and put my clothes in the hamper.

By the time I'm out of the shower, my sister is home, and she's already got dinner cooking. Any minute my parents will be home, dinner eaten, and back out. It doesn't get dark until nearly nine, so I can be home at 10. Wow! A lot can happen in that hour of darkness.

I'm not going to call for Whitey. I feel too weird. If I run into him and he stops and talks to me like nothing happened, well OK. But I'm sure as hell not going to start something with him. I don't know what to say. As soon as I picture his face in my mind, all I can think of is that blank look on his face. That empty stare and those zombie-like words. "Who is it? Who is it? Who is it?" I had to run. I couldn't just stand there. What was I supposed to do? I couldn't do anything. I couldn't help. I had to run away. I couldn't look at Whitey for another second knowing the truth. Knowing the whole awful truth of what happened. I couldn't look.

Once school is out, not only are a lot of kids away for the summer, but some are at a day camp or maybe away for a week or two, or even hanging out with different kids for some reason. Things are always changing during the summer.

I'm not going to call for anybody tonight. I'm going to walk down to the park and see who's there. That's who I'll be hanging out with tonight. Whoever is there. One way to get there, is to walk down the cow path, which goes next to the lot where we built our magnificent Wiffle-ball field out of Stella D'Oro cookie flour. And there they are. I don't think they even went home for dinner. There's Hector pitching his special Steve Hamilton folly floater Wiffle ball off our "mound", still covered from nappy head to holey "skip" sneakers in flour. Paul Donnegan is on the other team, with a bunch of really little kids. Probably 4th and 5th graders. Hector and Paul are yelling at them to do better, don't be a baby, faster, catch it, hit

273

it, throw it, slide, think! Passing down the skills we all learned from the big kids.

I just sit down on the board nailed across two wooden milk crates... our bleachers. The game is over, Hector's team winning 24 to 20. Hector runs around the field shaking everyone's hand for a good game.

The little kids want to keep playing, but Paul and Hector join me for a walk to get some sodas. And by the time we get to the store after stopping to talk to various people along the way...Barbara Boulevard (a retarded girl who lives in Paul's building)... Lenny Rabinowitz (one of the only Jewish teenagers on the block, who looks and acts just like any other Irish hitter teenager, except he looks more Italian than they do which is a real plus)... Olive (a very short and ugly woman with 3 year old who will "do it" for five bucks)... and even a short conversation with Mr. Walsh, sitting on his front stoop, warning us that the niggers are trying to take over, and we better be ready for them when they come off the "el" with their knives. He recommends baseball bats with nails sticking out of them.

Drinking Cokes on the street corner is a show in itself. Watching people come home from work, drunks coming out of the bars, and the assorted nuts who live in basement apartments on the block. Before you know it... it's almost dark. And time to walk over to the stands. Time to let the evening really begin. It could be a whole new crowd over there, being that it's summer.

And it is. I can see from the fence that there are only two groups of kids there. Unlike just a couple of weeks ago when there were 5 or 6 of them. One group at one end, of mostly younger high school kids, and at the other end, older high school kids and up.

Me, Paul and Hector know the younger crowd. Even though Paul and Hector are still in grade school, it's OK, they're cool. Usually if you're good in sports, and you aren't afraid to smoke or drink, you're cool. Jimmy Joe, Ralphie, and BB are there. I haven't seen them in a while.

"Hey, Vinny, where's Whitey?" Jimmy Joe calls down to me as we come up the steps to the top part of the stands.

274

"I don't know. I haven't seen him," I yell up.

"Me neither," Jimmy Joe replies.

I can see that the guys look a lot more comfortable with their Marlboros and their cans of Rheingold. And they're not making a big deal out of it, either, you know, like kids do when they first start out smoking and drinking. They could be their own fathers. Except for the music playing on the transistor radios. Echoed deejays like Murray the K, and Cousin Brucie, play the Beatles, Dave Clark Five, Roy Orbison, The Beach Boys, The Four Seasons, Peter and Gordon, The Supremes, Chuck Berry, and Gerry and the Pacemakers nonstop. No Frank Sinatra, or Nat King Cole or Peggy Lee, or even Elvis Presley. That's the music of our parents.

The evening turns from twilight to dark summer night. The beer cans and cigarette butts pile up. The laughs grow louder, the curses dirtier. I'm not drinking or smoking. I don't know why, I'm just not. And the dumber everybody gets, the closer I am to just going home.

But suddenly a tap on the shoulder, and a tug of the hair on the back on my neck gets my attention. Whitey.

"Where you been, Vinny?"

It's Whitey alright, but he sounds different. Like somebody else. Like somebody who doesn't know me that well.

"Hi, Whitey, where've YOU been?" I say, standing up and turning around to face him. I see he's just gotten a haircut. Short. Like Brian used to wear. But more striking is the fact that he's not wearing his black glasses. And without them, he's a dead wringer for Brian. Something I never noticed before.

And from out of the shadow behind Whitey, someone else appears. Symington.

"Hey, little Schmidt! Where's your beer can, you little queer?"

Symington sure hasn't changed. I don't reply. Knowing that Symington knows my brother will find him and kick his ass if he messes with me, I have a certain amount of bravery. Not much, but enough.

Symington grabs a beer from a bag on the ground,

shakes it up, holds it by his mouth, opens it with a can opener, and shoots the entire thing down his throat, with a considerable amount dribbling down his neck, into his ginney tee and down his chest. When he's done, he lets out with a deep primal yell. And much to my surprise, Whitey does the exact same thing, right after him. I think they're both polluted.

"Come on!" Symington screams in Whitey's ear, "we're going 8 ballin'!" Symington then pulls out an 8 ball from the pool hall out of his pocket. 8 ballin' is when you bust a large plate-glass store front window, or a home's picture window with an 8 ball. "Who's coming?" Symington yells to the crowd of younger drinkers. Jimmy Joe, Ralphie and BB look at each other, and agree. 8 ballin' is for them. I've got to go. Just to keep an eye on Whitey.

I've known guys who go out and bust windows and stuff. The first rule is, don't do it in your own neighborhood. You could get caught if someone recognizes you. So it's up to Riverdale, where the rich people live. Symington is definitely the leader. His drunken troops behind him, off to destroy. Every once in a while, Symington will urge his eager troops to shut up. Don't attract attention. It's like a secret mission. Whitey's ignoring Jimmy Joe, Ralphie and BB, and probably doesn't even realize I'm there. He's sloppy drunk, following Symington like a puppy dog.

Then there it is. The target. A luxury apartment building on Johnson Avenue. A huge plate-glass window through which you can see a gorgeous lobby with carpeting, a chandelier, even chairs with upholstery. Stuff that wouldn't last five minutes in a building on our block. Symington demands silence, "Sssshhussh, you assholes." He looks around, and sees nobody, nothing. The coast is clear. He pulls the 8 ball out of his pocket and holds it up in front of his face, looking straight at Whitey. "Do it, Whitey! Do it, Whitey!"

Whitey looks like a crazed animal. I know he's got to be blind without his glasses. He reaches out and has to grope for the stolen black 8 ball. He rears back and, with a guttural grunt, throws the ball with all his might, "Do it, Whitey, do it, Whitey!" Symington keeps yelling. It's sailing...high....up....oh shit....it misses the plate-glass window entirely, but crashes through a big apartment living room window, sending glass flying. And suddenly an older woman's voice shatters the quiet of the street with a blood-curdling scream. Shit! We all start to run. Symington is laughing his ass off, but the rest of us are quiet with one thought on our minds...escape. Then a face appears through the broken glass. An old lady with a look of hatred on her face. "You bastards! You little bastards! Police! Police!"

Fortunately, we know the area well enough to cut through alleys, over fences, through yards, and empty lots back to the park.

The anonymous windows of rich Riverdale apartment buildings now had a face. And I was scared. What if someone was hurt. Hurt bad. What if it was someone I knew. What if she saw me. I couldn't help but think how awful I would feel if I had to face my parents if I got caught doing something like this. What the hell am I doing?

But the rest of the guys were celebrating with more beers and cigarettes, and hooting and hollering and reliving the excitement of "Do it, Whitey, do it, Whitey, do it, Whitey." I can't believe how Whitey is eating all this up. It was real easy for me to slip away unnoticed.

It's after ten now. I should go home. I wonder if Alfie is still at the deli. I don't know why Whitey's not working with Alfie at the deli. He probably could sweep up or something. I haven't even seen him stop by there. I can't believe he doesn't hang out with Alfie all the time. He's probably one of the coolest guys in the neighborhood. He dresses real cool, has long hair, listens to The Beatles, goes away to college and has a job. Not like most of the guys around here who still get buzz cuts, or slick back their hair with a tube of Brylcream a day. Or still listen to The Cadillacs and Bobby and the Juniors. Mostly high school drop-outs who get fired job after job. If he was my brother, I'd want to hang out with him.

The lights are off inside the deli, but I can see some light coming from the back hallway. It's probably Alfie. If I was to go talk to him about Whitey, I'd really feel like a squealer. But maybe I don't have to really say anything that would be telling on him directly. Maybe I could just talk to him and mention that I saw Whitey over at the park, and now I'm going home. And if he asks me anything else, I'll just cover.

I take a nickel out of my pocket and hit the front door glass sharply with it three times. Here comes Alfie out of the back with a mop in his hand. He unlocks the door, and lets me into the darkened deli. "What can I do for you, Vinny? I'm a little busy right now. I've got two roast beefs ready to come out of the oven for tomorrow."

Think fast. Now I have to say SOMETHING. I'm on the spot. "Ah. Whitey's over the park hanging out if you're looking for him." I say, probably sounding a little retarded. "Yeah, is something wrong?" Alfie says lowering his eyes and staring into mine like a nun trying to stare the truth out of you.

"Well, he's with Symington, and ah, they're in the stands." I couldn't tell him what I really wanted to. I just couldn't. I feel like a rat.

"OK, thanks, as long as he's staying out of trouble," Alfie says as he puts his hands on my shoulders, turns me around, and points me towards the door. "Let me know if you guys get into trouble, see you later."

I feel like a real jerk now. Alfie thinks I'm a total asshole. I don't care if it's late. I want to go back to the stands and see what happens tonight. Something tells me there really could be trouble.

The crowd is a lot bigger and louder now. I don't even see Whitey or Symington. Ralphie is sitting down right next to all the action, looking like he's a few breaths away from throwing up. "Ralphie, have you seen Whitey?" Ralphie's eyes try to focus on me to figure out who or what I am. Suddenly that look of recognition flashes across his face. "Vinny! How you doin'?"

"Great, have you seen Whitey?"

"He and Symington....went to sniff glue. I think."

Damn. There's just something about sniffing glue that's

messed up. Everybody I know who's doing it is really screwed up. Symington's been doing it a long time. Whitey hasn't. I'll wait to see what happens.

The activity seems to go through cycles. For twenty minutes everybody seems loud and unruly. Then that dies down, and people get kind of quiet, and then a minute later, everybody's going nuts again. And just as everyone is on the second cycle of going nuts...here comes Whitey and Symington, really messed up, from the direction of the railroad tracks.

Symington jumps up the steps and lets out a rebel yell. Whitey does the same. "Let's get some queers!" Symington screams to the drunken mob like he just invented the light bulb.

"Yeah!" Whitey yells, with the other drunks chiming in.

I have a really sick feeling. A hopeless sensation. My world is out of control. I actually feel like crying. It's easy to disappear into the night, through the park, up 238th Street, past Whitey's building to mine. I'll probably get my ass kicked, but I don't want to go inside. I feel like something needs to be done. I've got to do something. But what? A long walk is a start.

It's amazing how quiet and pretty this neighborhood is at night. Big, smelly buses only come every hour or two, hardly any cars at all. No kids screaming cops and robbers, or arguing over stick ball balls and strikes. No radios blasting. You can actually hear crickets and see lightning bugs. You'd think this was a quiet block, with peaceful people living out their ordinary lives. It feels like the country in the dark of night.

I think I'll go down to "White Tower." I can sit there, eat a burger, have a Coke, and decide what I need to do.

"White Tower" has the usual assortment of Broadway end-of-the-#1 IRT-characters. Tired workers, drunken Irishmen, a hooker, and a bum or two. You're OK as long as you keep a stool apart from the next person.

I'm two bites into a five-bite burger when the little, weird guy we know as "gay Pierre" comes running into the place, holding his face with blood pouring down. "Those little pricks! Call the cops!" He starts pulling napkins out of the holder, and the white paper becomes a deep dark red once pressed to his lip. "Those little fuckers jumped me!"

Crap. We all know "gay Pierre." We know he's queer. We know all the men who cruise up along Broadway next to the park after dark are queer. Guys pull up in cars and park, and a queer will just either get in and they take off, or they walk into the park together. I guess "gay Pierre" met up with Symington and company.

"But I got one of the little fuckers with my knife. I hope he bleeds to death. I was lucky I got away."

I dropped my burger and ran out... I paid when served. Who got stuck? Symington? Whitey? Or one of the slower, fatter, drunker guys like Ralphie? I ran across Broadway, through the park, towards the stands. I don't hear anything. I see don't see anyone. I start to walk down the length of the stands, the cinder ash of the running track crunching under my feet. And down at the very end, I can see the dark outline of one person standing alone at the top wall, looking out across the Bronx at night. Whitey.

I stopped. I know it's got to be him. I'm afraid. I don't want to face him. I don't want to talk about us seeing Brian die. Him standing in shock... me running. Crying. I can't face talking about the funeral, the burial. I don't want to know why he can't hardly look at me. Why he's hanging out with Symington. Sniffing glue. Breaking windows. I'm not his brother. My brother looks out for me. My brother will kick anybody's ass that messes with me. And he always told me, if anybody bullies you who's bigger or older, just get yourself the biggest, ugliest stick you can find and go after him. Then let him know so he could kick his ass.

I quietly walk up the steps one by one. I get to the very top, just a foot behind Whitey. "Hi, Whitey."

Without turning around, Whitey replies, "Hi, Vinny."

I go alongside Whitey and look out over the wall, towards the ""el" and towards the hills of Riverdale, with their luxury hi-risers creating a skyline. I don't look right at Whitey, but I can tell he's been crying.

"It's all my fault, you know," Whitey whispers.

"What is?"

"That Brian got killed."

I feel like hot wax has just been poured down my back. I don't know what to say. I'm terrified. I want to run and cry.

"It's nobody's fault. It was an accident."

Whitey turns and looks at me. I can see the redness of his eyes and his face. Too much beer, too much glue, too much Symington, too much pain.

"I had the keys. He wouldn't have died." Whitey starts to cry. Wail. So hard that his mouth is open and drool is coming out.

I guess I should have some kind of speech for him. Like Ward Cleaver or something. But all Mr. Cleaver ever had to give speeches about was not sharing with Larry Mondello or not spying on Wally holding hands with a girl. The Beaver never saw Wally splattered in the courtyard with picket fence sticking through him, gurgling his last drunken breath of life in an ocean of his own blood. What the fuck would Ward have to say about that?

"Come on, Whitey. Let's go for a walk," I say in lieu of a speech. I put my hand on his shoulder and slowly step down the stairs onto the cinder track and through the darkness of the park path towards the lake, with only the sound of our feet, our breathing, and Whitey's occasional sobs.

The walk to the lake is about 10 minutes. I guess we're pretty nuts doing it alone at night, but the park is really empty. I don't feel afraid for some reason. I've got too much on my mind. I don't care.

"Did anybody get stabbed?" I ask Whitey, not really wanting to know the answer.

"Not really. Gay Pierre had a little baby knife that couldn't slice a banana. He tried to stick Symington just before he kicked him in the balls."

"Symington kicked Gay Pierre in the balls?"

"No, gay Pierre kicked Symington in the balls. He dropped like a sack of potatoes and we all split."

Whitey has a pint of "Southern Comfort" in his back

pocket. And every five minutes or so he takes a swig and then a bigger swig. I can't stand that stuff. And shortly after each swig, he gets into another crying jag and starts to mumble stuff about it being his fault.

"Alfie!" He shouts. "I've got to find Alfie. I know where he is. Come on."

Now Whitey's leading the way. We go past the lake to a path I've never been on at night. There are no lights at all. And it really goes through woods. Up the hill that leads into the part of park that is in another neighborhood, what we usually call JT, where mostly Jewish families live. There's probably a corner of the park where the Jewish teenagers go when they want to hide and do the things that they do in the park in the dark. I've heard the Jewish kids don't drink as much as Irish kids, but they take more drugs. Especially marijuana.

Whitey stops just before the woods end about 20 yards from a playground. "Look, there he is." Through a clearing in the bushes, we can see a group of 4 or 5 guys sitting on a bench, at the back of the playground. Not rowdy, drunken, screaming, bottle-breaking, pissing-on-each other kids. Kids quietly passing around a cigarette. And in the middle of them is the only blonde of the longish hair bunch, Alfie. His truck bike just off to the side.

"They're taking drugs," Whitey says with anger in his voice.

"Let's go."

I grab his arm. "Whitey, wait. And do what?"

"Alfie's taking drugs and I've got to stop him. Brian said so. Come on." Whitey takes off running towards Alfie through the bushes, I chase after him, there's an 8 foot chain-link fence around the playground and Whitey jumps up and starts to climb over it. I've got to go with him. Now we can see the shocked look of the four guys and Alfie watching us in amazement and smell the sweetness of their pot.

"Whitey!" Alfie says bewildered.

"Stop! Stop!" Whitey is screaming as he hoists himself over the top of the fence, and starts to climb down. "Stop it! Stop it!" Whitey says as he leaps down the last four feet of fence and runs over to Alfie.

Whitey stands in front of Alfie panting like a bull ready to charge.

"Brian knew you were taking drugs, didn't he?" Whitey says at Alfie.

"You're drunk, Whitey," Alfie says quietly.

"So what! Brian knew it! You're taking drugs!" Whitey says.

Alfie raises slowly. Laughing. Whitey's clenching his fists. He walks over to Whitey.

"This isn't taking drugs, Whitey," Alfie says as he pulls a Marlboro hard top out of his pocket, revealing several joints mixed in with the cigarettes. "This is just smoking pot. You want to know what taking drugs is, Whitey? I'll fucking show you what taking drugs is!" Alfie starts to roll up his deli clean white shirt he's still wearing, unbuttoned, and holds his arm out. "This is taking drugs, Whitey!"

Alfie shoves his arm into Whitey's face. I can see little black pimples. I think they're needle marks. From shooting up dope. Real dope.

"That's right, you own fucking brother shoots dope, Whitey. What do you think of that? One brother a cop and the other a fucking junkie! Face reality, you little jerk. This is the real world. Not you and you're little fucking friends. I shoot dope. And you know what? I was home when Brian tried to get in that night."

I'm in a dream state. This can't be happening. Whitey looked as shocked as when Brian was dying in front of him.

"I was home. But I was so messed up, I didn't hear a thing. I was home, Whitey. I could've let him in! But I was out-cold, strung out. I couldn't have let him in, Whitey. I couldn't because I was so stoned." Alfie stops dead in his tracks. His tirade over. He walks over to Whitey. Looks him in the eye. "I could've let him in," He says softly to Whitey as they embrace and cry together.

I don't think the other four guys on the bench knew me or Whitey. They sat in stunned silence.

It must've been five minutes of weeping. Together.

283

Deep wet sobs and drool crying. The kind that gives you a really bad headache.

"Go home, Whitey. I'll be OK", Alfie says as he walks over to his bike and hops on.

I walk over to Whitey and we head out to the street.

"My brother's a junkie..." Whitey says as he trails off into tears.

"Don't worry, Whitey. He'll be OK. We'll all be OK."

For some unknown reason, I really believe it. Whitey and I walk home together for the first time since Brian died.

It sure gets hot in the city in the middle of July. Whitey and I are going down to Review today. We're going to show the guys down there where "Charlie's Hole" is in Van Cortlandt Park. Tibbets Brook runs through Vannie and into the lake. We fish in the lake for fun, but you can't swim there. It's brown. And everybody knows that the bottom is thick muck and loaded with broken bottles, shopping carts, and rusty old beer cans. Charlie's Hole is about a mile walk up the railroad tracks. The brook runs really fast at one point and fills up a rock-lined hole about the size of half court basketball. The water is crystal clear and cold as hell, even on the hottest day.

I can walk right into Whitey's courtyard now. But I don't look up. I take the squeaky old elevator up to the top floor to call for Whitey. I know Whitey's going to answer the door because both his parents are upstate while his father is in the hospital. Alfie's gone to a special place on Long Island to get off drugs. He's not actually a junkie. A junkie is addicted to drugs, usually heroin, I found out. Alfie was mostly smoking pot, popping pills, and shot up "speed" a few times. I guess that's not as bad as being a junkie, but he decided to get some help. Believe it or not, Father O'Shaughnessy helped him through Catholic Charities to find somewhere that would help him. And the whole thing is free.

Before I could finish my second knock on the door, it swings open with a big, smiling Whitey Shelley. I don't think I've seen him smiling like this in months. And he's waving a piece of paper.

284

"Guess what this is?" he says as he taunts me with it.

"You won asshole of the year?"

"No, schmuck! I'm not on the waiting list at Hayes anymore! I was accepted!"

"Alright!"

And a minor celebration begins. Complete with root beer toasts and an entire box of Mall-o-Mars.

Me and Whitey are going to Cardinal Hayes. I heard it's super strict there. The priests are supposed to be OK, but the Christian Brothers will punch you out for almost any little reason. Even failing a test. It's scary, but it might just work.

So it's off to Charlie's Hole with the younger kids for a swim. Maybe tomorrow we'll hop the freight and go to the pool at Tibbet's Brook Park or take the #1 bus to Yankee Stadium. Or go fishing down at the Hudson River. Or take the train downtown and try to get into a game show. Or maybe go up to Orloff Avenue where Carrie, Donna, and Eileen started hanging out. Maybe we'll even go up to Pigeon Park where there are some cute new girls. I don't care if they're Jewish. Cute is cute. Or maybe just get some of the guys together for stick ball, curb ball, call ball, or king/queen, as always, with moons up. And when we run out of spaldeens, there's no need to worry. There's always sewer balls.